BILLY
STROBE

BILLY STROBE

JOHN MARTEL

DUTTON

DUTTON
Published by the Penguin Group
Penguin Putnam Inc., 375 Hudson Street, New York, New York 10014, U.S.A.
Penguin Books Ltd, 27 Wrights Lane, London W8 5TZ, England
Penguin Books Australia Ltd, Ringwood, Victoria, Australia
Penguin Books Canada Ltd, 10 Alcorn Avenue, Toronto, Ontario, Canada M4V 3B2
Penguin Books (N.Z.) Ltd, 182–190 Wairau Road, Auckland 10, New Zealand

Penguin Books Ltd, Registered Offices: Harmondsworth, Middlesex, England

Published by Dutton, a member of Penguin Putnam Inc.

First Printing, September 2001
10 9 8 7 6 5 4 3 2 1

 REGISTERED TRADEMARK—MARCA REGISTRADA

LIBRARY OF CONGRESS CATALOGING-IN-PUBLICATION DATA
Martel, John S.
    Billy Strobe / John Martel.
        p. cm.
    ISBN 0-525-94618-7 (alk. paper)
    1. Corporations—Corrupt practices—Fiction. 2. Male friendship—Fiction.
    3. Ex-prisoners—Fiction. 4. Law firms—Fiction. I. Title.
    PS3563.A72315 B55 2001
    813'.54—dc21   2001021334

Printed in the United States of America
Set in Sabon
Designed by Eve L. Kirch

To Frederick Hill
Esteemed Agent, Honorable Gentleman, Good Guy

ACKNOWLEDGMENTS

I want to thank the many people who contributed to the writing of this book: Carole Baron, Brian Tart, Jay Martel, Mary Eggleston, and especially Fred Hill and Barbara McHugh, for their suggestions, editing, and encouragement; George Beckwith and Doug Young, for filling in the many gaps in my knowledege of current criminal law and procedure; Don Eggleston, for getting me deep inside Soledad prison by means reasonably likely to ensure that I would get back out; Danny Martin, author of *In the Hat*, for sharing his involuntary and more extended experience behind the walls of Soledad; Dave Amis, the consummate Okie, for his stories and a lifetime of friendship and generosity; Dave and Jackie Allaire, for their aloha spirit whenever my own printer broke down on Maui; Paul Bergman and Michael Asimow, authors of *Reel Justice*; and, most of all, my friend, lover, typist, copy editor, photographer, and beloved wife, Bonnie, for her obsession with detail and her unfailing support.

PART I

INSIDE

The vilest deeds like poison weeds
Bloom well in prison air
It is only what is good in man
That wastes and withers there

—Oscar Wilde

1

They call me Billy Strobe, but not for long, thank you. Soon as I become a lawyer, I plan to go by William, mainly because it's got a more professional ring to it. I can't expect to help folks if they don't take me seriously.

I realize people don't think much of the law profession these days, and I reckon I can't blame them. But it's the system—a machine designed by the rich to chew up the poor—that folks should be down on, not the law. The system is religion, the law is spirituality. Take your pick.

Anyways, I'm set on becoming a lawyer, and not just because that's what my daddy was, but more in spite of what he was—what people back home *thought* he was—which I'll get to later on.

Lucky for me, I've never put much stock in what people think. Hell, those same people back in Enid, Oklahoma, were all the time telling me I was setting my sights too high. But take a look: I've already made it two-thirds the way through UCLA Law School and finished in the top 10 percent both years. My piece in the law review on injustices in the California Penal Code made the Metro section of the *L.A. Times* a year ago.

I don't mean to be bragging. The truth is, I had a head start on my classmates, being as how I grew up in the law, nursed at the titty of the blindfolded Lady of Justice, you might say. When other dads were teaching their kids how to shoot a basket or bat a ball, I was reading writs of habeas corpus and memorizing the Bill of Rights. I think even Ma knew Dad's first love was the law.

Dad was a courtroom movie buff, too, and he was always quoting things about the law from books and films, like what Paul Scofield said in *A Man for All Seasons*: "I'd give even the *devil* benefit of law, for my own safety's sake." Dad also liked that letter Dana Andrews wrote before they lynched him in *The Ox-Bow Incident,* where he said, "Law is the very conscience of humanity." Words like these stuck to me like money in a rich man's pocket.

So between my upbringing with Dad and seeing nearly every courtroom movie ever made, no big surprise that the law was in my bones, and when I got a shot at a scholarship out West, I took to law school as natural as a tick to a cat's ass. For me, the law was not a living; it was life. All my heroes were lawyers, my dad of course, but also guys like Atticus Finch in *To Kill a Mockingbird* and Henry Fonda in the first *Twelve Angry Men.* (Jack Lemmon was good, too, but I preferred the original version.)

Anyways, law school was just another movie for me, and I loved every minute. Being realistic, however, I knew that my last year of law school was going to be tougher than the first two, seeing as how I'd have to finish by correspondence.

Once I'd started serving my three- to five-year sentence at Soledad Maximum Security Prison for grand larceny.

Maybe I should explain this last thing, a piece of bad luck that landed on me a few months ago—July 26, at 3:30 in the afternoon, to be exact about it.

I was hoeing up weeds outside the Westwood rooming house I managed for free rent and ten dollars a day when these four UCLA frat rats—popular guys who had never paid me any mind when we were all in undergraduate school together—showed up in Harmon Alexander's cherry-red Jaguar, all smiling and shouting Hey, Billy, and What's up, Billy, like I was their best friend.

It was hot that day, too damn hot to be outside hoeing up weeds. Looking back, I should have been suspicious right off because it was also too hot to be driving around in an open convertible shouting What's up, Billy, to an outsider like me.

Mr. Dog, my brown-and-white mini-mutt, got to his feet and hauled in his tongue long enough to growl at them. I should have done the same.

You're wondering how I could testify at my trial as to the exact time of day and the place where I was standing when the four of them approached me with their harebrained idea. I guess it was like the way my dad, Joe Strobe, knew right where he was when President John F. Kennedy was killed. And like the way I can remember exactly what I was doing when I heard the shot that killed my dad. Twelve years old, coming out of the kitchen, carrying a Coke and a hot dog with melted cheddar and grilled onions that Dad always claimed was as good as Nathan's at Coney Island, where he took Ma on their honeymoon. Anyways, that's where I stood when the gun went off and Ma let out a scream that has lasted fourteen years so far.

Back to those four frat rats approaching me. As the Jag's tires settled into the curb, I spotted the Alexander brothers sitting up front but couldn't make out who was in the back. I shielded my eyes with the hand not holding the hoe because the late afternoon sun, unchecked by so much as a puff of a cloud, was ricocheting off that Jag's windshield and flying at me like splinters of burning glass.

Harmon Alexander—he's the fat brother—cut the engine, which kept on popping and crackling over the awkward silence as they all sat there for a minute. I began to feel silly standing there leaning on my hoe and squinting at them through the shimmering waves of heat dancing off the Jag's hood. I could hear them talking among themselves and could smell oil burning on the engine's manifold, smell the softening asphalt out on the street.

L.A. was having a bad air day.

"What's shakin, Billy?" said Steve Alexander, Harmon's younger brother, teeth white and perfect as piano keys and holding out his hand as he unwound himself from the passenger side of the car. "How 'bout you taking a break and having a beer with us?"

As Steve approached, Mr. Dog commenced to barking, so I had to ask him to sit and be still. Still shielding my eyes, I'd run out of hands, so I dropped the hoe and shook with Steve and said hey back, then made mistake number one and said sure I could use a beer. Looking back, I reckon the idea that these hotshots wanted me to hang with them threw me off balance. Truth be told, I didn't even feel like a beer right then, but off we went to the Rose Queen, me squashed in the back between two blond surfer types. The hot wind blew cold on my damp skin, and I worried I had dark rings showing under the armpits of my denim tank top. I doubt any of these white-shoes had ever sweat much in their whole damn silver-spooned lives except maybe for Milton Janson—the guy squashing me from my left—who had made third-string all-American defensive cornerback his senior year.

The Rose Queen was a throwback to the college hangouts of another time, reeking of sawdust, testosterone, and old beer, shin-banging dark despite a hanging garden of fake Tiffany lights. Serious conversation was discouraged by the booming bass sound of heavy metal music, waves of window-rattling laughter, and earsplitting shouts of *Yesss* followed by high fives that pierced your brain like cracks off a bat, followed by the obligatory clanging together of beer mugs. I never could abide this undergraduate bonding ritual, which I guess was modern kin to the sharing of blood, but considerably less painful, at least until the next morning.

The waitresses at the Rose were all hot young ladies in minis and halter tops who made peanuts for hopping their assigned pockmarked wooden tables, dreaming about getting "discovered," Westwood being only a few miles outside Hollywood. A minority of them were local girls also known to be willing to stir up something with a college boy that might lead to security and wedded bliss. I felt sorriest for these townies, who fantasized that all roads led to Rome but were more likely to end up on a beach blanket in Venice—the one in California—lucky to be spared the clap.

Anyways, there we were, me still feeling uneasy and ready for that beer though I never hankered much for drinking, despite being 100 percent Irish. There was some more What-you-been-up-to-Billy bullshit—as if they gave a rat's ass—then toasting to "success" with mugs of beer delivered by a semi-cute girl with a round, grown-up face, who reminded me of Bonnie Bedelia in *Presumed Innocent*. She also had a nice rear end that Steve patted without repercussions other than a dirty look. Then the boys got to the point, which was a plan to make a lot of money without having to kill anybody.

The idea was that these four rich kids would steal confidential corporate information from their dads' briefcases and desk drawers—legal opinions about proposed mergers and acquisitions—and then buy up a bunch of stock in anticipation of big run-ups when the news became public. Since the guys were going to provide the secret stuff and the capital, I was wondering what they expected me to contribute other than guilt and anxiety, which as an Irish Catholic I had plenty of to spare, or my corporate legal knowledge, which was in short supply since I hadn't taken the third-year trade regulation seminar yet. They were all staring at me now, even Steve, waiting for my reaction, my sophisticated expert opinion, which I told them was that they were all crazier than a pack of rats in a coffee can. I guess I was already feeling my beer and remembering how much I disliked privileged punks like these guys.

"We didn't bring you here to insult us, Strobe," said Steve Alexander, turning to stare at a waitress's fine legs as she walked by.

"Shut up, Steve," said Fat Harmon, "we brought him here to listen to him. Go on, Billy. What's the problem?"

I glared at Steve, but his eyes—half-closed, like a snake eyeballing a field mouse—were still busy trailing the waitress while his head bobbed to a deafening Pearl Jam tune. Fat Harmon saw my disgusted look and shrugged in tacit agreement, plainly wishing he had been born an only child. I guess I liked Fat best of the four of them, though that wasn't saying much. He had the same curly blond hair and dark blue eyes as Steve and would have been as good-looking but for an accident of metabolism leading to an extra hundred pounds or so.

"It's called illegal insider trading," I told Fat, and laid out the basics of Securities and Exchange Rule 16b, a law that makes it both a state and federal felony to use insider tips in buying stock. The fourth kid, named Oliver Sutton, piped up and said so what, nobody was going to get hurt and there's no way we could get caught anyway.

I tried to explain how the market did get hurt by insider manipulation, but my arguments sounded hollow even to me, the "market" being a pretty impersonal thing to get all worked up about. So I ended up focusing on the getting caught part.

"That's where you come in, Billy," said Steve Alexander. "Your name can't be traced to any of our fathers' names, plus everybody knows you're some kind of ace on criminal law, and that could come in handy. We'll cut you in for a full twenty-five percent share."

I must have raised my eyebrows at that, there being five of us at the table, so Milt Janson—he was the all-American cornerback—explained that the Alexander brothers were splitting a twenty-five percent share because they had only one father to steal secrets from.

Steve Alexander quit looking at the waitresses long enough to give Milt a hard look, but Fat Harmon and Oliver Sutton kept smiling agreeably. I could tell Steve and Milt seemed at odds, but the semi-cute waitress arrived with our second round of beers and Steve was all smiles again, laying on a tip that could have paid for my dinner.

After the waitress left, they all sat there staring at me again, and it's stupid, but I guess I was still a little flattered at being hustled by these campus celebs, plus they hadn't even used their best argument for sucking me in, which was that I was about to lose my scholarship because of cost-cutting at UCLA. I was working a short night shift as a warehouse security guard to help support my kid sister and a mother who had picked up in the alcoholic department right where Dad had left off when he died. Joe's suicide had left me head of the household, aided only by food stamps and ANC—Aid to Needy Children—as in me and Lisa. But that gets into a whole 'nother story that concerns what happened to my father, the most notorious trial lawyer in the history of Enid, Oklahoma. Like I said, I'll get more into that later, except to say now that he got set up and framed by a shiftless partner and an evil client and that clearing my dad's name would be my first project when I became a lawyer. Anyways, the point is, these fat cats had got me to thinking what it would be like to have my family set for life and for me to be able to stay in school and follow my dream.

Cutting to the chase, get this: During the four-week trial, the *Los Angeles Times* dubbed yours truly, Billy Strobe, the "brains" behind the Billionaire Boys Club II, which is what the press began calling us when the story broke. I thought that was a bit much, since we were never accused of killing anybody like the original Billionaire Boys Club was, plus which we never got past $1,300,000, though we had high hopes. At least we'd made it well over the $500,000 minimum for qualifying as an aggravated white collar crime under Penal Code Section 186.11 (2), thus entitling each of us to up to five years in state prison and a fine of up to ten million dollars if we got caught, which of course we did.

As for me being the brains, hell, if I'd had any brains, I would have listened to Mr. Dog and not gone for beers that day in the first place and—here's mistake number two—wouldn't have been the only one whose name the Club's trading account was registered in. Of course it had to be that way, and I'll admit it had made me feel good to see my name—William Joseph Strobe—right there on the monthly broker's account reports, and doing pretty damn well, too, until the roof fell in.

Milton Janson's father turned us in. His own goddamn father! My dad wouldn't have done that with a loaded gun to his head. Loyalty was everything to him. He understood loyalty, and say what you want about Joe Strobe, he always put his mouth where his money wasn't—never once denying a person in need—and winning nearly every case he took on except, unfortunately, his own.

Anyways, my problem with the Billionaire Boys Club II was that though I may have been the smartest, I was also the least connected, and when the scam went south, my four new best friends quickly caved and confirmed the press's notion that I was the big dog with the brass collar, the architect of the whole damn scheme. Their parents paid huge fines and each of them pulled a year of misdemeanor county time, which they only served four months of. But the judge made an example out of Billy Strobe, Boy Master Mind, and hit me with a felony. Guess I shouldn't have been surprised. Dad taught me a long time ago that the system will beat you six ways to Sunday if you're short on money and long on guilt.

2

So after a quick stop at purgatory—the San Quentin Reception Center, aka Q, aka Quentin, aka Bedlam, USA—I was consigned to full-on hell at Soledad. I knew something about Soledad Prison—now technically known as the Correctional Training Facility—because when I was a kid, my father gave me a copy of *Soledad Brothers*, written by a famous inmate there, Black Panther George Jackson. Dad said it would help me understand why he, Dad, worked so hard and why he never had time for me and Lisa. I told him that the stuff in there must have been made up because we didn't live in Red China, did we? Joe Strobe's eyes went blank as dull stones, and he said, "George Jackson did."

I had a seat on the window side of the gray refurbished school bus as we traveled through the Salinas Valley. I'd heard it was supposed to be a pretty place, but the December fog was so heavy the driver had to keep the wipers going for the whole trip. I stared out the wired-up window next to me, catching an occasional glimpse of the lead-gray December sky, but about all I could see was a railroad track running parallel fifteen yards off to our right, and field after field of straight rows of cultivated soil, plain old dirt. Winter's cold breath had exposed miles of steel irrigation pipes, sticking out of the ground like gray bones scattered across acres of desecrated graves.

Everything looked gray; even the guards' faces were the color of pewter, and the only signs of life I saw the whole trip were three Mexicans in a fog-shrouded artichoke field, tossing the remaining late-season chokes over their shoulders into heavy containers strapped to their bent backs. A few miles later I saw a dozen Herefords that looked as colorless and dazed as the people on the bus with me.

Still, I might have appreciated the Valley more if I wasn't so damn scared and if the skinhead across the aisle would have stopped staring at me and if my ankles hadn't been manacled to the floorboard with a chain running up my crotch connected to handcuffs that bound my wrists too tight, and if I hadn't been sitting next to a scowling kid who

talked to himself out loud for the first sixty miles and smelled like he
had pissed his pants.

Joey Harrison was his name, and he looked even younger than I
did. He had been next in line with me when we arrived at Quentin.
I heard him give his name at check-in which is how I knew it. He was
probably in his early twenties like me, skin like milk chocolate, and
sadly good-looking, though a little weak in the chin department. He
wore an empty hole in his earlobe, and a shaved head to make him
look tough, but it didn't work. Joey looked like a mongrel dog that
had been hit upside the head too many times. He didn't say a word
to me all the way to Salinas, too busy arguing with himself, I guess.
Then he went quiet, but still wouldn't answer me. I figured it was because I was white, but learned later that there is zero trust in prison;
everybody's critical, down on themselves and everybody else, wal-
lowing in suspicion, fear, anger—you name it. In prison, the less said,
the better.

Still, I tried to draw him out as we got near to Soledad because
judging by his prison tattoos—the kind made from burning wire and
ballpoint pens—he'd been in before, and I figured I might learn something from him. I told him I had been to law school and heard they
might let me enroll in correspondence school once I got to Soledad. He
grunted to show he had listened.

"I heard the school might even give me a free ride," I added, but he
still didn't say anything, just began shaking his head like I was crazy,
looking straight ahead, his eyes burning into the side of the guard's
face four rows in front of us.

"You got a ride comin, all right," he said at last, so softly I wasn't
sure he was talking to me.

"What?"

A small bubble formed at his full lips and then disappeared when
he gave off something like a smile. "You got no fuckin idea in the
world what you be headin for, counselor. Correspondence school?
Sheee-it."

I shrugged and waited a while before trying again; then I told him
I knew prison would be rough—I'd heard plenty about beatings and
rape inside—but reckoned that focusing on the future was better than
pissing into the wind of the past.

Still looking straight ahead, he said, "It's the present you'd best be
worryin about, white meat."

A tractor pulling a plow caught my eye off to the left, cutting fur-
rows as straight as prison bars. Crows followed, feasting on dislodged
bugs and earthworms.

"Hell yes, I'm worried," I said, my chains rattling as I lifted my hands for emphasis. "I've never been so scared in my life. But I'll fight if I have to. I've got a strategy, and I'm going to stick to it."

That got a rueful smile out of him. "Strategy? The only strategy in the can is to get yourself a jocker." The smile faded, and he added, "Best do it quick."

I didn't like the direction this was taking, but asked him what a jocker was.

"A pitcher, fool. A Man. Somebody to protect you."

"From violence?"

"From violence up your butt."

That stopped me, and the part of my breakfast I hadn't already thrown up at Quentin started roiling in my stomach like a pack of garter snakes.

"No champagne and violins, white fish. Talkin gang rape. You got three, four days at most to get yourself a Man. Then they be swarmin around you like flies on shit."

He told me he'd been inside before and knew what he was talking about. When I asked him what this "protection" would cost me, he gave me that same knowing grin, and all of a sudden I was throwing up in my hands, picturing that poor bastard McCullough in *And Justice for All,* who killed himself because of what they were doing to him. The difference was that this wasn't some movie; this was really happening.

"Oh, *shee-it,*" said Joey, when he saw what I'd done. The guard up front stared at me as if I had merely blown my nose, and then demonstrated what I should do by rubbing both his hands down his pants leg. No burp bags on the Soledad Express. Thanks a lot, I thought, but that's what I ended up doing. Now I smelled worse than Joey.

We traveled the rest of the way in a tense, terrified silence, rolling down Highway 101, which glistened darkly from the blanket of moisture that continued to hold us captive. The smell of Joey's piss and my own vomit was making me sick again. *Pitcher, jocker*—Christ, this was going to be worse than I thought.

Apparently tired of dispensing prison wisdom, even to himself, Joey acted like he'd gone to sleep. But nobody really slept on that bus, except maybe the guards.

I glanced over at one of Joey's fragile arms, like a caramel stick in an orange wrapper. No doubt which end of the pitch he'd been on.

3

As we passed through the drab yellowish walls of Soledad, my first surprise was the silence and the empty yard. I'd seen movies about the taunting of new fish and was ready for the worst.

"Fog lock-down," murmured Joey. "Best time to escape."

I guess he meant that when the fog was in, so were the prisoners, but my relief faded soon after I was escorted toward my cell in an area known as CTF North, on the third-tier block of a building called Shasta B. The sun had broken through, the cell doors were racked open by a guard using the locking box at the end of each tier, and I was suddenly surrounded by the clamor of the other inmates—sounding more crazy than guilty, though most of them were probably a bit of both—shouting and swearing at each other, crying and singing, anything to drown out the fear and pain in their heads. George Jackson said in his book that the racket made by inmates was so they wouldn't hear "what their mind was trying to tell them."

My mind was telling me that I was in big trouble, and I cringed in my cell with the door closed, relieved but surprised to see my cellmate was still asleep. Surprised because not even the dead could sleep in cell block Shasta B. It was like being inside a garbage can with people beating on it with baseball bats.

A quick word about the cells at Soledad. Unlike what you see in the movies, there are no bars on the doors of the cell blocks here. Instead, there's a steel door with a glass window about four by six inches, though most of them have been smashed out. Inside each cell, two inmates are crammed into a space about six by ten feet that had originally been designed for one person. A guard told me that Soledad was designed for a total population of 2,981 inmates and presently had over 7,000 men in captivity.

On the right side of the door as you entered a cell there was a miniature toilet where we shit and washed our socks and underwear. On the back wall was a barred window and the two narrow sleeping pallets, no more than twenty-seven inches wide. There was a stool for getting up to the top bunk, shelves like an orange crate on the left side, and that was it.

My cellmate—"celly"—turned out to be another fairly new fish, a harmless black kid, fat and younger than me, lying on the bottom sleeping pallet and slamming his head into the wall so hard his pallet shook. Trying to get himself back to sleep, I reckon. He never stopped, in fact, and kept me awake the first night moaning something like *ah-dintdoit* over and over in a mournful, raspy voice, prompting derisive shouts and made-up songs that never stopped, even when the guards finally showed up around 3:00 A.M. and kicked him around a little. We were on the third tier, and I was afraid they were going to throw him over the rail, but they threw him back in the cell instead. The beating made him moan all the louder, and I could smell his vomit, which made me nauseated again. He began to hit his head against the cement wall some more, but couldn't seem to knock himself out to sleep. I offered him some water, but he pushed me away.

I tried to shut my own brain off to what was happening that first night, but nothing worked. I tried singing, sang all the words to every country song I knew—and I know a whole lot of them—but that didn't work either. I couldn't stop my heart from pounding in my ears, or calm the nerve endings that sparked like they were short-circuiting through my whole body. Eventually, I tried hitting my head against the wall like the fat kid, but it didn't work for me either.

At 5:30 the guards came and kicked the kid around some more, then poked me one for trying to stop them. Then they dragged him away like a sack of grain, still moaning *"ahdintdoit, ahdintdoit!"* I never saw him again, but I later learned his name was Gary and that, like some other inmates who couldn't take it anymore, he had eventually paroled himself by diving over the rail from the third tier.

Understand, I'm telling a story here, not complaining and damn sure not making excuses. Hell, if the dog hadn't stopped to lick his ass, he would 'a caught the squirrel. And if I learned anything from my dad, it's that you do the crime, you do the time, especially if you're poor. Like my hero Waylon said, I had put myself on a downhill road to nowhere.

For all that, I knew I'd have to survive it somehow, hopefully with my humanity and independence intact. I'd heard from my dad what institutionalization does to people, but my optimistic nature told me that with a little luck, I'd survive and soon be free again.

Hell, some people never know freedom, like my sister, Lisa, who got diagnosed with multiple sclerosis in her senior year of high school, a disease that became a prison for her worse than anything the California Department of Corrections could ever dream up. The doc told us no test was conclusive for MS, so I think there's hope, but her fatigue and pain have turned her a little bitter, same as all prisons do. She is also in what they call "denial," always pointing out she doesn't have bladder problems and wasn't overly hot all the time like a lot of MS folks are, claiming she's just got "a touch of bad arthritis" and that the doc was wrong about her having MS. I reckon she could be right, and, hell, let her think whatever she wants to was my thinking, though it fairly drives Ma nuts.

See, Lisa is still with Ma back in Enid. Doubt Lisa will ever leave Enid. Fact is, she probably won't even leave the house, though Lord knows Ma's no barrel of chuckles to be around. Ma was fun once, and beautiful, too, but when Dad killed himself, she came apart, and now alcohol had slowed the messages from her brain worse than MS had slowed Lisa's.

The day after I arrived at Soledad, our cell doors were racked open, and we were sent out to the recreation yard. It had looked plenty big when I had walked through it the day before on my way to my cell block, but when 1,500 men from CTF North area poured into that same yard, it shrank up real quick.

I wasn't surprised to see all the inmates segregating themselves by race, mainly Latino, black, white, and Asian. The only thing they all had in common was the denim blues—guards all wear khaki—though the cons who could afford them were allowed running shoes and either gray or white tops. I walked uneasily toward the white guys, stiff-legged in my brown, prison-issued boots. Close up, the white guys looked the scariest of the lot—long hair, no hair, tattoos, scars—but nobody paid me any mind, thank God, and as soon as I could locate the telephones, I got in line. It felt good to have something to do, even if it was no more than standing in a line. There was a bank of eighteen phones in the yard to serve 1,500 men, and only fifteen of them worked. It took me an hour before I reached the head of the line, and I had to keep reminding myself to be cool—I had nothing but time. When the next phone finally opened up, a black dude in his thirties, wearing shades, white Nikes, and a gray sweatshirt, walked right in front of me and grabbed it. I started for him, but felt a firm tap on my shoulder from the guy behind me.

"Excuse me," he said in a quiet but commanding voice. "You best not do what you be thinkin."

He was as tall and slender as a Zulu warrior, around six feet six inches, an OG—prison parlance for "old guy"—who looked seventy but was probably no more than fifty.

"He took my phone," I said.

"It ain't *your* phone or his neither," the tall man said, giving me a sad, patient smile. "Neither of you ain't got nothin to call your own anymore. You ain't got nothin in here but regrets and some crumbs of respect you gonna have to get the old-fashioned way. That man cut in on you? He earned his respect by murderin a man who didn't ask permission to work in on the bench press he was usin. Put the bar down on his throat and crushed his windpipe. Since then, he be a shot-caller for the Bloods. You'll have yo' chances to earn respect boy, but I'd advise you not to be dissin that particular nigger."

I was still fuming, but I stayed in line. "He damned sure dissed *me*," I said.

"Sure he did and he got your dander up, too, din't he? But lemme tell you somethin, boy. Most of us got here in the first place 'cause somebody dissed us and we wasn't smart enough to roll widdit. So put that Harry high school shit behind you if you wanna survive in CTF North, not get squashed like the hot young pissant you 'pear to be."

"You're dissing me right now," I said.

He gave his head a little shake. "What I'm doin is savin your homesick white ass. Hell, kid, what good's a telephone gonna do you if your throat's been cut?"

Another phone opened up, and I went for it. My fingers were trembling so bad I misdialed Ma's phone number the first time, which cost me an extra prisoner-per-call flat charge of $7.50 plus the long distance. I tried again, and Lisa answered. I had called a little too late in the lunchtime cocktail hour to catch Ma in a lucid state, so I broke the news to Lisa that I was in Soledad and had no grounds for appeal. She took down my address.

"It's a great fucking life, isn't it?" she said dryly.

"It's not the end of the world," I said.

"What do you know about my world?" she said, and I could picture her lips pressed together in a pale line, her pretty face scrunched up in pain.

"I was talking about my own situation here. In prison. Are you feeling bitchier than usual today, Lisa?"

A flock of low-flying crows circled the yard, scolded us, then headed south.

I heard a little cry out of her that never made it into words.

"What's wrong, sis?"

She snuffled a little, and then said, "Just about everything, with you in prison."

"I know it. How's the pain? You hurting?"

"No worse than usual. I'm just being bitchy, like you said. I guess we're angry because first we lose Dad, now you. Plus Ma and I are at each other because I want a dog and she won't allow it. Says we can't afford it and I can 'barely manage myself, let alone an animal.' "

I decided to stay clear of that one.

"Billy, I'm twenty-one years old, old enough to drink in a bar—if I could drink—and vote—which I do, by absentee ballot—and I can't even have a goddamn dog when I want one!"

She let fly with some other problems, and I could feel a guy inching in closer and closer from behind. I huddled nearer to the phone and finally got a word in edgewise.

"I'm sorry about all this, Lisa," I said, getting frustrated and trying not to show it, "but truth is, I got a few problems of my own presently."

Whatever I'd called home for, I wasn't getting it. What I was getting was a ration of shit from someone who was upset, too, and not only at Ma about some damn dog. Both of them were mad at me for breaking the law and bringing more shame down on the family name. And then there was money, always money.

"I guess you do have a few, at that," she said. "So enough about me. How are things in the big house during this era of modern and enlightened penology?"

That was more like Lisa: emotional but usually coherent, self-centered yet sensitive and caring when she wasn't hurting too much herself, and brilliant, always brilliant. Since I've never been able to match her way with words or her sarcastic wit either, especially when I could tell she was in a bad pain cycle, I settled for telling her I was doing okay.

"You sure?"

"I don't really know yet," I said. "But you and Ma will have to cut back for a while."

"Cut back on what?" she said, chuckling but not meaning it. "I suppose we can start by forgoing the raisins we put on the cornflakes we eat three times a day; then, when the heat goes off for failure to pay the gas bill, we'll simply light ourselves on fire. And who needs electricity? We'll just—"

A new line of guys behind me pushed closer, looking like they were going to send *me* long distance if I didn't hang up soon. But even though Lisa kept ragging my ass, I hated letting go of my connection with her, with the outside. My new reality was crowding in on me.

I felt another tap on my shoulder. Actually, it was more like a karate chop. I turned and nodded at the stocky Latino, then told Lisa I had to sign off, that I loved her and that she shouldn't build walls around her hopes and dreams.

"How clever," she said. "A prison metaphor. I feel better already."

"Could you cut me a little slack here, Lisa. Hell, it's nearly Christmas."

There was no response at first, but even in the din that surrounded me I could hear her snuffling again, fighting off tears.

"It's that . . . shit, Billy, I'm so damn scared, with Ma coming apart, you in jail, and me all . . . oh, Billy, I'm so sorry. . . ."

It broke my heart to picture her at the beat-up kitchen table, elbows on knees, head down, shoulders hunched around the phone, her pretty face lined with pain, at war with a disease she didn't deserve. That's when the Latino reached around me and emphatically hung up the telephone for me and I walked off, feeling worse than before.

Soon after I'd returned to my cell, I had my first visitor, his presence signaled by the sharp scent of cologne, then by a stomach that preceded the rest of him by a good six inches. Was this squat, fat-assed stranger my new celly? My second thought was that the food must be better here than at Quentin. My third thought was despite his unimpressive appearance, I'd better not take him lightly. He wore an expression like a block of ice, the kind of face that would never betray aces in a poker game.

"Hello, Billy," he said, and while I was wondering how he knew my name, he held out a hand that was warm and dry and surprisingly small. "My name is Don Campora; most people call me 'the don' or 'don-Don.' Anyway, I'm sort of the welcome wagon around here."

I didn't know whether to laugh or order a beer and pizza. What I said was, "Much obliged, sir, but I'm a little weary at the moment."

"Of course, of course," he said, smiling and using his hand to plaster down a patch of errant hair on his nearly bald head. "I'll only be a minute. Tell me what you did on the outside, Billy."

I told him I was a law student, figuring maybe I could get some information out of him about correspondence school.

"How long have you studied law?"

"All my life," I told him. I explained that I'd also had two years at UCLA Law School and was looking to finish by correspondence.

"You going to be a jailhouse lawyer here, Billy?"

"If people need help," I said, "I'll try to give it to them."

Campora nodded, then made himself comfortable on the lower bunk, not looking like a guy who'd only be a minute. "That's the way I am, too, Billy. I help people. In fact, I'm thinking we might be able to help each other."

"Well, thank you, sir—and no offense—but I'm tuckered, and I'd be much obliged if you'd leave my cell."

I could see I was getting off on the wrong foot with this guy because though he kept smiling at me, his eyes, which were small, closely set, and dark as coal, suddenly sparked a little. Pig eyes, lit up from behind.

"You look like a nice young man," he said, "and you've got some balls, too, that's obvious. But I'll be blunt. I run things here. I run the cons, the gangs, even the guards. I decide who goes to the hospital, who goes to the Hole. I decide where people work and how many packs of cigarettes it costs to get somebody killed. Okay?"

"Sure," I said. "It's okay by me."

"Good. Because now we've got that straight, I want you to do a little favor for me. I want you to come over here in front of me and drop your pants."

"Sir?"

"You heard me," he said. He leaned forward and slammed the cell door shut. "I want to see if that thing between your legs is as pretty as the rest of you."

So Joey knew what he was talking about. I was nervous, but not panicked. Adrenaline had overwhelmed my fatigue, so I knew I could take him one-on-one. I'm a little over six feet tall and wiry strong from roughnecking oil rigs in eastern Oklahoma and two years building roads and hauling base rock and asphalt between college and law school. I'd throw the fat little bastard out my cell, give him time to cool down.

"That ain't going to happen, sir," I said, "so get out of my cell."

"I guess I've not made myself clear, kid," he said. Then, in a quiet tone, like a man ordering breakfast, don-Don Campora explained that he was making "claim" on me.

"I'm going to be your protector, kid. You should consider yourself lucky."

"I can take care of myself, sir, starting presently if you want to see." I added the last touch of bravado to conceal the fact I was having second thoughts.

He kept smiling. "The guys here are going to take a shine to you, Billy. They'll like the way your dark hair is swept back like a movie star, and they'll love those pretty blue eyes, too."

He moved in closer. "Indian eyes, that's what they are, Billy, pale like an albino's. Know what it all adds up to?"

I stared at him.

"It means the line of black jockers will stretch from here to the chow hall waiting their turn at the handsome young white fish. Without me, Billy, your asshole will be the size of a Buick within three days."

He watched me closely, and I tried to meet his eyes and not seem ruffled by what he was saying.

"You'll never have a better offer, Billy, even if I gave you a choice, which I'm not going to do. You'll be completely safe with me, Billy. I'll rarely lend you out, and I'll let you stay a man."

"Stay a *man?*"

"You heard me. Most of the jockers here will want you to be a woman to make them feel they're still okay. They'll give you a nickname, Bunny or Rose, make you grow your hair, shave your legs, the whole trip. I know who I am and won't make you do any of that shit."

"You won't make me do anything else either, sir."

Campora kept smiling friendly-like, and I pictured him shrugging and walking out. But that isn't what he did. What he did was cluck his tongue sadly and rise to his small feet, slowly, as if it pained him. Then he walked up close to me and, like a magician producing a flower, made a knife materialize in his right hand. Actually, it looked like a screwdriver that had been filed into a stiletto, but whatever it was, it was sharp, pressed up under my chin, and painful.

"You're not getting the point, Billy," he said, and then proved himself wrong by puncturing my skin with the steel tip of the stilletto. I could smell his sour breath on me and see those pig eyes glowing, putting out heat as he began to push his crotch against my leg, humping me like a dog. My calves were cramping, and I realized Campora's blade had forced me up on my toes, my back against the upper pallet. My heart was about to pound a hole in my chest.

"So you need me more than I need you, kid, and goddamn, I need you a lot. So drop 'em!"

One of the things I'll never forget about that moment is how men kept peering through the small Plexiglas window in my unlocked cell door and not one of them helped or even seemed to pay attention to what was happening. One of them was a guard. They were circling my cell like jackals, waiting for the show to start. I was on my own.

"Don't feel guilty about this, Billy, because like I said, you have only one choice, and I'm it."

"That doesn't seem fair," I gasped, the cold steel blade nudging my Adam's apple every time I spoke.

He smiled at that, kept grinding against my leg. "Fair? Why is that, Billy?"

"Giving me just one choice when I'm going to give you *two.*"

"*You* giving *me* choices?" he said, his sallow face a twisted smirk. "That's good, Billy."

"Yes, sir," I gasped, literally looking down my nose at him. "The first one—if you're the one who's still alive at the end of all this—is to fuck a corpse, because that's the only way you're ever going to fuck me."

He stopped moving against me. At least I had his attention. "Even there," I continued, finding unexpected strength in my raspy voice, "you might have a problem, because I plan on ripping your dick off before you can finish me."

Campora stopped smiling then, and I felt the point of the shank break through my skin again, deeper this time, causing blood to mushroom across my shirt. His eyes narrowed to slits then as he grabbed my privates with his free hand and squeezed hard on them. I couldn't help but let out a yell.

"I don't like that choice much, Billy," he said. "Can you tell?"

The fatigue, fear, and searing pain in my testicles were getting the best of me. I felt dizzy, but knew I had to stay on my feet and keep talking. "I didn't think you would, sir. That's why I'm . . . hoping you might consider the second one instead . . . which is to walk on out of my cell and . . . let me get to work on a brief that will get you out of here . . . out of Soledad."

His laughter crashed into my face with a sound like collapsed scaffolding. "Listen, punk," he sneered. "There are plenty of jailhouse lawyers in here, and I own all of them. They'll write me a habeas corpus brief for a carton of cigarettes."

"That may be true," I said, sounding more calm than I felt, though my vision was going dark from the pain. "But it looks to me like your particular *corpus* is still rotting right here inside Soledad."

The pressure increased on my balls, but I knew I'd better keep talking. "Tell me something, Mr. Campora. Did any of your jailhouse lawyers get straight A's in law school? Did any of them even *go* to law school?"

"Book learning ain't everything, kid; in here, it's *nothing*."

"I'm not talking ivory tower bullshit, Mr. Campora; I'm talking about experience and brain power. The kind it takes to make things happen outside, where the courts are."

He relaxed the pressure below, though I could still feel the blade pressing against my throat.

"Believe me, Mr. Campora, any writ-writing dipshit can get himself thrown into prison; getting people out takes a different talent."

His eyes narrowed as he came up on his toes so his face was closer to mine. "If you're so goddamn good at getting people out, shyster, how come you're here?"

"Not for long," I said. "I'll be walking out the door right behind you, Mr. Campora, I guarantee it."

I had his attention, so I kept the words coming, faster than ever. "Any of your amateur writ writers observe over one hundred jury trials and appeals? Any of them write for the law review at an accredited university? How many wrote a dozen successful appeals as an extern at UCLA the way I did?"

Campora cocked his head sideways, appraising me in a different way; he seemed to consider my words for a few seconds, then broke into something like a real smile. He grunted, then suddenly turned, pushed me aside with surprising strength, and sat down on the lower bunk, thinking things over. I wiped the blood off my throat with my sleeve and took some deep breaths. He seemed to have forgotten I was there, but after a minute or two, got up and put the shank back down into the front of his pants.

"Like I said, kid, you've got moxie," he said, jabbing a finger at me. "Okay, here's the deal: I'll give you six months to get me out of here. During that time you've got nothing to worry about because you'll be under my protection. I'll give you Earring, who everybody in the joint is afraid of. The man's six feet five, weighs two eighty-five, and bench presses four hundred. You can't miss him."

"I'm much obliged, sir," I said in my most diffident tone, not wanting to do or say anything to upset the delicate balance that was being struck.

"Don't fall all over yourself, fish. That's just the good news. The bad news is if I'm still here in six months, I hand you over to Earring for bloody seconds when I'm done with you. You got it?"

I nodded.

He started to leave, and then added, "Your new celly is quite a character. A lifer, in for murder, but he was a professional, a mechanic for hire, so not to worry. He's harmless. Just keep your cell deadlocked for the next couple of days after the screws have racked the tier doors open. By then the word will get around that I'm behind you."

It was clear that Don Campora—or the don or don-Don or whatever the hell he was called—could also rightly be called the de facto warden of Soledad Prison.

"Got it?" he said.

"Got it," I said, and began to breathe again.

4

I was relieved a few hours later to see that true to Campora's word, my new cellmate was an OG, so fragile he looked like an X-ray of himself. He entered my cell, dropped a stool he'd carried in his right hand, and offered a formal bow. In his other hand, he cradled a blanket full of his belongings. He introduced himself simply as Dickens and claimed to be an ex–British naval officer who had read everything written by his namesake and that he had memorized both the Old and New Testaments. I told him he couldn't prove it by me, since I'd read little of Charles Dickens and, being raised Catholic, knew more catechism than bible.

"Fear not, young sir," he said, in what sounded like a cultured, British accent that was probably fake like everything else here. "Thanks to the bountiful grace of God, it's never too late to salvage an open heart and mind from Satan's shipwreck of sin." He then cast a red-eyed glance around my tiny cell and added, "So this is my new humble abode. Well, I'll not deprive you of your obvious preference for the crow's nest."

I didn't contest the point, and he spread his gear out on the lower bunk, gabbing all the while and spouting all sorts of biblical admonitions. When I admitted I wasn't much of a churchgoer, he said, "In that case, 'Add to your faith, virtue, and to virtue, add *knowledge*.' That would be II Peter, 1:5, Master Strobe, and that would be *you* to whom the good Saint Peter was speaking!"

Dickens didn't seem dangerous, just crazy, and I figured I could do worse. Later, during our walk to the chow hall for dinner, I mentioned my plan to offer free legal services to the inmates.

He spun around and slapped a hand on each of my shoulders. "Ah, yes! Bring my soul out of prison!" he shouted, "that I may praise thy name!"

When I stared blankly at him, he gave me a curious glance. "Psalms 142:7," he said. "Goodness, lad, you are truly a work in process, a desert of nescience, a veritable tabula rasa. But fear not, for 'I will rejoice in thy salvation.' That was Psalm 9:14, Billy Strobe. You may wish to take notes as we proceed with your education."

I told him I'd consider that.

Outside the mess, I saw more than a thousand hungry inmates milling around in a freezing rain, waiting for their chance to form a single line and enter a hall that could handle less than a third of the population at CTF North at once. I was starved, as my lunch bag had contained four slices of white, stale-tasting bread, with nothing inside but mustard. Dickens explained that someone had either been pissed off or flat forgot to put in the meat. The problem is that California prisons served only two meals in the mess hall. The lunch bag is passed out with breakfast—miss breakfast, no lunch. So there was nobody at the chow hall to protest to, and the mustard sandwich had left me hungrier than I was before.

The mess hall at dinner was a loony bin—uncontrolled shouting, shoving, slapping, and the clanging and banging of hard plastic utensils on aluminum tables. When I finally got inside, shaking from cold, I took my tray from a square hole in an aluminum wall and followed Dickens toward a table with four aluminum seats and attacked my food, which tasted like aluminum, too.

I spotted Campora in the white section, holding court and involved in animated conversation. He winked at me, and I nodded back. Sitting across from him had to be the guy he called Earring. The man's neck was the size of my thigh, and his broad back and shoulders were nearly as wide as the table. His sleeves were rolled up, exposing bulging forearms as big as hams. A greasy ponytail hung down his back, though it looked like he was balding up top. An earring dangled from one ear. I couldn't see his face and didn't want to.

Dickens motioned to a seat next to him, and I took it. It was strange in this house of chaos to see Dickens offer a silent grace, then approach his meal with the most gracious manners, all the while humming "A Mighty Fortress Is Our God" and dabbing his mouth with a paper napkin he had shaken out as if it were fine embroidered linen like Ma used to set out on Sunday afternoon. I wondered how many people this mild-mannered man had assassinated before he was caught. Across from us, a tall, gaunt fellow with a hideously burned face ate with his fingers. What he was eating was what the menu described as *steak*—a piece of burnt animal flesh not much bigger than a half-dollar—and, for dessert, *cake,* consisting of hardened, day-old cornbread that water wouldn't soften.

Risking another unwanted biblical lecture, I asked Dickens why there were only four guards, armed with nothing but belted nightsticks.

"Wouldn't matter if there were fifty of them," he said.

He then caught the eye of one of the guards, a young black man, and motioned him over. To my amazement, the guard responded.

"James," said Dickens to the guard, "would you be so good as to explain to our young fish what would prevent the rabble in here from overpowering the four of you should it be their desire to do so?"

James nodded and turned to me, his face expressionless. "Nothing," he said. "You could take us anytime you wanted to."

"And James," said Dickens, "tell Mr. Strobe what assistance he can expect from you four guards should he be attacked by another inmate in here."

"None whatsoever," said James. "You're on your own." Lines delivered, he walked away.

"So why *don't* you take them?" I asked as soon as the guard was out of earshot.

"Soledad has a no-hostage release policy, so we'd never get through the main gate. Did you see the gun towers around the perimeter of the outside wall? Put simply, we would be shot to death. We choose, therefore, to coexist with the guards *en détente*."

On the way back to the cell block, I decided to tell Dickens about my confrontation with Don Campora.

"So that's why I was moved," he said, giving me a grave look. When I told him I had headed off any violence, he smiled and added, "Well, lad, you were blessed with good fortune. The don is famous for coming on with the bloody trick bag—getting you in his debt with favors—and when that doesn't work, out comes his famous shank, then, if you'll pardon me, out comes the . . . other thing."

He stopped walking and took me firmly by the elbow. His eyes glowed with intensity. "Never be *anybody's* punk, Billy! Once you're turned out, even a single time, you're finished here in Soledad."

"What do I do if Earring isn't around?"

"Respectfully decline the suitor's overture," Dickens said, rubbing his nearly bald head. "If that doesn't work, then it is truly 'a time to kill'—Ecclesiastes 3:3."

"I should *kill* him?"

"Without thought, guilt, or peradventure of doubt. Think of yourself as Shiva, the third god of the Hindu Triad, the Trimurti, the destroyer of ignorance, desire, ego, and death."

"I thought you were pretty much a Christian man, Dickens."

"I am a man of God in all His forms."

"Nothing wrong with hedging your bets, I reckon."

"That's why you'll need a blade, young Billy, which Father Dickens will provide when I return to my humble trade."

"Which was?"

"Before a brief stint in the Hole, I was—and again shall I be—the prison's leading manufacturer of both spiritual ambrosia and weapons of mass destruction. Loaves and fishes, lad, and arms with which to smite Satan's progeny."

I was confused by all this and said so.

"Shiva teaches that out of destruction comes renewal and re-creation. A second chance, if you will."

He chuckled, leaving me to guess, as he always did, whether he was serious, putting me on, or simply insane. But I thanked him, and we headed back to our cell, where I knew I would sleep despite the ongoing racket. By ten-o'clock lock-down, I had already dozed, but was awakened by a loud clanging sound. Dickens assured me it was just the night guard—a guy named Borkstead who, of course, everyone called Dork Head—racking all the tier doors shut. I began to feel safe for the first time in days.

But not for long. Dickens urged me out of the bunk, handed me a small mirror, and instructed me to keep an eye out for Dork Head through the small broken opening in the steel door. I figured the old guy had either gone simple or maybe wanted to whack off in relative privacy, so what the hell, I'd play along. I held the looking glass out through the cell door window, watched and listened, but heard nothing . . . until I heard a grating sound behind me, the sound of Dickens turning his stool upside down and unscrewing one of the legs. Out of a hollowed-out leg appeared a syringe, a metal spoon, and some waxed paper from which he removed what looked like a small black marble. I'd heard that over 80 percent of the cons here were on drugs, mostly heroin, but never pictured Dickens as a user. Where would he find a vein in that bundle of twigs he had become?

"Christ, Dickens," I shouted, "put that shit away! It's my ass, too!"

There's a rule at Soledad that if your celly is caught with drugs, you both go down.

"Silence, my dear novitiate," he whispered. "And please refrain from taking the name of the Lord thy God in vain. There is no cause for concern, for I'm preparing a sufficient amount for both of us."

"I don't *want*—"

"Please be so good as to keep your voice down. The entire tier will be clamoring for a taste and alert the pig in the process."

I could smell something like vinegar as Dickens cut a small piece off the marble into the spoon, and I saw that he had lit a pair of matches under the spoon.

"*Dammit, Dickens!*"

"For heaven's sake, lad, *shut up!* You're going to get us in trouble!"

The irony of his comment silenced me momentarily, and I could see the heroin was already melting in some water he'd put in the spoon. I didn't know whether to try to stop him or keep my watch at the front of the cell. By the time I decided to stop him, he was jamming a needle between his toes. Suddenly a whoop went up in the cell next to ours.

"Hey *motherfuckah*, share the wealth!"

"Dickens, you honky dishrag, open up your stash!"

"We smell nectar, motherfuckah, save some for us or we come get you tomorrow."

It was passing from one cell to the next like gossip, mirrors popping through broken cell door windows.

Dickens didn't look up as he spoke to me. "Congratulations, Strobe, you deplorable young arsehole! You've awakened the masses. We're done in. See if the screws are coming."

I didn't have to. I could tell by the new outburst of catcalls that Dork Head was on the prowl, confirmed by a glimpse of a CO uniform starting up the steel stairs to our tier on the third floor.

"It's the *guard*, Dickens!" I shouted, but the expression on his face told me that the approach of Lucifer himself, driving a thundering team of fire-breathing horses, couldn't distract him now. I raced over, grabbed up all the other paraphernalia and was hiding it under my mattress at the precise moment when Dork Head arrived at our cell.

Busted.

You're never alone in prison, and it begins to work on you right away, especially if you're a loner like me. I reckon that's why the isolation at the Adjustment Center—sometimes called O Wing, but generally known as the Hole—was a relief at first. But soon the walls closed in around me, and after my first forty-eight hours, I would have welcomed a visit from Adolf Hitler.

Food was slipped in once a day through a three-by-ten-inch slot in the bars of the Hole. It was up to me how to dole it out to myself. The Hole had no ventilation and was always either too hot or too cold. I couldn't concentrate. Although they allowed me two books, there was no light for reading after 10:00 P.M., and time weighed heavy on my heart.

I was allowed exactly thirty minutes of "out time" every twenty-four hours to shower and exercise after passing through a sally port where I stripped, bent over, spread my cheeks, and coughed. I began to hallucinate at some point in my third day or night: rats everywhere as big as dogs with mouths like alligators, waiting for me to go to sleep.

By the end of my third day in the Adjustment Center, I was definitely adjusted and ready to avoid trouble at any cost, including a new willingness to snitch on Dickens if he kept running drugs out of our cell. Here's a fact typical of the upside-down world of prison life: The worst thing you can be accused of inside is being a snitch, yet everybody is a snitch.

After a month back in the general prison population, I began to slip into something close to a routine. Well, not a routine exactly, because prison is like a grenade with a loose pin: there's going to be an explosion, and you hope it's some other guy sitting on it when it goes off. Living with all this fear and distrust, I was determined not to let myself become hardened like the rest of the guys here, but it was easy to see how scar tissue could dull feelings and harden hearts.

On the plus side, my application for correspondence studies at the Golden State School of Law was approved, and I was even granted a hardship scholarship, courtesy of a Montgomery Street white-shoe firm probably trying to grab some cheap public relations exposure. I wished I had the guts to tell them to shove it, but the free ride would mean I could send everything I earned in the shops to Ma and Lisa. Funny how things work out. I took a chance with the Club because I was about to lose my scholarship, and now, in a different kind of club, I had been granted another one.

I began developing a clientele among the inmates, which was easy because I didn't charge anything, since most inmates are poor and I had no interest in cigarettes, the universal prison currency. Don Campora remained my top priority, of course, and if he was leveling with me, the arresting officers had technically screwed up on his Miranda warning, providing potential grounds for a new trial. The overreaching cops may literally have saved my ass.

Within the next several weeks, I was working six other active files, six real people I was helping. I had found something of value in this moral swamp; I guess you could even call it a cause. Something I could sink my teeth into, carrying on in a small way the work my dad had done. All of them were dead-bang guilty, of course, though not one of them ever admitted it. But they were also men who never had a real chance in life, stillborn into a system they couldn't beat. All things considered, despite a rocky start, I was working toward some sort of balance at Soledad.

That's when the new guy showed up and turned everything inside upside down.

5

Darryl Orton arrived at Soledad on the first day of spring, with the force of a March wind. I wasn't there when the bus unloaded, as I never participated in the prison greeting ritual for newly arrived fish. I didn't see him until the next day when he walked into the rec yard like he owned it. Anyone could see right away this stranger had a two-by-four on his shoulder, maybe a monkey or two riding on top of that. Didn't talk to anybody, wouldn't even look at anybody, but the way the man put one foot in front of the other shouted out loud and clear: Don't fuck with me.

He appeared to be around forty, about six-three and 190 pounds, with straight rust-colored hair cut short. Kind of a Nolte look, but leaner, his face all hard angles with leathery skin drawn tight over prominent cheekbones. He had a nose that had gotten in the way of too many punches and a three-inch scar over his right eye, which I later learned were symbols of survival right here at Soledad, where he had spent a previous four-year hitch for the botched armed robbery of a convenience store when he was in his early twenties. He wore a pair of rimless glasses that looked totally out of place on his granite face.

It was cold in the yard, and I watched him making a beeline for a seat at the end of one of the wooden benches on which light from the late afternoon sun still slanted against the east wall. This could mean trouble, for that was an area favored by members of the Nuestra Familia, a prison gang that years before had spun off from the Mexican Mafia—the EME—over a single pair of shoes and had been at war with the Mafia ever since.

Prison life is more socially structured than an anthill. The COs—correctional officers—see that everything is done on schedule: eat, sleep, exercise, and work. You belong to a gang for protection much like minority high school kids do growing up in barrios that stretch from Harlem to Watts and up north to nearby Watsonville. The gang is your family, your only family, and you owe its members complete allegiance. You may have to kill someone to get into some of the gangs, like the Mexican Mafia. Only OGs like Dickens and a handful of cons can manage to stand on the sidelines, but as Soledad's only free, full-service, equal-opportunity jailhouse lawyer under don-Don's protection, I was able to straddle the structure.

But here was this white loner, walking into sure disaster his first day in the yard, no more than thirty feet from the NF's bench, and nobody saying a word of warning to him. This was no surprise, because cons don't stick their necks out in prison, and they damn sure don't cotton to a fish who carried himself the way this guy Orton did. The man had the kind of presence that tended to shame the fading remnant of pride in every con's psyche that hadn't quite died yet; the kind of self-assurance that can set an inmate's brain to dancing in red ants and stinging nettle. Why? Because a con wants everybody around him to be as housebroken as he is.

Besides, inmates loved a good fight anytime, or even a bad one, since there's no TV out in the yard, and they eventually got bored trying to pump themselves up on monkey bars once the weights were taken away after that windpipe murder, or bouncing balls around and bullshitting each other.

"I think that's Darryl Orton!" I heard a white OG say.

"By God, you're right," said another. "Must be ten, fifteen years."

So he had been in before. Okay, what the hell, he knows what the deal is, no use sticking my neck out. I'd always valued my white ass, especially where people like El Matar and the NF are concerned. So I kept quiet, even though I could see he was going to have to walk right past me. As he approached, damned if he didn't pause for a second and look right at me with an unsettling gaze that seemed strangely familiar. I wanted to walk away then, not stay for the carnage, but something told me I was about to stretch the limits of my protection arrangement with Campora. I had to warn this guy about the bench.

There's an expression in prison called "working the corners," where cons, sometimes even natural enemies, will put their heads together to ward off violence that may play into the hands of the guards or be undesirable for some other reason. I was hoping don-Don would see what I was about to do in that light. Besides, hadn't that tall black dude, who I had come to know as Tom Collins, saved *my* ass that first day at the phones?

"Could you hold it there a minute, sir?" I said as Darryl Orton started past me. As I spoke, I reached out and touched an elbow hard and dry as a bleached desert bone, and he spun back on me like he'd been hit with a cattle prod.

"What can I do for you, kid?" he said. Though his manner was brusque, his eyes revealed a gentleness that, like the spectacles shielding them, looked hopelessly out of synch with the rest of him. I opened my mouth, but before I could say anything, he had sat himself down on the bench. I took a step toward him, but one of the NF gangbangers pushed me aside, and El Matar himself walked up to Orton and stood glaring at him, hands on hips.

Matar was scary, not just because of his massive girth and position in the NF, but also because of his sheer ugliness, his oversize head, skin like crushed base rock, and an unexpected mop of long dark hair partially covered by a black-and-gray bandanna. Despite all this, Orton paid him no mind, so Matar leaned close into the stranger's lined face.

"*Fuck off,*" El Matar said in a voice like exploding metal fragments that brought Orton to his feet in preparation, not deference. Matar was known to be pretty frugal in the word department, but he added, "This is *my* bench, fish!"

Darryl Orton was tall like I said, but even he had to look up to meet the hard gaze of the NF shot-caller.

"No shit?" the stranger said, looking puzzled as he bent over and began inspecting the bench, all twelve feet of it, both front and back. El Matar stood there, arms folded over his massive chest, looking perplexed, as the new guy kept studying the bench like a man considering an expensive purchase, even kneeling down every once in a while so he could check out the underside. El Matar was clearly losing patience but didn't seem to know what to do.

Orton finally rose to his feet, dusted off his knees, slapped his hands together, and said, "Funny, señor, I can't find your name on this here bench anywheres." Then he smiled and plopped his ass right back down on the end of it, which happened to be the only place against the east wall where the sun was still shining.

I was aware a crowd was building around us and glanced up at the tower to see what the screws were up to, which was nothing. El Matar meanwhile regained his cool and nodded in the direction of three fellow NF members who joined the leader and formed a semicircle around the stranger.

"You want to see my name, asshole? Maybe I carve it on your forehead before I kill you." This rare outpouring of words revealed that the new guy had really gotten Matar's goat.

Cons moved in close around the scene, drawn by curiosity and the promise of violence. I heard somebody else whisper, "Yep, that's Darryl Orton, all right."

The air was surging with the kind of electrical tension that follows the first hit of an earthquake, when everybody gets close to a doorjamb, waiting for the next shaker to hit. Even more frightening was the way the yard had been sucked barren of all sound; no grunts from the exercise bars, no music from the Bloods' zone, not even a whisper from the trees outside the walls. Nothing.

I spotted Earring and wondered how long he had been standing near me. He had hardly been out of my sight, nor I his, since the day I got out of the Hole. He had never said a word to me, but he needed no introduction. I'd never seen a bigger, uglier brute. A half-inch-wide white scar tapered out of his disfigured right eye up into his massive, misshapened forehead, and a Fu Manchu mustache drooped down a jaw the size of a Buick headlight. Other than Matar himself and the Zulu guy at the telephones, he stood taller than anyone in the yard. My protector—for the present, at least. Would he allow the NFers to kill a white guy? Could he stop it if he wanted to? He was standing with a couple of skinhead Aryan Brotherhood thugs watching things develop, but they seemed to have decided to stay out of it, which meant big trouble for Darryl Orton. The blacks, of course, couldn't care less, having learned from the whites on the outside the passive art of allowing undesirables to go right ahead and exterminate each other.

I inched closer, drawn to the heat but still safely back from the flame, feeling sorry for the guy but not about to push my luck any further. This Orton fellow had made his bed and would have to lie in it. Maybe die in it.

I started to move back a little, but as the Latinos closed on him, damned if Orton didn't slowly rise to his feet and look between two of them, straight at me again. But his once-gentle eyes were suddenly a pair of blue steel guns trained on my heart. I tried to look away but watched him as he carefully pocketed his glasses, spat to one side, gave his head a quick little shake as if to say what the hell, then spun around and launched five white knuckles that sent El Matar backwards into the grasp of his friends.

It was on now, and still no movement from the COs or the tower guards. Within seconds, the whole yard converged in a circle around the bench. I didn't want to watch, but I couldn't bring myself to walk away either. With El Matar temporarily neutralized, standing there with strings of blood and mucus hanging from his nose and mouth, the new guy took after another NFer with what looked like a professional combination of punches. When the third one got him in a neck grip from behind, Orton broke it by throwing an elbow deep into the guy's solar plexus. The Latino bellowed in pain, and everybody in the yard began yelling. Bodies pressed in on me, screaming, sweating bodies, thirsty for blood, a few of the whites shouting "Or-*ton*, Or-*ton*." I realized I was yelling his name, too, roaring like the rest of the animals.

But then El Matar rejoined the fray and nailed Orton right on the jaw, and you could see he was good as finished. The Aryans moved in a little closer, which kept the other NFers on the sidelines, and a pair of guards moseyed in from the west shack, hands on sticks, which kept the knives out of play. The Aryans had silently communicated that they could live with the status quo, and the guards had moved in close enough to say go ahead and bang the fucker, just don't kill him. And no weapons.

But the NFers didn't need weapons. They had the new guy down on the ground, kicking him in the kidneys and working his face over real good. He was bleeding badly, but blood wasn't enough for the black and brown cons. They wanted the stranger dead and started shouting at El Matar.

"*Peel him!*"

"*Kill the motherfucker!*"

"*Finish him!*"

Jesus, I thought, a guy they didn't even know. Did these guys want to see a death to convince themselves *they* were still alive, or had they been buried alive in hatred too long to see much difference between the two? Gradually, the shouting merged into a single voice, a chant that sounded like "Gran'em, gran'em, gran'em!" In prison, *grinding* a con meant to annihilate him, beat him into an unidentifiable mush.

Suffocating bodies pressed in around me, and the smell of urine and sweat, together with a noise level off the scale, was giving me vertigo. I began pushing back against the wall of nameless flesh when a strange thing happened. My legs, heavier than tombstones, had started pushing the rest of me not to the rear of the crowd, but to the front, toward the Latinos, toward the new guy. I guess I was going to have to stand with this stranger, try to lend him a hand, despite a heart pushing through my chest and arms hanging limp with fear at my sides. Still, I surged forward into the fray, the moth now racing toward the flame, common sense, even my terror, subdued by the communal bloodlust and brutality.

But not my lack of skill. I got in only one punch before something clobbered me on my left ear, sending a searing pain through my body. As I turned to see who had hit me, one of Matar's NFers, a Latino about my size, teeth bared like an animal, suckerpunched me in the mouth, rattling my teeth together and starting a light show behind my eyes. When he hit me again, I dropped like a sack of potatoes. By the time I came to, Darryl Orton was being roughly packed off toward the infirmary by two inmates, and NF members were helping their leader up onto the contested bench seat. Then Tom Collins, my Zulu warrior, all six feet six of him, was helping me to my feet.

"Hope you fight better in a courtroom than you do outside a' one," he said, and moved away from me like I was contagious. Blood still streamed from El Matar's nose, but he leaned back, spread-eagled his arms across the top of the bench, and crossed his legs as casually as if hanging out on the beach at Acapulco.

A few days after the bench brawl, I sat down for breakfast next to Darryl Orton in the chow hall's white section. This was not an act of courage, for it was already understood that this was my jailhouse lawyer routine with new cons. Besides, I knew that the one guy El Matar feared was Earring and that good ol' Earring always had one of his psychotic eyes trained on me, the one that was a full half-inch higher on his slab of a face than the other one.

Orton didn't look up or seem to care who had sat down next to him. He seemed to have the ability to focus completely on whatever he was doing at the time, which in this case was eating something loosely called breakfast. When I could take the silence no longer, I asked him how he was doing.

He looked up and gave me a little sideways smile with a mouth still so swollen I couldn't see how he was able to chew. "The SOS ain't improved none," he said, referring to the creamed chipped beef on toast we called shit-on-a-shingle. He lifted a soggy piece of burnt toast and let it ooze back onto his plate, chunks of last night's pork fat sliding off his tray.

"Recycled mystery meat," he said, "smothered in gravy so thin a man could drink it through a straw."

"Lunch is worse," I said.

"I know it," he said, and glanced at me for the first time. Without the swelling, probably not a bad-looking guy, although his glasses, miraculously salvaged but broken and pieced together with Scotch tape, sagged on his cheeks and gave him a look of vulnerability. "You the dumb asshole tried to help me the other day?"

I was surprised he'd even noticed, let alone characterized my puny efforts as a serious attempt at help. I felt my face reddening as I told him that with help like mine, he could end up dead next time.

"No matter, you tried. You some kind a' do-gooder?"

"No," I said, "but you looked like you could use some help."

"You must be new. A guy don't stick his neck out in prison. Besides, you don't know me from a load of hay."

I didn't answer him right away, for my brain had been knocked backwards in time by an expression my mother used on my dad whenever he'd bring street people home. "You don't know that man from a load of hay," she'd say, and start talking about how she was barely able to put enough food on the table for the four of us, let alone feed some vagrant, usually Irish, who Dad had met in a bar on the way home. Then she'd take her plate and eat in the kitchen. Dad would shrug and deliver his sermon about the Catholic Church's social commitment to the poor, always in a voice that was sure to reach the kitchen, while me and Lisa tried to figure how anybody could confuse a person with a load of hay.

Ma had a point: we were always short of money. That's why I started my repair business, going around the neighborhood, fixing everything from broken rakes to lawn mowers. Made me feel good, and I made a few dollars at it, too. I got into food mixers and curling irons next; then, when Dad died and money disappeared altogether, I learned how to fix copy machines, shavers—you name it. Couldn't hardly get into my bedroom for all the stuff I was working on.

Funny, but long after Dad was gone I'd be looking at a mixer or mower I'd fixed and hear him say, "Damn, son, that's wonderful how you can do that." Hear his deep sandpaper voice, could smell the whisky on his breath, feel his strong hands on my shoulders.

Darryl's voice interrupted my thoughts. "Anyway," he was saying, "I'm much obliged."

"I was just trying to even up the odds a little," I told Darryl, trying to sound cool.

"I reckon you were," he said, not looking up, "though it'd take a stopwatch to time your effort."

I felt my face burning again, though this time not with pride. "I can fix those glasses for you," I said, ready to change the subject.

"Look, kid," he said, in a tone that betrayed impatience. "You probably mean well, but my glasses are fine the way they are."

"I could heat them up, then dowel them with a paper clip," I said. "It's simple."

"Don't sound simple to me," he said into his plate.

"No trouble. Fixing things comes natural to me," I said. "Neighbors called me Billy Fix-It when I was growing up."

"Billy Fix-It, huh?" said Orton. "You gonna be a repairman when you're out?"

"A lawyer," I said, shaking my head, "like my dad. Well, not like him, exactly. He was a trial lawyer. Put me in front of a group, and I'm a goner."

Darryl frowned. "Yeah, I saw an example of that a few days ago."

I shrugged and felt myself reddening again. The guy was likable, but something about him made me feel like a little kid. "Yeah, well, sometimes it's better to fall off the bottom of the mountain than the top. How *was* the infirmary, Mr. Orton?"

"I get your point, kid," he said, wincing as he tried to bite into a piece of hard bread. "But do me a favor, don't ever mention the word *lawyer* in front of me, okay? I don't like lawyers."

I told him he would have liked my dad, Irish Joe Strobe, the best trial lawyer in the Southwest. He listened—or seemed to, I wasn't sure.

"Anyways," I said, "I'll be a behind-the-scenes lawyer, lending a hand to folks like tenants and minorities, anybody getting cheated by the system." I heard myself sounding like the do-gooder he'd accused me of being, so I decided to acquaint him with the range of legal services I offered and be on my way.

"Billy Fix-It, Esquire, huh?" he said in a sardonic tone. "Gonna finish your hitch here, then go out and fix the legal system, right?"

He seemed to be baiting me, so I shrugged and said, "In the meantime, there's plenty about it that's broke right here."

He nodded, grimaced, touched a cut lip that was still oozing, and pushed the tray away impatiently.

"I was trying to warn you about that," I said. "The NF will throw down on anybody tries to sit on that bench."

He pulled his upper lip back as best he could and reached into his mouth for something, then dropped whatever it was into the tray with a little clinking sound. My stomach rolled when I realized what he had pulled out of his teeth was a tooth.

"Yeah?" he said, rising from the plastic chair. "Well, it ain't over, kid, so I suggest next time you look the other way."

I had decided that much on my own, but he wasn't finished.

"What I'm sayin, kid," he said, "is if I want your help, I'll ask for it." While I tried to say something more clever than go to hell, he added, "And that ain't likely."

Well, screw him, I thought as he walked away, though I was more curious than ever about him. What was with that bench? And what was he in for this time?

But I knew better than to ask. Prison etiquette. It wouldn't matter much, anyway. Darryl Orton struck me as just another decent human being who had been run over by life somewhere along the way. Like Mr. Dog, whose sentence at the L.A. dog pound I'd commuted at the eleventh hour. Mr. Dog eventually got over his slinking around, but it's a scientific fact that humans have better memories than canines, though not as much good sense.

Darryl Orton proved that to be true late the next afternoon; when I entered the yard, there he was, sitting at the sunlit end of that same damn bench.

6

The NFers were ready this time, and it looked like it would be over quick, partly because Darryl allowed one of them to maneuver behind him. It was Querto, a tough little *Norteño*, one of my new clients who had been a middle-weight contender before criminally assaulting the referee at the end of his final fight. A professional boxer's fists are deemed a "dangerous weapon" under the California Penal Code, but the assault charge in the ring soon became irrelevant because later that same night he went after his manager in the manager's own kitchen, slicing and dicing the poor guy with a carving knife.

By the time I arrived at the bench, it appeared that Querto had snuck around behind Darryl and grabbed his arms, then jerked them upward, pinning them between his chunky lats and oversize upper arms. Another NFer, a huge bully called Peligro, rushed Darryl from the front but was met by the heel of Darryl's shoe. Caught him right in the jaw, and there was no mistaking the sound of broken bones as the Latino crumbled to his knees, then toppled sideways on the asphalt, slowly, like a tree falling.

Then El Matar and two other NFers were all over Darryl, fists, elbows, and knees flying. I felt that same tremor of fear I'd felt three days earlier, a weakness that ran right down into my legs like I got when trying to speak in front of a group, only worse.

But I felt anger, too, anger at Darryl's stubborn stupidity, and part of me was thinking good riddance. Of course, it didn't matter what I was thinking, for several of the Latino gangbangers had formed a tight wall around the area that not even Earring could have penetrated. As I was shoved backwards, I caught a glimpse of a dark crimson stain spreading like spilled wine across the gray dirt, and I figured they were going to kill him this time.

Just as I was giving up hope, I felt something sharp jab me in my back, a CO's nightstick, the most welcomed pain I'd ever suffered. Suddenly everyone scattered as guards crashed through the circle and hauled both Darryl and Peligro off to the infirmary. Darryl was about to be grateful his SOS gravy was thin enough to pass through a straw. Peligro, too—word filtered back that they had wired his jaw shut and he'd be out for six to eight weeks.

I didn't see Darryl for two weeks, and the buzz spread around the yard that the screws had lost patience and put him in a strip cell—solitary confinement—for a full week after he was released from the infirmary. Charged with resisting attack, I guess. Your prison justice system hard at work.

Darryl Orton didn't realize it, but he was about to become a client of the law offices of Billy Strobe.

"Strobe," Dork Head shouted at me as I was coming out of the cafeteria a week later, "get your ass up front. You got a visitor. It's your mother."

I went to the visitors area and, without needing to be told, stripped, spread, and coughed. I was used to the mortification, but wondered how much my mother would be put through. The drugs not smuggled into prison by guards on the take were often brought in concealed in the vaginas of female visitors.

I got dressed and entered a huge room full of orange stack-chairs, and there she was, looking pale and upset, sitting off to one side.

The last person I had ever expected to see at Soledad was my mother, and the last thing I wanted to *do* at Soledad was cry in front of her, but one look at Amy Strobe, and I was fighting tears, my lips too unsteady to say anything. She just sat there looking uncomfortable and embarrassed, both hands folded tight over the top of her black purse, not a tear in sight. Good. Her tears would have marinated the toughness I had begun to foster in myself.

"Ma, how did you— Where did you get the money?"

This was stupid. Here's my mother, my first-ever visitor, and I'm babbling about money.

"I'm glad you came," I finally managed.

"A kind gentleman from some law firm in San Francisco—a Mr. Whitmore—wrote and said they were underwriting your correspondence course. They thought you could use a visit and sent me a ticket. Tourist class, of course." A smile with a trace of disdain brushed her last words, though she and Dad had hardly traveled anywhere, let alone first class.

"They sent you a round-trip ticket?"

"Yes, and hotel reservations, paid in advance. Provided a car and driver here and back."

It seemed I had become a project for some Montgomery Street law firm, like saving the rain forests or laboratory animals.

"Well, it's great to see you, Ma. You look real good."

She touched her hair, embarrassed by my obvious lie. "The guard thought I was Cameron Diaz," she said, and I smiled at her self-deprecating joke.

She seemed unable to look at me, but I guess she must have because she said I wish I could say the same for you, William. Ma was the only person who had ever called me by my given name. The tone of her voice was measured, as it had always been since Dad died, lacking any trace of emotion, triggering a flood of memories that bristled like sharp quills. She seemed sober at least, thank God, though her eyes were red-rimmed and her face was puffy.

"The gentleman said you were going to graduate from law school right here in jail. That's good, William. I suppose we should thank God for small favors."

Amy Strobe had developed a gift for masking reproach with a compliment, but it was always the snout of disapproval that soon poked its way through the thin veneer of praise. Never mind, I was determined to stay positive, despite the fact that seeing my mother staring back at me across that three feet of space, she might as well have been in China. The whole thing was unreal, *surreal*, yet her presence in the midst of the human detritus surrounding us, the vastness of the short distance between us, somehow moved me a notch closer to acceptance of the horrible reality of my new status.

"I'm getting good grades, Ma," I said, like I was back in high school.

She fidgeted on the hard chair and kept looking around her, that disapproving look I'd seen ever since Dad died. "You'd think they'd make a person more comfortable."

"Sorry, Ma," I said, forcing a smile, wishing she might try one on herself. "Are you okay?"

She gave me her are-you-insane look and said, "I'm perfectly fine. How could I not be, visiting my only son, the felon, here in the underbelly of the underbelly?"

"I'm sorry, it's—"

"Oh, don't apologize, William. It's really a *lovely* experience, well worth getting my bosom mauled by a two-hundred-pound lesbian Clydesdale."

"How's Lisa?" I asked, sure Ma would eventually calm down if I did.

"Well as can be expected."

"Does she still play her flute?"

"She watches TV. Symptoms about the same. When are you getting out, dear?"

"Ma, I just got in. I'm hoping for maybe three years, assuming I keep my nose clean."

She slowly shook her head, lips tightly compressed, staring at me as if I'd told her I was riddled with cancer.

"Three *years*?" she said.

I nodded, afraid she was going to cry, like the old Ma would have. Reach out and touch my face the way she used to after Dad had tanned my hide. The old Ma would cry if I was held after school for an hour. But new Ma straightened her shoulders and looked disdainfully at the next table, where a Latino woman was in animated conversation with an older, contrite-looking prisoner.

"Well," she said at last, her chin trembling. "At least *you're* taking your medicine. I admire that much anyway, William."

Jesus, I thought, wondering if my mother had flown all the way from Enid, Oklahoma—*tourist class*—to hammer one more nail into the coffin . . . no, into the rotted remains of Joe Strobe, one who had failed to "take his medicine."

"I'm glad he's not around to see it," I said, "but he'd be fighting for me if he was, make no mistake about it, Mother."

"If he was sober enough to find you."

I felt sweat breaking out on my forehead. "I'd be proud to be as good a man as Dad was. Why not let him be, Ma?"

"You should be grateful I won't," she said, meeting my eyes for the first time. "Most men don't see their father's feet of clay until they've wasted most of their own lives trying to live up to him."

I let it go. I'd never won an argument with the new, unimproved Amy Strobe, and knew I wouldn't win this one. I also knew her rigid pose was a prop to keep her from falling apart, so I would continue to accept it. Still, I longed for the old Amy, the one who wrongly thought her only son was always right, whose unconditional love for me used to irritate both Dad and Lisa, the Amy Strobe whose quick wit and kindness had once filled our dysfunctional little home with what passed for happiness. The Amy Strobe who wasn't systematically strangling her own organs with methyl alcohol.

Amy Martin Strobe had once been a seventies radical, smart, beautiful, and Dad's "soul and inspiration," as he often told us. But she was also a well-born girl from a well-off family, and never could accept the poverty that Dad's commitment—and drinking—had consigned us to. When he left us penniless, "damning himself to eternal hell" by his suicide, she vowed never to forgive his cowardice, and by her commitment, damned herself to hell right here on earth.

"Is Lisa responding to her new physical therapy?" I asked, struggling to find safe ground.

"Lisa wants to die," said Amy Strobe, as casually as if describing a new sweater. "She wants the whole world to burn up in a nuclear explosion. 'Then we'd all be equal,' she says."

"Don't you want to talk to Dad?" I ask Lisa, eight years old, four years younger than me. I tell her I think I know where he might be hiding. Waiting for us to find him.

"Dad's dead," Lisa says simply, and goes back to her flute fingering chart.

"Maybe it's not such a bad idea," Ma said, rescuing me from my reflection.

"What's that, Ma?"

"A bomb," she said, her sad gaze sweeping the visitors room again. She took a deep breath, then gave out a little sound that was supposed to be a laugh. "I'm sorry, William, you must think I've gone to the bow-wows, all this bleak talk. Now tell me what I can do for you. Anything at all."

"Letters would be great, Ma. Just to let me know you're taking care of yourself."

She slowly rotated her head from side to side; then she let it fall into her hands. "I'd better," she murmured. "If I don't, who else . . . who else will?"

She broke down then, let the tears come, swaying back and forth, whispering something over and over that sounded like, "My William, my Sweet William."

I had forgotten she called me that when I was a kid. I was her flower, her Sweet William. She reached out and clasped one of my hands in hers and squeezed it with desperate force. "If only they would take me instead," she said. "Do whatever they wanted with me."

"Shh, Ma, it's not so bad here. I'll be fine."

"No you *won't*," she said. She released my hand and fished in her purse for a hankie. "This is a godless place."

I told her I loved her, and she nodded, eyes closed, tears still streaming. Then, just as quickly, she glared accusingly at me through those wet, red-streaked eyes.

"Why?" she said. "Why did you steal, William? Did you think so much of your father and so little of me that you had to prove you shared his weakness? That you, too, were *flawed*, a 'chip off the old block'?"

My head had started to ache, and I felt the need to return to my cell. No, not my cell, just someplace where I could lie down. She had pulled me onto the roller coaster of her emotions. I felt a spasm of grief as I realized that me and Lisa were losing our mother.

I said nothing, and an awkward silence fell across our lowered heads.

"I'm sorry, honey," she whispered finally. "Your mother's behaving badly. I feel terrible you're in this situation." Then she again said, "Is there anything I can do for you?"

"You've got every right to be upset, Ma. I was stupid, and you and Lisa are paying for it. I'll make it up to you."

"Not to worry," she said, straightening her shoulders. "At least I was able to get out of Enid, visit San Francisco again. I haven't been farther away than Nebraska since that godawful trip to Nuevo Laredo back in 1978, which your father considered to be exotic international travel."

She had a point. Joe was a sole practitioner until he took in Amos Blackwell, an office lawyer. He would never trust another trial lawyer with his caseload, and what with a general shortage of funds, Ma never traveled much once they were married. She dabbed at her mouth with the tissue and replaced it in that same frayed black purse she wore everywhere—like a badge of honor—then snapped it shut in a way that signaled an imminent getaway. I leaned in close to her.

"I'm working here, Ma. Helping people. Fixing things. They only pay forty-two cents an hour, but it adds up. I'll keep sending whatever I make."

She nodded and rose to her feet, and suddenly I didn't want it to end, didn't want to return to my cell. She stood there awkwardly for a few seconds until I realized she had forgotten where she came in.

"The door's over there, Ma," I said.

She nodded, lids lowered, knuckles white around her sad purse, then glanced toward the exit and told me she'd have to get back to Lisa in the morning. I said sure, and she said good-bye, William, and kissed me on the cheek. Then she turned away to leave but didn't move, except for her shoulders, which began to shudder violently. One eye on the guard, I turned her back around and put my arms around her, and the floodgates opened again.

"Oh, William, my Sweet William," she cried loudly, over and over until everyone was looking.

"Shh, Ma, it's okay," I said, but she kept screaming and tugging, then clawing until a matron had to come in and pull her away from me. I tried to stop the matron and two guards were on me in a second. Ma seemed to have got a hold of herself by the time they reached the door, and the matron let her wave to me. Then she was gone.

I turned and kicked my chair against the wall, catching the hard edge on my shin. I also caught the attention of one of the guards again, who gave me a hard look but let it go. A spot of blood appeared though my denim pants midway up my shin, but I didn't feel the pain.

7

By the end of my fourth month at Soledad, with spring in full bloom outside the prison walls, I became more depressed. Nature was renewing itself, young UCLA girls would be getting into their short skirts, guitars and bongo drums would be heard all over the campus in celebration of spring, and I was in Soledad Prison, losing time out of life that could never be reclaimed. I tried to distract myself with my studies and caseload. I was doing well at Golden State Law School and polishing my third brief on Campora's motion for new trial. My first brief was bumped on procedural grounds: filed in the wrong court. I'd have to get on top of these technicalities if I was going to be an effective Trojan horse inside the system someday. My second brief had made some headway, but time was running out with don-Don.

I was preparing briefs now for nearly a dozen other inmates, but still couldn't interest Darryl Orton in one. Stubborn old fart wouldn't even accept the grievance application I'd prepared after he had been beaten by guards and put in the Hole without medical attention after merely defending himself in the yard. To top it off, one of the offending guards had written up Darryl for "resisting" in what's called an "accusation."

"We could take the offensive," I explained. "Sue the guards for assault and battery and the warden for permitting it."

"I've already got to deal with being wrote up for defendin myself when they clubbed me," he said.

"Yes, but that accusation will have to be approved by the shift supervisor," I said.

"Who will rubber-stamp it," he said, and I had to agree.

"But then it will be passed on to a screening officer."

"Who will read me my rights and tell me to go to hell."

Darryl knew more about the system than I realized. "Yes, but meanwhile, Darryl, we'll file a grievance report—"

"That'll be sent to the Grievance Committee, who will reject it and send it on to the warden, who will reject it and send it on to the CDC, who will also reject it. Am I right?"

I shrugged and said, "But then we can file our lawsuit for special and punitive damages, injunctive relief from retaliation, and ask to get the guard fired. What do you say?"

"I reject it," he said simply, and then walked away.

The next day I asked Dork Head—who I think was feeling a little guilty about being the guard responsible for getting me sent to the Hole my second day—what Darryl Orton was in for.

"Rape-murder," he said, his squat body rocking back and forth on his oversize heels like always, scanning the yard as he spoke. "Big deal in the newspapers early this year."

"Lifer?"

"You bet, kid, and I'm sure he'll be needing your services, if he doesn't get himself killed first."

"Do you remember him from before?"

"Why, sure. You don't forget Darryl Orton. That seat on the bench was his when he was here long ago, and I guess he wants it back, God knows why. His problem is that we've had nearly a complete turnover since then, different type of clientele, too. Kids. Gangs. No respect."

"Why don't you guys step in faster next time? You know he's a dead man if you don't."

Dork gave his head a quick shake. "Don't push me, kid. You best be worrying about your own ass. Word is your protection is about up with the don."

My mouth went dry as field cotton, picturing Earring holding me down while Campora . . .

Dork Head kept rocking, his head on a swivel, and I had the crazy notion to ask him how much it would cost to let me go. I swear if someone had approached me with an escape plan, I'd of gone for it. I was suffocating in this place and had to get free.

"As for Orton," Dork Head continued, "we can't concern ourselves with every asshole who insists on getting himself killed. Besides, I suspect he's too smart to go through all that again over a lousy seat on a bench."

I wasn't so sure about that, but I saw several cons eyeing us, so I ended the conversation. It doesn't pay for an inmate to be seen as being too aligned with management.

When Darryl got out of isolation and had his yard privileges restored, I reluctantly urged him to join the Aryan Brotherhood—which had struck a truce with the Mexican Mafia—before Matar and his

Nuestra Familia could get around to killing him. Like all prisons, Soledad was run by race-based gangs, each vying for a piece of the action. In prison, the action was drugs. The L.A. Crips had controlled crack cocaine, but the Mexican Mafia was moving in—though hampered by intraracial struggles between the *Norteños* and the *Sureños*, plus its ongoing battle with Nuestra Familia. Then there were African American groups such as the Black Guerrilla Family—the BGF—and the Black Gangster Disciples, all wanting their fair share, not to mention miscellaneous white biker gangs. All in all, a perfectly logical setting for rehabilitation, right? No wonder 70 percent of parolees eventually returned to the California Department of Corrections. As Tom Collins liked to say: "What's gettin 'corrected,' here? Obviously not us."

Darryl's reaction to my advice was a wry smile. "Never was much of a joiner, Billy."

I noticed that this was the first time Darryl had called me by my first name.

"You'd better become one," I said. "The guards are getting tired of what's going down in the yard. I'm handling a case now where they used a Taser gun on my client."

"That won't kill you."

Darryl knew damn well the guards were capable of using the Taser on an inmate's testicles. He also knew that guards at Soledad would sometimes pit "hard rocks"—troublemakers like himself and Matar—against each other like gladiators, then shoot them from the tower when they wouldn't stop on command. Sixteen inmates were murdered in California prisons in 1997 alone.

"If you keep up with the bench craziness, Darryl, the NFers *will* kill you—unless the guards get fed up and kill you first. Link up with the Aryans. They respect you, and you'll get the Mexican Mafia on your side in the bargain."

"You worry too much, kid."

"May I ask you a personal question, Darryl?"

"Sure, so long as it ain't too personal."

"May I ask why that bench is so damned important to you?"

"Sure you can ask."

"Well?"

But he was walking away, heading for the yard.

The don had managed to get me assigned to the library so that my efforts in his behalf would not be interrupted by the physical demands of the upholstery or machine shops. He had also bribed one of the COs to have me assigned to appliance repair on a freelance basis and to get my full twenty-two dollars a month on top of that just for clerking at the library. It doesn't sound like much, but the top income by any inmate at Soledad was forty-eight dollars a month for a black dude who cut hair. Anyways, add in what I had started charging clients who could afford to pay a buck or two, and I was able to send around thirty-five dollars a week back home. Not much, but enough to keep their lights burning.

To ease the day-to-day pain of existing between fear and the boredom, I developed a schedule of working on briefs in the library during the day and studying law after lights-out, which at Soledad was midnight. I felt most secure late at night, with the tier doors racked shut, Dickens zoned out on drugs, and my case book propped on my knee to catch the wedge of light that slanted through the cell window from the floodlights that emblazoned the horizon outside.

Working in the library during the day gave me the opportunity to begin piecing together the jigsaw puzzle Darryl Orton had turned out to be. He lost his yard privileges so often he'd begun hanging out there. But trouble was never far behind Darryl Orton.

"Look at this, Billy," Tom Collins said one day, loud enough that Orton was sure to hear it, "a growed-up man misleadin hisself with some book claimin to be about 'American' music."

Darryl ignored him, kept his eyes trailing his finger across a page he was studying. Watching his lips laboriously mouthing each word tugged at my heart.

"The dumb honky don't even know the only real American music is jazz, plain and simple."

Orton still didn't look up, but broke his typical silence. "I reckon that's true," he said, turning a page, "for people who cotton to jungle music."

Collins smiled wryly at Darryl's remark and hitched his head to one side as if deflecting a right cross to the chin. "Better'n that three-chord Okie shit," he said. "You an Okie, Orton? You look like one and quack like one, so you are one, right? One of them Okies from Muskogee, am I right?"

When Darryl said nothing, Collins persisted. "Speak up, my man. Where you be from?"

I didn't like the direction this exchange of cultures was taking. The first rule of prison is take care of yourself, don't worry about anybody else. But what about others you had come to care about? Poor old Dickens killing himself on drugs. Darryl always flirting with trouble, never backing away, somehow surviving despite his best efforts to get himself killed.

I guess the reason I kept reaching out to Darryl Orton was because

I hadn't anybody else to talk to, leastwise anybody I respected who wasn't full of bullshit like all my clients were, or stoked on drugs like Dickens and Tom Collins. Darryl didn't do drugs *or* bullshit, and when he spoke, people listened. The man was to me an island in a sea of hell-fire.

As for Collins, I should mention that despite his fifty-some years, most inmates were a little afraid of him, partly because at six feet six inches, he was the tallest man in Soledad, and known to have been a gang leader, killer, and club boxer. But mainly it was because of a caustic wit that could tie any victim into knots of frustration.

"Here," said Darryl. "I was born here."

"No shit?" Collins said, turning to me. "Billy! This here Oakball was born right here in this library."

"Here in the Salinas Valley," said Darryl, unperturbed. "Born in Salinas."

"You got to be kiddin," said Collins. "You hear that, Billy? We're gonna start callin this man John motherfuckin Steinbeck!"

Darryl shook his head, his eyes still on his book, on the words trailing the finger on the book.

Collins started nodding his head. "Wait a minute, here," he said. "Now I get it. Your kin be dust bowl Okies, am I right?"

Darryl cut his eyes up at Collins. "You know your history better'n you know your music."

"Did you play country and western yourself, Mr. Orton?" I said, trying to ease things.

"Country," said Darryl, nose back in his book, "not western."

"Like there's a difference," chided Collins.

Darryl exhaled impatiently and said, "Is there a difference between Dixieland jazz and bebop, Mr. Collins?"

"Oh, Jesus help me!" said Tom Collins, his forehead corrugated in disgust.

Darryl Orton took off his glasses, still Scotch-taped together, and rubbed his eyes, the way my dad did when he heard something stupid, which, around our house, was as common as rainwater. I decided to jump in and show Darryl Orton I was an Okie, too, and that I knew my country music.

"There *is* a difference, Mr. Collins," I said. "U. 'Utah' Phillips used to say that when playing in Nashville, you had to wear a new hat, while in the West, you had to run over your hat with a truck before you went on stage with it."

Darryl Orton looked at me, smiled, then looked at Collins and jerked his head once in my direction as if to say, listen to the kid.

But Collins leaned toward Orton, his fingers—long, but thick as rolls of quarters—splayed across the library table. "Look, rube," he said, an edge creeping into his voice. "If it gives you honky hicks somethin to do between bowlin and stock-car racin, I gots no objection. Just don't be callin all that Okie little-black-train bullshit real music."

Orton closed his book shut without a sound, rose to his feet, then aimed those gentle blue eyes back at Collins and spoke in a voice so quiet we both had to lean in closer. "It's all music, sir. No need to take sides where music's concerned."

I asked Orton if he played professionally, and he smiled ruefully and stared out past a row of books into the rec yard. "I used to."

Plodding ahead, obviously encouraged by having interrupted Darryl's studies, Collins said, "Well, whatever. I still say country music's got nothin to do with jazz and damn little to do with music."

Darryl shelved his book, more loudly than he had closed it, finally betraying his frustration, and started to walk out. He then glanced back at Collins. "Both your music and mine come out of pain, sir," he said. "Workin men without work. Families without food and medicine. I'll grant you the dust bowl was better than slavery, but it weren't no cotillion party neither."

I was so stunned to hear Darryl Orton string all those words together at once that I failed to notice that Collins had moved around and blocked Darryl's way, and that his eyes were sparking.

"My music's roots was in *Africa,* Mr. Motherfucking Steinbeck," he sneered, "on slave ships and cotton fields. Your music's beginnins were Grand Ole Opry in Nashville, where the only chains you heard rattlin were made outta gold, mined by African children."

Darryl started to say something, then stopped, shook his head. "There's a bunch of books here, Mr. Collins," he said at last, back to sounding as if each word had to be pried out of his mouth. "You might try readin some of 'em."

"He's right on that, Mr. Collins," I said. I was trying again to lighten up the growing tension, but also signaling Tom that if this thing went beyond words, I'd have to side with Darryl. "Nashville wasn't the center of country music until the late forties, early fifties. In the twenties, it was Atlanta, then Chicago during the depression years."

"Well, la-di-fuckin-da," said Collins to me, but still glaring at Darryl.

"It's true, sir," I said. "My dad told me about how country music caught on in Hollywood through the war years because folks had come to California from all over the Southwest—Texas, Missouri, Arkansas, Oklahoma—bringin their guitars and fiddles and starving kids with them."

Collins made a comic-sad face and started playing an invisible violin, but I ignored him and added, "Many settled right here in the Salinas Valley, the ones you were talking about, Mr. Collins."

"Bunch a' Okie white trash," said Collins. "That's all they was."

Darryl Orton winced a little at that but kept his cool, and Collins looked suddenly like he realized he had crossed an imaginary line that exists sometimes even in prison. Maybe he was thinking what I was beginning to think: that Darryl Orton's father had been one of those starving kids. He let out a deep breath, then said oh well and gave Darryl a friendly sideways tap on the arm and moved out of his way. I let out a deep breath, too.

"Was your dad a musician, Darryl?" I asked.

"Yep," he said, starting toward the door again. "But he made his livin pickin artichokes and lettuce, not pickin a guitar." Then, as Darryl was almost out the door, he glanced over his shoulder, smiled at Collins, and added, "For slave wages."

Collins smiled back at Darryl's barb and nodded a salute, and I realized that even in this sterile, intolerant hellhole, the power of words could ripen grudging respect into friendship.

Sure as taxes, Darryl and Collins became friends during the next few weeks. Darryl opened up with me a little, too, though he steadfastly refused to discuss the law, lawyers, or his case. On other subjects, particularly music, he began to talk freely, which in Darryl's case meant stringing maybe two or three sentences together at once. I think he was impressed that someone my age knew about Lefty Frizell, the Maddox Brothers and Rose, George Jones, Merle Haggard, and other country greats. He knew about all the current country stars, too—Clint Black, Garth Brooks, even Tim McGraw and Lee Ann Womack.

Darryl said that when he was a kid, he'd used his dad's Fender and opened for Hoyt Axton down at the Palomino Club in North Hollywood just months before Axton died. Biggest payday he ever had.

"Ever cut a record?"

"No," he said, and grunted out something like a laugh. "But if every A-and-R man's broken promise was a forty-five single, I'd have twenty albums out by now."

I told him record people sounded worse than lawyers.

"Lawyers are scum," he said, and spat to one side. "Ain't nobody worse than lawyers."

I was afraid that was the end of our conversation, but then he asked where I'd learned my country music. I told him it started while growing up in Enid, hearing it on my dad's car radio. I could clearly picture Joe Strobe, hair thinning but still dark under a tan fedora he always wore, hunched over the wheel of his Plymouth, fingers tapping on the wheel to the music, his old tweed sport coat hanging on him like burlap.

I smiled at Darryl. "Whenever an old Patsy Cline tune would come on, he'd tell me about her going down in a plane in 1963. Just thirty, he'd say, just thirty. Over and over, he'd say it, then he'd give his flask a workout."

Darryl nodded to indicate he understood where Dad was coming from. "Dad talked about her all the time," I added. "I was only ten or eleven, so I thought he must have been a good friend of hers."

"Her singin made everybody think they was a good friend of hers because she touched people. That's what good music does."

The next time I wrote to the San Francisco County Clerk to order documents for a writ I was working on, I put in a pro bono request for copies of Darryl's trial transcript, together with his arrest and probation reports. I'd help the son-of-a-bitch whether he wanted it or not. Without singing a note, something about this weird loner had touched me.

8

Summer at Soledad was like Devil's Island without the water. The sun burned the rec yard asphalt into molten sludge by midday; then a late afternoon cloud cover would darken the hot sky and trap the heat beneath its suffocating mattress, turning the air into water. My shirt would be wringing wet from the humidity by the time I reached the rec yard.

The library had no air conditioning, of course, but it did have a fan, and during the dog days of July, Darryl and I logged a heap of library time together, me polishing up a new attack on Campora's conviction, surviving one day at a time under a three-month extension of the don's protection, and Darryl plodding through a beat-up edition of the *Encyclopaedia Britannica*, one page at a time. He had made it halfway through the Ds—pretty good considering he had to hold his glasses on with one hand and basically teach himself to read as he absorbed everything from the function of an abacus to the rococo architecture and sad history of Dresden.

The library was the most underutilized room at Soledad, the cons preferring TV. That was another thing I admired about Darryl. I never once saw him watching television. I guess he noticed I didn't hang around the TV set at night either, and when he asked me about it I reminded him I was spending every spare minute studying to be a lawyer.

"That's a bad reason for doin a good thing," he said.

"I don't figure I need a good reason not to waste my time watching TV," I said, not about to reveal my real reason to a guy with a mind as open as a clenched fist. The real reason I didn't watch was women. Girls.

Think about it. TV sitcoms, the courtroom movies I used to love, cop shows, even commercials—gorgeous women everywhere. You spend a few months in prison, you don't want to be reminded about a woman—her gentleness, her voice soft as rainwater, the rush you felt cupping a hand under her warm breast the first time, exploring her hardening nipple with a longing finger, then losing yourself deep inside her, and later, afterward, touching her hair and watching her sleep, wanting to know everything about her, all her secrets, seeing her panty hose hung over the shower the next morning. Well shit, see what I mean? I guess you'll have to trust me on this: sexual thoughts and anything that arouses them were unwelcome in prison, at least for me. I tried to crowd that stuff out with thoughts of freedom. Freedom was my aphrodisiac and my orgasm; freedom was all I thought about.

"So why don't you watch TV?" I asked Darryl.

He thought about it for a few seconds and then said, "Television is like a virus." He tilted his head to one side. "Enters your blood at night and eats away whatever peace you've managed to muster durin the day."

The lunch bell went off, and he headed for the door, where he turned and added, " 'Course as between a virus like television and a cancer like lawyerin, a man'd be better off with the TV."

Darryl had mastered the art of changing any subject into an attack on lawyers. I had sworn I wouldn't get sucked in again, but couldn't resist.

"Listen, Darryl. The law may have gotten you in here, it could get you out, too."

He croaked out a laugh at that. "The law is a trip wire for the poor, sonny, the whole system built to keep us in our place."

"Okay, the system isn't perfect, I agree with you there. But that isn't the fault of laws. Rich or poor, as long as there's evil, we all need the protection of the law."

"Rich or *poor*? That's a good one, Billy."

"Well, I stand by it. The reason the lady with the scales of justice is blindfolded is because she doesn't care if you're rich or poor."

"Well, she might not care," said Darryl, bristling, "but her cops and judges cared enough to let my daddy's baby sister die west of Barstow, then starve out my great-grandma near Tehachapi and my great-grandpa east of San Bernardino, all because they were poor. Fifty years later, the blind bitch went to work on me. Couldn't see the difference between a guy waitin in his car for a pack of smokes and a guy inside a store beatin up an Iranian and stealin his money! Pack 'em both up and throw 'em in Soledad. Equal justice for all."

"I just *said* it isn't perfect, Darryl, but the law—"

"The *law*!" said Darryl, and spat close to one of my feet. "You tell me one law made by a poor person. The law is a broken record warnin poor people not to tamper with the natural order of things—the natural order of things bein that the rich get richer and the poor go to jail. Stealin fruit out of a field? Hell, man, throw the book at that dust-bowl Okie."

I was stunned. He was talking about his father's trip out West as a child. The little girl would have been his aunt; the "dust-bowl Okie," his great-grandfather.

Then he turned the harsh light of his eyes back on me. "What did the law ever do for you, poor boy? Look around you. See any of those rich kids here? The ones was in that scam with you?"

As ususal, Darryl had me thrashing in the net of his logic, had me thinking how the legal system had eventually killed my own dad, just as it had killed Darryl's aunt and great-grandparents. But I wouldn't give in. "You've got to have laws, Darryl. Believe me, it's the system that's messed up."

"The system you're studyin your ass off to become a part of?"

I tried to explain the difference between laws and systems that enforce the laws, and how the way to try to fix any broken system was from the inside, but I wasn't making much sense under his gaze, even to myself.

"You love fixin things, don't you, kid?" he said, his tone softening as he broke an awkward silence. "I hear you fixed the air conditioner in the chow hall."

I told him that maybe what had happened to him during his own trial could be fixed as easy as that air conditioner. I watched uneasily as his shoulders stiffened again.

"Do I have to draw you a picture, kid?" he said after a tense silence.

"I come in here owin nothin to nobody and I plan on keepin it that way. So drop it!"

I was having more trouble with this guy than Jimmy Stewart did with his clients in *Anatomy of a Murder*.

"Look Darryl, I know you've got good reason to distrust lawyers, but we're both Okies, okay? You can trust me."

Darryl Orton laughed. "Never heard of an Irish Okie."

"Yeah? Well I was born and raised in Oklahoma, not Salinas, California."

He crinkled his features and swatted at a fly. "Bein an Okie is a state of your mind, not what state you're born in. Plus, my daddy moved us to back to Oklahoma when I was no more'n six. You're just another lawyer to me, kid, so back off."

"No, dammit, I won't," I said. "Everybody needs a helping hand sometime, Darryl, especially in here. Trust me, I'm figuring out how the system works. Maybe I could get you out of here."

He shook his head. "What I'm gettin is plumb wore out from you cryin over my spilt milk. I eat regular, I sleep warm, and I ain't complainin."

"Bullshit, Darryl. You eat *shit* three times a day and sleep every night with a lunatic eighteen inches above your head. If you're *not* complaining, you're as crazy as Dickens."

Darryl's lips tightened, and he leaned in close to me. "Maybe so, but if you don't back off, kid, so help me, I'm gonna have to pop you one."

I knew he meant it, so I shrugged and went back to a brief I was working on, and he went back to studying the *D*s in the *Britannica*.

Ten minutes later I caught my mind wandering into hostile territory, things like the way Campora's new deadline was closing in on me and worrying about Dickens, who had just got roughed up again by a dissatisfied customer and fretting about how Mr. Dog was doing with his new master and wondering if I'd be able to get a job outside with a degree from a correspondence school, *if* I got outside, and if I did get back outside, wondering whether I'd still be someone I'd even want to know. Stuff like that.

I caught Darryl glancing up at me, looking contrite, a look I'd never seen on him. He shelved his book and rubbed his temples with the thumb and forefinger of his large right hand. Then he spread both hands, palms up.

"I came on a little rough there, kid," he said. "I know you mean well."

I shrugged.

"I've been thinkin about . . . Well, hell, if you still want to fix these glasses, I could do without 'em for a day or two if you're sure it ain't too much trouble."

I said sure, casual-like, to cover my surprise. He looked a little embarrassed as he handed them over.

"And I wish you luck with your studies and tryin to fix the system," he added as he turned to leave.

I was touched and probably thanked him too enthusiastically because he seemed embarrassed.

"Yeah, well," he said, "if you really wanted to be cool, you'd stick to air conditioners."

When Darryl's trial records arrived weeks later, I was shocked to see the way he'd been railroaded. It hadn't been a trial at all.

He had been working weeknights as a janitor in a financial district complex where a fortyish Chief Financial Officer was murdered at night in her office. Nothing stolen, but rape was a possibility. There was "bruising to the labia majora," but no semen, so "possible phobic personality" became part of the perp's profile. The victim was three months pregnant at the time of her murder, and the usual suspect—the estranged husband, who stood to collect $500,000 on a double-indemnity policy—was picked up for questioning. He had been seen in the victim's office late the same day she was killed. But there was someone else in the Synoptics offices that night: the janitor, an ex-con who was working on the Synoptics floor the night of the murder. Although he claimed he had actually logged out of the building before the pathologist's "most probable time of death," the picture changed. The estranged husband suddenly had himself a bulletproof alibi from his current girlfriend, plus the cops found out that Darryl had just deposited one thousand dollars in his bank account, the highest balance he'd had in his whole poverty-ridden life. He claimed the money was given him by a dude who approached him at the Saddle Rack in San Jose during a break and said he liked what he had heard. The guy said he was producing a CD in L.A. and wanted Darryl to play guitar and sing backup behind some country chicken who might also cut one of Darryl's songs. The money was to pay his expenses down to L.A. Darryl had even bought his ticket to L.A., but of course that looked to the cops like part of the Great Escape plan.

Anyways, it turned out that when the L.A. cops showed up at the producer's sorry excuse for a recording studio, the guy—who not only made records but had one, including county jail time for drugs and money laundering—was spooked and denied everything. Five will get you ten the thousand bucks was hot out of the laundry, which, of course, left Darryl out in the cold.

So at this point the cops began to view Darryl as a low-budget contract killer and tied him into a Synoptics illegal stock manipulation scheme the victim was in all the way up to her garter belt. Yeah, she was wearing one. And would you believe the scheme was an insider trading scam? My specialty.

But it gets worse: the murder weapon, a paperweight with the victim's blood on it and prints wiped clean, was found behind Darryl's locker in the basement! Just where he'd hide it after killing someone, right? Jesus. Bonnie Bedelia pulled off a better frame-up than that using a cocktail glass and Harrison Ford's semen in *Presumed Innocent*. Hell. Even Spencer Tracy did a better job of it using nothing but a burnt ring in *Fury*, a 1936 clunker. I remember the date because it was produced the same year my dad was.

So the finger now pointed straight at the janitor. The victim's husband, Frank Hinton, was released with apologies, and Darryl was formally charged and booked.

Justice moved swiftly after that. Darryl manifested no "phobic personality" other than a love of country music, which I reckon was close enough for the DA. The trial judge forced Darryl to accept assistance from the public defender, who warned Darryl after hearing the prosecutor's opening statement to plea-bargain or start making out his will. Darryl took the plea-bargain and two weeks later, found himself back in Soledad.

Armed with this information, I decided to take the risk of getting "popped one" and make one last approach to Darryl. Although I now had more than a dozen clients, this was my first chance to do some real justice in a clear case of obviously inadequate counsel. Nothing would stop me.

"You can't want to stay in a place like this for the rest of your life, Darryl," I told him the next day while we strolled around the yard. We walked past some blacks playing three-on-three basketball and other inmates doing push-ups in the area where the weights had been before they were taken away. We paused near the empty handball court.

"Every lifer at least *tries* to get out," I added.

"Only way I'll get out is in a box," he said, then gave his head a quick shake, turned, and started walking away.

"Or parole."

"I'll be dead by the time my shot comes up."

"Then you've got nothing to lose by letting me try to get you a new trial."

He stopped, turned toward me, and said, "You know why you're all the time pesterin me, kid?"

I shrugged, taken off guard by the question.

"You think you can stay human in here by bein kind to the animals; always helpin the likes of people like me."

I denied it, of course, maybe a little too quickly. Maybe I felt busted. "You're crazy, Darryl."

But the wise old bastard gave me a wry smile. "You're gonna have to save your own soul, kid. I ain't gonna help you."

I told him I was helping him because I thought he was innocent.

"Nobody's innocent," he said, "once they growed up."

"I'm talking crime, not philosophy," I said. "Your lawyer didn't even make an opening statement! They handed him the ball, and he punted on first down."

Darryl shook his head. "Am I gonna have to pop you one, kid?"

"You were framed, Darryl. I know it can happen. *Let me help you, goddammit!*"

He hit me then. The son-of-a-bitch hit me, right on the chin. Knocked me up against the wall of the handball court.

"Christ, Darryl!" I said, looking around to see if the screws were paying any attention. All I could see were several Latinos pointing at us and laughing like jackals. No one else seemed to notice.

"Shit, I'm sorry kid," he said, genuinely upset. He smoothed out my shirt, which did little for my jaw, and added, "You okay?"

I said something to him like hell no I'm not okay and fuck you and your threats and you always walking off whenever I offer to help you. Then I added, "You know what your problem is, Darryl?"

Still contrite, he gave me an amused smile. "I can hardly wait to find out."

"You think anybody who gives a shit about you is a do-gooder. Well, all I've ever offered you was a second chance; but consider that offer hereby goddamn *rescinded*."

Darryl shook his head. "Hereby rescinded? Fuckin lawyer talk. Look, son. Try to understand I really don't *want* another chance. I'll just end up fodder for your fuckin legal system again." He spat out the last words as if a bug had flown in his mouth.

"Fuck you, Darryl," I said, when I could trust my voice if not my originality. "Stay right here until your miserable ass rots into dust for all I care."

"That's my intention, kid, whether you care about it or not."

"Good," I said, feeling a hot flush on my face. "And don't forget to get the shit beat out of you at least once a week over that raunchy square of redwood. Eventually they'll kill you, which is fine because all you really want out of life is death anyway. Am I right?"

Darryl gave his head a quick shake and said, "I only want my seat on the bench, kid, and if you opened your eyes one time, you'd see I don't have to defend it no more. It's over."

I knew he was right. "Congratulations, Darryl, you wore their fists out on your face, and for what?"

We were still standing in the handball court. His back was leaning against the wall beside me, thumbs hooked in his pockets, looking down at his brown boots, saying nothing. A minute or two passed without a word, making me uncomfortable. Darryl always seemed to enjoy silence as much as some folks liked to gab.

He looked up at a threatening thundercloud and then shoved both hands deep in his pockets. Then he spoke. "Whether inside or outside, a man's got to have somethin that's his and nobody else's. I got nothin left outside, but here, that 'raunchy square of redwood'? That's *mine*, Billy. It was mine when I was here before and it's mine now that I'm back."

While I tried to think of a response, he added, "What've *you* got in here that's really yours, kid?"

"Hope," I said without a second's hesitation, "and a determination not to let all this place make me hard, not to let it change me."

"Hope in a place like Soledad is courtin hopelessness," he said. "As for change? You've already changed, kid; you just don't know it."

Now it was my turn to walk away, but I felt his hand on my upper arm, and I turned around. I was ready this time, but he just stood there, averting his eyes, looking a little sheepish, not saying a word.

"You know I'm right about your case, don't you?" I said finally into the silence. "You were framed, Darryl. Believe me, I know how easily it can be done. To *anybody*."

He actually smiled then, but it was that wry, sardonic smile that no longer fooled me. "Ah," he said, "I get it. *You* were framed, kid. You, me, Dickens, Earring, Campora—all of us was framed."

"No. I deserve to be here, and so do they. But my dad was framed, and it cost him his life. So I know from personal experience how easy it is for an innocent man to get framed."

He shook his head, and I could see his eyes were laughing at me. "And even easier for a guilty man to claim it," he said.

That's when I hit him, hit him hard, though my aim wasn't so hot. Caught him on the side of his throat and ear, but enough to back him up hard against that same handball backstop.

"My serve," I said coldly.

He gently rubbed his ear and said, "And your point, too, I reckon," then gave his head a little shake and added, "All right, kid, let's hear it."

"Hear what?"

"About your dad. Seems like he figures pretty important in all this."

I took a few deep breaths, and we started walking again. After a few minutes, I cooled down and told him about how Joe Strobe had taken in a partner a few years before his suicide, a business lawyer named Amos Blackwell. During a trial of his partner's wealthiest client, the partner phonied up a letter that allowed Dad to get the client off. Dad thought it was legitimate. When the DA exposed the scheme, the client and Dad's partner both testified it was my dad who had forged the signature on the letter and he was convicted.

"He shot himself dead in his bedroom the night before he was going to prison. Blackwell took over all the partnership assets and left us with squat. I had just turned twelve."

Darryl nodded and considered what I'd told him.

"Anyways," I said, "first thing I do when I'm a lawyer is to go back to Enid and clear his name."

"Billy Fix-It," Darryl said, almost to himself, "restorer of good names and reputations."

"You want to get hit again?"

"You're gettin mean, kid. You'll be a regular hard-rock mother-fucker by the time you get out."

He was probably teasing, trying to relax things, but his words bothered me. "You're crazy," I said, and walked away, nursing an ache in my jaw and a bigger one in my heart. Opening up about Dad had triggered painful recollections. I squeezed my eyes shut, trying to block out the memory, but there was my father again, fully dressed in his best suit—a blue pin-striped number—lying face up on the bedroom floor, blood and bits of flesh and bone splattered against the grasscloth-covered wall behind him. He was still breathing, but part of the side of his head was gone, and those wide blue eyes were staring up at a twelve-year-old kid too damn scared to even touch him, let alone try to fill his lungs with life-saving oxygen from his own. Or to slow the flow of blood—deep red like the carnation he always wore—slow it down with a sheet or something while waiting what seemed like weeks for the paramedics Ma had called to show up. Or even to hold his quivering hand and beg him not to leave us.

Looking back, I think it was guilt that caused me to deny he was dead for over a year, sometimes seeing him in a crowd of men, feeling him tuck the blanket around me at night, knowing he was somewhere in the house if I knew the right place to find him. I'd make up stories at school about things we were doing together, trying to mask the feeling that I was as responsible for his disappearance as sure as if I'd pulled the trigger myself.

Which was before I quit feeling guilty and started hating his cowardly guts for abandoning us.

Which was before I quit hating him and decided to become him.

9

It's funny; after all that talk with Darryl about not watching TV, and there I was in front of it a week later. I had heard *The Verdict* was going to be on, and couldn't pass it up. That had been my dad's very favorite movie, and we'd seen it together not long before he died. Afterward, I asked Dad if it was okay what Paul Newman did, paying off a mortician, pestering a grieving widow, and breaking into a mailbox looking for evidence.

"When you take up the fight against Satan, son," he said, "whether it's big firms like James Mason's or prosecutors for the State of Oklahoma, you'll have to battle 'em tooth and nail and fight fire with fire. The Lord only helps those who help themselves."

It always made me proud when he talked to me like I would be doing this myself someday. He was always great about that. It would also unnerve me a little, because he would quiz me as he talked, as if I was in a school situation. Looking back, I think I felt like he was God and I was Moses, being handed lessons on tablets of stone, so that when I grew up and took on Satan's government prosecutors, his wisdom would be engraved on my memory.

I've mentioned that my dad had a weakness for movies. He used to tell me it was because trial lawyers and moviemakers were in the same line of work, figuring how to capture an audience's interest and trust, no matter how crazy their story might be.

"We're both trying to make our hero out to be sympathetic and likable," he told me on a day I'll never forget at the Red Hen Café, the day we'd seen *The Verdict*.

Dad bought me a Coke and himself a shot of some kind of whisky and a beer. I remember thinking he must have been thirsty from the movie, because both disappeared quicker then he could order another.

"You also have to keep the plot moving forward," he said, making a sour face from the whisky and wiping his mouth with the back of his hand, "but you can't overdo it. Juries get bored like any other audience, then they get irritated and turn against the side that's boring them."

When I asked him if it was getting the jury's attention that won the verdict, he turned the question back on me, as usual. I answered that it seemed like you had to at least start out that way.

"Exactly, son," he said. "But then you have to get them to *act*. How would you do that, son?"

I knew the answer to that one because it was his favorite question. "You tell them a story," I said.

He smiled at me as the waitress came up. "A gold star for my son," he told her, "and another round of drinks for me."

It's funny how drunk Dad must have gotten in those days without me ever realizing the connection between those numerous "rounds of drinks" and the way he would change after drinking them.

"The big firms like James Mason's in that movie we saw, and the government prosecutors I tangle with every day? Well, they may have all the power, son, but they can't tell a story to save their arses, so busy they are papering the walls of the courtroom with documents and exhibits and general confusion. Then your dad stands up and tells them a story that would bring the birds weeping out of the trees. You understand me, son? While the prosecutor is trying to win the minds of the jurors, I creep in and steal their *hearts*."

"But what kind of story do you tell the jury when your client is really guilty? Like that robbery case you won last week?"

"Hush, son," he said, laughing, "that was a father-son privileged communication."

He took several deep swallows from a fresh bottle of beer, belched, and said, "Okay. After I had 'em warmed up, I gave the ladies and gents of the jury some simple variations on the oldest theme in the book: little guy with big dreams runs into obstacles not of his own doing, hits hard times, gets pushed to the limit, makes a mistake or two like we've all done, then *pow!*"

Dad hit the table with his hand at this point, and some people next to us jumped. But Dad didn't notice or slow down a bit, just held my gaze and slipped into his Irish brogue.

"So all of a sudden, ladies and gentlemen, this poor lad finds himself the target of the biggest bully on the block: *the government*."

The people closest to us were listening now.

"At this point, Billy, I've usually got the sweet ladies' eyes glistening. Then I rise to me full five and eight, puff out me chest, look each one of them square in the eye, and ask who amongst them wants to cast the first stone? If they can't meet me eye, I know I've got 'em."

"They feel sorry for your client?"

"Yes, indeed, son, and so they should. So they should."

"Then it's feeling sorry for your client that won it?"

"Nay, that's just one patch on the quilt, as your grandma used to say. See, the government is always talking about *justice—justice* that demands punishment, *justice* for the poor victim's widow, the jury as an instrument of *justice,* and so forth. But tell me, son, what's the meaning of *justice?*"

I puzzled hard over the question, one he'd never hit me with, and then said, "Fairness?"

"Fairness?" he said, and studied the ceiling for a second or two. "Not bad, son, but the problem is that fairness to a plaintiff may mean bankruptcy to a defendant, am I right? And fairness to the prosecutor may mean something different to the guy strapped into a chair full of electricity, belching smoke rings out his arsehole.

"That was a trick question, son. *Nobody* can answer it. I've been at this game for twenty years, and I can no more define *justice* than pick up a bead of mercury in my fingertips. But what I do understand, son, is *in*justice, and that's what I focus the jury on, and *that's* how I get jurors to act. *In*justice is something we all understand because it's happened to all of us, even if it's just somebody slipping in and stealing your parking place while you're trying to back into it. I tell them that the justice the prosecutor waves in front of them is a lovely ideal, something for us all to think weighty thoughts about over a stout before dinner. But now you're in the jury box, I says to 'em, and you've got to deal with a specific and concrete *injustice* that's about to be done to this poor soul who's already been dealt one bad hand after another by fate."

Dad was in his glory, and half the people in the Red Hen were watching and listening now, not wanting to miss a single word.

"I look each juror in the eye again and I say, 'You, my fellow citizens, are all that stands between this poor man and that terrible *injustice.*'"

Dad's dark brown eyes were sparking now, and the words were flowing like grain out of a silo. He paused only to polish off another shot and a beer. Even the waiters and waitresses were tiptoeing around, so's not to miss a word he was saying.

"So just *do the right thing* is what I tell 'em! *There's a wrong here that's got to be set right,* and *that's* why you're here, dear ladies and gents, *to right a wrong!"*

He smiled at the waitress as she set down a beer and another shot. My second Coke was still full.

He turned to me. "And when do I tell them that, son? At the end? During argument?"

"No, sir," I said, proudly, playing to the crowd a little myself. "You tell them right off the bat."

"And why is that, son?"

"Because jurors make up their minds early in the trial."

"Exactly!" he said, and I beamed. "After that, they only hear the evidence that confirms their original gut instinct, and the rest goes out the window like slop for the pigs."

When he wet his whistle again, first the shot, then the beer, I heard another voice, a big man two tables over who I figured must know my dad.

"So, Joe Strobe, is that how you got that crook off last week? The guy what was caught in the act like a fox with feathers in his mouth?"

Dad turned around slowly and then said, "Well, if it ain't me old friend, Brandon Murphy." Dad's expression was glowing, and every eye in the restaurant was on him. "You stay out of trouble, Brandon, because the only way I'd ever be able to get you off is if half the jury was Irish and the rest was your immediate family!"

Everybody laughed at that, and Dad held up his beer to the crowd, and they clapped for him. But not Brandon Murphy, whose face went red as the cherry in my suddenly empty Coke glass.

I thought it was over, but the man piped up again. "Answer my question, Strobe. You call it *justice,* gettin a guilty man back on the streets? A thief who gave old Jon Burns a heart attack while in the act of robbin him blind?"

Dad looked like he was going to ignore Brandon Murphy, but his question hung in the air like sheep rot. You could have heard a flea fart in the room, it got so quiet. Dad smiled at the red-faced man, took a slug of beer, and asked me to stand up.

"Stand up, Dad?"

"On your feet, son." Dad was still giving Murphy the hard gaze I'd seen too many times myself when he was mad. People around us were looking as uncomfortable as I was feeling.

I got on my feet, scared and about to pee my pants from two Cokes and nervousness, wondering what my dad was up to.

"Ladies and gents, your attention please. My beloved son, Billy Strobe, though only in the fourth grade, is about to ask Brandon Murphy a question about the justice he's so interested in. We will then eagerly await his answer."

I started to remind Dad I was in the fifth, almost the sixth, grade, but suddenly realized that every eye in the Red Hen was now on *me*. "Can I sit now, Dad?" I whispered, but he whispered back that I was to ask the man "the question about justice."

But my mind had gone totally blank. I couldn't have given Mr. Murphy my own name. I held out a pleading hand to Dad, a beggar's hand, sweaty palm up. "*What question, Dad?*" I whispered, fighting back the first tears of embarrassment as my mind swirled inside itself.

"Jesus, Mary, and Joseph, son," he whispered, "the question we just discussed! The one nobody can answer. *What-is-justice?* Don't worry, he won't be able to answer."

How many times have I relived that moment? Three words. All God was asking of his eager servant was to say three fucking words. But as I turned and looked into the raw, angry face of Mr. Brandon Murphy, I felt the room begin to sway. I leaned against the table and felt the first warm trickle down my right leg.

"Wh-wha-wh . . ." I was dizzy, my head full of bees, my heart pounding so hard in my throat my voice couldn't get past it. I'd passed Dad's pop quizzes, but here I was flunking the final.

Then I felt Dad's warm hand on my arm, gently guiding me into my chair. "It's okay, lad," he whispered. "Is it all right with you if I ask him?"

He gave me a warm smile that told me he was sorry for embarrassing me, which made me feel even worse for having let him down. I nodded, though I knew I'd never get past it. Never.

Dad gave my hand a little squeeze, then turned to the red-faced man and said, "Tell us, Brandon Murphy, what *is* justice? We'd all be very interested in your answer."

The rest is a blur. Murphy scratched his head and stammered some kind of answer and Dad shot something back and then everybody at the Red Hen was laughing.

Everybody but Brandon Murphy and me.

Over the next several weeks at Soledad I struggled to keep up with my law studies at Golden State Law School, while filing four motions for reconsideration, three motions for new trial, seven writs of habeas corpus, and one appeal, plus helping a half dozen inmates with grievance procedures. I also began drafting a motion for a new trial for Darryl based on the trial record I'd got, though I never really expected he'd let me file it.

It was tough keeping my heart in it, between the relentless heat, the sickening stench of the place, too much noise, too few supplies, shit for food, and shitheads for company. I couldn't help longing for the simple pleasures I had once taken for granted: driving a car, taking a quiet walk, playing with my dog, taking a date for pizza, shooting hoops with a friend, catching a movie.

To distract myself from these aching reveries full of self-pity, I tried to stay focused on my studies. I figured I'd take the bar exam in prison, then, if I got out alive, get a job with a public interest law firm. Darryl laughed when I told him this, but stopped after I showed him my first semester grades. Straight A's.

In fairness, the optimism that fueled this strategy was possible mainly because Campora had remained true to our agreement. Thanks to being exempted from rape and most of the day-to-day violence of prison, I had been able to struggle through a maze of bureaucratic bullshit and, with only a month to go on my extension from don-Don, filed the best motion for new trial I'd ever drafted. But now, with only three days left on my deal with the devil, there was still no word from the court, and I was losing hope.

The next day, with only two days left, I was working on a desperation telegram to the court. I was in my cell with the door open to get some air and wondered why a parade of cons kept passing by and looking in at me. Many of them gave me sad looks, but others leered, and I wondered if they had been promised a shot at me after Campora and Earring finished. The word was out.

Looking back, I'm not sure when I made the decision to kill don-Don when he came for me, nor can I pinpoint when it was that other peoples' lives had ceased to have the value they once had. Survival was all I cared about now, and I knew I would die before I would be punked out.

Getting a weapon would be no problem, given the fact that my celly was an arms dealer, running a virtual weapons factory in our cell. Dickens had a confederate working in the machine shop who would put axle grease on the end of a seven-inch piece of welding rod every few days, then conceal most of it up where the sun don't shine to smuggle it out past the guard. Dickens paid his supplier five packs of cigarettes per rod and went to work sharpening one end on the dank-smelling concrete floor of our cell. Then he'd sell the shank, complete with leather handle, for dope or one and a half cartons of smokes or bottles of quality pruno, a homemade fermented brew popular among prisoner alcoholics. So Dickens spouted his scripture, sharpened rods, and shot up—hour after hour, day after day. Of course, if somebody had the proper "trade," Dickens could also make a zip gun out of metal tubes taken from a stolen chair leg that was capable of firing .22-caliber bullets.

"For old times' sake," Dickens said that night, handing me a crude shank including leather. He also gave me some information.

"It is my unpleasant duty to inform you, Master Billy, that there is a 'note' out on that Orton chap," he said, the words slightly slurred. " 'Ah, well, what man shall not see death,' he added, his balding head bowed. "Psalms 89:48. Sorry. I know Orton was a friend."

Past tense. Jesus.

One of the catch-22s of prison life is that any day you might get an anonymous "note" ordering you to beat up or kill somebody. You have no way of knowing who sent it or why he sent it to you. All you know is that if you didn't follow instructions, you'd get beat up or killed yourself. Dickens explained that somebody was going to have to kill Darryl Orton to save his own life, and Darryl's only recourse would be to try to kill the guy caught in the middle.

"What kind of person would kick off a chain of events like that?" I asked Dickens.

He didn't answer me at first; then he met my eyes with an expression that chilled me. I noticed that the pupils of his eyes were dilated and his lips were moving without anything coming out. When the words came, his voice was dreamy and distant: " '. . . and I looked and beheld a pale horse: and his name was Death, and Hell followed with him . . .' "

Dickens's biblical references often went right over my head, but I caught that one. Though not as directly as I would later.

I raced to the yard and found Darryl on his bench, despite thunderclouds building over the west wall and some autumn showers not far off. He already knew about the note, of course, for nothing stays secret long in Soledad.

I asked Darryl what he was carrying, meaning how was he armed.

"I'm carryin a world of hurt," he said, giving me his crooked little smile.

"That's a decent country song title, but I'd like an answer to my question."

"I don't need a weapon and won't carry one," he said, then smiled again and added, "I'd hate to get in trouble with the law."

I knew Darryl had neither the money nor cigarettes to buy a shank. Another reason he was often in trouble with the guards and had no commissary privileges was because he refused to work in any of the shops. Darryl wasn't lazy, but he was convinced the state was trying to convert prisons into forced labor camps like in the old Soviet Union, and he stubbornly refused on principle to be a part of it.

"I'll get Dickens to make you a deal."

He shook that off like I knew he would.

"Okay, how about we melt down some plastic spoons and reshape the goop into a blade? Or maybe we melt the end of a toothbrush, then stick a razor blade into it? That would give you a straight razor."

"Toothbrush? That's real smart, Billy. If he attacks me with a bonecrusher, I'll come at him with a sparklin smile."

A bonecrusher is a special shank made from something like a sharpened screwdriver. It's called a bonecrusher because it can penetrate bone, not glance off a rib on the way to the heart.

"If it's one of Matar's goons," I said, "you'll need a bonecrusher yourself."

"You're full of wisdom today, kid. Makes me wish I'd taken up college."

"Dammit, Darryl, I'm going to lend you some money. You can pay me—"

"Forget it. I'll borrow your imagination, kid, but not your money. If Billy Fix-it has any bright ideas on how a bonecrusher might be made, let me know."

Frankly, I was a little surprised Darryl would accept even a small amount of help.

"I'll come up with something," I said.

He put a hand on my shoulder, the way Dad once did, and said, "You're a good kid, Billy. I'm sorry about calling you a do-gooder the other day. I reckon it's in your nature."

I felt myself reddening.

"I ain't used to people like you. As for the bonecrusher, you'd best make one for yourself while you're at it. Word is your time is up with Campora in forty-eight hours."

My hands went cold all of a sudden. "I'll be ready for him," I said, sounding pretty convincing, "and I'll figure something out for you."

"Take your time, son. I doubt they'll kill me before morning."

I was all the way back to my cell block before I realized that Darryl was acting like a man who wanted to live.

My first stop was the don's cell. Campora would know who put out the note and maybe who was on the spot. He could even cancel it if he wanted to. But the first thing he did was remind me I had forty-eight hours left before he owned me. Not that I needed reminding. I had been at Soledad 234 days, the longest ten years of my life, and not a single one of those days had passed without a tortured image of being brutalized and sodomized by Campora, then Earring.

"I called the court," I said, meeting his hard, dark eyes with effort, "and the clerk said the decision was being processed this week." Despite my despair, I glanced up hungrily at the collection of cheeses, packaged meats, and pastries spread across Campora's upper bunk. He had a cell to himself, of course, even had a TV and a small refrigerator rumored to contain Far Niente Chardonnay and Crystal Champagne, as well as fresh meats and frozen desserts he sometimes shared with guards.

"He tell you what they've decided?" Campora asked. I noticed he had grown a mustache, a thin black line above his thick upper lip, but I decided not to compliment him on it. Campora was a man who saw through flattery, particularly bald-faced lies.

"She sounded encouraging." I hoped he wouldn't see through that one.

"Good. I'll tell you this much about your friend," don-Don said, moving so close I could smell his cologne, "which will come as no surprise to a smart kid like you. It's El Matar. Those NFers are crazy motherfuckers, and even I would have trouble stopping this if I wanted to, which I don't. So here's what you do: Mind your own fucking business, kid, which happens at the present to be *my* business. Your time's about up, and in case you've been too busy to notice, I'm still a prisoner of the California State Department of Corrections. No more extensions, Billy Strobe, not one day, not one hour. So get your ass back on the phone and quit worrying about some deadbeat lifer who's as good as dead anyway."

As I walked away, I turned and saw him tapping his watch with his index finger. I was down to hours now.

I stewed all day about how I could get some heavy plastic, something hard and bulky enough to melt down into a bonecrusher for Darryl. It hit me the next morning when I was putting on my deodorant—yes, many of us inside still cared about how we smelled— and in less than an hour I'd scavenged a half dozen discarded deodorant cylinders from the recycling dock and pried the hard plastic balls out of the ends. I'd need another five or six to make a decent bonecrusher and would hit the commissary after lunch and buy some new ones.

I went out to the yard to tell Darryl I had solved the problem and spotted him walking toward the handball court with that confident stride I could ID a mile away. I spotted something else, too: it was that shithead Querto, moving up fast behind him, a hand under his shirt.

I tried to shout, but my throat was shutting down on me like it did when I tried to speak in public. Querto was only twenty-five feet behind him and closing hard. It was like that nightmare when you're heading off a cliff and you try to scream but nothing comes out. I started running toward them and finally managed to gasp, "Darryl! Behind you!"

Darryl turned—but too late. Querto came up with a hard overhand thrust, and I watched the shank rip deep into Darryl's chest. Even now I can picture him pitched backwards as if hit by gunfire, see the spectacles I'd repaired flying through the air, hear a loud *whoosh* sound from Darryl's mouth as the air flew out of his chest. Nobody else saw it, at least nobody acted like they did. Querto casually walked away from where Darryl, bent over but still on his feet, stood looking down at his chest, both hands on the leather handle of the shank.

I was moving fast toward Darryl, but I suddenly realized that he was moving even faster away from me, gaining on his assailant! And by the time Querto heard him coming, Darryl had somehow pulled the weapon out of his chest and plunged it into Querto's throat.

I couldn't believe what I thought I'd seen, or how fast it had all happened. Not one con in the yard had so much as turned around. And now it was Darryl's turn to casually walk away.

"Darryl!" I said, trying to catch my breath as I fell into step beside him. "Why the hell aren't you dead?"

He said nothing, but pulled his shirt up enough to reveal the prisoner's version of a bulletproof vest: two layers of magazines held in place by a sheet tied around the torso. There were small traces of blood showing on the pages of *National Geographic*.

"I'll take you to the hospital," I said.

"No," he said. We both knew that revealing an injury contemporaneous with Querto's death would tie the two events together. So I helped him to his cell and was relieved to see that only the tip of the shank had traveled all the way through the Nairobi article plus a copy of *Fortune* that was underneath the *National Geographic*.

It struck me funny somehow, knowing Darryl could barely read, and as I applied a makeshift bandage to his chest, I told him I hoped he'd finished the Nairobi story.

He nodded and smiled weakly in my direction. "Just in time," he whispered. "Somebody wants to cancel my subscription."

For once, he didn't seem to want to be left alone, asking me questions and such, so we talked about his kinfolks coming West, and I told him stories about my dad.

"How old were you," he asked, "when he shot hisself?"

"Twelve."

"Must have been tough, growin up without him, without a father."

"It was, but I was old enough to know what kind of man he was, and his spirit has stayed with me."

"I know what you mean, kid. He's in your bones. That's good."

We sat in silence, then he said he wanted to sleep for a while. I nodded, but paused at the door of his cell. "You don't really want to live like this, do you, Darryl?" I said.

He met my eyes, then let out a noisy sigh of resignation. "Okay, Billy Fix-It, I give up. Go ahead and try to save my worthless ass if it'll make you feel any better."

With less than twelve hours left on my deal with Campora and no word from the court, I got a wake-up call. No, it wasn't a horse's head next to my pillow.

It was the tail of a weasel, *under* my pillow.

Despite the burst of adrenaline exploding in my brain, I got Campora's message: First, that he had the power to enter my cell whenever he wanted. Second, that I was weaseling on my deal and he'd soon be around to collect.

I had to confront him, for this was the kind of violent prison foreplay that, if ignored, would be like bending over in front of him and spreading my own cheeks.

10

Which is exactly what I was doing an hour later in the visitors wing sally port, because I had my second visitor in eight months. Call me Mr. Popularity.

A CO pointed toward a guy sitting against the wall in a navy three-piece herringbone. He appeared to be not more than a few years older than me, but he looked so damn healthy and clean I wanted to hide, walk right past him. He handed me a card and introduced himself as Neil Whitmore of the law firm of Price and Jamison, my "sponsors" at Golden State Law School. He was my "liaison" and had meant to come by sooner.

"I'm much obliged for your help, sir," I said, wondering what he was up to. "It was nice of you to send my mother out here."

"It was our pleasure, Mr. Strobe. I wanted to come down and tell you how proud we are of your fine record at Golden State. May I call you Billy?"

I said sure and took a look around me at the other civilians. Being in the huge visitors room for the first time since my mother's visit, surrounded by at least twenty visitors—some of them decent-looking women—was like coming off the desert into a green meadow. Whitmore wore a suit, which set him apart, plus a fancy white shirt with a pale peach-colored collar and splashy blue tie they'd never allow inside. No colors in prison.

"Tell me a little bit about your life here in prison, Billy," he said, and I told him pretty much what I thought he wanted to hear. He asked all kinds of personal stuff but mainly seemed curious about prison violence, so I told him about my first night with fat Gary and how he'd eventually done a header off the third tier. This made his eyes glow with excitement and made me feel dirty somehow for telling the story. Then he turned the conversation toward sexual abuse, so I made a dumb joke about our animal ranch division. The guy was beginning to irritate me with his morbid curiosity, and I felt like asking whether he'd ever been butt-fucked, but kept my mouth shut. It's not like the guy was a pervert; he'd just been to too many movies and wanted some inside stuff to talk about over cocktails, some bang for his buck. I was the one being weird.

Sensing my reluctance to open up, he got down to business. "So, Billy, is it fair to say that our financial support has assisted you in achieving your goal of graduation from law school?"

I said sure it was fair to say that.

"And that you couldn't have attained your goal without it?"

I reminded him I hadn't attained it yet, and he said, yes, yes, yes, of course, but you know what I mean. I realized I was sweating, but nodded to indicate I knew what he meant. He had whipped a small notebook out of his inside coat pocket and I noticed an NW monogram on his shirt pocket. He kept staring at me, with his clear blue eyes, waiting for me to answer his question.

"Well, I'm hoping to graduate soon, and without the firm's financial support, I doubt it would have happened so quick," I said, and he smiled to show that he could live with that.

I realized that the reason this guy was making me uncomfortable was that he was in *my* house, yet ten times more at ease than I was. I tried pretending that he was the convict and I was the visitor, and in a few minutes, I would be thanked for coming, then be escorted through two sets of clanging, sliding bars out onto the street, where I would take in a deep breath of free fresh air, hop in the waiting van, and be driven to the circular driveway at the Central Facility Entrance Building where my silver Jaguar convertible would be waiting. I began to feel better.

Mr. Whitmore was saying something about me writing a letter thanking them so they could put it in the *San Francisco Recorder.* "It can be brief," he said. "My address is on the card."

"Do you drive a Jaguar convertible by any chance, Mr. Price?" I said.

"My name is Whitmore, Billy. Neil Whitmore," he said. "The firm's name is Price and Jamison. And no, I drive a BMW."

"Sorry, Mr. Whitmore. I'd be glad to do whatever I can. Maybe you could put in a word for me with the parole board." In prison, you scratch somebody's back, you expect to get scratched back.

"I'd be pleased to do so," he said, putting his notebook away.

"I'd be much obliged, sir. May I be frank with you?"

"Why, yes, of course," he said, though he looked uncomfortable.

"Well, I'd appreciate it if you could look in on my mother and sister again. I'm not sure . . . when I'll be out or even if . . ."

Mr. Whitmore ran manicured fingers through his short, curly blond hair, then looked around like he was afraid someone might have heard me. I think he read the message I was reluctant to send. He had read my fear.

He leaned in close. "I'll talk to some people, okay? I have an idea. You keep your grades up and stay out of trouble. And sure, I'll give your mother a call."

I thanked him, though I didn't really expect anything out of him. He seemed in a hurry to leave, so I made it easy for him. We shook, and I was escorted into the sally port, where I took a deep breath, then stripped and spread my cheeks. It's hard to concentrate when someone has a rubber-gloved finger up your ass, and despite my prison cynicism, I kept wondering what the man meant about "talking to some people" and "having an idea."

Back in my cell, I figured the most suitable venue for my client conference with don-Don Campora was one totally lacking in privacy, like a mess hall full of people with four guards nearby. So I waited and spotted him dissing some skinhead at his table. I got out of the chow line, moved in quickly from his left, and dropped the weasel tail into his potatoes. I put my mouth close against his ear just as he noticed what I'd done.

"We have a legal problem here, don-Don," I whispered. "Our agreement included protection so I wouldn't be 'distracted,' remember? Well, waking up with weasel body parts in my bed tends to be 'distracting.' The legal significance of this is that you've materially breached our contract, excusing my performance. I am willing to continue, but only if I have a one-week extension. Is that acceptable?"

Campora laughed unnecessarily loud to make sure everyone would think we were just fucking around. He tossed the tail into Earring's plate like it was a game and everybody laughed. "Billy boy," he whispered back over his shoulder, "you've had your extension, and now you've had your little boy snit over my friendly reminder; so now I want you to go sit the fuck down before I have Earring break both your legs."

"A week's extension," I persisted, "or I withdraw the pleading that could be your ticket to ride. You saw it, you know it's good, and I think we'll win. But if I don't get my week, I call the court and pull the plug on you."

He laughed again, watching the tail tossed around the table, but I saw a spark in his eye. "You're going to be a fucking shyster, all right," he snarled between his teeth. "Okay, you got a three-day extension. But no result by then, I come visit."

I leaned in closer. "*Seven* days."

He looked straight ahead and chuckled out loud again. Look guys, my punk lawyer won't stop joking around with me. So I bit down on his ear, but kept talking through my teeth. "Just keep smiling, Campora, or I'll take off a piece of your ear." I saw beads of sweat popping out on his forehead. "One week. Seven days. Just blink your eyes twice if we have an understanding. *Now!*"

I bit down harder on the rubbery cartilage, tasting the sourness of his flesh, then the sweetness of his blood.

Finally, as negotiators like to say, Don Campora blinked.

Later that day, as a freak late-September storm raged outside, the fires of hell burned in my cell as Dickens helped me melt seven more deodorant balls into the mother of all bonecrushers, not much thicker than a fountain pen, but nine inches long with a tip like an ice pick and as hard as tempered steel. I had given Darryl his; this one was for me, bolstering my protective armament, in case Campora decided that a promise extracted under physical duress wasn't binding. I had been very careful to make sure nobody saw what I was doing to don-Don, because a public, physical attack on a made man was suicide, and I knew it. Not that I expected him to forgive and forget, even if nobody else was aware of it and even if I did get him freed in time, which was not looking likely. So I spent the next five days in my cell, not even going to meals. The only time I went out was once a day to call the court clerk, who would patiently tell me, "Nothing yet, Mr. Strobe."

At night, I put my mattress against the rear of the cell and sat straight up with my bonecrusher in my hand and the short shank I'd bought from Dickens under my mattress. I dozed a little, but only when I could hear Dickens snoring. I was most worried about a Molotov cocktail, but when it didn't come after the third night, I figured that Campora was granting me the extension.

When the mail came, with only twenty-eight hours to spare, it was both good and bad. The good part was an order from the Superior Court of the City and County of San Francisco, granting my motion for new trial in behalf of Donald Giovanni Campora. I wept with relief when I read it, then wept with grief when I read the second piece of mail. It was from the friend watching my dog for me. Seems that Mr. Dog had been hit and killed by a car while trying to cross Wilshire Boulevard.

He had been heading north, toward Soledad.

Dickens produced two tiny airline bottles of scotch he'd been saving for a special occasion. I didn't mention Mr. Dog to Dickens. We had so few occasions for celebration inside, I didn't want to disappoint him.

"Here's to a very promising young chap," he said, rising to his feet, "Master Billy Strobe."

I thanked Dickens and asked him why he'd never let me help him with an appeal.

"I've planned my own escape," he said as casually as if telling me he was off to dinner.

"You've *what*?"

"It's as good as done."

"But how?"

"Job 3:21."

That's all he would say on the subject, and I didn't want to encourage the discussion. Dickens was too frail even to think about busting out of high-security prison.

It was dinner hour, and I went to the chow hall to deliver the good news to the don. I quietly apologized about biting his ear, but he was so overjoyed he didn't even hear me. I directed his attention to the last line of the order granting a new trial, and I thought the mean bastard might break down and cry. Instead, in front of two hundred inmates, he took my face in both hands and kissed me full on the mouth. Being a lawyer isn't all roses.

Ten days later, on the fifth of October, don-Don was transferred out of Soledad. He paid me a farewell visit to tell me he appreciated what I'd done and that he had a "little surprise" for me. Then he added that I had brains, balls, and a job waiting for me if I made it out.

"*If* I made it out?"

"You think I was going to forget this?" he said, pointing to a tiny nick in his ear. "Good luck, kid."

"You going to turn loose Earring on me, don-Don? That's my surprise?"

He shook his head. "You don't have to worry about Earring," he said, and walked away. "Not for the next three months. I might need you for some follow-up."

I put his address in my pocket and thanked him, not wanting to piss him off again now that things were looking up. A month before, my last midterm exam grades had come in: straight A's again. Earring was apparently still protecting me, and Darryl was staying clear of the yard.

But what did Campora mean by "a little surprise" he had for me?

I finally cornered Darryl for our first client conference. It wasn't hard to find him, as he was now almost always red-tagged to his drum. Prison lingo for cell confinement. Querto had been murdered, and the screws hear the rumors, too, though they couldn't prove anything.

Rabbit, Darryl's cellmate, was masturbating in the top bunk, and Darryl made him leave. We closed the cell door and locked it. First, I explained my approach to winning him a new trial—inadequate counsel—but reminded him this would just be the first battle, not the war. He should be thinking ahead about how he could win a verdict at his new trial if I was successful in getting him one.

"How we supposed to do that, Counselor? Tell the jury I'm too nice to kill anybody? Is that your plan?"

"Part of it," I said, "and too smart to hide the murder weapon behind your own locker."

He nodded.

"Didn't *anybody* see you enter your trailer camp that night?"

Darryl hesitated for a telltale second and then shook his head.

"You're lying," I said, feeling like I was getting pretty good at this. "Who were you with?"

"Never mind that."

"Dammit, Darryl, help me out here! And tell me something else while you're at it: Why didn't you ask to see a lawyer right off?"

"Hell, Billy, you know I hate lawyers even more than I hate cops. It's a lawyer got me in here the first time."

"No, Darryl, *you* got yourself in here the first time."

"Maybe. Anyway, they had my prior felony this time, so I knew I was dead anyway."

"A convenience store when you were in your early twenties. That's nothing."

"Tell *them* that."

"How did that one go down?"

"I caught a ride home from a gig with a guy I played music with who stops at a Seven-Eleven for smokes and comes out runnin with two bottles of gin, plus forty-six dollars and change."

"A drummer, right?"

"Naturally, though I've known some weird-ass bass players, too. Anyway, he did a paradiddle on the Iranian's head using brass knucks, which upped it to armed robbery."

"And once busted, the drummer became a lead singer?"

"Like a bird. Gave me up like a bad habit. By the way, I had took half the forty-six dollars."

"Oh, shit."

"I know it. I was fixin to get married and didn't expect him to get caught."

I shook my head. "Twenty-three fucking dollars."

"Yeah, well, I guess I was countin on luck, and I got it. All of it was bad."

"How did he get caught?"

"They made him on one of those cameras over the cash register."

"Another reason you hate TV."

He shrugged; I decided to keep pressing.

"I've seen you getting letters in a colored envelope. Are they from a woman? Maybe a woman who was with you that night?"

"This is bullshit," he said, as his chair noisily skidded back.

"Come on, Darryl. Talk to me!"

"That's it, kid. Forget the whole damn thing."

He was gone, but I was grinning. The son-of-a-bitch had an alibi. Now I just had to find out who she was.

11

An unfulfilling week later, while sweating my final grades from Golden State Law School and getting nowhere with Darryl, I was called to the warden's office. I figured it had something to do with don-Don's release, but when I walked in, Warden Fletcher, a tall man with a spare, bent physique, was all smiles and pointing at a gray-haired stranger who said he was Edward Crocker, dean of the Golden State Law School. Crocker, a pleasant-looking, pudgy little man who looked like Costello to the warden's Abbott, told me how pleased he was to meet me at last and then handed me my final report card. All A's.

"Mr. Strobe," he intoned, while pumping my hand, "you are the first graduate in the eighteen-year history of our institution to achieve straight A's by correspondence."

"Well, thank you, sir," I said, as much taken aback by the "Mr. Strobe" as by my good grades. "I'm much obliged to you for coming all the way down here to tell me that."

"That's not why I've come, sir," he said, and the warden gestured for us both to sit down as he ambled around his desk, sat himself in a cracked Naugahyde swivel chair, and lit up a stogie the size of a corncob. The indoor no-smoke rules obviously didn't apply to everybody.

Mr. Crocker cleared his throat, looking pleased and uncomfortable at the same time. "Golden Gate Law School, in conjunction with the California Department of Corrections and the San Francisco Bar Association, represented by a Mr. Whitmore and several others, have arranged an early release for you, Billy."

I felt the blood rush out of my head. What kind of stunt were they pulling? I glanced at Warden Fletcher, who had that same silly smile glued to his mouth.

"He's telling it straight, Strobe," the tall man said, seeing the distrust in my eyes, knowing I'd been here long enough to earn it. "They want to make you the poster boy of second chances. Put you on the TV and everything."

Mr. Crocker cleared his throat and frowned a little, but not at me. "We think you could be an inspiration to inmates throughout the state correctional system, Billy, and yes, we would like to feature you on a national television tour as the standard bearer for a new paradigm in penal rehabilitation."

I kept looking from one to the other of them, looking for some sign that this was a practical joke, that "Edward Crocker" was a con from another cell block. I refused to commit myself, cards close to my chest.

Crocker continued. "Following that, we have the assurance of the Committee of the State Bar Examiners that as a 'non-reporting' parolee, you will be permitted to take the bar exam. Moreover, the San Francisco Bar Association and some of the largest firms on Montgomery Street have informed me that you will have plenty of job opportunities in San Francisco."

If this was some kind of trick, it sure was an elaborate one. My face must have continued to show suspicion, because Warden Fletcher leaned forward and handed me a paper. "It's all here in writing, Strobe."

It was a letter of intent, signed by a CDC honcho, the president of the San Francisco Bar Association, Douglas R. Young, and a bunch of lawyers.

I learned later that all major law firms have "marketing directors," whose job it was to find issues that will get press exposure to their firms and ensure a continuing source of supply of brain power from law schools noted for their liberality on social issues. Issues like me.

My heart was pounding. This was real. An early out! I was trying to decide whether to tell Crocker about my fear of speaking in front of groups, but decided that in front of this particular group, the only words I'd better be speaking were, "Thank you."

A week later, I was getting ready to ride the merry-go-round, every prisoner's dream. That's what they called the slip of paper that a released con had to get all departments to sign off on: the laundry, library, education, cell block, recreation yard, the works. They don't want you walking out of the place with one of their fine plastic plates or a tick mattress under your Salvation Army suit coat.

I knew the word would get around soon, so I was determined to set a new merry-go-round speed record. I got everything done in one afternoon but the laundry. I also knew that going to the laundry even in the early evening for sign-off was risky, but I was due to be released the next day, and laundry was the only thing left on my merry-go-round.

The laundry was located up near the west gate off the main corridor, which at this late hour echoed with only the lonely sound of my own footsteps. It was too damn quiet, but as I turned off the corridor, I spotted the late-shift laundry room con and felt better. He signed me off after checking his log, then hurriedly disappeared out the back, which should have told me to disappear, too.

When I turned around, there they were. Carlos Ortez, El Matar's first lieutenant, and two others, one of them circling quickly to block off the back door. That was Arthur Gómez, light skinned, smaller than me, but he had a shank, and there was no point rushing him. Hell, Ortez alone might have been enough to do the job, but I guess he owed his buddies a romp.

"Beely Boy is leaving us, *mis amigos*," said Ortez, who then turned his dark eyes on me. "Think of this as your going-away party, motherfucker. You're just going somewhere different than you thought."

Usually I could manage speech with a group of only three, but not now. I suspected that raping and killing a white boy like me had as much to do with a power struggle with Earring and the Aryan Brotherhood as anything, but either way, I was dead meat.

My thoughts tripped to my mattress, where I had left my bonecrusher. It would have been nice to take one or two of them with me. I could have whipped it out of my crotch, like Campora had done that first day, then plunged it right into Ortez's throat. The others might even have lost interest after that.

"First, Beely Boy, we got to pay off a little debt to an old amigo of yours."

Ortez ran his thumb gently along the edge of a scary-looking blade that looked like a kitchen knife ground into a scalpel, a perfectly honed instrument of pain. I started to say something, but my throat had seized up. So this was don-Don's "little surprise." I stared dumbly at Ortez, shaking my head from side to side, until his thugs grabbed each arm, bent me over at the waist, and threw me down hard, facefirst on a laundry table. A hand, probably Ortez's, grabbed my hair and forced the right side of my head hard into the table. As terrified as I was, I remember thinking that at least my pants were still on.

But out of the corner of my eye—oh *Jesus,* I saw the scalpel.

"Such a pretty face, Beely. Such nice blue *ojos!*"

I shut my eyes then, unable to watch what he was going to do to me. I fought against the hands that pinned each of my arms, but to no avail.

"Easy, Beely-Boy," came Ortez's voice. "Steady now, or you just make it worse!"

I clamped my eyes tighter, unwilling to think about what was coming next.

What came next was like an electrical shock to my left ear.

I opened an eye and saw an amused expression on Ortez's face. His thugs jerked me to my feet and on the tip of Ortez's finger was a small piece of cartilage he had taken from my ear: don-Don's revenge.

Was that it? Was it over?

"Okay, Beely. We got that out of the way, eh? So, let's start *my* party now, okay? We gonna play house. So you wanna be *mamá* or *papá?*"

I said nothing, stunned into a despairing silence as hope drained out of me.

"*Answer,*" he shouted, and hit me hard in the stomach, doubling me over. He said something else—I think he wanted an answer—but I couldn't speak. So he rabbit-punched me and something popped in my neck, but I kept my feet.

"*Mamá* or *papá?*" he demanded, but everything was getting hazy.

I shook my head, then took a blow to my right ear, felt the searing pain all through my body. That must have been the third guy, the one I didn't recognize. Probably new. Dazed, I felt cold concrete on my face and hands, and realized I was down. Hands were all over me, roughly turning me on my back and pulling my pants down around my ankles. I started kicking wildly until something like a house fell on my jaw, followed by an explosion of light. Consciousness leaked away. *Don't let go!* Now someone had his hand on my balls. Another hand roughly pulled on my cock, then poked me in the pelvic area with what felt like an ice pick or a stiletto to stop my writhing. I heard myself groaning, at least I think it was me. I tried to stay with the overhead fluorescent lights in the battered ceiling because I knew if I lost consciousness, I'd lose everything.

"*Momentito, hombres,* we want Beely to enjoy his party. Okay, Señor Beely, last chance. You wanna be *mamá* or *papá*? See, I give you choice."

Someone pulled me up roughly into a sitting position. I was gagging on blood from cuts in my mouth, the hearing gone in my right ear. They were all laughing as Ortez grabbed a fistful of hair and jerked my head back.

"Choose, *motherfucker!*" he shouted.

"Papa," I whispered, and they all laughed again. Through swollen eyes I saw that Ortez had his fly open.

"Okay, *papá,*" he sneered, no longer smiling, "come over here and suck *mamá's* dick!"

They all laughed at that. Unable to speak, I shook my head, but Ortez backhanded me and told them to flip me over. They jerked me to my feet, then slammed me over a sink, facedown, one of them pinning each of my arms again. Ortez kicked my legs apart. I struggled like a rabbit in a trap, because I knew what was coming next.

But what came next was a familiar voice that rumbled into the room like the hooves of calvary horses in the final reel of a western.

"Ortez!" came the voice. "My Lord, you sure ain't got much of a pecker on you for bein such a huge asshole."

I realized my left arm was free, and I saw that Darryl had hit one of the NFers with what looked to be a length of pipe. By the time I turned, instinctively pulling my pants up, Ortez and the other guy were all over Darryl, trying for the pipe. But Darryl sank his elbow into Ortez's face, then swung at the other one, who ducked and took the blow on his shoulder. Then the first guy Darryl had hit was back on his feet going after Darryl, too. Everybody seemed to have forgotten me, so I did my best to clear my head and jumped into it, putting an armlock around Gomez's head. I gave it a hard twist, but he caught me with an elbow before I was able to break his neck, and now I had to deal with the third guy's shank, which I handled, thanks to some soap flakes I scooped up out of a bin and threw in his eyes. He staggered away, and I gave Gomez a kidney punch that bent him over. Somebody hit me, and another burst of pain shot through my head and I spat up some blood. I wiped my swollen eyes, which were hooded by tears and mucus, and saw that two of them were running for it and that Darryl had Ortez on his back. He had produced the bonecrusher I'd made for him and had the point against the NF lieutenant's throat. The Latino's eyes were shut tight, and his face was contorted with fear, waiting to die.

"Kill him, Darryl!" I heard myself shouting. "Kill the mother-fucker!"

I would spend many sleepless hours in the future thinking about those words and the raw hatred beneath them, thinking about my bitter disappointment when Darryl pulled Ortez to his feet instead of finishing him.

I eyed an abandoned shank ten feet away, but Darryl shot me a warning look and I stayed put.

"Drop your pants, amigo," he told Ortez, and the big man looked as surprised as I must have. "Now!"

He quickly obeyed, desperately ripping at them until they lay crumpled in a pile at his feet.

"Take 'em off," Darryl ordered, and Ortez stepped out of his trousers. "Shorts, too, everything."

Darryl put his bonecrusher in his belt and picked up the pile without taking his eyes off Ortez, who was bleeding heavily from his nose and mouth and shaking with cold and fear. I was bleeding, too, but only from flesh wounds, including some that were oozing blood through my recently retrieved pants. Blood from the notch in my ear ran down my neck in rivulets and onto my chest.

"I was noticing your clothes is kind of dirty, Carlos," Darryl told him in his slow drawl. "Take a look at that underwear, will you? Didn't your mama tell you that you might get in an accident someday? Better give me your shirt and socks, too. Wouldn't take much to cover up that little pecker of yours."

Now it was Ortez who was dumbstruck as he watched Darryl drop his clothes into one of the huge washing machines and start the wash cycle. The Latino stood watching, stark naked, looking as vulnerable as a child and not as big as I'd always thought him to be. Nudity, the great leveler.

"Okay, amigo," Darryl said, "it'll be a while, so you git on back to the cell block."

Ortez looked in my direction as if he expected me to plead his case. "I . . . I cannot go back like—"

"You prefer more of this?" said Darryl, picking up his pipe and lay-ing it across the bridge of Ortez's bleeding nose. Ortez gave a quick shake of his head.

As Ortez hurried off in nothing but his unlaced shoes, Darryl looked at me for the first time.

"You gonna survive, pard?"

I nodded, then tried to thank him, but he seemed mad at me, too.

"Won't do you any good gettin out tomorrow if you're in a pine box. Keep bein stupid, and that's how you'll end up."

I nodded and found my voice. "You won't make it either, Darryl. Not after this. You should have killed him. He can't let you live now."

But Darryl gave me a wry smile and said, "I'll be able to take care of myself, once I ain't got you to worry over. Come on, kid, let's git while we can."

I felt like I was going to lose it then, break down and cry right in front of him. I guess he was afraid I was about to hug him or some-thing, so he spun around and walked off in a hurry, me close on his heels, feeling a growing, unreasoning anger alongside my gratitude. When he turned off toward his cell block, I grabbed him by the arm, hard, and spun him toward me. He flinched, looked surprised.

"Why didn't you kill the bastard?" I demanded.

He considered my question for a few seconds and then said, "They can keep you up on their stage, kid, but that don't mean you have to sing their tune."

I thought at the time he meant the NFers. Later, I realized he was referring to the prison system. Either way, I knew he wasn't going to say more on the subject. Darryl never explained himself.

"Listen, Darryl," I said. "I won't try to thank you. That'd be just words. But your life isn't worth squat here after what you did tonight, and I swear I won't quit till you're out of here, too."

Darryl shrugged. "Hell, kid, my life ain't never been worth squat."

"That's not the issue. We had a deal, Darryl. Is your word worth squat, too?"

Darryl cocked his head to one side. "I'll stand by my word."

"Okay, but you've got to help me. We both know the system may be fucked, but it's all we've got to work with, and it only helps those who help themselves."

"That's got a familiar ring," said Darryl, with a quick smile before he turned serious again, "but you can forget that alibi angle. You're just gonna have to go out there and find out who really killed that lady."

Every step I took the next morning stabbed me with pain. I felt like my arms and legs were held together with burning wire. But each step also carried me closer to freedom, so I wasn't about to turn myself in to the infirmary. Instead, I gimped out of the mess hall after breakfast and picked up my "dress outs," a cheap brown suit and a pair of black plastic shoes that didn't have any give to them. Poor as we were in Enid, Oklahoma, I'd never had to wear plastic shoes, but I took them without complaint. They also gave me bus fare to San Francisco and fifty dollars in "gate money."

I said good-bye to Tom Collins, Dickens, and a handful of others.

"God be with you, Master Billy," said old Dickens, smiling beautifully, wiping tears from his eyes.

"And with you, Dickens."

He let out a cackle. "Not to worry about old Dickens," he whispered as I was giving him a hug. "True to my word, I'll be out soon. Prison hath no walls . . ."

"My lips are sealed," I said, holding back a smile.

I told Darryl good-bye and presented him with a used guitar I'd bought from another inmate. Darryl wished me luck but refused the guitar.

"There's no music for me inside prison walls. Hold on to it for me."

"I'll keep it tuned," I said, but as I walked away, I could tell he never expected to see me again.

A half hour later, one month short of a year after I'd been imprisoned, I was riding free and unchained on a Greyhound bus through the Pastures of Heaven, not once looking back at the Walls of Hell.

PART II

OUTSIDE

Stone walls do not a prison make
Nor iron bars a cage . . .

    —Richard Lovelace,
     To Althea from Prison

12

You could put me down as the least likely kid on your block to suddenly show up on national television and manage to remember his own name and avoid having an accident of a personal nature. Which is about all I managed, but I survived somehow, chauffeured like the pope to TV studios in L.A., Dallas, Atlanta, Chicago, then over to Philly, and finally, New York City.

At least I knew Darryl wasn't watching.

I'd never had the money to travel, so when Edward Crocker first mentioned the tour possibility—he was the guy who had given me the good news in the warden's office last month—I figured it would be an opportunity to see the USA and try to conquer my fear of public speaking in the bargain. Maybe it would even be fun, which is a thing I'd fairly forgotten how to have.

It wasn't fun. Seemed like all I saw was airports, taxis, hotels, and TV studios, then more airports. There wasn't even a spare day for me to stop off in Oklahoma, though I was talking to Ma and Lisa by telephone at least twice a week.

The weather was at war with us. Winter in full battle gear seemed to be waiting at every stop, so I did little between appearances other than eat and sleep. Travel definitely isn't what it's cracked up to be, and talk show hosts should be forced to watch themselves on TV. Airports should be against the law.

It seemed impossible that I had spent only one year in prison, for it had become a way of life, a mean structure for survival. It was as if I'd been in a foreign land and on my return had forgotten how to speak English. And along with my cheap suit and fifty bucks, I'd brought my fear outside with me.

I feared, in fact, just about everything. The traffic seemed heavier and faster, the buildings higher, the sun more blinding, the smells more powerful, even the crush and glut of people on too-narrow sidewalks was uncomfortable.

On the other hand, to be able to close the door and set the dead bolt in my hotel room after a TV appearance was like a gift from God. I would take off my shoes and feel the lushness of the carpet under my bare feet, hop in bed stark-ass naked and swim in the freshly laundered sheets. Smell the free hotel lotion and rub it all over my pale body while watching old movies. Room service. Real coffee. Telephones. Chocolates on my pillow.

The telephone was best of all, talking to Lisa and Ma in complete privacy without people like Carlos Ortez hovering and clearing throats every ten seconds and leaning so close their putrid breath seemed to rise out of the receiver, befouling the words.

Lisa told me that Ma cried in front of her for the first time since Dad died when I called from a pay phone the day I got out. I was able to call often once the tour started because Edward told me I could charge two ten-minute calls home every week on his credit card. I'd try to call early in the morning, of course, hoping to catch Ma clear-headed enough to rag at me for not coming straight home to Enid when I had got out of prison.

I'd try to explain that I had no money, not a dime of my own, and was living on Edward's expense account. "Let me talk to your Mr. Crocker, William," she'd insist, and I'd tell her he was attending a meeting. Then I'd promise to come home soon as I finished the job interviews Edward had lined up, got hooked up with a law firm, and saved some money.

The conversations were always pretty much the same. Ma would start out asking me when I was going to get out, and I'd keep telling her I was already out and on the TV. Then she'd remember and ask me if my shirts were clean.

Lisa told me once I looked handsome but kind of "jumpy," which irritated the hell out of me because the jumpy part was so goddamn true. Amazingly, no one else seemed to mind. I had warned Edward Crocker about my problem talking in groups.

"How's your memory," he had said.

"Too good," I said, and he gave me an understanding smile.

"Then think of everything they might ask you and memorize some clever answers, you know: 'What was your worst experience?' 'What is your biggest regret?' 'What have you learned from—' "

I told him okay and I reckon I got away with it because ol' Edward, who traveled everywhere with me, kept rubbing his hands together and saying this had become a "damned successful project." He would wind me up and put me in front of a camera or a crowd, and I'd turn red and sputter things like it's great to have a second chance in life and thanks a lot everybody. Lucky for me, the hosts were pros, used to dealing on the air with everything from retards to odd jungle animals. If they were pissed off, they concealed it, even during dead-air moments when a question seemed to fade on the way to my mind like smoke scattering in the sky. That little red light would come on, and a curtain would drop somewhere between my brain and my mouth.

No matter, they'd usually wish me well afterward; then me and Edward would be off to the next city.

One thing that came out of my nervous performances was confirmation that I was destined to be an office lawyer, nowhere near a courtroom. But that wouldn't stop me from working to free Darryl and redeem my father's good name, though it might complicate my quest at times.

New York being the last stop on the tour, Mr. Crocker took me to a fancy place after *The Today Show* called Aquavit, which had huge colored kites hanging from a fifty-foot-high mirrored ceiling and dinners that cost seventy-four dollars, not even counting tax or drinks.

Funny how a crowded, romantic place like this can make you feel more alone than being in a cell. Not that I didn't like Mr. Crocker, but it seemed a shame not to be sharing all this with a girl. I'd seen a lot of pretty women on this tour and had such a set of horns on me I had to turn sideways to get though a door. Problem was ol' Crocker had been chaperoning me like some damn Miss America candidate, assuring me I'd have plenty of time to "sow my wild oats" when the tour was done. I think that meant getting laid, so I told him I was more into reaping than sowing at this point, and he laughed and ordered up a bottle of bubbly called Dom Pérignon to make the best of things. He raised his glass, repeating that the "project" (that was me) had been "damned successful."

I had become the poster boy of second chances.

Back in San Francisco, the tour finished, I got a second-floor studio apartment on Bush Street on the edge of the financial district. It was roomy but had only a few small windows, which was okay because I was not accustomed to having a lot of light. All I wanted was privacy, a double lock on the door, and room to move around in, plus I was spending most of my daylight hours in the library anyways, studying for the state bar. I tried to establish a routine that would take the place of the one I'd had on the road with Mr. Crocker—which had taken the place of the one I'd had in prison. In other words, I realized I needed routine in my freedom, some structure, and was uneasy with anything that violated it. I was eager to get a job, a place to go every day.

Mr. Crocker called to tell me he was holding a batch of interview offers from top firms all over the Bay Area.

"I don't get it," I said.

"You're a hot commodity," said Mr. Crocker, which I took to be a step up from being a "successful project."

"You're smart, Billy," he continued, "and you've paid your dues. You've also become a PR item firms can exploit to get their name out front, particularly with law schools. Of course, they'll treat you like dog meat once you actually accept their offer and go to work for them, so enjoy rush week. 'Pluck the day!' "

Sure enough, during the next few weeks, I found myself being hustled by all kinds of white-shoe hotshots. I was living high on the hog, getting recognized at posh places like Aqua, Postrio, and Jack's, and fun spots like Hawthorne Place, Moose's, Bix, and Le Central. The corporate lawyers I met seemed like pretty regular people, not the mean-spirited flaming assholes I'd figured they'd be. Which raised the question of my standards of comparison. Maybe I was now judging people against the likes of Campora, Matar, Ortez, and Earring.

I decided to go with the flow for the present. What's the harm in being friendly and having a good time after what I'd been through? So I plucked the hell out of the day and the night, too.

After about three weeks of this, I came in one night from a great meal at Rose Pistola in North Beach, feeling full and boozy, my ears sore from hearing what a great guy I was.

So why was I so miserable?

I knew why. While I was scarfing lamb chops and champagne, a guy who had saved my life was dining on shit-on-a-shingle and wearing magazines around his belly. This alone was enough to fill even a renegade Catholic boy with guilt, but there was something else gnawing at my conscience. Other than sending Ma and Lisa a little money and calling regular, I hadn't found enough free time to go to visit them. And what about my plan to clear Dad's name?

I turned on the light and grabbed my bar course outline for torts, hoping to study myself into drowsiness. I ended up taking a couple of the sleeping pills Mr. Crocker had given me when we were on the road. The bottle was almost empty.

I drifted off about two o'clock, but a couple of hours later I shot upright in bed, still half-asleep, sweating, shaken by the dream-image of my father's likeness, his face bruised and bloodied, sitting on the edge of a metal slab and a tick mattress.

I got up, took a pee, and found myself thinking about what Darryl had told me that day after I'd hit him on the handball court when he'd implied my father was guilty. He'd said I had gone hard, and I had told him he was probably crazy because the truth revealed in his words was too damn staggering to take in. But I *had* gone hard, had made myself hard to keep from giving in to the daily terror that lurked behind the eyes of every man in prison. *Kill him,* I had shouted in the laundry room that day Darryl saved me from Ortez, and that was after only one year of institutionalization. *Kill the motherfucker!* But Darryl, a convicted "murderer," wouldn't play the tune I was requesting. He hadn't just saved my life; he was trying to save my soul. Time would tell.

I looked at myself in the mirror over the washbasin and saw somebody who looked like he'd gone more soft than hard.

I took a cold shower, put on a fresh T-shirt and chinos, and dug a box out of the closet that contained my prison files. It was time to get cracking on what I'd come here to do. Darryl could be dead by the time I passed the bar or even got a job. As for Dad, I was sure he wouldn't mind me temporarily shuffling my priorities.

I carried the box into the kitchen and cleared my bar study materials from my worktable. I spread Darryl Orton's files out on the table, sifting through the mass of paperwork until I found the name of his alleged victim, Deborah Hinton, and her employer, Synoptics Corporation. That got me thinking. Synoptics was where she worked, where her friends were, and where she was killed. Got to be a way in there.

I had no meetings the next day—which made me feel a little uneasy—so I set the alarm for 9:00 A.M. and this time went right to sleep. At 9:20, my metabolism jump-started by day-old coffee, I called the receptionist at Synoptics.

"May I speak to your legal department?" I said.

"We have no 'legal department,' *per se,* sir," she said, sounding proud of the fact. "May I connect you with our general counsel's office?"

I said thank you, ma'am, and found out in short order that Synoptics referred nearly all its legal work to outside law firms. I couldn't pry a single one of them out of the tight-ass on the phone, so I had another cup of coffee and called back, trying to lose my Okie accent this time.

"May I speak to your public relations department?" I said, and she said one moment please, nice as pie.

"Public affairs," came a tired woman's voice a few seconds later.

"Good morning," I said, in a light tone. "I'm doing a research proj-

ect for the *San Francisco Recorder*. Are you familiar with our law pe-
riodical?"

She was. I could hear a spoon clinking in a cup.

"I'm writing an article on the top ten law firms in the greater Bay
Area," I said.

"We're not a law firm, sir."

"I know that, but we've selected Synoptics Corporation as one of
the top Bay Area companies we're surveying."

"Oh?" she said, suddenly interested. "How can I help?"

"Well, we're preparing a study on the satisfaction of these companies with their legal counsel. May I ask if you're generally satisfied
with yours?"

"Why, yes," she said. "Quite satisfied. You see our company, which
started back in . . ."

She then gave me half the history of mankind and the importance
of Synoptics in its evolution. I practically had to start yodeling to get
a word in.

"That's fine, ma'am, but our story has to do with outside general
counsel. May I ask who your outside law firm is?"

"Stanton and Snow has been our lead outside counsel for all fourteen years of our existence, and I think you could quote me as saying
it has been a mutually rewarding relationship. You see, we're the
largest U.S. provider of integrated—"

"I believe you said that," I said, feeling the heat of impatience
flooding my body, "and I'm much obliged for your time, so thank
you—"

"Rice is my name. Thelma Rice. That's *R-I-C-E*." Her coffee was
kicking in, plus she smelled the possibility of seeing her name in the
paper. I couldn't turn her off. "Is there anything else I can tell you? May
I send you our brochure? Give me your name and address and—"

"No, ma'am, that's all I—"

"We are the fastest growing company in the Silicon Valley and one of
the first providers of integrated software to make the Fortune 500—"

"Christ, lady, I guess I'm the one put a quarter in you, but would
you give it a rest?"

I reckon I shocked myself about as much as I did her, but at least
she stopped yapping. I hung up—then wondered whether I should
hang myself. I realized that among the things I'd lost in prison were
courtesy and patience.

But now I knew where I wanted to go to work.

13

I caught up with Edward Crocker later that morning over at Golden State Law School, and he arranged an interview with Hale Lassiter, Stanton and Snow's senior partner, who said he had seen me on TV.

"S & S is Montgomery Street's monarchy, Billy, the blue-blooded, bluestockinged Brahmins of the corporate establishment."

"Sounds like a perfect fit for an Okie ex-con."

Edward looked worried. "It's a rigid culture, Billy."

"I've *been* in a 'rigid culture.' But would *they* want *me?*"

Edward chewed on a pencil for a few seconds and then said, "Lassiter is a man who recognizes your PR value. Welcoming a highly publicized outsider into their hallowed halls will help overcome their image of cronyism and stodginess. I've also heard they may be having some cash flow problems. They lost a big contingent fee case a year or two ago, and some partners and associates left the firm, taking blue-ribbon clients with them. They could use the PR boost you'd give them, but you might not want to join a firm that's seen its best days."

"I don't care about that. Just wish me luck."

Two days later, dressed in a sincere blue suit, new black wingtips, and a red power tie—not the Soledad threads, but stuff Crocker had bought me out of the tour travel budget—I felt sufficiently disguised to invade Troy.

I walked the eight blocks from my Bush Street basement apartment down to the Western Bank Building on Montgomery Street and stood before the forty-story, gleaming glass-and-steel edifice. An old cripple hawked newspapers out of a stand in front nearly as big as the cell I'd lived in at Soledad.

It was a typical January day in the city, and I could see my breath as I gazed skyward to the top floor where my fate—and perhaps Darryl's as well—might well be decided. People were pouring into the building like ants into a honey trap, jostling so close I could smell their lidded coffee and hear music bleeding out of their earphones.

Once inside, an oak-paneled elevator—dedicated exclusively to the top six floors occupied by S & S—swept me up to the penthouse, where an elegant English lady offered me tea or coffee, which I said no to because I was wired enough already. I sank into an old-style leather reception chair—one of six—and took in the splendor of the reception area, the most impressive I'd seen in all my interviews. But now that I had passed through my brief post-prison Sodom and Gomorrah phase, I saw this posh facade for what it was: a fancy cover for a book about avarice.

As for Lassiter, I was ready for the worst. Edward Crocker had told me the guy was in his mid-fifties, smart and richer than God, a business lawyer by training who was now a top trial lawyer, primarily serving the surviving dot-coms and other high-tech companies in the Silicon Valley. In short, Lassiter sounded like the ultimate economic animal, the very soul of the S & S greed machine. I wondered how long he would make me wait until he sent one of his secretaries out to fetch me.

I leaned back and tried to relax, but the mahogany walls surrounding me suddenly seemed as foreboding as those I'd endured for the past year. Hypnotic cones of light from the ceiling canisters cut through the rich darkness of the reception area and I half expected Lassiter to materialize out of the lush carpet like a snake bearing an apple.

I briefly considered flight, but then out came the man himself, in shirtsleeves for Christ's sake, looking like Charlton fucking Heston with eyebrows like toothbrushes and a jaw like a bucket. He was tall like me, but bigger, with a healthy mane of gray hair and large, gentle eyes.

"Hello, Mr. Strobe," he said, his voice deep and friendly. "Thanks for coming."

I thanked him for the invite, and he escorted me straight to the coffee machine, where he poured some for both of us in Styrofoam cups! Then he sat me down in his office like I was Bill Gates, not Billy Strobe.

Lassiter's office took up a large corner of the top floor and faced both to the north—the Golden Gate Bridge, the Marin Headlands, Mount Tamalpais, and Sausalito—and to the east—the Bay Bridge, the East Bay Hills, and Mount Diablo. The east wing appeared to be his conference area, with a bar and a closed door that looked like it led to a private bathroom. We were sitting in what appeared to be his working office. Mr. Lassiter was lodged behind a bulwark of fine oak. I sat in front of the desk in one of three large client chairs. The wall behind him was covered with honor plaques and photographs, several picturing him with an attractive woman about his age posing in formal wear, ski clothes, snorkel gear, and once with a pair of golden Labs. No kids that I could see.

Did you see that game Sunday? he asked me, making a face. Pretty sad, I agreed, having read the Rams butted the 49ers all over the field. Damn salary cap is killing us, he said, thank you very much, Carmen Policy. I agreed. Did you get to see broadcasts of any of their games in prison? I didn't. Was I really from Oklahoma? I was. He'd be damned. Did I follow the Sooners? Not too much anymore. Well, they had a hell of a season, didn't they? Yes, sir, and it was about time, I said. And so on.

This wasn't so bad: a couple of good old boys talking football in an office big enough to scrimmage in. I kept waiting for the tough questions, but then we were into the elections, the Academy Awards, and what kind of music I liked.

"Your golden Labs?" I asked him, indicating the photo. Billy getting personal.

"Aren't they beauties? But that's my real treasure standing next to me." He pointed to the woman. "Wife Laura. Celebrated our thirty-fifth anniversary last month."

I didn't ask him about the absence of any children in his pictures. Billy learning when to keep his trap shut.

When he finally got down to business, he asked me what questions I had about the firm. I asked the usual things: what I'd be doing if I came to S & S, what kind of challenges the firm offered, what sort of contribution I might be able to make, whether I would be allowed to do any *pro bono publico* work—questions I'd picked up from Mr. Crocker designed to create the appearance of a curious, ambitious, and enlightened mind.

"We pride ourselves on our public service commitment," he said, "and we expect our business-side associates to bill around eight hours a day."

That sounded reasonable, but I would learn later how many hours you had to work in a day to actually bill eight of them to a client file. Most law firm associates, especially new fish, worked nearly all their waking hours, six or seven days a week.

Anyway, there I was, Mr. Billy Nobody from Enid, Oklahoma, graduate of Soledad Prison, and there was this Montgomery Street hotshot OG with a loose tie and his sleeves rolled up, revealing forearms like a longshoreman's, treating me like a visiting prince. I kept waiting for him to reveal himself to be the prick I had expected and that he sure as hell must be to ramrod a firm of over two hundred lawyers, but he just sat there smiling, seemingly unaware of himself, so soft-spoken I had to keep leaning forward to hear him. After a while, I couldn't stand it anymore.

"I reckon you'd like to know a bit about me," I said, "you know, about my . . . background?"

"I know what I need to know," he said, giving me a smile like the uncle I never had. "I just wanted to be sure that you know what you'll be getting into, if you come to work here."

"If that was an offer, sir, I accept."

He smiled, shook my hand, and said, "Welcome aboard."

"Will I be working for you, sir?"

"That's what I want to talk to you about. I'll be your so-called 'mentor,' but I'm doing mainly litigation these days, so you will be working mostly with Rex Ashton and Malcomb Wilcox, business law partners. Ashton will be stopping by to meet you."

I must have shown some disappointment.

"Rex is a senior partner, a member of the firm's executive committee, and a co-chair with me of the firm's M & A group—Mergers and Acquisitions. He can be a taskmaster, but he's probably the smartest lawyer in the firm, and our M & A group is the firm's top profit center. You'll learn a lot from Rex Ashton. Wilcox is the third member of the firm's executive committee and heads the wills and probate department."

I had the feeling he wasn't telling me everything. The bride was too beautiful, as Dad used to say when he had a case that looked like a slam dunk for the defense.

My pessimistic speculation was interrupted by a noise behind me, and I turned to see a smallish but fit-looking man in his mid-forties blasting through Lassiter's door with the force of an Oklahoma twister.

"Is this the famous Billy Strobe?" he intoned in a resonant and heavily sardonic baritone voice that didn't fit his slight frame.

I almost said "guilty as charged," but reconsidered under the circumstances—the circumstances being as how he didn't look to be a man with a sense of humor.

"Yes, sir, I'm Billy."

"This is Rex Ashton, Billy," said Hale, in a tone that lacked enthusiasm.

Ashton advanced and gave me a handshake that can best be described as, well, competitive. There was no goodwill in his grip. The man reminded me of some of the steel-eyed cons I'd known inside, always sizing you up, control freaks, probing for the weakness we all have buried somewheres. He was also a guy who just missed being good looking and probably resented it. An otherwise fine-featured

narrow face, it was his nose that did him in: sharp and sloping right
out of his forehead, putting me in mind of some kind of rodent. His
hair was not so great either, too coal black to be natural, and combed
up high over his forehead from the side to hide a hairline in disorderly
retreat.

"Glad to meet you, Mr. Ashton," I said, telling my first lie of the
day. "I'd be obliged for the opportunity to work with you." There
went my second.

Ashton smiled broadly at this, revealing a large mouth with small
teeth. "Some would call it a sentence to cruel and unusual punishment,
not an opportunity," he said, the words unrolling from his lips with
the reluctant precision of tightly coiled wire. He beckoned me back
into my seat with an imperious wave of a small hand. *Cruel and unusual punishment.* I wondered how much bad prison humor I could
look forward to at S & S.

"So, Mr. Strobe," he continued, taking a seat beside me, "how
much do you know about me and my M and A group?"

"Not much, sir," I said, noting the "*my* M and A" group. I wanted
to glance at Mr. Lassiter, but resisted.

"How much do you know about mergers and acquisitions, generally?"

"Just what I learned in my corporations law course, Mr. Ashton,"
I said, hoping he wouldn't know I'd taken it by correspondence.

"You didn't take the mergers and acquisitions seminar?"

"It wasn't offered, sir."

He gave me a hard look, and I figured I was being tested by a man
who already knew a lot about me and didn't like what he knew. Time
to go with the truth.

"It was a third-year course when I was a freshman at UCLA," I
added, "and Golden State didn't offer it when I was in prison."

"Doing your third year," he said ambiguously, the hint of a smile
on his pinched face.

"Doing my third year of law school," I said, determined not to play
games with him or let him piss me off, "while doing my first and only
year of incarceration. I graduated just before I was released from
prison."

His eyebrows rose at my frankness, but he wasn't put off balance.
"Who said you were released?" he said. "You'll be working for me!"

He laughed at his joke, though his mouth didn't open, producing
the effect of a ventriloquist's dummy in a state of human constipation.

"I warned him, Rex," said Hale, interceding with his own forced
smile and a clipped tone, "that you were a bit of taskmaster. I didn't
tell him you aspired to be a warden as well."

"Somebody has to do it," Ashton snapped back, staring hard at me, "inundated as we are these days by Ally McBeal wannabes and refugees from *L.A. Law* reruns."

"I'm not familiar with those shows, sir."

"My God, Hale," he said, "we've been sent our very own tabula rasa! Perhaps there is hope for the profession after all."

Hale glowered at his partner. "Billy was asking me what he'll be doing here."

Ashton waved his small hand dismissively and faced me. "Studying for the bar is what you'll be doing. It's one of the toughest bar exams in fifty states with roughly a fifty percent failure rate. With your, ah, scholastic background, you'll need to work hard."

"Billy was on the law review at UCLA, Rex, and graduated from Golden State with straight A's. He'll have no trouble with the bar exam."

"I hope not," Ashton said, then smiled wryly and added in a stage whisper, "for your sake as well as his, my friend."

"Do you have anything else, Rex?" Lassiter said, his face reddening.

Jesus, these guys were like a couple of cons in the rec yard, fixing to throw down on each other. What was going on here?

Ashton turned his narrowed dark eyes back on me. "Come see me when, and if, you've passed the bar, young man. Then we'll try to make a lawyer out of you. Meanwhile, I'll leave you to the more benign devices of Messrs. Lassiter and Wilcox."

At least he had spared me another prison gag. Abruptly, he lifted off from his chair. "Must run. When can I have your report on the Paul Dexter case, Hale?"

"Later," Lassiter said, and this time I did steal a glance at his tight lips and clenched jaw.

"That's what you said last week."

"*Later,*" Lassiter repeated. Ashton shrugged and walked out.

Hale Lassiter exhaled and stared into his huge clenched hands. "I apologize for Rex's manner, Billy. He has moods."

"May I speak frankly, sir?"

"You are more than entitled."

"What does the man have against me? Is it my record?"

"It's not you, Billy, believe me. It's a long story, but you're entitled to the truth. Rex Ashton wants this office."

"Sir?"

"Stanton and Snow is a democracy. We elect a presiding partner every two years. I'll stand for reelection next year against Rex, with whom I've been sparring for all five years of my administration."

"I don't mean to be nosy, sir, but should this affect my decision?"

"That's for you to judge, Billy. What you need to know is that Rex opposed your hiring, then insisted on working with you when I over-ruled him. As a concession, the partners felt he should be allowed that privilege. I must confess that he may wish to see you fail, so that he can impugn my judgment in hiring you."

Well, that was more like it, I thought. The bride was not only too beautiful, she was beginning to look like a bag of antlers.

"After observing Rex's attitude today," he continued, "I must also tell you that if I were in your shoes, with all your opportunities, I might go elsewhere."

"Is that your advice, sir, or your preference?"

"It's merely advice," he said, rising to his feet. "Advice I sincerely hope you'll reject."

I nodded and got up, extended my hand to him. "If you're willing to bet on a dark horse, sir, just tell me when the race starts."

Hale Lassiter smiled broadly and said, "How about next Monday?"

The following week, on the twenty-fourth day of January, slightly a year after I had been wrapped in chains and consigned to Soledad Prison, I became an employee of Stanton and Snow, counselors to Synoptics Corporation. I was paid a salary of $100,000 a year for studying for the midyear bar exam and showing up once in a while for a research project if I felt like it. I had become the proud owner of a 1993 Probe two-door hatchback and three new suits. I felt like Tom Cruise at the beginning of *The Firm*. Fucking Cinderella.

On the downside, everybody knew who I was and what I had been. Hale figured we shouldn't try to make my sordid past a secret since I'd been on the TV and all. Tongues would be wagging soon enough, and I could become a "distraction." So I was introduced to the 80 partners, 137 associates, and 294 staff members of Stanton and Snow in the firm's newsletter:

Meet our new business associate, William ("Billy") Strobe, an honor graduate from Golden State Law School! Mr. Strobe's unique background, including one year at a state correctional facility, will provide S&S's white collar crime group with an unique dimension of experience and the rest of us an opportunity to get to know a fine young man who has put his past behind him. Our firm is honored that Mr. Strobe has chosen to join us over all the other offers he received. His office is on the 37th floor, next to Mr. Rothschild. Stop by and get acquainted!

There was a postage-stamp-size photo of me off to the side, smiling hard so it wouldn't look like a mug shot. A few partners and two associates stopped by to "get acquainted," and not one of them mentioned my dark past, probably because the article said I'd put it behind me—as if there was somewhere else you could put the past.

My first visitor was the guy mentioned in the newsletter. "I'm Mace Rothschild from next door," he said, entering my interior office. "You've made me a celebrity. First time I've been mentioned in the firm's newsletter since I started three years ago."

Mace was a tall, skinny kid with flaming red hair who put me in mind of a broomstick on fire. His hair started too soon above his eyes so that his abbreviated forehead gave him the look of a creature of questionable intelligence, though the dark-circled eyes beneath the brow were alert and friendly. I later learned he had the highest LSAT in the history of Yale Law School.

We shook hands, and he told me we wouldn't be neighbors for long. "I'm scheduled for a window," he said, and explained that if you survive three years at S & S, they move you to an outside office.

I tried to picture myself working ten hours a day for three years in my elegantly appointed, grasscloth-walled, leather-upholstered, lush-carpeted, windowless cubicle, breathing recycled air under the relentless glow of fluorescent lights. The only consolation was that I wouldn't have to share it with Dickens.

"With partnership—four or five years after that—you get *two* windows," he continued, "though statistically, only two and one-half associates out of ten make two windows."

The kid was full of information.

"Where do the other seven and a half go," I said.

"Some go out their single window," he said, flashing a smile with uneven teeth, "particularly the ones assigned to Rex Ashton."

How did he know that? Must have a grapevine here, like in prison.

"I'm also going to be working for Mr. Wilcox in probate," I said.

"Lucky you. Less than a week here, and you've connected with all three members of the executive committee."

"Wilcox is the third member?"

Mace nodded. "He's not the brightest crayon in the box, plus he's an Ashton stooge."

I didn't feel lucky at all. Maybe it was rookie paranoia, but I felt more like I was already under executive surveillance.

Though I had few visitors, I was fair game once I was outside my office. People at S & S didn't seem to want to know the ex-convict, but they did want to get a look at me. I felt like a person with leprosy or terminal cancer; nobody knew quite how to deal with me. I was older than most of the associates, had not graduated from a top-ten law school like the rest of them, and, of course, was an ex-felon on parole. Wherever I went, I could feel eyes on me—lawyers, secretaries, paralegals, whatever—staring at the hardened criminal right there in their midst. Some would smile nervously when I looked their way, most would avert their eyes. Hale assured me that this would wear off shortly, so I minded my own business and stayed out of trouble, the way I'd tried to do at Soledad.

To be fair about it, these people were under the gun, without the spare time to even stay acquainted with their own families, let alone play meet-the-freak. Most looked as tired and damaged as Mace, the only associate who seemed up for friendship.

"Are all big firms like this?" I asked him a couple of days later. "Mr. Ashton says I'm expected to bill twenty-four hundred hours a year."

"Hey, you'll be making $125,000 a year with a guaranteed $20,000 bonus as soon as you pass the bar," he said, as if that answered my question. He collapsed into my lone client chair, looking like a young version of old Dickens. If he was any thinner, he could qualify as the "half" associate who would graduate to two windows.

"Law firms are having to compete for talent with the high-tech firms that have been cannibalizing the top young people. So we're the beneficiaries!"

I had to smile at the foolhardiness of someone so smart. "I reckon I'd rather be the beneficiary under your life insurance policy," I said.

Over the next two weeks, I settled into a routine of studying for the bar and doing a few research memos and, before I knew it, I was backing up to the pay table for my first S & S check, half of which I sent to Ma and Lisa, who, incidentally, I still hadn't visited. The second thing I did was draft papers to the court with my supporting affidavit, moving to have Carlos Ortez transferred out of Soledad, away from Darryl. The third thing I did was use some of the other half to hire an investigator named Barney Klinehart to start investigating Darryl's case. I'd heard from Mace he charged reasonable rates and was one of the best in the business. He had been one of the victims of the current district attorney's purge of the local offices' best deputies and investigators, career folks who had been deemed politically incorrect after a hotly contested election. The rest of my check went for rent, car payments, and eats.

Klinehart came up to the office on a cold day in early February. His presence shrank the size of my cubicle even more. No more than five feet six, he weighed in at more than 250, and I feared for my teak client's chair.

"What can I do for you?" he growled, wiping sweat from his forehead with a wet handkerchief. I wondered if he'd live long enough to do much for me or anyone else.

"I need some work done on a murder that took place nearly two years ago. Her name was Deborah Hinton."

"Chief financial officer for a high-tech operation called Synoptics," he said in a clipped East Coast accent.

My face must have registered my amazement.

"I got one of them pornographic memories," he said, and then snickered to be sure I caught that he was joking. "I'm a walking encyclopedia of useless information."

"What else do you remember?"

"The Hinton woman," he said, staring upward, as if details of the case might be revealed in the pitted acoustic ceiling tiles. "She was killed by a delivery man, right?"

"Maybe," I said. "They claimed it was the night janitor."

"Yeah, yeah, yeah," he said, nodding his head furiously and wiping it at the same time. "The janitor. Now I remember."

I told him I wanted him to update the activities of Dr. Frank Hinton, the estranged husband of victim Deborah Hinton, and then try to find a hole in his alibi. I also asked him to check into any financial problems Hinton may have had, considering the large insurance policy he had collected on. I told him to interview the superintendent of the TechnoCenter Building where the rape-murder took place to discover who, other than Darryl Orton, might have been on the Synoptics floor of the TechnoCenter Building the night of Deborah Hinton's murder. I told him Frank Hinton was there in the late afternoon according to the police report and maybe the building log would show what time he left. I also told him that the autopsy showed Deborah was pregnant, had been either raped or involved in rough sex, and to see what he could find out about her love life.

He listened intently, though I realized he had never once met my eyes, a strange quirk for an investigator. Then he shook his huge head so hard beads of perspiration flew through the air.

"Save your money kid," he said, rising with great difficulty to feet that looked too small to support his weight. "Hinton didn't do it. My memory's clear on this. The janitor admitted it."

"He pleaded guilty, he didn't admit it."

Klinehart glanced up somewhere around the area of my forehead and said, "You're a lawyer, all right."

"And you're supposed to be an investigator, Mr. Klinehart. So investigate."

He was already at the door, but turned and measured me for the first time with small, penetrating eyes that seemed to pop out of his puffy cheeks. "I'm not comfortable wasting either my time or my clients' time."

"You're wasting both presently, sir. The janitor did not kill Deborah Hinton. Here's the file and a retainer of five hundred dollars so that you'll be comfortable while you're finding out who did."

The eyes popped wider. At first, I thought it was the mention of money, but it was me he seemed to be regarding with new interest.

He waddled back, grabbed the file, but left the check. "I'm a little backed up at the present time," he said, "but I'll do what I can. Call me Barney."

He held out a small hand, and I took it.

The next thing I did was file a request, complete with check, for the trial transcript in the case of *State of Oklahoma vs. Joseph Strobe*. I didn't have the time or money to go home yet, but I had to get the ball rolling on clearing the family name.

I then turned all my attention toward passing the bar. The statistics didn't favor night school or correspondence graduates, and Edward had agreed with Ashton that I was now fighting the odds. So as much as I missed Ma and Lisa, I knew I wouldn't get home now until after the bar exam. They were disappointed, but I promised to head for Enid the day after it was over.

Weeks later, the bar exam finally behind me, my resolution to head home was instantly shattered, for I was now fair game, a full-time, first-year, Montgomery Street rookie. In prison lingo, I was a fish, Rex Ashton's bitch.

Edward Crocker had warned me that when the exam was over, the party would be over, too, and I could count on long days and being treated like dogshit stuck to the bottom of Rex Ashton's finely cobbled English wingtips. Still, I was surprised to be summoned by Ashton so soon because I'd only taken the bar, not passed it.

I had already nosed around, trying to find out as much as I could about Ashton and learned he was the firm's biggest "rainmaker"— producer of fat-cat clients—as hardworking and reliable as the twelve-cylinder Rolls he drove to the office seven days a week. Also as personable: a cold, never-married, ferret-faced little man with a little mustache and a big ego. It was an open secret that he had in fact been actively lobbying for Hale's job for a year, and I had no doubt that Hale was correct in predicting that a failure on my part would give Ashton ammo at the next annual partners meeting. But I suspected there was another reason Ashton wanted me to work for him. He planned to keep an eye on me, given the fact I'd have access to sensitive IPO—initial public offering—information. I'd spent a year in state prison for stealing exactly that kind of information, so I reckon I couldn't blame him for that.

Hale had called Ashton the smartest lawyer in the firm, and Mace Rothschild had called him the biggest asshole in the firm. But I didn't give a hoot whether he was smart *or* an asshole, because I had also learned that Rex Ashton was the lead lawyer for Synoptics, which meant I was a step closer to my goal of getting inside the TechnoCenter Building.

"Consider this a warm-up, Strobe," Ashton said, gazing at me from behind a fortress of ebony that must have cost more than the U.S. average national income. The desktop was barren, but for a Mont Blanc pen in a black marble holder engraved with his name in gold and a single file folder. Like Hale Lassiter, Ashton had a corner office, but it looked south and east, and what met the eye on entering it was not bridges and water, but the Moscone Convention Center, the Mission District, and the cluttered detritus of urban living.

My first assignment involved a client named Zebra Corporation, which, according to Rex Ashton, wanted to back out of a signed facilities lease worth hundreds of thousands of dollars a year. I tried to take notes, but words shot from Ashton's small mouth like a machine gun, employing legalese I'd never heard of. Trying to follow his line of thought was like catching fish with bare hands.

"Sir, would you mind slowing down a bit?"

"I'll try to speak slower, Mr. Strobe," he said biting off each word, "if you'll try to think faster."

When he finally wound down, and asked me if I had any questions, I didn't know where to start. So I didn't.

"Have your research memo in my office tomorrow at eight," Ashton said, "and be certain the law supports the answer the client wants to hear."

He then signaled the end of the meeting by focusing his dark eyes on a second file folder on the credenza behind him. In his mind, I had already left.

"Tomorrow?" I asked, trying to convey the impossibility of his request without actually saying no, which I'd been told by Mace Rothschild was a word that had never been uttered by an associate at S & S more than once.

"You apparently have difficulty with your hearing, Mr. Strobe," he said without turning around. "I hope you are not similarly handicapped in your writing and research skills."

My next question could get me thrown out of the firm on the spot, but I had to know the answer.

"Would that be a.m. or p.m., sir?" I said, as diffidently as possible.
He turned partway around, flashed me a murderous glance, jerked his head in the direction of the door, and then returned his attention to his file. I took this to mean A.M.

By the time I got back to my office, Ashton's secretary or law clerk had already deposited on my desk six inches of Zebra Corporation's annual reports, ledgers, journals, and other financial statements, plus four correspondence files and an inch-thick lease agreement, signed by all the parties. Sweat broke out across my forehead, for I knew I couldn't even read all this stuff in the allotted time, let alone make sense out of it, research the law, and write a memorandum setting forth conclusions I wouldn't have time to draw. I reckon the smartest lawyer in the firm knew that when he gave me the assignment.

I decided I'd better get some advice. This wasn't easy for me, as I'd always been a loner like I said. But I realized I was going to need a friend at S & S, an ally. I liked Mace Rothschild right off, though he was a bit of a wise-ass and, other than being a liberal and a confessed ex-computer hacker, he had little in common with the likes of me. For one thing, he came from a wealthy background. For another thing, he was smarter than me, at least better educated, with his Order of the Coif plaque from Yale Law. He was also a worrier; an intense kid with thick glasses that made his eyes bulge like a codfish. He described himself as an East Coast liberal geek and he loved hearing me tell stories about my dad's informal free law clinic.

"That's the reason I went to law school," he had told me the week before I took the bar, during lunch. "I'm not sure what happened, but I ended up here instead."

"The nineties happened, I reckon," I said.

"A new generation of yuppies," he said. "Carriers of the dot-com virus, an epidemic of greed."

When I admitted to him how I sometimes stole food from the chain supermarket where I worked after my dad died, he asked me what chain. When I told him National Best Foods, he started laughing.

"What's so funny about having to steal to eat?" I had asked.

He couldn't stop laughing and I was getting pissed off, but he finally managed to tell me that his dad owned the whole damn company. Then I was laughing, too, which caught disapproving looks from the glum faces around us in the lunchroom.

Maybe this coincidence of me ripping off his dad was a slim reed to build a friendship on, but Mace was funny as hell and an outsider like me, radical in his own way, serving the rich and hating them at the same time. He was also a goldmine of gossip on insider firm politics—

some of it fool's gold, of course, much of it rumor, but all of it pre-sented with the assured force of indisputable fact.

I knocked on Mace's door and walked in. He told me to have a seat, and I told him my problem. He clucked his tongue sympathetically.

"First thing you have to understand is you're looking at Chapter One in a book he's writing, called *Breaking Billy's Balls.*"

"It may be a short book."

"He's not so bad once you learn to worship and adore him. I'll lend you my knee-pads."

"Any other suggestions?"

"Just one," he said, and thrust a plastic bottle in my face. "It's Dexedrine. When you develop tolerance, I'll move you up to Benzedrine."

"You really take this shit?" I said, shoving his hand away.

"Lots of us do. My brother is a pharmacist in Queens."

"I'll stick with caffeine, Mace, and you damn well ought to do the same. This is dumb. It's *bullshit.*"

"To each his own," I heard him say as I walked out of his office.

He knocked an hour later, staring at me over the pile of documents I was reading.

"Look, cowboy, I'm not a pusher going around corrupting young girls, okay? It's just the way it is here at 24-7. As for your project for Ashton, I've got my own problems at the moment, but call me around midnight, and I'll help you out. Okay?" He was holding out his hand.

I took it. "Thanks," I said. "Look Mace, I'm usually not so judg-mental. But go easy, okay? It's stuff like those bennies you're taking that passes for small currency on the inside."

He nodded. "Okay, cowboy, how about this as a working hypoth-esis: I won't hold your background against you if you won't hold mine against me. I've *got* to make it here, okay? It's just the way it is. Don't ask me why."

"Okay, podner, but I got to tell you, Stanton and Snow is beginning to remind me a hell of a lot like the last place I served time in."

"Point made. Now I suggest you set aside a discrete problem out of Ashton's project for me to analyze when I come back in an hour or so."

"It's not your war, Mace," I said, sounding as stubborn as Darryl Orton, "and like you say, you've got your own problems."

"Consider it a one-time introductory offer. I insist."

I nodded. "For a junkie, Mace, you're a good guy."

Mace turned serious. "Hey, cowboy, this is just the beginning. You're going to be ridden hard and put away wet. If Rex Ashton wants you, he'll get you."

"I've been told that by people before," I said.

Mace nodded like he understood what I'd meant, but gave me the sort of sympathetic smile a pallbearer gives a widow. We both realized I had barely arrived at S & S, yet was already targeted for failure. At least I knew Ashton's game; now I had to find a way to hang in long enough to do what I'd come here for. And when Ashton did get me, I'd have to find a way not to take Hale Lassiter down with me.

I was tempted to ask Mace what he had heard about the murder of Deborah Hinton, but Synoptics was one of the firm's biggest clients, and I couldn't trust anyone with my true intentions at S & S, not even Mace. I was on my own.

14

I worked all that night and laid Ashton's project on his desk at 7:30. That's A.M. I then returned to my claustrophobic office, closed the door, and was letting my head fall on the desk when a messenger delivered an envelope from Barney Klinehart. Bleary-eyed, but excited, I ripped open the envelope and quickly scanned the one-page, one-paragraph report. I was awake now, but angry, too. I grabbed the phone and punched out the number at the top of his cheap stationery.

"This is *it,* Barney?" I asked. "This is what I get for five hundred dollars?"

"No," he said, in his metallic Brooklyn accent, "you also get to piss and moan at me. Plus, you got two more hours coming—a hundred fifty dollars' worth—but you oughta forget about it."

The last three words were rolled together into one barely comprehensible exclamation that sounded like *fogehbowit.* I'd never been East and wondered if they all talked like Klinehart.

"Why didn't you talk to Suzy Threadgill?" She was listed in the police report as Frank Hinton's alibi witness.

"I *did* talk to her," he said, and I could picture his small hands extended as if holding a pizza. "The problem is *she* wouldn't talk to *me.* Understand? Fact is, she calls up this Nordstrom security guard, who gives me the heave-ho onto Fifth Street. Very unprofessional."

"And what about the log book for the TechnoCenter Building?"

"The book for that particular month was never collected by the cops, and now it's gone."

"Only for that one month?"

"Yeah. I confirmed it with the building office people."

"Doesn't that sound a little too coincidental to you?"

"I charge more for rank speculation."

I told him I wasn't in a mood for comedy, but he chuckled anyway and said yeah, Suzy Threadgill probably lied to the cops and sure, somebody probably snatched the log book. I could tell he was with me now.

"They've got their log on computer as of late last year," he added, "but not back then."

"So Suzy Threadgill stonewalled you, and there's no way to prove what time Frank Hinton left the building?"

Silence.

I told him that I was pursuing another angle, trying to get inside Synoptics. I added that my days might be numbered at Stanton and Snow and that we had to move fast. I told him to try to find the security guard on duty the night of the murder, then to question everybody in the east wing of the TechnoCenter Building and try to come up with someone else working there that night. He warned me the trail was probably too cold for that now, but I had time coming, so he'd give it a shot if that's what I wanted.

That's what I wanted, I said, and put my head back down on the cold hard desk. It was a little past 8:00 A.M., and I figured it would take Ashton an hour to read my memo and maybe another half hour to come up with something nasty to say about it.

Ten minutes later my phone was ringing, but it was Hale Lassiter, asking me to join him in his office in a half hour to discuss a problem that had come up involving Paul Dexter at Synoptics. "Rex will be joining us later."

Synoptics! I felt a rush of anticipation. Maybe I could find a way to get involved in the case. I jumped into the pleadings file on the office network and learned it was a case brought by the Justice Department, claiming violation of the U.S. Foreign Corruptions Act, something I knew next to nothing about.

I grabbed a cup of coffee, downed it black, surfed Lexis and Westlaw for fifteen minutes, then poured another cup I didn't need and hopped an elevator two floors up to the eagle's nest. Maybe I could pull this off. Maybe.

"Go right in, Billy," said Eileen, Hale's secretary. "Mr. Lassiter and Ms. Mathews are waiting."

Ms. Mathews? I had heard of the mysterious and reclusive third-year workaholic trial associate, and there she was, sitting across from Hale and next to a chair Hale beckoned me to. Usually when entering Hale's office, I was drawn to one of the north windows, a vista opening to the Golden Gate, Alcatraz, and, of course, the Bay itself, usually crammed in early spring with sailboats and commute ferries.

But today, it was Dana Mathews I noticed. Though seated, she looked to be five six or seven, thin, yet filled out in the right places, with the greenest eyes I'd ever seen on a dark-haired girl. Could she be Irish? I stared into those eyes and suddenly felt weak in the legs. As she stood up, I took in the raven hair tumbling down over her shoulders in long kinky curls, framing a fine-featured face with a slightly uptilted nose, and full lips curving slightly upward at the corners. She walked purposefully toward me with the athletic grace of a ballet dancer and took my hand. Her touch went straight to my groin, filling me with embarrassment, for I was standing, too.

The funny thing about her was that she seemed to have worked hard at *not* being gorgeous. She wore no makeup, and her hair looked somewhat wild and uncontrolled. Her long legs were concealed by pants, and her breasts by a blazer. Still, she had failed to hide a raw, natural beauty that excited me beyond anything in my experience.

"We've got a problem with a case that's escalating into something ugly, Billy," said Hale as I put both hands in my pockets to conceal my own escalating problem, "and I may need some one-shot legal research. Dana's on the trial team and will provide her assessment after Rex gets here. The company is upset because a piggyback class action was filed yesterday."

I figured the class action would complicate and delay things, but they all knew that. Besides, I was probably there as nothing but a note-taking potted palm anyway. So I just nodded and tried to look smart.

"So feel free, Billy," Hale continued, "to give us your reaction to the facts as you hear them from a business law angle. I'm not after a sophisticated legal argument; I want your gut reaction at this point."

That was a relief, for I had squat legal sophistication to begin with. It was also an invitation that sent the blood in retreat from my genitals, returning up my spine and back into my brain. I had to think my way into this case and onto the Synoptics trial team.

"Rex is close to Jason Moncrief, the CEO of Synoptics, and serves as liaison on all Synoptics matters." He turned to Dana Mathews and said, "Did Rex mention if Paul Dexter will be here?"

"Not to me," she said, her voice soft and melodic, yet professional.

"Dexter, Billy, is the regional head of all Asian operations for Synoptics Corporation. He's been charged by the Justice Department with bribing foreign government officials in Taiwan to induce preferential treatment on Synoptics contracts."

"I've heard of the company," I said as casually as I could manage. I had also heard of Jason Moncrief, a well-known San Francisco philanthropist and patron of the arts, as well as top dog at Synoptics.

My thoughts were interrupted by the door bursting open and Rex Ashton shooting through it like a bull out of the chute. He mumbled a hello to Hale and removed a gold pocket watch from his vest, which he glared at as if we had been late instead of him.

He threw a leg over the corner of Hale's desk and perched himself there, so that despite his shortness of stature, he was looking down on all three of us. He then reviewed the facts of the case, which were simple enough. Paul Dexter was accused of seeking illegal preferential treatment on a Taiwan nuclear power project subcontract. Trial was scheduled to commence before the end of the year, and S & S had recently come into the case, replacing another firm. Dana was there because she would be second-chairing Hale at trial. I reckon I was there as a pencil monkey, in case they needed some last-minute research or their coffee cups refilled.

"Jason Moncrief is unnecessarily worried about this pissing contest," Ashton told Hale, "but I'd like to hear your views."

Hale, probably tired of straining his neck to meet Ashton's elevated eyes, rose to his feet and began pacing along the east window, through which the morning sun was glowing like a nuclear furnace. Ashton blinked and stared into Hale's blurred profile and said, "Well?"

I wondered if Hale had intentionally positioned himself against the window, the sun at his back like a fighter pilot, the trial lawyer back in control. He smiled down at the squinty-eyed corporate practitioner across the room.

"It's more than a 'pissing contest,' Rex; it's a dangerous case. I'll break it to Jason if you're concerned that he'll shoot the messenger."

Ashton glowered at Hale. "*Dangerous?* You can't be serious."

Ashton's dark eyes shot toward Dana Mathews. "Dana?"

"I agree with Hale," she said. "First, it looks like Dexter did in fact give money to the Taiwanese government official. Second, the lawyers we replaced have botched the discovery, including Dexter's deposition in which he clearly lied. Finally, it's a jury trial, Rex, with a competent assistant U.S. Attorney on the other side. He wants Paul Dexter to do time and Synoptics to pay huge fines. The case could very well go his way. As for who should break the news to Jason Moncrief, I'll do it. If a messenger is going to get shot, better a private than a general."

So this was not only a damn pretty woman, but a smart and ballsy one as well. That's when the yellow flag came out. After what I'd been through the past year, working side by side with a woman like Dana would be as tempting as a honeybee tree to a starving bear. A guy could get stung, or at least distracted, and I couldn't afford either right now. So I'd to stick to business, and the business of the day was how to throw myself into the alien waters of this complex case without drowning.

Ashton obviously wasn't as impressed with Dana's little speech as I was. "*Go his way?* Are you both telling me that we could *lose* this case?"

Dana glanced at Hale, who nodded back.

"In all probability, we *will* lose," she said, her gorgeous green eyes unwavering as they met Ashton's harsh gaze.

"Wonderful," said Ashton, his narrow shoulders hunched, his lined skin blossoming red. "Bloody fucking wonderful! Well, I'll break the news to Jason myself, but I wish we had known all this earlier. Christ, Hale, I've been pushing for a resolution of this problem for weeks!"

You didn't need a Rosetta stone to translate that remark: Ashton would blame Hale for everything that was about to go wrong.

He sighed and slid off the desk.

"May I throw out a different view?" I said, drawing surprised looks from all three of them. Nobody said anything, so I kept talking. "I wrote a paper on the Foreign Corruptions Act at UCLA and have kept up with current applications." This was a lie, of course. Everything I knew about the Act I'd learned on Lexis an hour ago.

"Oh?" said Ashton, looking mildly amused. "So what do *you* think about all this mess Dexter has created?"

"I think," I said, looking straight into Rex Ashton's intense dark eyes, "that he could walk. Synoptics, too."

Ashton actually started to smile, but muscle memory eluded him. "Please expand on that, Billy," he said, calling me by my first name for the first time.

Jesus, what was I getting myself into? I didn't dare look at Hale.

"I don't question the trial team's analysis, sir, and I'm obviously the new kid in town, but I think the government has a tough burden in these suits under the case law. In addition, Mr. Dexter should be able to explain that the alleged bribes were all a misunderstanding, an accounting department error. What was intended was merely an advance payment of taxes, tariffs, government medical insurance, whatever. For a fallback, we could employ the 'when in Rome' defense, combined with some heavy flag-waving."

"What the hell is that supposed to mean?" asked Ashton.

"That would be a strategy that asks why American business should be punished by its own government for adhering to traditional foreign customs and practices. The jury has to be taught that any American company that doesn't pay the expected toll can't cross the bridge and will be effectively barred from foreign markets, leaving them to the Japanese and Germans, who are not similarly inhibited."

"I see," said Ashton, crossing his legs and stroking his mustache, "we make the anti-corruption act seem anti-*American*." He seemed torn between resenting my intrusion and thinking I might be able to help. But he was no more torn than I was, hearing myself defending Corporate America from well-deserved charges of fraud and bribery.

"We then ask the jury," I continued, "if that's how they want their Justice Department lawyers spending their time and their tax dollars: boycotting American business and labor from foreign markets. Throw in some trade deficit figures and turn our experts loose."

Ashton was nodding, so I kept talking. "As for the class action, the corporation should immediately appoint a special 'unbiased' litigation committee to consider whether the suit is in the best interest of the corporation. The answer, of course, will be no."

Ashton looked at Hale. "Can we do that?"

Hale nodded in affirmation. "We're considering that, and also asking that a costly bond be secured by the named plaintiff."

Ashton looked back at me, the attempted smile forgotten.

"But what of the lies in Paul Dexter's deposition?" said Ashton. "Isn't your optimism a bit naive, or are you assuming he did *not* lie?"

"If Mr. Lassiter and Dana say they were lies, sir, they were lies."

"Then how in God's name can you theorize a victory?" said Ashton, again directing his frustration at me. "Do you have any *rational* basis for what you're telling me, Strobe?"

So much for the first name. I'd have to take the next step out on the plank.

"Dexter is rich, sir, Synoptics is even richer, so they have Stanton and Snow in their corner. I don't question Dana's assessment of the U.S. Attorney's talent, but he'll be no match for her and Mr. Lassiter. Remember how Robert Frost described a jury? 'Twelve people who decide who has the best lawyer.'

"The file shows we've also got Reiko Hasuike, the top jury consultant in the country, a quarter-million dollars' worth of graphics the government can't afford to match, and professional experts who have been bought and paid for to confuse the jury into a state of reasonable doubt. Nothing has been left to chance."

"You sound more confident than the people who are about to try the case," said Ashton, still skeptical. "Why should I take comfort from the optimism of a first-year business associate who hasn't even passed the bar yet?"

"You shouldn't," Dana said, in a voice that was patient but firm, the way Ma used to talk to me and Lisa when we had screwed up. "The government poked gaping holes in Dexter's explanation for the payments, and our experts *can't* explain them."

"Maybe so," I said, thinking, in for a penny, in for a pound, "but the criminal justice system was made for people like Paul Dexter. Powerful guys like Jason Moncrief are used to getting away with murder, and my guess is he'll walk, no matter what he did. We've got the best gut argument—America first—and an unlimited budget to sell it."

Dana rose from her chair and looked down at me, more bemused than challenged. "He'll walk under our system only if we can raise a reasonable doubt," Dana said, "and we don't think we can do that."

I felt Ashton's eyes on me, and knew I couldn't back down now. I said, "You talk about the justice system as if it were a science, Dana. Our justice system is only a few degrees north of witchcraft, and it can be manipulated. Remember the Dream Team?"

Dana's jade eyes flashed then, but her voice remained calm. "It's called the adversary system, and it's served us well for two hundred years. To paraphrase Winston Churchill on democracy, it's the worst system in the world, except for all the others that have been tried."

A true believer, I thought, but I figured I'd said enough for now, surely too much as far as she was concerned. So a strained silence fell across the room before Hale spoke up. "Let's continue this philosophical discussion later," he said, "and get on with the task of preparing for trial."

But I was beginning to hope I knew Rex Ashton even better than his partner did, because Ashton was still staring at me through those dark ferret eyes.

"I agree, Hale," he said, hands clasped behind his back as he headed for the door, "and although Strobe's viewpoint might represent little more than boyish exuberance, I'd like to see him added to your trial team."

Hale agreed. Dana raised an eyebrow. I struggled to hide my excitement and tried to forget that I had lied about authoring a paper, said more than I believed about the prospects for victory, and probably pissed off a very interesting woman, who *wouldn't* forget.

But the camel's nose was now under the tent of Synoptics Corporation.

Later, I made a beeline for Mace's office. As excited as I was about getting on the Synoptics team, I needed to know more about Dana Mathews.

"She's a third-year associate like me," he said, "but she's on the fast track to partnership."

Fast-track is associate-speak at S & S for making partnership in five years instead of the standard six or seven. Mace had explained that the grail of early partnership is occasionally granted to a particularly brilliant and achieving candidate.

"Where does she hail from?"

"She said she was from the Midwest. Ohio, I think."

"Smart, beautiful, and upper-class," I said. "She's bound to love me. The contrast between us will be irresistible."

"Don't even think about it, cowboy."

"Why? Is she in a relationship? I saw no rings."

"She's single," Mace continued, "but she's all business and never dates S & S people. Maybe doesn't date *anyone* for all I know."

"Are you describing an ice princess?"

"Not necessarily. She's friendly, a good person actually, just keeps to herself. She has a small daughter."

"She's really got a kid? Who was the husband?"

Mace shrugged. "It's strictly rumor, but there may not have been one."

"Sounds more like gossip than rumor."

"A distinction without a difference. The story involves a guy from out of town, a quickie Reno marriage, and an even quicker Reno divorce."

I poured myself some coffee from Mace's private Colombian beaker he made fresh every morning. "So why the rumors?"

"She went full term as a first-year associate here. Nobody ever met or even saw a *Mr.* Mathews."

"If all that's true, Mace, wouldn't it be two strikes in a place like this?"

"True. On the plus side, she's got Hale Lassiter in her corner, but single-mother-raising-bastard-child is not high on the Stanton and Snow most-desired-attributes list. Still, she's brilliant, dedicated, and apparently headed for early partnership. Sounds as if she impressed you."

"What's not to like? She's got class, balls, she's smart, and she's gorgeous."

"I agree, though I might reverse your order of attributes. Of course, I've seen her legs and you haven't. Definitely a hotty. Sexy, but somehow maintains a professional bearing."

"I got a dose of her 'professional bearing' today, though I guess she can't allow herself to be pushed around."

Mace chuckled. "Being an unwed mother on fast-track in a misog-

ynistic outfit like Stanton and Snow is like Jesse Jackson trying to become president of the NRA."

Now that I thought on it, there weren't a whole lot of women partners at S & S, maybe three or four out of eighty. I resolved to cut Dana
Mathews plenty of slack, and hoped she'd do the same for me.

"Here's some unsolicited advice, cowboy," Mace continued. "Hale
and Laura Lassiter are like surrogate parents to Dana. Not that she
gets favored treatment at the firm; hell, she doesn't need a break from
anyone. But Hale and Dana are tight, so don't fuck with Dana if you
want to keep Hale in your corner."

Then he gave me a toothy grin and added, "Or fuck her either."

"Fat chance," I said, but the thought of it made my legs go weak
again.

The next day—a Friday—I finally broke out and headed straight
for the airport and my long-overdue trip home. I must have been wore
out, because I fell asleep right after breakfast was served and again
after my connecting flight into OKC had taken off. Next thing I knew,
we were about to land.

I felt a warm tug in my stomach as I looked down at section lines
framing a patchwork of cattle grazing fields and harvested grain. Once
on the ground, the plane taxied by bales of uniformly bundled grain
and the familiar oil pumps, ceaselessly pumping black gold from the
earth, looking like a scattered flock of those novelty water-dipping
birds.

I picked up a rental car and headed north ninety miles toward
Garfield County. With an hour to go before sundown, I had reached
Enid, passed Boggy Creek, turned off Highway 64 then to S. Twenti-
eth Street, and pulled up in front of Ma's house.

I had always thought we had lived in a decent part of town, close
to the bus station and all, but our part of the neighborhood was looking tired now with scattered RVs and broken-down pickups, yards
grown over with weeds, and homes hard in need of paint, including
ours, a 1,300-square-foot, tongue-in-groove wood frame house built in
the forties. Enid had been bypassed by the new prosperity. The population was over 50,000 when I was growing up there; now it had less
than 47,000, if that tells you anything. Still and all, home looked good
to me.

I popped the trunk, grabbed my bag, and had taken just a few steps
onto the cracked sidewalk when the memory of one of my worst days
rushed toward me from out of the past, the morning after Dad's conviction.

He was still out on bail, sleeping off a hangover in their bedroom, while the rest of us moped around the house like we had the flu. Ma's eyes were red-rimmed, with bruised sacks under each of them, and there was a foreboding silence around the breakfast table. Even the old RCA radio, usually spouting the morning news, sat silent on the counter.

I was the first out the door for school, hoping the other kids hadn't heard yet, worried how I'd be treated, afraid they wouldn't believe me when I told them my dad was innocent.

But I never made it past that damned front sidewalk, for when I glanced back to see if there was anyone to wave at, I saw it there, scrawled in huge, spray-painted letters, three feet high, clear across the front of the house.

CON

I ran back inside to ask Ma what the word meant and why it was there. She rushed past me out of the kitchen, drying her hands on the front of faded jeans, then took a quick look outside and muttered something I couldn't hear through lips that seemed almost purple against the sudden chalkiness of her face. She then shooed us back inside, a firm hand on each of our backs.

"What's a *con,* Ma?" I asked, but she was on her way to wake Dad. Lisa and I were ordered to our rooms, and now I knew something else bad had happened.

After a few minutes, I heard a sound out front and pulled the curtain back for a peek. There was Dad outside in the freezing air with nothing on but a pair of pants, red-faced and talking to himself, scrubbing the daylights out of the front of the house.

Graffiti had made it to Oklahoma.

I shook off the memory, pushed the doorbell—which didn't work— and opened the front door.

"Anybody home?" I said, and stepped inside. The living room was as it always had been, a place for everything and everything in its place: the clutter of too much furniture, the sofa with the faded afghan to cover cigarette burns, the fireplace with a gas heater inside the firebox, Lisa's favorite leather chair that had once been in Dad's office, assorted bric-a-brac including carved gnomes and the Virgin Mary, a large picture of Jesus with sacred heart exposed, two fake Tiffany lamps, the worn oblong area rugs covering the sturdy but pockmarked hardwood floor, the ceramic cat with a nonworking clock in its paws, a large bookcase containing an ancient set of the *Encyclopaedia Britannica* plus Dad's old law books and numerous hardcover novels and paperbacks, photos everywhere.

I suddenly felt a sudden, deep sense of . . . what? Loss? This was the place where I'd grown up, built my own house of dreams which, ambitious as they were—jet pilot, millionaire movie actor, NFL quarterback—could never be realized. But you don't know that when you're a kid. When you grow up, you best either live in reality or in a dream world; some people keep slipping back and forth, but that can be hazardous to the health. I learned that from the Billionaire Boys Club II.

For all its clutter, this run-down, antique house, the only real home I'd ever known, was still the only constant in my life, and despite the ration of grief I could always count on from Ma, the seeming durability of the family home never failed to fill me with a secure and comfortable drowsiness, instilling a sense of my own durability.

I turned and saw Lisa coming out of the kitchen. "Hi, Mugsy," she said, and threw her arms around me. "Good to see you out of stir. You must be wreaking havoc with the recidivist ratio, not to mention all the broken hearts you left behind at Soledad."

"I left your name and number on the bathroom walls," I said, and kissed her on the cheek. "You'll have visitors."

I heard a high-pitched sound and saw Ma hurrying toward me out of her bedroom, nearly stumbling, as she threw her arms around her prodigal son. Maybe money *could* buy love, I thought, or at least forgiveness.

"You're home, son," she said, and after we had taken each other in, her hands firmly planted on my shoulders, she pronounced me too thin, and led me by the hand into the kitchen where a hot meal waited.

In the harsh light over the table where we ate, it was clear that Amy Strobe was well into a dance of death with John Barleycorn. Though relatively rational, she was frighteningly unpredictable: up one minute, down the next. She ate nothing and excused herself from time to time to "freshen up" in her bedroom. After dinner, Lisa and I watched TV. Ma went off to freshen up and didn't return. Lisa just shrugged, as if to say business as usual.

I knew that my sister, the innocent bystander, could not hope to maintain her own fading motivation to get out of bed each day, living with a woman who had given up. We'd have to get Ma into a clinic.

"It's too late, Billy," Lisa said the next day as she walked me toward my car. But I knew that was her own fear talking, fear of being left alone at home with nothing but the ghost of Joe Strobe and a host of bad memories.

Back at Fort Misery, the days hung heavy as I waited for the bar results. I'll never forget the relief I felt the day Hale came in to shake my hand and welcome me to the bar. I was sworn in a few weeks later and was now formally licensed to lie. Rex Ashton had already made me his bitch, punking me out mentally on every assignment. I wasn't sleeping much, but I was determined not to give him any cause for complaint.

On the plus side, I was bumped to $125,000 a year plus a guaranteed bonus of $20,000, thanks to a firm in Palo Alto that had recently blown the lid off the traditional unwritten salary cap for starting lawyers. I wondered what Darryl would say if he found out that recent law graduates, who knew next to nothing, were drawing this kind of salary. But I was happy to take the money, as my preliminary research showed that getting Ma into a first-rate recovery clinic in Oklahoma City was going to be expensive.

I kept accidentally running into Dana whenever I could arrange it. She was courteous but distant, obviously not interested in getting to know Hale Lassiter's project. I had apologized to her about coming on strong in Hale's office that day. She just said, "Fine, you're forgiven," shook hands businesslike, then walked right off. If she treated all men like she was treating me, she might stay a single parent—or whatever the hell she was. Anyways, I was more determined than ever not to get sidetracked and to keep my eye on the brass ring—the one tightening around Darryl Orton's neck.

My problem was that it was almost summer, and though I was an official junior member of Paul Dexter's defense team, I still hadn't made it through the doors of Synoptics Corporation. I had remained nothing but the designated research monkey, armed for battle with laptop, Lexis-Nexis, and green eyeshade. On top of that, Hale told me all sides now wanted to settle, which meant the litigation was in limbo, as were my hopes of getting inside Synoptics.

Klinehart wasn't getting anywhere either, so I arranged a visit with Darryl, hoping to get the name of the woman I was sure he was with the night of the murder. If I couldn't break Frank Hinton's alibi, maybe I could come up with one for Darryl.

It was remarkable how different things looked traveling down the Salinas Valley on U.S. 101 in your own car with the windows open and the music playing, from when you're manacled to the floorboard of a broken-down school bus, slogging through winter fog with thieves and cutthroats for company.

I had set out early morning from San Francisco, just as the sun was rising like a crescent of fire over a horizon called Oakland, doing its slow burn through the predawn darkness. The oncoming headlights from a sad parade of commuters blinked off two by two, and I cranked up the volume on my radio for the chorus of an old Joe Silverhound tune, "The Handwriting on the Wall," one of Darryl's favorites, hoping to drown out the clatter of blaring horns and straining engines.

The yearnin time, the burnin time is over,
It's my last chance, and I'll blow it, I'll throw it, all awaaaay,
I prayed that your love had blinded me, but through these misty
*   eyes I still see,*
That same handwriting, still there on the wall,
*   The handwriting there on the wall.*

I knew now that there were all kinds of prisons. Prisons that crawled along freeways. Prisons with mahogany-paneled walls and thick carpets where the inmates were seduced by trick bags full of money, urging the rendering up of marriages and health for promises of even more money. Then, of course, the more traditional "correctional facilities" like the one I was heading for, where whatever good that might still dwell in a man was swiftly "corrected" out of him.

I ain't talkin bout four-letter words in some subway station
Or a calendar markin time on some prison wall
No I ain't talkin bout post office rewards for police information,
I'm just talkin bout wantin to stay, but leavin it all.

By the time I hit the central coast and entered the eighty-five-mile-long and fifteen-mile-wide Salinas Valley, the red horizon had cooled a pale blue, streaked vanilla by occasional bands of clouds that looked like fading contrails of a jet plane. I was driving up the middle of the Salinas Valley: more than a half-million acres of flat, fertile farmland, protected on either side by the Gabilan and Santa Lucia mountain ranges. Steinbeck country, the breadbasket of America.

All I had seen on my first trip was bare ground and steel irrigation pipes, but the land was now dense with ripe vegetables—mainly artichokes, lettuce, and broccoli—and floral products of all kinds. The fields were also dense with workers harvesting the crops, nearly all of them Mexicans and many of them illegal, serving the landlords with immunity until their work was done, then exiled back across the border into even worse poverty. They roamed the fields like foraging cattle, picking, slicing, and pulling—their backs bent at ninety degrees, probably longing for darkness and the waiting truck they'd be herded onto—then returned to hovels as bad as we had at Soledad.

My nerves began to jump when I saw the sign that read CORRECTIONAL FACILITY TURN RIGHT, and my stomach was seizing up bad by the time I turned into the circular driveway in front of the Central Facility Entrance Building. Behind this check-in center loomed the pale beige walls of Soledad Prison, running at least three football fields from north to south, beyond which I knew lay fear and hopelessness.

I thought about how the cruel beauty of the surrounding valley mocked this man-made abomination.

As I entered the massive Soledad visitors room—about the size of a tennis court—I was pointed in the direction of Darryl Orton. It was weird seeing this room for the first time through the eyes of a visitor. It seemed more shabby, the lighting duller, the smells stronger.

I barely recognized Darryl. He looked like he'd lost fifteen pounds and was as pale as the yellowish-beige walls around us. One of his eyes was black and swollen and a mottled bluish bruise mushroomed on his cheek. His thinning hair looked matted and unclean. I felt consumed by shame that I had dressed that morning in a Polo button-down shirt, chinos, and pair of new Ferragamos, one of the disguises I had affected to avoid detection at Stanton and Snow. Darryl didn't seem to notice as he rose to his feet with pained effort.

I swallowed hard and tried to say something, but all I could do was extend my hand. He took it, then took in my discomfort and said, "Jesus, kid, you look *terrible.*"

The sweet son-of-a-bitch was trying to put me at ease.

"You look worse now than you did in here," he added. "Did some ambulance you was chasin back up all of a sudden and run over you?"

I managed a wry smile.

"Your face is as white as a plate," he continued. "That law firm you're workin at must have you in solitary."

I told him he wasn't far wrong, then said he didn't look so good himself. "You got a new battle scar," I said, glancing at serrated tissue that ran from between his eyebrows up at a forty-five degree angle until it disappeared into his hair line.

"Nothin serious, Billy. Cut myself shavin."

"You shaving your forehead these days?"

He ignored my remark. "You doin okay out there, kid?"

"Was it Carlos Ortez?"

"Ortez got a court-ordered transfer. You have anything to do with that?"

I shrugged and said, "That's about the only thing I've accomplished."

I handed him a bag full of fruit and some roast beef sandwiches I had picked up at a deli in Salinas and a new CD player with discs by George Jones and Garth Brooks. He put it all on the floor between his feet and then nodded his appreciation. I asked him about Dickens, and he said he was "gettin crazier than a shithouse rat," always talking about his imminent escape from Soledad.

"We gave the old fart a birthday party last night," Darryl continued, and started to laugh until pain reminded his face to forget about it. "He turned sixty, so we give him a half-pint of Scotch. Long after lights out, his celly sees him leanin over the head at midnight, drunk on his ass, tryin to take a whiz and talkin to his cock."

"He's talking to his penis?"

Darryl winced as he started to laugh again. "Dickens looked down and said, 'Prick, you'd be sixty today if you hadn't died.' "

We laughed together; then I told Darryl I was sorry he was still stuck inside and confessed that things were moving slowly on the outside.

"So the Great Crusade is in lock-down," he said smiling. "No matter. I'm doin fine."

I admitted I'd pretty much run out of leads on the Hinton murder.

"Now there's a surprise. I figured you'd come to fetch me out a' here."

"I haven't given up," I said, sounding defensive.

"Hey kid, don't worry yourself. The good Lord despises impatience the way the Devil hates virtue."

I asked, "How's Tom Collins?"

"That dried up old licorice stick? Still driving everybody bat-shit with his witty bullshit, though he finally got hisself clobbered by some punk who couldn't take a joke."

"Give him my best," I said.

"I'll do it. And thanks for this, too," he said, putting his hand on the food. "But you best hold on to the music box. Every time they put me in the Hole, anything that's worth the takin is gone by the time I get back."

I didn't argue with him, and we talked some more about the people closest to me.

"How's your celly?"

"If it weren't for Proposition Thirteen, Rabbit would be in a mental institution. The damn fool claimed a cockroach was in his dinner last night and got us all to look at it, which turned out to be a bean like the others on his plate. 'Them other ones ain't cockroaches,' he says, 'them's beans disguised to look like cockroaches. This here one is real.'

"He don't bother me much personally and won't be around long anyhow because he takes it up the ass from anybody wants him. He's already tested positive. I offered to give him some protection, but he said no thanks. When he's not gettin laid, he's whackin himself off. Must do it five times a day, says it's the only way he knows he's still alive. Disgustin."

I listened, surprised to hear Darryl talking so much, and figured he needed to get stuff off his chest. Eventually, I worked the conversation around to what I wanted to talk to him about.

"I need to know the name of the woman you were with the night of the murder."

"Don't know where you get your thoughts, kid. Must be hell livin in your head, all that crap stirrin around."

"I'm not blind, Darryl. I've seen when you got those letters, and you've all but admitted you were with someone that night."

Darryl smiled ruefully and shook his head. "It's been good seein you, kid, but I gotta get back to my studies at the library. I'm almost up to the Gs. Did you know that durin the French Revolution in 1789, the good citizens found only seven prisoners alive by the time they stormed the walls of the Bastille?"

I told him I didn't, privately wondering if the story was a subtle rebuke.

"Yeah. I'm gettin smart in here, Billy. Anything you want to know from *A* to *F,* you just ask."

"What letter does *her* name start with?" I said. "Her name's all I want to know."

"Good-bye, young Billy. You take care now."

Sweat formed across my forehead. I was losing him. What would Dad do in this situation? He could get water out of a stone.

"Come on, Darryl," I pleaded, "What's the harm in it?"

He leaned forward, his gaunt features twisted into a stern mask. "You forget about her, Billy. Either that, or forget about me."

"Then give me a reason, dammit."

"I got my reasons." His skin seemed to tighten over twitching jaw muscles, and I knew he'd never tell me her name.

"Darryl," I said, watching his face contort again, this time with pain as he struggled to get to his feet. "I just got here. At least tell me what I can send you?"

"Good wishes," he said, and walked away.

I drove back onto Highway 101, then headed north, feeling helpless and depressed.

15

It's not surprising that guys getting out of prison are pretty fucked up sexually. I'd been lucky not to get punked out inside, but instead of making love to magazines like most cons did inside, I had tried to shut down all thoughts of sex. Maybe that was a mistake, and I admit it didn't always keep me away from myself, but it's the way I picked to keep my sanity.

But as the weeks passed now that I was out and suddenly had some money in my pockets, I began hanging out at least once a week in singles bars, SOMA spots like Harry Denton's, Elroys, and Eddie Rickenbacker's. My first opportunity at getting laid, soon after coming off the grand tour, had been a disaster. Mr. Happy went limp while I was trying to fit him with a raincoat. Jesus.

But I shook it off and it didn't take long cruising the Tiffany jungles before I found a girl or two who made me feel regular again. The ratio of straight girls to straight guys in San Francisco put the odds in my favor, but it bothered me that I kept thinking of Dana Mathews, no matter who I was sleeping with.

All in all, looking back on my first six months at S & S, I was doing okay. Being a young and single, downwardly mobile Montgomery Street lawyer on the make in San Francisco definitely beat rooming with Dickens and dodging don-Don. Beat it all to hell. I never forgot for a minute how lucky I was to be a free man, earning a good living so I could help out my family and, with the exception of Rex Ashton, working with surprisingly decent people who had accepted me for what I was.

The day after my visit with Darryl, I scalded the Garfield County Clerk's office about the delay in getting the transcript I'd ordered in *People vs. Joseph Strobe*. The guy promised to put a tracer on my request. I then left a message for Barney Klinehart. He called back within an hour to tell me he had accomplished nothing other than pissing off everyone he had talked to at the TechnoCenter. He was at a dead end and again urged me to give it up. I told him to keep snooping, but felt stalled on both Dad's and Darryl's cases.

Mace popped in, and we took off for the weekly staff meeting in the conference center. I steered us to seats as close to Dana as I could find, but if she noticed me, she didn't show it. I guess I wanted to give her one last chance to show me there was a warm heart beating under those perfect breasts.

As Rex Ashton entered to conduct a seminar on current merger and acquisition matters, she looked my way, smiled, and raised her hand. I felt a pleasant shudder in my loins and smiled back, but then watched her expression change. I glanced to my left, saw one of her friends waving back at her, then quietly slouched down in my chair.

"Well, people," Ashton was saying, "have we all read the advance sheets this week?"

Advance *sheets*? I wondered if someone should tell him we have computers now.

"Who wants to update us on what the court said in *Havers versus Lancaster International* this week on the issue of director's liability for failing to uncover insider trading?"

Not a hand went into the air, and I knew why. The case had been published late yesterday and I'd found it on Lexis only because I was researching a memo I'd handed him this morning. I wouldn't give him the satisfaction of raising my hand. Not that it mattered, because Ashton had already selected his prey for the day, and for once it wasn't me.

"Ms. Mathews? Why don't you enlighten us. On your feet, please."

Dana rose, but slowly. "I haven't read that case," she said, "but I assume the court upheld the lower court's decision to the effect that directors have a responsibility to act reasonably and affirmatively to discover insider abuses."

"You *assume* that is what the court did? Is that what you'd tell me if I were a client?"

"If you were a client," she said, reddening, but standing up to him, "I'd have definitely read the case in preparation for our meeting."

"But I'm *not* a client," sneered Ashton, "merely a humble senior partner in this law firm." He scanned the room. "Can anyone help our Ms. Mathews?"

I rose quickly and said, "I'd like to help, sir, but she doesn't need it. The case, published just yesterday as you know, held exactly as she said, emphasizing the duty of the board of directors not to sit around scratching their butts while the officers looted the company."

A sprinkling of laughter went up, but Ashton quelled it with a glare. "Earthy, Mr. Strobe," he said. "The kind of coarseness we've come to expect from you. Now, if you please, *sit down*."

I sat, and Ashton commenced his lecture on current developments in the field. I had taken two steps backwards in Ashton's eyes, but maybe a step forward in Dana's. It was clear that in Ashton's attempt to diminish Hale in the eyes of his partners, the cowardly bastard was broadening his attack to all associates Hale was mentoring, even Dana Mathews.

"Here she comes," said Mace as we stood in the hallway after the meeting, stalling. "Right toward us. By Jove, I think I hear violins."

"And I hear your mother calling," I said. "Get lost, Scarecrow."

I could smell her as she came up to me, a clean fragrance of freshly cut jasmine and boxwood that made me want to touch her face. Staring into her large eyes, I felt a touch of vertigo, maybe from the blood rushing out of my head, headed south again.

"What you did in there?" she said, her face closer to mine than ever before, a little pale from Ashton's lashing.

I nodded, smiling, waiting.

"Thanks, but please don't do it again," she said. "I can take care of myself."

She walked off, leaving me confused, pissed off, and shaking my head in wonder at the things I didn't know about women.

I told Mace the story at lunch the next day, and he reacted in his typically sympathetic manner by laughing his ass off. I thanked him and told him how lucky he was that we were in a public restaurant surrounded by witnesses.

"You embarrassed her, Billy. When you're on fast-track like Dana is, you don't want to look like you need rescuing from some smart-ass first-year *business* associate."

I leaned my elbows against my knees. "She should have appreciated it, or at least been decent about it."

"When you're carrying a fast-track caseload, you don't have time to even notice other associates, let alone appreciate them."

"She'll notice me," I said.

"Let me guess. You're going to hire a sky-writing airplane."

"If I do, it'll be to drop you out of."

The month was a blur, like the early summer fog that now often blanketed the City by the Bay. I was billing two hundred hours a month, right on "quota," thanks to Rex Ashton, and was on two teams with Hale and Dana, though I was doing strictly grunt work and getting nowhere near Synoptics. On the plus side, Hale had become more than a mentor, a sort of "father in law," never too busy to provide counsel, and beginning to treat me at times like the son he never had.

As for Dana, she was still friendly in our occasional team meetings, but I couldn't seem to connect with her. She was spirited and clever as hell in these meetings, and it struck me that maybe I'd just got off on the wrong foot with her. Or maybe it was the right foot but I'd put it in my mouth. Or maybe she was uncomfortable because of the way I couldn't help but stare at her a lot, at her cool green eyes, at the gentle curve of her neck when she tossed her long dark hair to one side while laughing at something, at the perfect proportion of her slender body, her narrow hips, high-riding breasts, and long legs.

I decided to have a talk with her, and one day in early July I knocked on her office door. Hearing nothing, I opened it and saw she was working at her desk.

"I came by to congratulate you on your window," I said, strolling in, uninvited. She said nothing. I turned and took in her larger office space, an extra forty square feet over mine. "Tomorrow, the world," I added.

Not even a smile. In fact, she looked uncharacteristically tense.

"Hello, Billy," she said at last. "Listen, I'm terribly busy. Can it wait?"

"I guess. Quick question, then I'll leave. Have I been coming on too strong? Is there some way we can get to know—?"

That's when I saw her, the cutest little girl I'd ever seen, sitting under Dana's desk turning the pages of a coloring book. "Act normally," I whispered to Dana, "we're not alone here."

"There's that to be grateful for," Dana said, still looking tense.

"Your daughter?" I said. "She's beautiful."

I meant it. Soft curls almost to her shoulders, large pale blue eyes, and a smile like her mother's. But her mother wasn't smiling.

"The flu shut down Sarah's day-care provider, and I couldn't find anyone at the last minute. As you can imagine, the firm isn't happy about baby-sitters moonlighting during the day as S & S associates. In fact, they're not happy about single mothers daring to aspire to partnership, so I would be grateful if you didn't mention this."

"This one would melt even Ashton's heart."

"He has none."

"True. Well, he'd have to make an exception," I said, kneeling down and extending a finger to Sarah. "Shake hands?" I said, but she shyly returned to her book.

"I'm in love," I said to Dana. I realized I'd been expecting too much from someone packing an even heavier load here than I was.

"Motherhood and work do not mix at Stanton and Snow," she

said, "particularly when it involves baby-sitting. Promise you won't say anything?"

"I promise, but look, Dana, I'd like to bury the hatchet with you. Maybe we've got more in common that you think."

"Consider it buried, though I'm curious. What do we have in common, other than being owned by the same masters?"

"Are you Irish?"

She nodded.

"Catholic?"

"Yes."

"Well, looks to me we're a pair of Irish Catholic lawyers working in a bluenose, blue-blood, blue-stocking firm, both with . . . unusual backgrounds."

She shook her head. "Forgive me, Billy, but I have trouble equating motherhood with a criminal past—"

"I'm sorry. I didn't mean it the way it sounded. I'm also sorry about the way I'm all the time staring at you."

"Well, thank you. Leering makes a girl uncomfortable."

"How about gawking? Are you okay with gawking?"

She smiled. "Billy, I don't date much, and I never date S & S people, so find yourself another girl."

"Do you like movies, Dana?"

"I adore movies, but I'm not going to one with you."

"Not even to see a rerelease of *To Kill a Mockingbird* at the Alhambra?"

"It's too scary for Sarah, and you're too scary for me. Am I going to have to call 911 to get you out of here?"

I held up my hands, palms out, to show how unscary I was, then asked, "What's scary about *To Kill a Mockingbird*?"

"Boo Radley."

"So you *do* like movies. Bet you don't know who played him?"

"Robert Duvall. It was his very first movie role."

"Will you marry me, Dana?"

"Not without having so much as gone to a movie with you, which I will never do." She reached for her phone. "I'm going to ask Hale if he has something for you to do."

I was changing my opinion about her, but her dim view of me seemed set in stone. "I'll go, but are you ever going to let us get to know each other better?"

She sighed and put her pen down. "I know you well enough, I think."

"You're put off that I'm an ex-con?"

"No. In fact, that's about the only thing I've liked about you so far."

"The element of danger," I said, but she didn't smile. "So what is it? I hardly drink, never gamble, adore your daughter already, and occasionally write my mother."

"Our values are different, Billy."

"How so?"

"I have them, you don't. When was the last time you went to Mass?"

She nailed me there. "I was twelve," I said.

"And I loved the way you danced your way onto the Synoptics team. You never wrote an article on the Corruption Act, did you." It was an accusation, not really a question. I was busted.

"Well, thank you for not sharing," I said. "Even Hale would be pissed if he knew. Look Dana, it was important to me to get involved, so I stepped over the line. But I do have values."

"Name one." Her hand was off the phone.

"I'll give you four. I love music, little children, old people, and small farm animals."

"And never being serious."

"That's five. Okay, you want serious? I'm serious about getting to know you, Dana. As for values, we've got different views of reality based on different life experiences. So what? You believe in the justice system, and I don't think it does much for poor people. Jonathan Swift—an Irishman like you, incidentally—had it right when he said laws are like cobwebs that catch small flies, but allow wasps and hornets to break through."

She smiled. "So there is simply no justice for the downtrodden in the world of Billy Strobe."

"There's justice, but it's got to be fought for if you're poor. You think the system hands it out to rich and poor alike, I don't. Maybe it's the different way we were raised."

I pictured her in a formal at her coming-out party, while I was scarfing ribs and bowling a line with high school friends in Enid. She was too nice to agree with me, so we sat in silence for a minute.

"Okay," I said, "for whatever reason, we disagree on whether the trial process works equally for everybody, but that doesn't strike me as grounds for divorce."

"Don't worry, Billy. I promise you'll never have to worry about me divorcing you."

I gave her a touché smile and she considered me for a few seconds, then said, "All right, Billy Strobe, what *is* your most treasured value? And don't give me the kids and animals number again."

"Loyalty," I said, "and trying to do what's right in a situation, once you get through the hard part, which is figuring out what's right."

She leaned down and gave Sarah a kiss, then turned her eyes back on me. "That's better. Look Billy, I appreciate you trying to improve our working relationship, and I'll try harder to accept our 'differences,' but I'm busy on a brief for Malcomb Wilcox over in probate, and it's due in one hour. Then I—Sarah and I—have a custodian of records deposition out on Van Ness an hour after that."

"Well, then," I said, "I think you should get busy and let me leave. One last question, now that it's clear we share common values. Why not go out with me? The three of us. A quick bite somewhere family-friendly, then early to bed."

"I think I know whose bed you have in mind." Her smile killed me.

"Yours, of course," I said. "And mine. I mean you in yours and me in—"

"Billy, I can't go out with you, really. We *work* together."

"I'll quit my job. Soon as I can find Hale."

She laughed, then so did Sarah. "Then I couldn't date you because I would have lost all respect for you. Never could stand a quitter."

"Okay," I said. "I'll get him to fire me."

"Then you'd lose all respect for me if I dated a person who couldn't hold a job."

And on it went, but I could tell she was beginning to like me. I decided I had come as far as I could for now and called upon a trait for which the Irish are not famous: restraint.

"Sarah, would you like to say good-bye to Billy?"

"Good-bye, Biwy," Sarah said, then leapt into her mother's arms and shyly buried her head. Dana noisily kissed the top of her daughter's head and her neck. Then Sarah stood up and kissed her mother full on the mouth. I had never seen such tenderness.

"Good-bye, ladies," I said, but stopped at the door. "Oh, yes, a value I may have left out, common to ex-con Okies: bullheaded, mule-minded, fire-walking perseverence."

"Good-bye, Billy," she said, not looking up. "Enjoy your movie."

I called Barney Klinehart later that afternoon and told him I was worried about Darryl and had a new idea on Suzy Threadgill, Frank Hinton's alibi witness. If Darryl wouldn't help me firm up his alibi, I had to destroy Frank Hinton's.

"We've got to break Frank Hinton's alibi," I told him. "How about you pull together a list of all her activities—health club memberships, bridge clubs, night classes, whatever—then maybe we can pin her down somewhere else the night she claimed to be with Frank Hinton."

"It's your money," he said, referring to the $1,750 he had gone through so far. "Any progress getting into the victim's place of employment?"

I admitted I had failed to crack Synoptics, then asked him whether he knew anyone at Soledad who could get us a look at incoming mail, specifically the name and return address of Darryl's mystery pen pal. I explained to him that mail was handed out by the unit cop at his office, usually after the 4:00 P.M. count.

"Not offhand," he said, "but I know somebody who might be able to make contact with such an individual." He added that it would be "expensive."

"Do it," I said, and hung up.

I then paid Mace a visit. "Hi, Scarecrow."

"You look like shit," he informed me.

"So I've heard."

"Try sleeping."

"I did. Just last week. Did nothing for me."

"How are things with Herr Ashton?" he asked. "Still using your head as a battering ram to get into Hale's corner office?"

"Andrew Beckett was treated better at his firm."

"Andrew Beckett?"

"The guy with AIDS in *Philadelphia,* played by Tom Hanks. You didn't see it?"

"Oh, *that* Andrew Beckett."

"I'm hoping the other partners will figure out Ashton's using me to get to Hale. You got time to gossip?"

"Always," Mace said, rubbing his hands together.

"I've heard the firm's in trouble."

"There have been rumors."

"The ones I've picked up are that S & S came close to financial failure last year—soaring costs, the loss of two major clients to New York firms opening branch offices here, plus a disastrous defeat in a contingent fee case the firm had invested six or seven million in. Have you heard anything?"

Mace nodded. "The prevailing coffee room rumor is that the firm's perennial executive committee members—Lassiter, Ashton, and Malcomb Wilcox—were under fire from the firm's Young Turks and that the firm was going down."

I remembered Edward Crocker's warning before my interview with Hale. "The firm was going bankrupt?"

"It was hemorrhaging money. But Ashton engineered huge no-interest firm bailout loans from himself and Hale Lassiter, personal cash loans of over five million each. That quelled the rebellion, since the partnership was now literally indebted to them."

"Is this why the partners are driving us so hard?"

"Loans have to be repaid, even to partners. You probably got more sleep in prison. I billed a hundred ninety-five hours last month myself."

"What would happen," I asked, "if we lose the Paul Dexter Synoptics case?"

"We lose Synoptics. We almost lost them a year or two ago when the Securities Exchange Commission began investigating Jason Moncrief for possible insider trading."

"Moncrief? The CEO?"

"Yeah, him, but it was all over as quick as it started. Case closed. So is this conversation. I've got a meeting."

I filed this information in my cluttered memory bank and said, "One more question, Scarecrow. What would happen if we do lose Synoptics?"

"We lose our jobs."

I walked out, sure that the key to breaking Darryl's case was somewhere inside the walls of Synoptics Corporation. Now I just had to breach those walls.

Three weeks later, I was in Hale's office when the phone rang.

"Yes, Paul, your trial has been continued until January. We're still trying to settle with the Justice Department and the class action representatives."

An angry metallic sound surged through the receiver, but I couldn't make out the words.

"It's true, Paul, but it's no big deal," Hale said. It had to be Paul Dexter on the other end, a very upset Paul Dexter.

"Jerry Cooper is *perfectly* capable of handling your depo review. He's a senior associate here."

Hale gave me a pained look as he again held the phone away from his ear and another protest blasted through the receiver.

"No, Paul, Dana cannot do it either. She'll be in Seattle arguing the motion with me. I assure you—"

The depo review they were arguing about, as I knew from Mace, was a procedure in which the lawyer assisted the client in identifying and correcting any "misstatements" he might have made during his deposition. In my view of the trial process, this meant correcting any answers in which he might have slipped up and told the truth. They didn't offer anything on this subject in law school, but I saw an opening and took it. I scribbled on a pad and held it up in front of Hale's face. Here's what it said:

Let me take it. Handled these as a UCLA extern. Please!

I hated lying to anyone, particularly to one of the most honorable men I'd ever known, but I had to get my investigation off the ground somehow.

"All right, Paul, listen to me. A trained seal could handle this assignment, but I'm sending my star associate"—he winked at me—"to walk you through it. His name is Billy Strobe . . . Yes, I said *Strobe*. He'll be there at nine a.m. He's very experienced at this and will spend as much time with you as you want . . . Good. I'll call as soon as I get back in town."

He hung up the phone. "You'll do anything to get away from Rex, won't you?"

"Anything, though you could have skipped the trained seal part."

He laughed and so did I, because I was about to breach Jericho's walls.

16

I had been doing my homework, preparing for my shot at Synoptics by having my hair cut at a styling shop within its walls. Hale had tipped me to the idea by mentioning that he walked south of Market twice a month to have his hair cut by Coco Lewis, "the Executive's Stylist," on the ground floor of the TechnoCenter.

Coco knew everything about everybody, at least in the TechnoCenter. She was in her thirties, nearly six feet tall in her knee-high laced up boots with two-inch soles and four-inch heels. She wore her dark hair short, usually streaked with blue, sometimes red, and miniskirts that barely covered her perfect ass. A gold bead was attached like a blister to her nose above her right nostril. I paid Coco the sixty-five bucks she charged because Hale agreed it would be good for my image, and I figured it was worth it to maintain my disguise as a normal young white male in pursuit of the American Dream on Montgomery Street.

With my passport into Synoptics finally arranged, I decided it was time for a haircut.

"So Coco, what's Jason Moncrief like?" I asked, once settled in her house of white walls, etched and beveled mirrors, art nouveau, and retro disco music.

"I don't speak ill of my clients," said Coco. "Far as I'm concerned, all of them are perfect. In Moncrief's case, he's a perfect asshole."

"I hear he's well off."

"Moncrief? Figure about two billion. He's also permanently tanned, tailored, and trimmed. The guy is an elegant marble statue of himself."

After hearing her ten-minute oral biography of Jason Moncrief—well worth the sixty-five bucks even without the haircut—I told her that I was sure she was the only thing Moncrief and I would ever have in common.

She knew little about Paul Dexter. "He doesn't come in here. Looks like his wife cuts his hair with duck shears. No wonder he's in trouble."

"Trouble?"

"Yeah, something with the government. That's all I know."

At my first pee and coffee break the next day with Paul Dexter—a chinless man of average height, with vague eyes, unruly hair, and ordinary intelligence who had been easy to con—I launched my reconnaissance of the Synoptics headquarters suite. The current CFO's office—presumably Deborah Hinton's former office—was down the hall only five doors from Dexter's. Posted at a desk outside of it sat a plain, perfectly round-faced lady in her forties, appropriately named Mildred Moon.

I introduced myself and confirmed that she had been Deborah's secretary.

"Shame about Deborah," I said, after I'd broken the ice.

She scrunched her features up like someone suffering a gas attack. "Oh, Lord, yes," she said, slowly shaking her head as if it was somehow all her fault. "Were you a close friend, Mr. Strobe?"

"We weren't all that close," I told her, "but I know everybody thought the world of her." I was barely a lawyer, but already bullshitting like a veteran.

"Not everybody," she said, pursing her lips and raising her eyebrows to be sure I knew she had said something clever.

"How right you are, Mildred," I said, and spotted Paul Dexter beckoning to me from his office. "At least, the police caught the guilty party in a hurry."

"Well," she said, giving me a sad-eyed smile, "I suppose so."

Was she doubting the speed of the catching or the guilt of the guy who got caught?

Dexter waved more emphatically.

"Let's talk more later, Mildred," I said, and she said sure and I rejoined Dexter, who winked and told me there were much better fish in the sea than "old Moon face." I returned his manly smile and we returned to work.

After another half hour of trained seal work, I decided to go for gold. "Is Mr. Moncrief in today, Mr. Dexter?"

"Yes, why?"

"Do you think we might have lunch with him? I'd like to ask him a question or two."

Dexter's narrow shoulders tightened, his almost nonexistent chin rose, and his milky eyes seemed truly alert for the first time. "Why do you want to talk to Jason? What do you have in mind?"

"I guess it's not that important," I said.

He tilted his head. "Then why did you ask?"

"It's simple, sir. He's the CEO of the company, with ultimate responsibility for all regions, including yours in Asia. His name has come up several times in your earlier deposition. I'd like to try to reassure him about our progress, verify his own lack of knowledge about the allegations. Routine stuff Hale will ask me about."

Dexter's thin shoulders seemed to relax. "I could check. He's a busy man, a hands-on CEO. Right now his hands are on me. Around my neck, actually."

"Maybe I could put in a good word about the way you handled yourself in the deposition so far."

"Yesss," he said, "that *would* be appreciated. Let me see what I can do."

The company cafeteria was a definite step up from the chow hall at Soledad. Brightly colored walls, modern tables for two and four with comfortable blue dining chairs, a choice of three hot meals, four desserts, a soft frozen yogurt dispenser, and all the popcorn you could eat. This was good groceries, and if I weren't confronting the lion in his den, I would have been happy as a pig in a melon patch.

Most impressive of all was the silence in the huge room. You could almost hear the New Age Brahmins chewing their free lunches.

"Keeps them at the forge, Mr. Strobe," said Jason Moncrief, as he caught my look, "with the result that our stockholders save money in the long run. Studies prove it's cost-effective."

Moncrief sat across from me, oozing poise and confidence, one of those average-size guys who somehow looked bigger than he was, particularly when exercising his rich baritone voice. His features seemed chiseled in marble, just as Coco had said, but his outstanding feature was a thick mane of silver hair. Although Synoptics was a typical high-tech company full of the typical young Asian and white-skinned hot-shots attired in T-shirts, jeans, and sneakers, Moncrief wore a lightweight traditional navy three-piece suit, a starched white shirt, and a tie that cost more than my shoes. His shoes also cost more than my suit, and his—well, you get the picture. Even his skin looked freshly pressed, and I figured him for a face job, given his nearly sixty years of life on a badly damaged planet.

I had checked his pedigree: ex-Dartmouth defensive tackle and team captain, former president of the Commonwealth Club, well-known philanthropist and perennial chair of the Bay Area United Crusade campaign, senior tournament tennis champion, and on and on—the longest bio I could find in this year's *Who's Who in the World*.

"So how does it look, Mr. Strobe?" he said after we had taken our seats.

I told him I thought we'd win, but spared him my rant about the justice system that had got me crosswise with Dana, and focused instead on my "America First" and reasonable doubt theories. As Moncrief and I spoke, I noticed that Paul Dexter had transmuted from the reasonably confident executive I'd spent the morning with into a quavering nerd, swiping beads of sweat from his forehead whenever Moncrief wasn't looking.

"Is it likely, sir," I said, "that the government would try to dig up that old SEC Hinton investigation that went nowhere?"

Moncrief gave me a withering look. "Why on earth would they bring up that old business? In point of fact, why the hell do *you* bring it up?"

This guy was tough, and it was my turn to wear Dexter's tightened shoulders and damp back. Another entry went into my memory bank in the form of a question: Why was Moncrief so sensitive about this "old business"? But for now, time to bail out.

"Maybe I should ask Paul," I said turning to Paul Dexter. "May we assume that you were not involved in any way with that SEC investigation?"

"My God," said Moncrief before Dexter could even untrack his tongue, "he's our senior man in *Asia,* for Christ's sake. He wasn't even *in* the U.S. at the time."

"Good," I said, swallowing hard. "I just wanted to be sure." I was looking and sounding stupid, and could imagine Dad rolling his eyes.

Moncrief grunted, urged me to get this "foolish damn case wrapped up," then democratically bused his own plates and utensils and stalked out of the room like he owned the place, which I reckon he more or less did. This was apparently a signal for others to return to the forge, for nearly everyone in the cafeteria got up, cleared their tables, and left, including Dexter, leaving me in the huge room with but a dozen late arrivals. I hoped Mildred might still be in here somewhere—she looked to be a person with a hearty appetite—and I found her on the staff side of the lounge. I grabbed a dish of raspberry yogurt and joined her.

She seemed pleased, until I told her I had been thinking about our conversation and wondered if she had some reason to doubt the janitor's guilt.

"We're not to discuss the matter," she said, continuing her assault on a plate of fettuccine primavera. "Bad for morale."

"I know that," I assured her, hoping she had seen me having lunch with the CEO, "but I'm a lawyer for the company, and you can talk to me. It's okay and strictly confidential."

She slowly opened up, recounting how Deborah had not been herself for two or three weeks before her murder. "Deborah had been so happy for several weeks, absolutely glowing. She was a beautiful girl, you know."

I said I knew.

"Then this SEC investigation came up, which, on top of the arguments she'd been having, suddenly threw her into a tizzy."

"Arguments?"

Mildred attributed most of Deborah's sudden dismay to a souring relationship. "Deborah was constantly quarreling over the phone with a boyfriend she'd been dating, saying things like 'You don't love me' and 'What am I supposed to do now?' "

So Deborah had been arguing with the not-so-proud future papa.

"The calls would usually end up with Deborah slamming the phone down. I could hear it through the door. I wasn't listening, you know, but . . ."

"I understand. Did you ever see this man or hear his name mentioned?"

Mildred shook her head and narrowed her eyes. Was she growing suspicious? It amazed me I had gotten this far with her. So far, Mildred was the perfect source: smart enough to remember things and naive enough to talk about them.

"Or what they argued about?"

Another shake of the head.

"How about her ex? Did Frank Hinton ever come to the office?"

"Well," she said, looking around, then leaning in closer to me, "he was here that day she was, you know . . ."

"Murdered? How long did he stay?"

"I don't know. It was around six o'clock, and I left for the day."

"And Frank and Deborah were still arguing?"

Mildred paused, compressed her features again, and gave her head a nervous shake. "I'm really not sure I should be . . ."

I feigned impatience. "Mildred, did you see who I was lunching with?"

"Yes."

"Well, do you really expect Mr. Moncrief to have to call you into his office and do my work for me because you won't have a confidential conversation with me?"

"All right," she said, leaning toward me again, "if you're sure it's all right."

She then pushed her plate away, exhaling as she did. "Deborah had been screaming at somebody on the phone—it may have been Dr. Hinton—then Dr. Hinton himself showed up after five o'clock mad as a hatter, screaming about the kids. The door was closed, but, well, yes, I could hear them."

"The day she was killed?"

"Yes. Dr. Hinton was accusing her of not being a good mother to their two daughters. I wasn't eavesdropping, you understand, it was just so *loud*."

I again nodded my assurance that she wasn't eavesdropping. "Well, I think Dr. Hinton thought Deborah was having an affair with Mr. Moncrief. Anyway, they were still at it when I left for the day."

So that silver-haired devil might have been dipping his pen in the office inkwell. My list of suspects had just doubled.

"Did you report this to the police, Mildred?"

"Some of it, sure, but they had the janitor by the time they got to me. They weren't interested."

"Listen carefully, Mildred. Were the arguments with the guy on the phone also about the kids?"

Mildred pursed her lips in deep thought. "I couldn't hear the words clearly, but she seemed, well, different on those telephone fights than she was with Dr. Hinton. Not that I was paying attention, you understand, but I think those calls were with the boyfriend. She sounded mad, but also kind of scared. At least that was my impression."

"Mildred, I need you to—"

"I'm sorry, Mr. Strobe, but I've really got to get back to my desk."

I put my hand on her arm. "Me, too. But Mr. Moncrief and I need two more things."

She waited.

"First, you're not to discuss this with anyone, understand? Jason doesn't want anyone to know about this investigation. We also want you to pull the phone records and give me a list of numbers of all of

Deborah's calls in or out that day on that last afternoon, say between three and six, October twenty-fourth. Okay?"

"Today? That was over two years ago."

"Today. Top priority. Get the records out of storage if they're not on the computer. Okay? Either Mr. Moncrief or I will stop by your desk in a couple of hours. Just hand us a note with the numbers. And mum's the word, okay?"

She frowned as she stacked her empty dishes onto her tray, but then gave her head a quick nod of agreement. I glanced around, realized my heart had been pounding.

I grabbed a glass of water and returned to Dexter's office. If Mildred Moon was only half right, and Deborah had been arguing with Frank Hinton for weeks, leading up to a face-to-face confrontation the day she was killed, maybe I had enough to try for a new trial. Was she pregnant by Hinton? More likely, he had found out she was pregnant by someone else—the boyfriend on the phone—and went bat-shit. Did he think Jason Moncrief had knocked her up? Was he jumping to conclusions? Was *I* jumping to conclusions?

Whatever, I was already drafting a new trial motion in my mind: a scenario of an angry Deborah, an even angrier estranged husband, furious at each other just hours before she was murdered. Now I just needed some hard evidence.

My optimism took a hit when I stopped by Mildred's desk at 4:15 on my way out after finishing with Dexter. She was shaking her head and looking like it was all her fault that there were no calls either in or out between 3:00 and 6:00 P.M. the day of the murder.

"I checked all back records," Mildred said. "She might have been on her cell phone, and I don't have access to those records."

I concealed my disappointment and thanked her.

"Did you ask Mr. Moncrief?" she said. "He and Deborah were always together. Maybe she made the calls from *his* office."

Always together. "Were they together a lot the day she was murdered?"

Her brow furrowed from the effort to remember. "Yes, most of the day."

"How come you remember that?"

"Because they were preparing for a stockholders meeting the next day. Didn't Mr. Moncrief tell you all this?"

"Of course," I said, "but he wants me to function in this matter independently. You know, double-check his memory, leave no stone unturned?" I then complimented her on *her* memory and added, "How is it you know that was the day Deborah was murdered?"

"Well, Deb was supposed to report at the stockholders meeting the following day, but she was . . ."

"I see."

"I also remember that Mr. Moncrief had gone over to the Western Bank Building late that same afternoon to meet with his lawyers before the stockholders meeting. His secretary was out sick, so I made the appointment for him at Coco's Salon downstairs for four o'clock. Mr. Moncrief liked to look his best for stockholder meetings. He was always so—"

"Right. So he was not in his office when you left at the end of the day."

"No, but I ran into him coming back into the building as I was heading for my bus. I remember wishing him luck at the meeting."

"That's right, Mildred. That's exactly what Jason told me. Do you remember what he said to you when you wished him luck?"

She paused, her lips compressed from concentration, and then said, "Yes. He wanted to know if Deb was still upstairs."

Back at the office the next day, I called Barney Klinehart, who said he would get Deborah's phone records from her cell phone server, along with Frank Hinton's office and home phone records from the phone company. Then he gave me a bonus. His friend's Soledad mail room contact had come through with the return address and name of Darryl's mystery friend. It had cost me another five hundred dollars.

"Her name is Bess Padgett. Want me to check her out?"

I took a look at my dwindling bank balance. Lisa had been hospitalized with a flare-up of MS-type symptoms for nearly a month, which had given me a bad case of the cash shorts. The doc said she may be suffering more demyelination—where the coating around nerves that keeps them protected from scarring breaks down. I had given the go-ahead for some newfangled vaccine, something about mononuclear cell-based immunoltherapy or whatever. Lisa had gone along, protesting all the while that she was just having another bad flare-up of arthritis and a touch of the flu. I had hired a woman to move in temporarily to keep an eye on Ma, but Ma had run her out of the house within an hour.

Anyways, back to Barney. I told him thanks, I'd take Padgett myself.

I decided to hit her cold, not alerting her with a phone call, and found her at a run-down trailer park outside of Union City, south of Oakland, off U.S. 880.

The summer sky was heavy with bruised, wadded-up clouds, and I could smell the stifling humidity in the air.

"Yes, I know Darryl Orton," Bess Padgett said, her dark hollowed eyes darting suspiciously over my head as I stood on the second step of her tiny ancient trailer house. All the paint was chipped off, and every piece of metal was corroded by rust. It rested on planks, no wheels. For all that, it wasn't any worse than the others stacked around it. This place even gave trailer trash a bad name.

The guilty, guarded tone in Ms. Padgett's voice practically invited a reading of her Miranda rights. A boy toddler clung onto his mother's robe with one hand and sucked his thumb with the other. Bess Padgett's skin was deathly pale and her narrowed-eye expression reflected a distrust born of a lifetime of disappointed expectations.

"Is he—?"

"He's alive," I said, and her eyes closed as in prayerful relief.

"Then may I ask your business here, sir?" she asked. She was strictly business again, pulling her bleached hair down across her pallid face to cover what appeared to be a bruise, while tugging her robe tight around her throat with the other hand.

The woman had been pretty once, maybe beautiful, but now she stared at me through vacant eyes too washed out to adequately match the anger in her tone of voice. The voice is what stood out in this drab setting, her polished diction.

"All right if I come in?"

"No, you may not come in. State your business, or I'll have to ask you to leave."

The little boy began pulling her out of the doorway toward the safety of the interior. He seemed frightened, about to cry.

"Darryl was with you the night of the murder he was charged with. I want you to help him."

She started closing the flimsy door, but I got up on the third step in time to block it with my foot.

"For God's sake, leave us," she said. "I *can't* help Darryl! If my husband finds you were here, I won't be able to help myself either. Darryl may not be a killer, but Jack *is*."

"I'm going to have to subpoena you, Mrs. Padgett."

She looked at me like I was crazy. "I won't appear, and I'll lie if I do."

Christ, now I had Suzy Threadgill probably lying to provide an alibi for Frank Hinton and Bess Padgett lying to deny one to Darryl Orton! More and more, life on the outside was beginning to look the same as life in the inside. Everybody lying. Everybody afraid.

"Listen, Mrs. Padgett, you don't have to worry about Jack, I can get you protection—"

Her unexpected smile was mocking, her tone derisive as she said,

"There is insufficient weaponry in the entire California National Guard armory to deal with Jack once he goes upside down. Jack is a cop who happens to be mentally disturbed."

"Are you saying your husband is bipolar?"

"No, he's a run-of-the-mill psychopath who fuels his temper with excessive volumes of methyl alcohol."

I was again struck by the woman's intellectual polish beneath her low-rent appearance. I handed her my card and asked her to call me if she changed her mind.

"We *can* protect you from Jack, Ms. Padgett, but there's no way we can protect Darryl in prison. Fact is, there's a race between the guards and inmates as to who's going to kill him first. He's lost the will to resist."

"That may be true, and it saddens me, but I can't help him."

"Why not let me take you and the child to a women's shelter?"

She let out a cynical laugh. "Perhaps you didn't hear me. Jack is a cop with access to information. He would track me to an underground vault in the middle of the Kobe Desert for the sheer pleasure of blowing my brains out for running out on him. Good-bye, sir."

She pushed the door so hard against my foot the thin metal began to bend.

"One last question. How did you meet Darryl?"

"I am—was—a singer. We met through music."

"How long have you known him?"

"Long enough to know Darryl never looks to anyone for help."

"Well, he's changed, Mrs. Padgett. I'm his lawyer, and he's asked me to represent him."

"Well, he doesn't want any help from me," she repeated. "For one thing, he never told you where to find me."

"Why do you think that?"

She relaxed her hold on the door, but not so much to constitute an invitation inside as to reflect a growing confidence. I had never seen a more articulate person in a more disastrous circumstance.

"Because I know the man Darryl is. You apparently don't." Her voice choked a little as she said his name. "Because," she added, "he . . . he knows Jack would kill me if he finds out. Consequently, I know Darryl would never have told you where to find me."

I was stung by the truth in her words, wondering what Darryl would do to me if he knew I was here, putting this enigmatic woman at risk. One thing for sure, I'd be the one needing the National Guard.

"Did you sing with his band?"

"Once or twice. You might say that my twisted path to country music was both unique and arduous."

"You were classically trained?" A guess.

She nodded.

"Don't get me wrong, Ms. Padgett. I love country music. It's just that, well, the way you talk and all."

She smiled at the tacit compliment despite herself. "And you're wondering how I came to . . . this?"

I felt my face going red at her frankness. The child now had his mother's robe in his mouth, but continued to protest my presence with whining sounds. But I *was* becoming increasingly fascinated by the "twisted path" that had brought Bess Padgett to a trailer park, married to a homicidal cop, and she seemed willing to talk about herself, as long as I'd leave Darryl out of it.

"If you must know, Mr. Strobe, I've a problem with men. Not men like you. Indeed, men quite unlike you. Tough guys. Men who are not good for me. Guys who like motorcycles, guns, and listen to country music. I was young when I met Jack, and he seemed exciting. His craziness even thrilled me. I interpreted his obsession as love. I was wrong."

"Then you met Darryl."

"Darryl was an exception, a decent man, so of course I couldn't possibly deal with him." She paused, stared off somewhere in the distance, then shrugged and smiled dolefully. "They don't teach you much about sexual pathology at Mills College."

I had heard of Mills; it was a women's college in Oakland.

"Can you at least tell me what time you met Darryl, the night before he was arrested?"

"He came straight here from work—he had finished early—got here around ten—I was waiting for him."

There it was: an alibi. At least something that should have been raised at trial, considering that the probable time of death pegged by the coroner's office was between 8:45 P.M. and 10:30 P.M. It would have taken Darryl nearly an hour to get to Union City from the TechnoCenter Building, leaving a window of less than twenty minutes for Darryl to have killed Hinton. The things Darryl hadn't told me would fill a courtroom. I felt a tremor of excitement.

"Where was Jack that night?"

"On the job, copulating a waitress somewhere I suppose. Look, Mr.—"

"Strobe, Billy Strobe."

"I ended it with Darryl that night anyway. We were in love—if one can call it that—but we both knew Jack would never let it rest. Darryl said he'd handle Jack but, well, there's no handling Jack. Jack would not think twice about burning this shack to the ground right this minute if he knew you were here talking about this."

"With his own baby in it?"

"It's not his baby. Anyway, I told Darryl it was over, which was quite painful for both of us."

I decided to deal my ace. "You're right, Bess, right about everything. Darryl doesn't know I'm here, and he would hurt me if he knew I'd tracked you down. But what you don't know is that Darryl lost the will to live the night he lost you and got arrested the next morning for something he didn't do."

She looked down at her child, avoiding my eyes.

"How many of us could have handled a double-whammy like that?" I continued. "He doesn't write you, does he? He's dead to the outside world, Bess, and now he's dying inside, too, and you're the only one can save him."

The little boy had been sniffling, and now started crying. She picked him up, though the effort nearly made her fall through the door.

"I'm sorry, Mr. Strobe," she said. "Darryl is not coming back; he and I know that now. Don't ask me to put at risk the only part of him I have left."

A cold shudder shot up my back. *Holy shit!* I was looking at Darryl's son! I stood staring at both of them in stunned silence.

"Mr. Strobe," Bess Padgett said, "if you see Darryl again, please tell him I love only one person on earth as much as him." She pulled the child close and kissed him on the cheek. "He understands."

She started to close the door, and I moved my foot out of the way, the subpoena still in my pocket.

17

There were three e-mails and five voice mails when I got back to my office a few minutes before five o'clock. Four of the messages were from Ashton's secretary. Two minutes later I was in his office.

"You wanted to see me, sir?"

"Three hours ago. Where have you been?"

I told him I had run a personal errand of great importance. He let it go and resumed reading a file, then swung his chair around so that his back was to me. I sat awkwardly for what seemed like five minutes, coughing and clearing my throat, before asking him if I should leave.

"We're waiting for Mr. Lassiter," he said to a window. This was a man with a permanent burr under his saddle.

Hale walked in looking unhappy, and I knew something was up. Ashton did the talking.

"Mr. Strobe, it has come to my attention that you've been nosing around Synoptics, asking questions about the Hinton murder. True or false?"

"I thought it might be related to the Dexter case, sir—"

"It's true then?"

"Yes, sir."

"Have you any notion of the time and money that Jason's company has expended to keep the lid on that unpleasant incident?"

"I don't, sir, nor do I have any notion why they would."

I watched Ashton's face darken into a dangerous hue, but Hale interceded. Hale, the peacemaker, the firefighter.

"For a very brief time, Billy," he said, "some of the officers of the company were under investigation for certain 'indiscretions' concerning the company's accounting methods. Given the fact that Deborah was the company's chief accounting officer, it was briefly and erroneously thought that these indiscretions might somehow be connected to her murder."

Her *murder*. Jesus, Mary, and Joseph. *Were* the two things connected? No wonder Moncrief was so defensive.

"Please let me handle this, Hale," said Ashton, who appeared to have calmed himself. "Jason is my problem, more than he is yours."

"But Billy is my 'problem,' Rex—more than he is yours—as you know better than anyone."

"Well, that may be," said Ashton, ignoring Hale's less than subtle challenge. "But I called this meeting, dammit, and I'll now end it."

While the firm's two senior partners fought over my carcass, I had time to try to think about where I'd got careless. Dexter? Mildred Moon? Jason Moncrief himself? I realized I was sweating, worried I might get fired just when I was getting somewhere on Darryl's case. I watched Hale rub his eyes, swallowing his anger at Ashton, something I suspected he was getting used to with a rat like Rex Ashton all the time chewing at his gut.

"Consider yourself advised, Mr. Strobe, *on the record*: Curiosity killed the cat and it could kill you here at S & S. Have I made myself clear?"

"Yes, sir," I said, relief flooding through me, safe for another few weeks anyway.

"Anything to add, Hale?"

"I think you've covered it, Rex," said Hale, regaining his trademark poise. "I might have said it differently, Billy, but I generally concur in what Rex has said. We can't have our best client finding out his own lawyers are currently fanning a fire he paid us years ago to help put out."

I apologized, thanked them both, and raced to my office. But Ashton didn't know that what I was really thanking him for was for revealing the connection between the insider trader scam and the death of Deborah Hinton that had at least temporarily interested the Securities Exchange Commission. It took several hours on my computer, but I finally found a single news article in a Contra Costa newspaper linking Jason Moncrief and Deborah Hinton as targets of an informal SEC investigation for insider trading—*just three weeks before Deborah was murdered.* Ashton and Moncrief had done a hell of a job suppressing the story. If I hadn't been focusing so hard on Frank Hinton, I might have figured out this angle earlier. Now my list of possible suspects had definitely doubled, as had my need for caution. If Moncrief was involved in Deborah Hinton's murder, things could get dicey. How high up did this thing go?

The next morning I entered Dana's office with two cups of cappuccino. If I was smart, maybe I could not only make some points with her, but also learn something about Jason Moncrief.

"Since you won't go out with me, I've come in to you, bearing your favorite coffee."

"Ah, the old trick bag trick: get them in your debt, then extract the sexual favor."

"Where did you learn about trick bags?"

She had momentarily forgotten I was an ex-con and appeared embarrassed. "My first assignment was a pro bono appeal for a death row inmate."

"I see," I said and held the paper sack up, giving it a little shake. "So is it working for me?"

"Depends. Where's it from?"

I removed the cups from the bag, triumphantly held them up for her inspection.

"From Peet's?" she said. "That's unfair, you bastard."

I shrugged, and put the cups on her desk. "I've seen you in line there."

"Okay, but don't expect to sleep over."

"Lord, no, woman, leastwise not on our first date."

"Good, and I want you to know I've had a *wonderful* time. Good-bye, Billy."

I pulled the cup back from her extended hand.

"I'm afraid I come with the coffee and stay until it's finished. No date, no coffee."

She smiled and beckoned me to a chair, seriously considering me for the first time, and more relaxed then when I had caught her baby-sitting Sarah.

"You've got the look and persistence of a trial lawyer, Billy Strobe. So tell me why an obviously ambitious man of your varied background has settled for shuffling papers all day? You *are* ambitious, aren't you?"

I smiled. "My daddy used to say the ripest fruit grows highest on the tree."

"That's fine," she said, "if you don't break any branches on the way up."

"If I do, it's by accident. You trial lawyers break 'em just for the fun of it."

"Not at all. We're simply marking a trail up and out of the dol-drums for our slower, paper-shuffling brethren at the bar."

I smiled and decided to try a different approach. Challenge her a lit-tle, Tom Collins style.

"We business drones are slow," I said. "You're right, we sweat and strain all the livelong day, bodies all aching and racked with pain, shuf-fling those papers that move the wheels of commerce through bureau-cratic red tape, making America the envy of the world. You trial lawyers, on the other hand, bring true glory and international atten-tion to the profession by persuading juries to free murderers one day and convict the innocent the next."

She made a face. "Are we getting serious here?"

"Serious dating is all."

"Okay, then, seriously, since I haven't finished my coffee yet, tell me why is it you chose to become a number cruncher instead of a real lawyer."

I decided to tell her the truth about my speech problem. It was harder than I thought, because the admission came out as a weakness, a failing, a side of my personality I realized I didn't really want re-vealed to her. But there it was.

"Only in groups, Billy?" she said. She seemed sincerely sympa-thetic, an unexpected silver lining in the confession of my disability.

I nodded. "Five, six, or more people. It varies, but if I get a sense they're paying attention to me, I clam up. It's okay. I'll be able to do a lot behind the scenes."

She shook her head. "You're not a behind-the-scenes guy, Billy." She paused, watching her own graceful fingers turning a pencil, "And you don't give a damn about 'the wheels of commerce.' I don't mean to be personal, but have you considered a speech therapist?"

"I would like nothing better than for you to be personal, Dana. As for a speech therapist, I think it's my head acting up, not my tongue."

I thanked her for her concern and eased us onto other subjects. Personal stuff—favorite movies, wine, books, restaurants—the kind of things people jawbone about on a real date. She had a way of pulling things out of me, and before long, I was telling her about Joe Strobe, my efforts to overturn his conviction and posthumously restore his good name. She seemed moved by my dad's story and told me she'd be willing to help, which in turn moved me. Next thing I was confessing my role in the Billionaire Boys Club II; then she was telling me about how Hale Lassiter and his wife had rescued her from hard times. It was clear she idolized Hale as much as he doted on her and a wave of unreasoning envy swept over me.

"Tell me about Sarah," I said.

Her face lit up. "She's finally out of the terrible twos, and even more independent than her mom."

It was obviously a topic she loved, and I was relieved she hadn't picked up on the morbid curiosity skulking beneath my casual inquiry. She continued to glow as she went on and on about her daughter, the joys and the problems.

"It's not all perfect," she said. "I don't spend enough time with her and there's always the anxiety of being 'found out' when necessity requires that I bring her in with me. Once when Sarah's day-care provider shut down for an emergency, I had to take her to a depo in Marin, and she cried the whole time. The receptionist at the plaintiff's firm tried to help, but I could hear her through the walls and had to bring her back in. She sat on my lap and drew pictures on my notes. Sometimes when my opponent objected, she would say: 'No, no!' "

"Guess she's going to be a judge," I said, and we laughed together. Eventually, I was able to shift our conversation again.

"Everyone seems touchy about that SEC investigation of Synoptics," I said.

"Really?"

"Yeah, Ashton particularly. Are you familiar with what happened over there when that lady was killed?"

"Yes," she said, her eyes alert. "Why?"

"Just curious," I said.

"No," she said, with a directness I would soon take for granted, "you have a reason for your interest. Would you like to tell me what it is?"

I guess I'd known all along I would tell her, partly because I needed her help, partly because I wanted to impress her that I was more than the empty, tongue-tied suit she saw before her. I didn't tell her all of it, of course, just that I'd met Darryl Orton in prison and hoped I might scare up enough dirt on Frank Hinton to help Darryl get a new trial. I let her think my coming to S & S was pure coincidence and that I fully expected to spend my entire wretched life here as a blue-stockinged plumber for the economic animals foraging the Silicon Valley.

"Will you tell Hale?" I asked.

I couldn't tell if she was looking at me with anger, curiosity, or pity. "I won't lie to him, but I don't feel an affirmative burden to blow the whistle on you."

"Good, because I've been warned by Ashton to cool it about the SEC investigation."

"Jason Moncrief is sensitive on the subject."

"For good reason, but I'd be much obliged if you could lend me a hand on this, Dana."

She looked surprised. "You want me to help you release a man who has admitted his guilt—"

"He copped a plea—"

"—and in the process help you toss our biggest client into the journalistic snake pit they have gone to incredible lengths to avoid?"

"Darryl Orton is innocent, Dana."

"Of course he is," she said, smiling so beautifully her teasing tone was almost lost on me. "Another innocent victim of our heartless and discriminatory system. No, Billy, from what I've heard about the case, your pal is right where he belongs . . . again. He did have a prior felony, am I right?"

"He was young and got caught up in something," I said, uncomfortable under her gaze. "As for the Hinton thing, he was framed."

She raised her eyebrows. "Wasn't everybody in prison either 'caught up in something' or 'framed'? You have more experience than I in this regard, but have you ever met a con who admitted his guilt?"

"You're looking at one."

That stopped her. "I'm sorry," she said. "But you don't seem . . . I mean you don't look like . . ."

"I may not look it," I said, "but if you're going to help me, you should know that I'm the Zodiac Killer and can never be sure when my blood lust will overwhelm my fragile discipline."

"I deserved that," she said, flashing her straight white teeth. "But seriously, what evidence do you have that he was framed?"

I shrugged. "I'm working on it," I said, and she shook her head again. "Dammit, Dana, I just know it happens." I sounded lame, even to myself. "It happened to my father, and if it happened to him, it can happen to anybody."

I saw doubt in her face, half expected her to say, "*If* it happened to your father," and felt overwhelming relief when she didn't. The last person who had implied that Joe Strobe was guilty got popped on a handball court.

"So," I said, "are you going to help me or not?"

"Not. I know nothing that could help you even if I wanted to, which I don't."

"You have information about Synoptics that could help, and I'm snake-bit there now."

She gave me a puzzled look, so I kept going. "Specifically I need to know more about the stock transactions that the police initially thought were connected to the murder."

"So look in the files."

"I can't find them. I've looked everywhere."

She raised both hands and fluttered her graceful fingers at me. "What makes you think I would know anything about the case?"

I got up, strolled over to her single associate's window and stared out at a brick wall and more windows. I felt my shoulders sag under the weight of her words, and my jaw tightened. My breath against the glass clouded my vision, but not my resolve.

"What makes me think that? The case files weren't where they should be, so I looked at the firm's time records. You showed up on the case time sheets every day for nearly three months, working with Hale during the SEC investigation. That's what makes me think that."

She met my hard gaze, appraising me over the lid of her coffee cup. "There's more to you than meets the eye, Billy Strobe."

I shrugged. "You're the one said I was ambitious, Dana." I was struck by how the casual cleverness of my remark, issued with a shrug of cool indifference, masked a disappointment and frustration so surprising, so powerful, that I had to restrain myself from taking her by the shoulders and shaking her.

She tossed her coffee cup, only half-empty, into her wastebasket and said, "Our date is over."

There was also more to Dana Mathews than met the eye.

"Don't bother walking me to the door," I said, and stormed out of her office knowing I'd have to find a way to scope out the Synoptics stock scam on my own. As for Dana Mathews, I reckon I'd been right the first time about staying clear of her, but the knowledge of it didn't ease the disappointment in my heart.

*   *   *

I returned to my office just as the afternoon mail arrived, consisting of the usual bar activity flyers, a half-dozen depo notices, four interoffice memos, and an order on a minor motion I had researched. There was also the usual array of impossible assignments from Rex Ashton, including a proposed contract he wanted drafted and faxed to a hotel in Washington, D.C., by 3:00 P.M., Pacific Coast time the day after tomorrow. Scanning it, I nearly tripped over a cardboard box on the floor I hadn't noticed. The return address was: County Clerks Office, Enid, Oklahoma.

My heart was pounding against my rib cage as I lifted it onto my desk, then warily ran my fingers around the sides and the top. It was as if my father's casket had been exhumed and delivered to my office. I grabbed a letter opener and slashed open the top, revealing fifteen volumes of trial transcripts in the case of *State of Oklahoma vs. Joseph Strobe*.

I shoved most of them in folders, told my secretary that an emergency had come up, and literally ran toward the elevator. I'd have to worry about Ashton's contract tomorrow; the transcripts were burning a hole in my briefcase, screaming to be read, and I had to have total privacy. I hoofed it up Pine Street to my apartment panting like a stuck hog, lugging my precious cargo. The guys who found the shroud of Turin couldn't have been more excited than me.

I loped through the front door and up the stairs, praying I wouldn't see Mrs. Alvarez, the widow in the apartment across the hall from me or worse yet, my landlord, Mr. Bharani, who had found out I could fix things. I didn't have to worry about making noise; Mrs. Alvarez was near deaf and Mr. Bharani lived on the ground floor, probably napping at this time of day.

"Oh, Billy," came a voice as I fumbled with my key, "just the young man I was hoping to see."

My prayers had, once again, gone unanswered.

"Hello, Mrs. Alvarez. Is your TV working all right?" I had set her up the week before with some earphones and an adapter that connected into her television set.

"*What?*"

I moved in closer and repeated my question.

"Something's wrong with the thingamajig!" she shouted back at me. I set my briefcase down and entered her apartment hurrying before she woke up Mr. Bharani downstairs.

It turned out that the batteries were dead in both her hearing aids. She was getting forgetful—could never remember where she kept them—so I had begun keeping extras at my place. Ten minutes later, I was in my own apartment, had made a fresh pot of coffee, taken my phone off the hook, and opened my briefcase. By two the next morning, I had finished volume ten, the rebuttal testimony of Amos Blackwell, the office lawyer from Oklahoma City my dad had brought in as a full partner, the lawyer my mother had distrusted from the day she first met him.

"He's got shifty eyes, Joseph," I heard her tell my dad one morning over breakfast, "and he's pretentious, too, with his big-city airs."

"Relax, Mother," Dad said, "you wear socks to court in Enid, they call you pretentious. He can't help it he's smart—smarter than I am, he is."

Blackwell would sure enough prove himself smarter than my father, for within a year, he went from the firm's new junior partner to sole owner of the business following Dad's death. He broke plenty of branches along the way as he shimmied up the tree of his own greedy ambitions, and the brilliant and unimpeachable key prosecution witness against my father was none other than Amos Blackwell himself.

On the plus side, the trial judge must have been surprised by the verdict, for he had not only personally polled the jury without being asked, but had practically cross-examined them, as well. His disagreement with the verdict was obvious, even before he sentenced Joe Strobe to the lightest possible prison term—three years—a month later. I figured the trial judge, a man named Charles Ryan, might provide the key to proving Joe was framed. I made notes in my journal.

Interview Ryan, obviously Irish. A friend? Drinking buddy? Or a straight ahead guy who figured Dad was framed?

I waited until 7:00 A.M., then called Lisa. Somewhere in the attic or garage was a box of Dad's old papers, stuff that might make more sense to me now that I was older and had the trial transcripts. She sounded peppy on the phone, like the drug therapy had helped, and I told her so.

"I've felt better recently," she admitted, "now that they've quit using me for a dartboard. I've graduated to semimonthly IVs."

"But the pain's less?"

"I guess so, but Billy, they're treating me for something I don't have! Not that I don't appreciate you making it happen."

"No problem, Lisa, and since you're feeling a little better, how's about sorting through Dad's stuff yourself? Then send me anything that relates to his trial or the trial they claimed he committed fraud in. Look for anything connecting Amos Blackwell to either case."

She paused. Did she resent being drawn into a quest she was opposed to or did she suspect I was trying to distract her from her troubles?

"Okay," she said at last. "I've checked my busy calendar, and will try to make time for your burdensome request."

I smiled, told her where the boxes were. I could tell she wasn't smiling with me.

"I need to tell you, Billy, that I'm doing this for you, not for him."

I swallowed. "I understand, sis. But try to keep an open mind, okay?"

"For *you*, Billy," she repeated, a metallic bitterness resonating in my ear, "not for him."

"Okay, I hear you," I said. "How's Ma?"

"The doctor just left, but he can't deal with her, and neither can I. He gives her a year. She threw up blood last night."

"Blood?"

"Internal hemorrhaging."

More silence. Jesus, this was just what I needed right now. I was in trouble at the firm, behind in all my assignments, had still not yet accrued any vacation time, and, between Lisa's medical bills and the high cost of living in San Francisco, still living hand-to-mouth. Yet, wasn't there always *something* holding me here? Wouldn't there *always* be something?

"I'm coming out, Lisa."

"When?"

"Tomorrow."

Hale was great about giving me two days off and lucky for me, Rex Ashton was too far out of town to squelch it.

I finished up Ashton's contract by 9:30 that night and faxed it off. I heard my phone ring as I walked back in my office and caught it on the fourth ring. As usual, it wasn't Dana apologizing and confessing her undying love for me—but Barney Klinehart, as usual reporting bad news regarding his efforts to break Frank Hinton's alibi witness. He had thoroughly investigated Suzy Threadgill's club memberships and social habits—hoping to put her somewhere else the night she claimed to be with Frank Hinton—and had come up empty.

"She ain't too active since her split-up with Hinton. Still belongs to Dave's World Gym, but she wasn't there that Wednesday night according to the log-in book, maybe because her aerobics class is on Thursdays. Her investment club meets on Tuesdays. She's got no regular activity on Wednesday nights, which was the night of the week Deborah Hinton was killed. Shall I go on?"

"I get the picture. Any *good* news?"

"No, but I got some more bad news."

"Listen, Barney, if you charge more for good news, just say so. I hear we're getting raises here."

"I didn't know that, so I've only been chargin you the bad news rate."

"If I'm paying for the jokes, you owe *me* money."

"Yeah, yeah. Anyway, I got the victim's cell phone records. Nothing between Frank Hinton and his ex. In fact, no calls at all to or from Deb Hinton's cell between three o'clock and six. Dead end, kid."

I hung up, disappointed, then turned my thoughts to my trip to Enid, hoping I'd do better with Dad's case than I was doing with Darryl's.

Ma was still tall, thin, and erect, but seemed thicker through the waist and hips than she was on my last visit after the bar exam. Her hair was short, unkempt, and had suddenly gone a drab, gunmetal gray. Her face was red, bloated, and dense with broken capillaries. She was upset right off when I told her I had to return to San Francisco the next day.

"Haven't changed a bit, have you, Billy? Come home just to put your feet under the dinner table and catch up on your sleep."

Her tone was easy and humorous, but we both knew she meant every word. We kept the conversation light as Lisa and I ate dinner and Ma drank herself to sleep. I helped her into bed, feeling a surprising strength in the bony arm that clung hard around my neck. She oozed a flowery gin odor from every pore. I could no longer picture her the way she looked when I was a young kid.

"She's much better today," Lisa said later, after she'd undressed Ma and tucked her in. "The doctor was in this morning."

"She's getting worse, Lisa."

She shrugged. "She went through hell today, trying to stay sober for your arrival."

I nodded.

"She made it till noon."

We had talked about the Oklahoma clinic at length. The bottom line was that Ma wouldn't hear of it, left the room every time Lisa brought it up.

"Keep working on her, Lisa. Prepare her. I've got the money—or soon will have. I'll come back and take her down there if I have to hog-tie her first."

Lisa looked out the window, tears forming in her pale blue eyes.

"And you, brat," I added, "are coming out to California to stay with me while she's in stir."

Lisa didn't move a muscle or blink a misty eye, not even a twitch. "One thing at a time," she said finally. "Tell me more about your job."

"Only if you'll play me something on the flute."

She made a face and said, "At the risk of shattering the hopes and dreams of music lovers all over the world, I've retired the flute. I've grown tired of the damn thing."

"You can't do that, Lisa," I said. "You're gifted."

"Wake up, Billy. Nobody plays the flute anymore," she said, but as she reached for her teacup with both hands, I flushed with mixed embarrassment and sadness. Lisa clearly no longer possessed the dexterity to finger the instrument. Her world was shrinking to the four walls of this sad little house.

I changed the subject, asked her if she had found Dad's papers in the attic.

"I found them, but I've not made much of a dent. The files are in hopeless confusion, and I'm organizing them as I go."

"Anything about Blackwell or the trial?"

"Lots about Blackwell, but nothing relevant to Dad's trial so far."

I knew this was hard for her. She had never forgiven Dad for leaving us, and unlike me, had taken his suicide as an admission of guilt for the crimes he'd been convicted of. I changed the subject again, this time to politics, and was glad to see she seemed to be keeping up with things.

"We've renewed our subscription to the *Daily Oklahoman,* thanks to you, Billy. Between that and CNN, I stay current, though God knows why, since the news is always bad and I don't really give a shit anyway. Indeed, prodigal Billy, I don't give much of a shit about anything."

I had to keep trying to motivate her, give her a reason to get out of bed in the morning.

"I know how you feel about Dad, Lisa, but I need your help."

"Billy, I'm barely able to help myself. Can't you see that?"

"What you're doing up there is important. I've got the entire transcript of Dad's trial, and I'm going to reopen the whole thing. I'm going to have a talk with Dad's old partner tomorrow. It's just a first step, but I want to see how Amos Blackwell reacts to a dose of reality. Will you keep at it?"

She exhaled slowly. "Do you want the truth? I've spent very little time in the attic, Billy. This project ranks pretty close to the top of my list of things I don't give a shit about. Our dear father was a drunk, a crook, and in the end, a coward as well."

I tried to shake off Lisa's harangue, which, if uttered by anyone else, would have been his or her last words. "Okay, Lisa, maybe he drank too much, maybe he couldn't face things at the end. But what if he wasn't a crook? What if I—*you* and I—could prove he never faked those documents, that he was framed by Amos Blackwell, or maybe by Blackwell and the client?"

"Dear blind, loyal Billy," she said quietly, her eyes fixed on me. "Is it so damned important to you?"

"It's damned important, sis, and I need you to help me."

"All right," she said, raising and dropping her small shoulders. "I'll help you prove yourself wrong if it will make you feel better. Let's hear your bizarre theory."

But I realized the energy had drained out of her, and by 8:30 at night I was sitting by myself watching TV, which had gotten even worse than I remembered it. I found a good old movie, but it was so riddled with commercials, I gave up.

My room was exactly the way I'd left it eight years before, but sleep wouldn't come. Worries about my mother and Lisa mingled freely with thoughts of my confrontation with Amos Blackwell. Lisa thought I was crazy, but I knew I had to avenge the evil that Amos Blackwell had done to my family. Then the dead could rest, and so could we.

The next morning over breakfast I decided to tell Ma I had obtained the transcripts of Dad's trial and was sure he had been railroaded by his own partner and his best client. Though sober, Ma let out a derisive cackle louder than a car crash.

"Stay out of it, son. Let the poor drunken soul rest in peace."

"I just want the truth to come out, Ma."

"Then face the truth about your father," she said, inhaling deeply on a cigarette she held in a shaking hand while waving the smoke aside with the other. Still, I was surprised at how much better she looked in the morning, despite her worn-looking robe and slippers.

"I *know* the truth about my father," I said calmly. "He was a good man, a public interest lawyer who honored the poor."

"He was a well-meaning man, leave it at that," Ma said in a cold tone, then refused to leave it at that. "Sure, he honored the poor. First, because being around them made him feel less like a failure, and second, because they comprised most of his clientele."

My head was starting to throb. Jesus, how I hated conflict with my family. Hated it worse than dealing with Rex Ashton. I had to get away.

"I know he was good to drunks," Lisa chimed in, "because he kept bringing the poor bastards home."

"There'll be no swearing in this house, Lisa Strobe," said Ma.

"Oh, Christ," said Lisa.

"That's *enough*!"

Lisa turned back to me. "Do you know why he was good to

drunks, Billy? Because that's what *he* was. Another drunken Irishman—first, last, and always, world without end, amen."

"Blasphemy," muttered Ma, off in pursuit of a match to light another cigarette. I reached for my pack of Rolaids, kicking myself inwardly for opening up the subject.

"The man you call his 'best client,' " said Ma, lighting up again, "was one of their few clients with any real money—and even most of those came to the firm thanks to Amos Blackwell."

"I don't care about that," I said. "My point is that Dad wasn't a crook, and it's time you both get over your bitterness, especially you, Lisa. Don't you see it's eating you up? Wrecking your life?"

"By all means, let's do get over it," said Lisa, giving me that wiseass smile, the one I'd told her would one day add homicide to my rap sheet. "Let's get over it before it wrecks my altogether perfect life."

"Stop it!" said Ma. "Stop it, the both of you! And William, *you're* the one who has to 'get over it.' You're the one unwilling to let the past sleep and the dead rest."

"I'm sorry, Ma," I said, "but I won't stop, whether you like it or not. I intend to sue Amos Blackwell's bony ass and recover every cent he stole from all of us!"

Ma kept staring grimly out the kitchen window, though there was little to see other than a neglected lawn, some overgrown rose bushes, and a decaying fence. Lisa, on the other hand, was giving me her full attention, a look that told me her grudging agreement to get serious about the project from the night before had just received a jolt of green adrenaline.

"You could do that?" Lisa said. "Recover money after all this time?"

"If he committed fraud and concealed it, the statute of limitations doesn't even start to run."

Oh, is all she said, but the whispered word was accompanied by the broadest smile I had seen in years.

"*Enough, William!*" Ma shouted at me, her face dangerously red. She then gave Lisa a sidelong glance that erased her smile. "You, too, Lisa. I want you both to let it go!"

I was angry now, too, fed up with their disloyalty. "Why don't *you* 'let it go,' Ma? I'm sick and tired of your constant harping on Dad."

She took a step toward me, her dead eyes suddenly sparking with light, and slapped me across the face. I was so surprised I didn't even feel it. Dad had taken the belt to me only once—I'd been caught in a lie, and he had cried with me afterward—but Ma had never touched me in anger. And now, she looked as stunned as I was.

But when she broke the silence, her voice was unremitting in its intensity. "Most young men grow up thinking their fathers are perfect and end up hating themselves because of it. You should be grateful to me for sparing you that illusion."

"Well," I said inadequately, still off balance from her act, "I'm not."

Another tense silence filled the room, as if a single spark would set the room ablaze.

"Mother," Lisa said at last, "maybe Billy has a point. We could use the money."

"*Everybody* could use money, but I won't have you digging around in old dirt, exhuming the poor man's grave. *Either* of you."

I put my arms around Amy Strobe and told her I couldn't give it up. Her arms hung heavy at her sides until I released her and she lurched off toward the kitchen.

I put on a fresh shirt, packed my travel bag, exchanged a tearful hug with Lisa, found Ma at the kitchen table holding a glass of gin-scented orange juice, and kissed her cheek. I then headed for the relative tranquillity of my rented car.

I drove straight to the address where Dad and Blackwell had rented space fifteen years before and saw that it was now called the Blackwell Building.

I entered and gave my card to the receptionist and told her no, he wasn't expecting me. My heart was pounding. I was surrendering the home field advantage, and my team wasn't ready yet. Still, I was determined to confront him, smoke him out, check his reaction, see what I was up against. Maybe he'd just admit everything and save us both a world of trouble.

Blackwell immediately emerged, barely recognizable. Now in his fifties, he had the face he deserved. He was, as I remembered him, still broad-shouldered and tall, but thick through the gut and ass, giving his chest the look of a collapsed tent. The man had gone from too thin to too fat in only a decade. His cadaverous head, perched on top of this ungainly structure, appeared too small—out of whack with the rest of him—so that as he took me in with red-rimmed eyes set deep in dark hollows, surrounded by skin that looked like a walnut shell, he put me in mind of one of those arcade photos they take with your head superimposed on whatever larger-than-life cardboard cartoon torso you selected.

"Billy!" he said, flashing an uncertain smile. "My God, it's you!"

The smile withered as he sensed my mood, but he offered me a chair. "Long time, no see, young man. How are your dear mother and sister? Louise, was it?"

"Lisa and my mother are as well as can be expected," I said, deciding on the direct approach, "given the fact that after convicting my father, you screwed them out of their interest in the firm."

"My Lord, Billy," he intoned without hesitation in his soothing baritone voice, eyebrows tilted in sympathetic concern. "Your father was like a saint to me, pure and simple, but surely you understand that I was under *oath* at that trial."

So Amos Blackwell knew I had obtained the trial transcript.

"As for your family, perhaps you were too young to realize that there *was* no 'interest in the firm.' Indeed, I was the one who helped out the three of you—whenever I could."

I took in the elegant antique desk he sat behind, the engraved Waterman pen set, the paneled walls. "Heavy guilt makes heavy demands for its expiation," I said. "We Catholics understand that, Mr. Blackwell."

The skin on his face seemed to tighten somewhat around his prominent cheekbones. "I have neither guilt nor reason for it," he said. "Didn't your mother tell you of the assistance I rendered while you were in prison for aggravated larceny in California?"

"What did you do? Keep her in gin?"

"As a matter of fact, I occasionally arranged for food and beverages to be sent to them during your time in custody."

Neither of them had mentioned this. I suddenly felt the need to get away from Amos Blackwell and back into the fresh air. I wasn't ready for him, and he wasn't going to give an inch until I was prepared to take it. I tried to think of what Dad would do in this situation, but drew a blank. I rose to leave.

"You may have changed my mother's opinion about you," I said, "but you don't fool me." He got up, too, and came up close to me.

"Listen, Billy," he said, still affecting a conciliatory tone. "Your father *was* a saint, like I said, but he was also a sinner like all of us. You understand? Ask your own mother. She'll tell you. Hell, kid, *I* didn't convict him, a *jury* convicted him, pure and simple, following a lengthy trial."

"In which he had no lawyer."

"He insisted on representing himself."

"You knew he had no money."

"Hell, Billy, neither of us did, and I had responsibilities, for Christ's sake! What little money I had went to raising a family. His money went straight to his liver. Your dad was a *drunk,* kid—a drunk and a perjurer who ran away from life because he didn't have the balls to pay his debt to society."

Waves of heat engulfed my body, and I knew I'd better get out of there quick. "I'd be obliged if you didn't say that again, Mr. Blackwell."

"I'm just telling it like it was," he said, his face so close I could feel his stale breath on me. His attitude had changed, and so had his tone of voice. "Still, despite all your drunken father did, I helped your family, and goddammit, you should be kissing my hand. Fact is, you should be kissing my ass."

I seized him by the lapels and threw him against the wall, knocking his framed State Bar certificate and some pictures to the floor with a loud clatter. I put a hand to his throat and pressed his chin upward so that his effort to speak came out in muffled grunts. His sunken eyes began to bulge out of their sockets.

My attitude had changed, too.

"I asked you politely not to say that again about my father, sir. Are we clear now?"

He managed to give his head a slight nod and I let him go. He staggered to his desk, clutching at his throat and panting for air.

"Get . . . out of here, you bastard . . . or I'll call a cop and . . . have you put back where you belong! Oh, you're a chip off the block all right."

"I hope so, Mr. Blackwell."

"You'll hope for more than that the next time I see you," he said, "and I suggest that you consider your status as a parolee before you assault me again. By the way, are you authorized to travel outside the State of California?"

I was, of course, but wouldn't give the prick the satisfaction of responding to him. I was on my way to the door.

"I didn't think so," he shouted after me. "But then you're Joe Strobe's son, aren't you! What do you care about the law? *You're all bums!*"

The receptionist was in the doorway, and I realized that Blackwell was deliberately provoking me now, wanting me to hit him in front of a witness. My hands had turned themselves into fists, clenched so hard my fingernails were cutting into my palms. He had somehow maneuvered quickly in front of me, blocking my way, so that all I could see was that smirking face, that jaw thrust within inches of my cocked right hand.

But then I remembered something Darryl Orton had said to me once: "Never wrestle with a pig. You'll just get dirty, and what's worse, the pig will like it."

So I shoved him aside and stormed out past the wide-eyed receptionist and two young associates.

I fumed all the way back to San Francisco, knowing that when I returned, I'd need more than faith in my father if I was going to beat Amos Blackwell.

18

Mace and I went for a drink after work the next day at Aqua, the firm's watering hole. Aqua was one of the most expensive restaurants in San Francisco. Four stars. They serve up real creative seafood dishes—Idaho trout, Chilean sea bass, Maine lobster, you name it. I know all this because Hale told me so. I've never eaten in Aqua, and probably never will, but I could afford their beer and liked the open spacious feeling, bouquets of flowers tall as a man, and dramatic lighting that made everybody look good, especially after those beers I mentioned. I was surprised to see Dana there, surrounded by friends.

"Still lusting after the boss's surrogate daughter?" Mace said, following my gaze.

"Trying to quit," I said, and ordered a Wild Turkey and water. "Got her down on me again."

Mace shook his head. "You could piss off Mother Teresa. Did you ride horses when you were an Okie?"

"Never. And I'm still an Okie. Why?"

"New hot Dana rumor. She's some kind of riding champ. Dressage, I suppose."

"Fits," I said, downing half my drink, picturing her in a little red jacket and black hat, sailing over the barrier to the applause of chardonnay-sipping fat cats with nothing better to do.

"Rough trip?" he said, eyeing my empty glass.

"To Enid? Yeah, got clobbered by the home team. You're a trial lawyer, Mace. Can I get exhibits released from my father's trial?"

"All appeals exhausted?"

"The case was tried more than a dozen years ago."

"Sure you can. Clerks like to get rid of old stuff cluttering their exhibit lockers. They'd be long gone by now in California, but things might be different in that cow county you hail from."

I nodded.

"How were your mother and sister?"

"Welcomed me like the proverbial bastard at a family reunion. My ma's real sick. I'm going to get her into treatment and move my sister out here."

But Mace was distracted. "Oh-oh," he said, peering over my shoulder, "are you wearing your flak jacket?"

"Why?"

"Dana Mathews is heading our way." I had told Mace about our last encounter.

I turned just as she reached us. She stopped and smiled at Mace. Then she turned to me and, as usual, my heart took a hit as her eyes came to rest on me. "Remember that case we discussed last week?" she said. "The one the SEC took an interest in?"

"How could I forget?"

"Stop by my office tomorrow when you get a chance. I have some thoughts."

I nodded slowly, said okay. Mace offered her a drink.

She shook her head. "Thanks, Mace, but I'm running late. See you tomorrow, Billy?"

"Good," I said, wondering what was going on.

"Bye, Mace," she said, and walked away, every eye in the place trailing her slim hips and perfect ass through the door.

"Progress, Studman?" said Mace. "Or work?"

"Definitely work," I said, and signaled the bartender.

I was up with the pigs the next morning and in the office by six, making periodic checks of Dana's office. On my fourth trip around seven-thirty, I saw her door was ajar, so I rapped and entered.

She smiled and nodded toward a client chair. "I was brusque with you the other day. I apologize."

"If that was brusque, I don't want to see you mad."

"I think I'm trying to apologize, Billy."

"Apologizing for being brusque or for lying to me about being on the Hinton SEC investigation team?"

"You are a difficult guy to apologize to."

She was right. I took a deep breath. "Sorry. I'm in a difficult situation. So is a good friend of mine. Plus Ashton's all over me. I've gotten nowhere clearing my Dad's name. Even Hale's pissed at me."

She said nothing and turned a pencil end-over-end for a minute. She was slowly shaking her head, but I don't think she was aware of it. She abruptly turned her head away, but not before I saw that her eyes had melted into clear green pools. "I want to help you, Billy, but I don't know how. I'm willing to tell you what I know about the investigation, though I can't see what good it will do."

"I'd appreciate it."

"It's not that I didn't mean what I said about your friend being guilty. Or about warning you that you *will* be fired if you go digging around into that old business again."

"So why are you handing me a shovel?"

"I feel badly about the other day and about not being truthful with you." She paused, gathered herself, and met my eyes. "I like you, Billy, and I admire what you're trying to do. But mind you, all this is— was—public record, so I'm not divulging anything confidential."

"I understand," I said.

"It all began when CEO and Chairman Jason Moncrief sold some of his stock at a profit during an uptick in Synoptics stock."

"Nothing wrong with that," I said.

"Normally, no. But in this case, the uptick had resulted from a deferred write-off on a failed operating division of the company. The deferral caused earnings of Synoptics to exceed Wall Street's expectations."

"You're saying that if the company had taken the write-off as it should have, the stock would not have gone up?"

"Worse, it would have gone down, because the entire year's profit would have been wiped out. In addition, deferring the write-off was clearly improper under any accounting standard."

"Let me guess," I said. "It was the company's chief financial officer who improperly deferred the write-off."

Dana nodded. "Deborah Hinton was the CFO, and she made the decision. It was, of course, completely without Jason's knowledge."

"How do you know that?"

"It would have been stupid for him to have sold significant amounts of stock knowing the numbers were rigged, and Jason is anything but stupid."

"How far did the investigation get?"

"The SEC closed its file within a matter of weeks for lack of corroborating evidence," she said. "Hale's approach was twofold: First, he argued—"

"That any CEO dumb enough to sell stock knowing it's illegal would be too dumb to have become CEO in the first place."

"Exactly. Second, we showed that the sums involved were relatively minor, at least to a man with hundreds of millions in liquid funds. In other words, he had quite enough money without cheating to get more."

I sighed inwardly at the naïveté of her remark. Nobody these days had "enough" money, *particularly* people with too much already. I thought about asking her how much it cost to keep one of her purebred jumping Morgans fed and trained. Instead, I asked her why the homicide investigators looking into the Hinton murder were interested in the transaction.

"It turns out that Deborah had also sold stock when it went up—the rise she had improperly created herself."

"So that's how Jason's own sales of stock came to light."

"Exactly. The homicide investigators suspected that Hinton might have fallen out of bed with possible co-conspirators—your friend, for example."

I laughed at that. "Darryl has a great deal of native intelligence, but he wouldn't know a stock from a bond or a wild pig's ass either."

"The police figured that out."

"But?"

"But by then they figured him as an assassin for hire."

"Hired by?"

"Deborah's unknown co-conspirator."

I wanted to laugh, but it was too absurd to be funny.

"And who was that?"

"That's where the theory unraveled."

"So the SEC closed its file," I said bitterly, "and the cops busted Darryl anyway, despite having no motive."

"People in America these days don't seem to need a motive or even a reason to kill each other. Besides, rape was a possibility."

I shook my head, thanked her for her help, and slowly rose to my feet. I was tired, and beginning to feel like I'd never make a living in the business of clearing innocent people's names. Better keep a day job, I told myself.

Dana said you're welcome and please be careful, and I decided to believe that she had misled me before in a good faith effort to keep me from falling into a hole I was digging for myself. She even seemed concerned about me; those teared-up eyes didn't lie. A part of me wanted to take her in my arms, but another part reminded me that the woman was out of reach, out of my league. She had warned me long ago not to compare my life with hers, and I should have paid her heed.

Back in my office, I tried to ignore the projects piling up on my desk and the files stacked on the floor against the walls, walls that seemed to have closed in a foot or two around me.

I took stock of where I was, which was basically back down to one suspect: Frank Hinton. I picked up a file, but images of Darryl twisting in the Soledad wind haunted my thoughts. Just before noon I grabbed my coat and headed for the elevator.

I wandered around the cosmetic concessions at Nordstrom's, watching the clerks painting women's faces into masks designed to seduce the men of their dreams. While I circled the area, I kept glancing over at the woman who met the description Barney had given me. It was Suzy Threadgill, all right, and I prayed that my train-wreck subtlety would somehow succeed in breaking Frank Hinton's alibi witness where an experienced investigator like Barney had failed.

I was ready, and when Threadgill sent off a freshly painted customer, I took a deep breath, walked up to her, and flashed a badge I'd picked up at a novelty shop on Market Street on the way to Nordstrom's.

"Ms. Threadgill? I'm with the San Francisco police."

She said oh my, but sounded more disappointed than concerned, which of course disappointed me. Here I was, bravely engaging in a parole-violating felony, and the best I got out of her was an oh my.

"We've reopened the Deborah Hinton murder case."

"Oh?"

"You see, Ms. Threadgill," I said, narrowing my eyes into a menacing glare, "we've got a little problem with your alibi for Mr. Frank Hinton."

"Oh my," she repeated, but this time she put some feeling in it. I was encouraged. "But the killer is in jail, isn't he?"

"So we thought," I said in a stern tone. "We realize now that we should have checked other possibilities more closely. Dr. Hinton's alibi, for instance."

"Oh." Suzy Threadgill was not a big talker, but she was starting to show her nerves. Time to go for it, kid, I told myself. Take the notebook out of your jacket pocket; move in a little closer.

"Yes. You see, Ms. Threadgill, we've done some checking and now have reason to suspect you were not really with Dr. Hinton the night of the murder."

Her unlikely gray eyes darted beneath what I suspected were colored lenses, highlighting her deeply shadowed cheeks and lips painted dark red.

"Why would you think that?"

"Because you were somewhere else that night," I said.

"And how would you know a thing like that?" She was a cool one, her masklike face betraying nothing.

"Easy enough, once we took the time," I said, and rattled off the list of her activities Barney had come up with. That got her heart pounding so hard I could see it in her throat. She paled and dropped into a stool, her narrow shoulders sagging into her flat chest.

How about that, Dad? Not too bad for an office lawyer?

"Well?" I said.

"I'm n-not saying anything m-more to you," she said. "In fact, I think I would like to speak to a lawyer."

I'd been one long enough myself to know that nobody *likes* to speak with a lawyer unless they're desperate or incredibly lonely or both. I had her going now, her thin, painted-on eyebrows drawn together in thought.

"Are you refusing to give me a written statement?" I said. "An officer of the law?"

"That's right. I want to speak to a lawyer. Now, please excuse me?"

I excused her and strode through the door onto Market Street. I hadn't broken Hinton's alibi witness, but I knew I had my man. Now I just had to find a way to prove it.

I hopped a streetcar back up Market Street to the financial district, planning on calling Barney and telling him the good news. My phone at the office was blinking, and one of my messages was from Barney.

"Klinehart," came the gruff voice from the other end.

"Barney, it's Billy Strobe. I've got great news."

"Tell it to somebody else, kid, I'm off the case."

"What?"

"Did you know about the DNA?"

"DNA?"

"You've been conned by a con, kid. There's a little something your prison buddy neglected to mention."

"Barney, what the hell are you—?"

"Hair follicles found in the victim's fingers presented a perfect match with DNA samples taken from your buddy's scalp."

I fell into my chair. "There's been some mistake," I said, my voice unsteady. "I've read the trial transcripts—"

"The deputy DA on the case never goes to trial with the quick and dirty PCA form of DNA analysis; always wants the more definitive RFLP, which takes longer. The problem was that the tests hadn't been completed by the time of trial. The RFLP results were ready, however, in time for the sentencing hearing. I take it Mr. Orton didn't mention this to you?"

I couldn't answer him, my mouth was too dry.

"Face it: Orton killed her. Look, Strobe, I gave up working on DNA cases two years ago; it's taking the client's money with no upside possibility. I'll send you my closing bill."

I still couldn't say anything.

"Don't beat yourself up, kid; we all get taken in once in a while."

He hung up. I had not felt so empty, so physically immobilized, since the day my dad died. My body had gone somewhere else. I didn't seem to be breathing.

19

"**W**hy *didn't you tell me?*" I demanded in a loud voice, leaning so close to Darryl Orton in the Soledad visitors center our knees were touching. "And please don't say, 'you didn't ask me.' "

"Chill out, kid," he said, though he looked pretty stressed himself. "What the hell's got into you?"

I don't think I mentioned before that in the center of the open visitors area at Soledad, up against the inside wall, sits a guard on a raised platform. I realized he was staring at me like he was getting ready to make a move. I decided I'd better "chill out."

The guard looked away, and Darryl and I lapsed into silence. I slumped forward, my hands clasped together, elbows on knees.

"The DNA," I said finally. "You didn't tell me."

Darryl met my eyes, gave his head a quick shake, and then looked away. While I waited for him to say something, I noticed he had lost more weight. His eyes seemed dull, glazed-over. A muscle danced under the skin stretched tight across his jaw.

"I trusted you, Darryl. More than that, you'd come to represent something I could count on in this fucked-up world."

Darryl smiled a little and said, "The nobility of the poor and downtrodden."

"This is not funny, Darryl. You owe me an answer."

"Okay, kid, I'll give you two of 'em. First, I figured you had my damn file, fact is you *told* me you did."

"It wasn't *in* the trial transcript, Darryl. The DNA only came out later, at the sentencing hearing."

"Well, excuse me all to hell for not guessing at all the things you didn't know."

I felt my anger beginning to drift. The old bastard had every right to assume I knew all the evidence against him.

"Second," he continued, "how am I supposed to know how they rigged up somethin like DNA? You're the goddamn people's lawyer. *You* figure it out."

"You can't rig DNA, Darryl. It's science."

"Yeah, I know. I've been through the Ds, remember?" He stood up. "Well, what the hell, now that my own lawyer has found me guilty, I guess we can forget about the new trial."

"I just need to—"

"Fact is, I'm up to the Js in the encyclopedia. Do you know what a jackass is, kid?"

"Sure, it's an undomesticated male donkey."

"That's real good, country boy. Mate that ass with a mare, you get a stubborn mule, which you sometimes have to hurt just to get him movin." He put a fist in my face and added, "So get movin, kid, before you get hurt."

I could feel Darryl's anger, but there was despair there, too, so I tried to stay cool. I glanced sideways to see if a guard was paying attention to us.

"I'm not quitting on you, Darryl."

"Hell, you quit the minute you heard that DNA bullshit. So screw you, kid, I'll take my chances on parole."

I met his hard gaze. "Listen up, Darryl, I've done some checking on that. There are twenty-two thousand guys in the California system with fifteen- and twenty-five-to-life sentences like yours presently up for parole. Guess how many of them got parole dates set in 1999."

He ignored me.

"I'll tell you anyway. One."

"One thousand?"

"One person, Darryl. The parole board reviewed 1,942 cases in 1999 and set sixteen for parole dates."

"Sixteen? What happened to the other fifteen?"

"The governor rescinded ten outright and sent the rest back to the Board for reconsideration. He's got the last word, and the nine fat cats on the Board who get paid $95,859 a year got the message. They rescinded four out of the six that was left, put one on hold, and let one stand. The governor can boot their asses if they don't play his tune."

"Which is?" he asked.

"Which is that it's not good politics to let you wild-eyed murderers back out on the streets once you're caged. Ask a guy named Michael Dukakis about a prisoner named Willie Horton."

Darryl grunted something and turned to walk away.

"Hold on, Darryl," I said, jumping up. "I'm saying that a new trial is your only shot at getting out of here."

He started walking.

"Where are you going?"

"Away from you. Back to the safety of my cell."

"Wait up, Darryl, I'm sorry, really, but my whole damn moral compass is spinning over this DNA thing. The least you can do is give me a while to let it all sink in."

He came back and leaned down close to me. "I don't know about your broke compass, but let me ask *you* somethin. Did you believe I was innocent?"

"Yes."

"Well, I'm the same guy you believed in before, dammit! I ain't changed one bit, for better or worse. But I reckon that's too much for a smart guy like you to figure out."

I got to my feet, jammed hands deep in my pockets. "Jesus, Darryl, I said I was sorry—"

"Want some advice, kid?"

I shook my head.

"Well, here it is anyway. Go back to your law firm. Get yourself a nice girl. Buy a house with a two-car garage. Have a couple a' kids." He straightened and added, "And forget you ever knew me."

I looked at him through dampening eyes, out of words.

"Shouldn't be too hard, kid, 'cause you never really did."

"Shit, Darryl—"

"Go on, get the hell out of here. Go find some other ambulance to chase; I'm wore out from runnin away from the likes of you and your bright ideas."

I was not sure how he had ended up being the angry one, but the man was sorely pissed. Or was he driving me away because I'd crushed the fragile seed of hope I'd finally nurtured in him?

"Listen, Darryl. I'm going through some difficult shit myself presently."

"Well, let me see if I can get a counselor over here."

"I'm not quitting," I said, ignoring his sarcasm. "There's a loophole in an otherwise stacked system that says you're entitled to the presumption of innocence and legal representation whether guilty or innocent; DNA or no DNA. Besides, I owe you, and you're my friend. So I'll keep trying—"

"Three reasons you won't: First, I got no more faith in the so-called system than you do. My misplaced faith was in you, kid, not some goddamn system, and you haven't even decided which side you're on. Second, you don't owe me nothin and never did. Third, as for bein your friend, I got no friends, least of all some goddamn lawyer who can't read a transcript. You want a friend, buy yourself another dog. You're fired, counselor, so go on; get the hell out of here!"

*   *   *

I drove back to San Francisco through a heavy downpour, awash in confusion. Darryl had become more than someone I owed, even more than a friend. Though he had joked about it, he had emerged as a kind of symbol to me; his travail—along with my dad's—had justified the life I was determined to commit myself to.

I tried to clear my head. Was he innocent? Was he guilty? As a lawyer, was I even supposed to ask the question? Or even give a damn under our system?

Christ, Dad, could you spare a little inspiration here?

I kicked my Ford Probe into second to pass some guy going fifty on the two-lane part of 101. I fishtailed as I hit deep water pooled on the on-coming roadway, but the car brought itself under control, and I slowed to sixty. My heart was still pounding twice that when I hit Salinas.

I found Mace in the library of Stanton and Snow, not an easy mat-ter, as the room was only slightly smaller than the entire Enid Public Library I had frequented as a boy looking up do-it-yourself tricks. He was in a carrel preparing for a motion he was arguing that same af-ternoon and wasn't happy about being interrupted.

"Tracked me down like a dog, didn't you, cowboy?" he said with-out looking up. "Speak and be gone."

"Listen, Mace, I need to ask your advice on something that only a hot young trial lawyer like yourself would know about. So be nice for a minute or I'll hit you."

"Flattery and threats will get you one quick answer to one quick question."

"How scientifically pure is DNA evidence?"

"Look in the dictionary under 'driven snow.' "

"What I thought," I said, noticing his reading light was sputtering. "Okay, say you wanted to frame somebody, how could it be faked?"

"That's a second question."

"Indulge me, or I'll take that book you're reading and shove it up your bony homesick ass."

"And a second threat. Okay. The answer is I don't know. Seriously, Billy, it can't be done."

He pretended to go back to his book, squinting, and bent over, but I knew he could feel my eyes on him. Then he straightened, looked at me, and said, *"What?"*

"Couldn't the lab get DNA mixed up or contaminated or whatever bullshit defense O.J. used?"

"Possible, but you'd never prove it. The only good thing that came out of the Simpson trial was that San Francisco and other jurisdictions cleaned up their labs." He gave the reading light a slap. It kept blinking.

"How about planting someone's DNA on the victim's body?"

He shook his head. "Possible, I guess, but the framer would have to know the framee well enough to cannibalize some DNA first."

"Your reading light is shorting out," I said.

"I wondered about that."

I took out my Swiss army knife and opened the blade, which Mace eyeballed, and he said, "I know you didn't like my answer, but don't you think stabbing me here in the library is a little excessive?"

I unplugged his lamp, pulled it apart, stripped the end of the wire to ensure contact, and retightened the screw. "That'll fix it," I said.

Mace looked impressed and thanked me. "About the DNA," he said, "if you're thinking of framing Ashton, don't bother. I can get you a dozen associates who would be glad to kill him for you outright."

"I'll consider that," I said.

Back in my office, I took stock of what I knew so far. Suzy Threadgill had lied, which she had no motive to do unless Frank Hinton had put her up to it. Add to that the argument Mildred Moon had overheard between Deborah Hinton and Frank just hours before her death and the fact that she was pregnant, maybe by her boss. Husbands, even ex-husbands, can't much like the thought of that sort of thing going on. So Frank Hinton, though feeling cuckolded, is suddenly consoled by 500K in insurance money as a result of Deborah's demise. He remains a suspect.

Then what about Deborah Hinton's deferred write-off? Was it a mere coincidence that she was murdered in the wake of the SEC investigation? And what was up with Jason Moncrief, who also took profits from Deborah's manipulation of Synoptics earnings, who was "always with Deborah" according to Mildred Moon, who Mildred had seen entering the building when she left work that night asking if Deborah was "still upstairs," and who S & S was sheltering under a cloak of silence?

And what had happened to the TechnoCenter Building log for the night of the murder? Just another coincidence? And who was Deborah Hinton's mystery boyfriend, the guy Mildred Moon had heard her arguing with on the telephone for days, leading up to hours before her murder? Damn sure wasn't the janitor, but who was it? Could it have been Moncrief himself? There was something I was missing here—something both simple and important—but when I'd try to grab at it, the damn thing would slip out of my grasp like a greased pig. I kept thinking it was something to do with those phone calls that Mildred had heard but Klinehart couldn't track down.

20

Sitting in my office the next day, I fell to thinking about Dad's case and decided to call Judge Ryan, who had presided at Dad's trial and was obviously upset by the verdict. I called the Enid Superior Court and asked for the judge.

"I'm sorry to tell you," the clerk said, not sounding sorry at all, other than about being interrupted, "that the judge died quite some years ago." While I was trying to think of what to say next, he repeated that he was sorry and hung up.

I called back and got the same impatient voice on the phone. I asked if the judge's clerk was still alive. He was again sorry to tell me that the clerk, Brandon Gettleman, had passed away a year after the judge's untimely demise.

"By untimely, do you mean he died in an accident?"

"Yeah, 'accident,'" he said, and his tone had evolved from impatient to snide. "He accidentally pulled the trigger of his .12-gauge shotgun while cleaning it after accidentally putting the barrel in his mouth. Look, sir, I've got about twenty people here, so I hope—"

My turn to hang up. I wondered if Judge Ryan might have left a widow and if so, whether he might have confided to her his misgivings about the verdict. I wasn't sure where it would lead me, but I called Lisa and asked her to do some detective work for me.

I then turned back to looking at the draft of a client's buy-sell agreement all morning without really seeing it when my scattered thoughts were interrupted by the phone. A single ring, meaning an inside call. Two rings meant the call originated from the outside, and my secretary would pick it up. If she felt like it.

"Strobe? Rex Ashton here."

It wasn't a long conversation, but by the time we hung up, I knew I'd be sleeping in the office again tonight. Most S & S associates kept clean shirts and airline shaving kits in their offices and there were cots in the staff lounge where you could grab an hour or two.

I was trying to focus my attention back on the draft agreement I

had been looking at but not seeing when the thing I'd been missing hit
me like a twister slamming into the side of a silo.

One ring. Two rings. Christ, there it was! How had we all missed
it? The reason there were no company or personal cell phone records
of Deborah Hinton's numerous arguments overheard by Mildred
Moon was because they were on her *inside* line! This meant that the
mystery boyfriend who had impregnated her and who she was fighting
with on the phone *worked at Synoptics.* And, I was willing to bet,
chaired its board of directors.

"Mildred? Hi, it's Billy Strobe. Remember me?"

Even on the phone, there was a wariness in her voice as she allowed
she did remember me. I could picture her big round eyes nervously
darting from side to side in her big round face.

"Listen, Mildred. I'm coming down there in a few minutes, and I
need some information out of the computer Deborah Hinton used. Is
it still around?"

It was a long shot, but worth a try. If I could find it, there are nerds
out there who could resurrect deleted e-mail messages like Jesus raising Lazurus. I held my breath.

"Mr. Strobe, that computer has been gone for years."

"Do you know where it went?"

"I have no idea, Mr. Strobe. It had been taken away by the time I
arrived for work the morning after Deborah's . . ."

"Taken away? That very morning?"

"Monitor, printer, everything."

"Did the police say it was for evidence?"

"It wasn't the police that took it," she said. "They already had their
suspect, remember?"

"Then who took it?"

"Didn't Mr. Moncrief tell you?"

"I must have forgotten, Mildred. Tell me *what*?"

"He took it away himself. James said he saw him trying to lift the
heavy monitor around six a.m. and gave him a hand."

"James?"

"He's one of our night shift word-processing people."

But I wasn't listening to her anymore. I was listening to the voice of
a friend from two days earlier.

I'm the same guy you believed in before.

I hung up the phone, feeling that old rush of electricity up my spine.
I was back up to two suspects in the murder of Deborah Hinton. That
was the good news. The bad news was that while proving a case

against Frank Hinton had been a battle, taking on Jason Moncrief would be a war, a nuclear holocaust.

People could get hurt.

I stayed in the office until three in the morning, then tried a final search of Ashton's, Hale's, and Dana's offices for the Securities Exchange Commission's investigation files. Nothing. The next morning, I called Andrea, head of the file department. I knew that questioning her might get back to Ashton, so I had been putting it off. Now I had to act.

"I've been looking for the Synoptics SEC investigation files for a couple of weeks, Andrea," I said, sounding casual, even bored. "They're not in the Synoptics file area."

"Hold on, let me check that," Andrea said. "Ah, here it is. The log entry says I was instructed by Mr. Ashton to send all those files down to the sixteenth floor."

"Good. Is that where closed files are held?"

"No, Mr. Strobe," she said patiently. "That's where the firm's shredder is."

As I walked toward Dana's office, I wondered if I was going back to the well too soon and once too often. Pressing my luck. But, I had to have the answer to a question only she might be willing to give me.

She was rising from her desk as I walked in, wearing a skirt for a change in deference to the warm, late summer day outside. I had only seen her legs twice before, and could almost understand her decision to keep them covered most of the time. They drew the kind of attention she didn't want: long, thin, and well-toned, tapering down to trim ankles. Showstoppers.

I rapped on her doorjamb. "Got a minute?"

"Why, you want to look out my window again?"

That was a joke; the long-awaited single window that looked straight into the brick facade of the building next door. Office assignments fell under Rex Ashton's domain, and this was a subtle slap at Hale's ingenue.

"No," I said. "I need to ask you why Ashton shredded all the records surrounding the SEC investigation of Jason Moncrief and Deborah Hinton."

She gave her head an impatient little shake; then her lips parted as if to say something. But she just stood there, arms folded under her small breasts.

"I'd also like to know why you didn't tell me the files had been destroyed."

"Look, Billy, I'm very busy, so please, let's not go through this again."

"Destroying those files left a trail of smoke. I'm looking for the fire."

Dana slowly rotated her head from side to side. "What's with you, Billy Strobe? Don't you have enough to do around here?"

"Oh, I've got plenty to do," I said, suddenly angry—angry at Ashton, at Moncrief, at Dana, but mostly at myself. "I'm busy dealing all kinds of grand and lusty blows for justice and the good of mankind. I'm working with Ashton on an initial public offering for a bullshit Internet company investors will gobble up though it hasn't made one dollar of profit in its four years of operation. By the time that one crashes, you, Hale, and I will probably have kept Paul Dexter out of prison so he can enjoy the under-the-table bribery cash he's probably raked off the top and stashed in an offshore numbered account. I'm also helping Ashton on a hostile takeover that will put four hundred and fifty people out of work when our client breaks up the company and sells off the pieces at a huge profit."

"Nobody's encouraging you to break the law around here, Billy."

"You sound like Vince Lombardi."

"Who?"

"Green Bay Packers coach, my dad's hero. He used to say, 'We bend, but we don't break.' We don't actually break the law here at good old S & S, Dana, we just bend it."

I reckon it was months of frustration that had set off this sanctimonious tirade, but I couldn't stop myself. Maybe I needed to know where this woman stood, once and for all.

"And to make sure the worker bees all feel good about the process, 'Here's a raise to a hundred twenty-five thousand dollars, kids, plus a twenty K bonus, so you won't ask too many questions.' Isn't that about it, Dana? Well, fuck it, there's got to be more to the law profession than this."

Dana's eyes narrowed with irritation. "There's plenty to do around here for anyone willing to work within the system instead of always looking for problems. Are you aware that this firm does several hundred hours of *pro bono* work for the poor every year? Or that the firm supported me to the tune of six hundred seventy-five thousand dollars' worth of time and costs to get just one man off death row during 1998 and 1999? And when it came time to argue the matter to the California Supreme Court, can you guess who stepped forward to handle it and spent a week of his vacation in preparation for the hearing?"

She didn't have to tell me it was Hale.

"But you hold yourself above the mere ebb and flow of commerce, right, Saint Billy? You'd rather spend time bitching about things you don't understand."

The woman had worked up a lather. "Tell me what I don't understand," I said.

"You want an example? Let's take the Hinton SEC probe you're so obsessed with. You apparently don't know that it's the standard practice of this and plenty of other firms that when the SEC closes its file on an informal investigation, the law firm's files are shredded to prevent a possible prejudicial disclosure to the public. *It's the way it's done, Billy.*"

I nodded, looking interested but noncommittal to mask my uneasiness at being lectured to. Being around Dana sometimes made me feel as awkward as a dog on a bike.

"There *is* no fire, Billy, there's not even any smoke! And by the way, the files were shredded, not burned. Your metaphors are as mixed as your obsessions. It's time you faced the facts: There is no evidence Orton was framed, and plenty of circumstantial evidence he wasn't."

And she doesn't even know about the DNA, I thought.

"So get over it, Billy, or Hale won't be able to keep them from running you out of here. You may not know it, but the firm has had financial problems—exacerbated by these large raises you accept and then complain about—which means the partners can't afford to get crosswise with Synoptics."

"And you can't afford to get crosswise with the partners," I said, needled by that raise remark. "You might fall off that fast-track carrying you toward a two-million-dollar-a-year income, right?"

Her eyes sparked, and as she leaned in close to me, I wished I could take the words back. "I'll work with you, Billy," she said, "because it's my job. Outside of that, I want nothing more to do with you."

"I'm just trying to make a point here—"

"You're trying to judge me," she said, tears of anger welling up in her eyes. "And you haven't earned the right."

I stared at her, but she had turned away, walked over to her window, and stood looking out at the wall next door, her arms folded again. My heart was already heavy with shame and regret. Who the hell was I to be judging anybody, let alone a single working mother, who had done nothing but accomplish what most every young lawyer in America aspired to? Maybe I had been justified in my suspicion of Dana for not telling me the files had been shredded, but now I was the one staring into the harsh light of judgment.

I retreated to my office, uneasy and tired, to commence work on an overdue new IPO assignment from Ashton. I tried to keep my mind on the financial projections in front of me but the pages blurred as my mind swirled with high-frequency confusion and ran the gamut of emotions from remorse about Dana, to concern about Hale, to suspicion about Moncrief and Frank Hinton, to hatred about Amos Blackwell, to guilt about Darryl, Lisa and Amy Strobe, and half the free world. I slammed the file shut at seven o'clock, packed my briefcase, and headed for Aqua for a quick beer on my way home to a frozen dinner and, I hoped, a clearer head.

I want nothing more to do with you.

I couldn't help but look around the bar for Dana, though I knew she wouldn't be there. I pictured her driving home from Sarah's day-care provider, the tyke belted into a carseat in back beside a briefcase full of work for Mom to tackle after she had fed and read to her darling. My heart ached every time I thought about Dana, and I didn't know whether it was guilt for the way I had acted or regret for having blown any remote possibility of a relationship with her. Is that what I'd really wanted? To be involved with a silver-spoon, by-the-book, Montgomery Street lawyer who probably spent her free time riding purebred show horses down at Woodside? Jesus, man, get a grip.

My eyes swept the bar. No Mace either, only a couple of associates I'd seen around and a bunch of other yuppies and Gen-Xers. I realized I felt lonely and even more out of place than usual, my spirits sinking lower than a snake's belly. I decided to drink and run, when I noticed an attractive girl halfway down the bar sitting with another woman. The pretty one seemed to be looking at me, though it was hard to tell because she wore sunglasses. Definitely kinky-pretty with short blond hair, almost a buzz cut, definitely different-looking, but undeniably sexy.

I looked around to make sure she hadn't been smiling at someone else, but there was nobody near me. The next time I caught her eye, I gave her a friendly smile, which she returned with one that knocked my socks off. But now what?

I suppose I could blame prison for getting me out of practice approaching girls, but truth is, I'd never been any good in bars. Even now, I felt stupid standing there by myself, so I looked at my watch like I was expecting someone.

The next time we exchanged smiles, she held up her glass in a mock toast. That did it. I walked over and said hello.

She said hello back, and we all exchanged names. Hers was Betty Perkins. The friend's name was Sandra Esquival. They should have switched names. Betty Perkins had an exotic, mysterious face, while Sandra looked as plain as a postal clerk.

"Strobe?" Betty said, her head tilted, giving me a mock-dubious smile. "That's incredibly polychromatic."

"It's what?"

"Prismatic, glowing, spectral, mysterious."

"I'm as mysterious as a hoehandle."

Sandra touched my arm, saying, "And as hard?" Which sent her into spasms of laughter.

"Ignore her," Betty said, and raised her sunglasses long enough to give me a glance that reached right down and grabbed my balls. I'd never seen a more wanton expression on a good-looking woman. "She meant that you appear to keep yourself in shape. I know this sounds trite, particularly in a bar setting, but what's your sign?"

"She does charts," said Sandra, reading my skeptical look. "I didn't believe all that stuff either, but the one she did for me, well, I'm telling you, it was me all *over.*"

We bantered a while, long enough I reckon for Sandra to judge that I wasn't a deranged slasher; then she took off.

"Was it something I said?"

"No," Betty said, laughing, "she's got to get home to her husband."

"So it's down to us," I said, trying to sound cool. The drink was already hitting me hard, and I was reaching out to this woman like a drowning man.

"Looks like it. Want to take me to dinner? I'll read your palm. Tell your future."

"Will it tell me if I'm going to get lucky?"

She gave me that sexy smile and said, "With your looks, you don't need luck. Let's get out of here."

Betty Perkins was obviously not saddled with the need for a lot of small talk, which was good because I'd already used up my meager quota.

As I reached down for my briefcase, I caught a glimpse of her fine ankles. One of them had a dime-size rose tatoo on the outside. Yep, this was a unique beauty, a little offbeat maybe, but the first girl I'd met or even seen other than Dana who instantly filled me with desire—plus this one seemed to like me, which may have been unnecessary since she appeared to be hornier than a prisoner.

We walked up to Bix's, had another drink at the bar and split a bottle of wine at the table with dinner. Only when we sat down at the table did she briefly remove her sunglasses to reveal penetrating, deep blue eyes.

I was feeling the booze, but she asked if we could have a brandy after dinner, and I said okay. I didn't think she was drinking to get up the nerve to take me home—she'd apparently read that part of my future the minute I walked up to her at Aqua. I figured she was drinking so she'd have an excuse in the morning for having taken a total stranger home the night before.

An hour later I sat on a bed in her apartment, watching her take off her clothes. She wasn't shy about it, I reckon she knew how gorgeous she was. Her breasts were large, but when her bra released them, they didn't fall a bit, just stood their firm ground above a flat and hard stomach. She had a couple more tattoos—one with several words—but I wasn't paying much heed to them. The last thing to come off was the sunglasses, and then only because I asked. She watched me as I took my clothes off, nodding and cooing with approval, then laughing as I had trouble getting my jockey shorts over Mr. Happy. Then I was on her like an animal. She didn't move much, which surprised me. See a woman this funky and you expect her to be an acrobat. Not that I was disappointed, being a bit old-fashioned myself when it comes to physical coupling. Anyways, we were both a little drunk and the first time with someone is always experimental. I came too fast but she didn't mind and we lay there quiet, me feeling the best I've felt in a long time. That's when I paid attention to what was tattooed under the black rose above her left breast. I traced the words with my finger.

That which nourishes me is killing me.

She laughed at my obvious question and told me it meant whatever I wanted it to mean and suggested we have a cup of coffee. I didn't push her on it.

I lasted much longer the second time with her on top, but she still didn't make it. She didn't fake it, either, though it would have been easy as crazy as I was. She smiled and assured me I was terrific and that she was just "a little bit too tired and drunk." But I suspected there was something else going on, another person in the room, and I wondered if her woman's intuition sensed it, too. Frustrating as it was, Betty's face had kept turning into Dana's.

Just after midnight, I told her I'd better get going and she told me I could stay over. I pleaded an early morning meeting, and she said okay.

At the door she kissed me and said, "You interest me, Billy Strobe, and I insist that you call me." We exchanged numbers, and I promised to call and meant it.

I started down Russian Hill to my apartment, feeling good, still a bit boozy. Betty was a little weird, with her mystical notions, but bright, pretty, and seemed to like me. Okay, she wasn't as gorgeous and witty and frustrating as Dana Mathews, but maybe time would take care of that.

I saw the guy just as I crossed Sacramento Street. I hadn't thought anything about it when I'd come out of Betty's apartment house, but that was three blocks ago, and there he was again, on the other side of Taylor, but definitely following me. Shit, just what I needed in my life, a beef with a jealous lover.

I decided to let him know that I knew he was there, so I stopped and looked straight at him. He ignored me, and I got a good look at him. He was medium height, stocky, swarthy, and mid-forties, with a dark raincoat too long for him. If this was a jealous lover, I didn't have much competition.

He walked on by, turned left at the next corner, and then kept going west on California Street until he was out of sight. I shrugged off my paranoia and continued home without incident, except for stepping in dogshit at the corner of Taylor and Bush.

21

I started down Bush Street toward the financial district the next morning with a light heart despite a heavy, aching head, and a mind still hard-wired to Darryl's case. But then I began fretting again about my last visit to Soledad, thinking about the worm of a muscle twitching in Darryl's jaw and the way his dull winter eyes glazed over when I accused him of holding out on me. I had been afraid to ask if he was still defending his bench, afraid even to wonder if he would survive long enough for my bungling efforts to save him.

I was also slacking on the case of State vs. Joseph Strobe, but what limited time I could steal from Ashton's projects had to go to the guy still alive. Darryl was on a deadline with death, and a few more weeks' delay wouldn't matter to Dad.

I suddenly realized that it would matter to me. So I punched in Lisa's number on my cell phone, heard her answer, and said, "Any luck finding Judge Ryan's widow?"

"And hello to you, Mr. Congeniality."

"Sorry, sis," I said, and she told me that Mrs. Ryan was currently living with her sister and brother-in-law in Beaumont, Texas.

"I've talked with her twice," Lisa said, "the first time on the phone." She paused to let the implication sink in.

"The second time at her home?"

"Sure," she said, and I could hear the pride in her voice. She had left the house, taken a bus to Beaumont on her own.

"That's terrific, brat. She have anything?"

"She said the judge never mentioned anything about the trial, or anyone else connected with it, but was never himself afterward."

"How long afterward did he kill himself?"

"About six months after the trial. He wouldn't discuss the case with her or why it had so depressed him."

"Never mentioned Joe Strobe? Or the verdict?"

"Not a word, though she knew it was eating him up. You want to talk to her?"

She was testing my confidence in her. "No point in it," I said, and could imagine her blushing with pleasure.

I sent her love, signed off, and my thoughts trailed back to Darryl. Although I was stumped on coming up with evidence sufficient to gain Darryl a new trial, my unconfirmed suspicions about both Frank Hinton and Jason Moncrief were building. Time to take inventory.

Hinton was still my number one suspect. Involuntarily estranged from Deborah, their legendary fights had intensified when she became pregnant by another man. Then there were those other 500,000 reasons for him to kill her, thanks to a double indemnity clause. Most important, he had undoubtedly bribed, cajoled, or threatened Suzy Threadgill into providing a false alibi, hardly the conduct of an innocent man. Threadgill was ready to break, and I'd use a wire on her next time.

Jason Moncrief remained a distant second candidate, mainly because his guilt required a bucketful of inferences. If, for example, he and Deborah Hinton were in cahoots on the insider trading fraud, and it was Moncrief who got her to defer the write-off, then I could imagine him getting pissed when she got greedy and traded some stock of her own during the swings she had set in motion, drawing the attention of the SEC down on both of them. Once that happened, what if he not only became angry, but also got concerned she would rat him out? Hadn't he asked Mildred the day of Deborah's murder if she was still up in her office?

And what if old Jason was Deborah Hinton's secret boyfriend? Those arguments she had with mystery boyfriend were on an inside phone, and he being married would explain why she had to keep him a secret. Might the distinguished CEO, husband, and parent have learned he was about to be a papa again? Might Deborah have balked at the notion of an abortion?

Finally, who had made money on Deborah's improper deferral *and,* before business hours, personally hustled the victim's computer out of the clutches of nosy homicide investigators who might have been interested in romantic e-mails, drafts of love letters, perhaps even details of the stock scam? So Moncrief was still a dark horse candidate.

Like I say, lots of *ifs* on both these guys—but if I played both bets to the limit, maybe I'd come up lucky with one of them. I remember Dad telling friends once that I was so lucky, if you threw me in the ocean, I'd come up with a fish in my mouth.

I also had to keep a third potential suspect in mind: the real boyfriend-impregnator if it *wasn't* Moncrief. I knew nothing about this candidate other than that he probably worked inside Synoptics and probably *wasn't* Paul Dexter, a dull, chinless wonder whose hair was cut by his wife with duck shears.

To complete the picture, I forced one more question out of myself: Where did Dana fit into all this? I stopped walking for a second. Did it make sense for her to have been so damn secretive about the SEC matter, while at the same time discouraging me every step of the way from helping Darryl? Had she been playing good cop to Ashton's bad cop? How far were these people, maybe including Hale, willing to go to protect Jason Moncrief, the firm's top client?

Last, but not least, had I dropped my guard with Dana Mathews too often and forgotten the prison code?

Don't Trust Nobody.

I realized I had stopped in front of the Bush Street male porn theater and had gathered a small but enthusiastic group of admirers. I started walking again.

All this thinking was making my headache worse, so I stopped at Peet's for a double espresso and popped two more aspirin. Then up the elevator to my office where, as usual, my message light was blinking. The last one was from Hale, wanting to see me, so I caught another elevator up to the top floor.

I didn't see him at first when I entered his office; then I spotted him over in his conference area, sitting alone with a cup of coffee in his hand. The shades were drawn, and a bottle of open brandy was on the small bar. I'd never seen him alone in his conference area, let alone with spiked coffee in his hand with the shades drawn at 7:30 A.M.

"We need to talk, Billy," he said. I came closer and saw that the

man looked plumb wore out. His face was pale, and I thought I
smelled stale cigarette smoke. He didn't offer me coffee, spiked or otherwise.

"Yes, sir?"

"Rex tells me you're running behind on projects again. I've also
heard that you have retained a private investigator named Barnard
Klinehart."

"True and true, sir," I said, my legs suddenly heavy with anxiety.
Had I mentioned Barney to Dana?

"Is he looking into the Hinton murder?"

"Yes, sir, he is. Was. That is, Mr. Klinehart no longer works for me.
His work is finished." I hated lies, even half-truths like this little
corker, but I couldn't let everything end now, not before I could get
back into Synoptics.

As my eyes adjusted to the half-light, my heart grew heavier than
my legs. The lines on Hale's face had deepened into grooves overnight,
and his broad shoulders sagged forward. I asked myself how it got to
a point where to save one friend from death, I had to jeopardize another friend's distinguished career. It wasn't fair; Hale was supposed to
have been a money-grubbing asshole. Then it would have been easy.

"Good," he said, his voice a tired croak. "Then I can report to the
executive committee that he *and* you are finished with whatever the
hell it was you were doing?"

What could I say? So I said it. "Yes, sir."

"Excellent," he said, staring into his cup. "Then perhaps you are
now free to explain this obsession with the Hinton matter, particularly
given your knowledge of the client's sensitivities on the subject?"

"Well, sir, I was under the impression we were encouraged to par-
ticipate in *pro bono publico* work on our own free time."

"Yes, but through the *firm's* program." He rose, poured himself
some plain coffee, and commenced to pace around the room. "I have
to go along with Rex on this one, Billy. We cannot have our associates
running around willy-nilly, moonlighting on their own, can we? Particularly in the criminal defense area, where we have no experience
outside of white collar. Splashing around in alien waters like that could
put our malpractice insurance at risk."

"I understand, sir."

"It pains me to tell you this, son, but Rex Ashton and Malcomb
Wilcox are ready to let you go. For the present, you're on probation."

I doubted there were any other associates on Montgomery Street on
both probation and parole. I took a deep breath, tried to stay calm.
"Yes, sir, and thank you."

I looked at my mentor. God knows what it was going to cost him in next year's presiding partner election to have vetoed Ashton's attempt to fire me outright. I wished I could offer my resignation to spare him further embarrassment, but where would that put Darryl Orton? And Amy and Lisa Strobe?

"Do you understand, Billy? It's two strikes."

"I do, sir," I said, my stomach churning again, spin cycle. "I also understand that Mr. Ashton has been throwing me nothing but curve balls."

He sat down again and slowly nodded. I noticed one of his shoe-strings was untied, but didn't say anything. I stood.

"I won't let you down, sir," I said. "I want to make it here."

"I want you to, Billy. More than you could possibly know."

I knew. Hale Lassiter, the firm's leader and one of the deans of the San Francisco bar, was also standing at the plate with two strikes against him.

I'd have to move even faster, and from this day forward, I would trust nobody, not Dana, not even Klinehart. I was on my own.

22

I spent the next few weeks catching up on some of Ashton's projects, forcing myself to cool it with Darryl's motion for new trial. To throw the wolves off the scent, I followed up on some additional exhibit requests in Joe Strobe's case and called Lisa to see how she was doing on Dad's attic papers.

"There's nothing up there even remotely connected to his trial, Billy," she told me after we'd caught up on the usual health issues.

"Bullshit, Lisa," I shouted into the receiver, "he was *pro per,* for Christ's sake! The case files *have* to be up there."

"I don't even know what a *pro per* is, Billy Strobe, and I hope you treat your other secretaries with more courtesy," Lisa said. "Snapping at the messenger won't produce files that don't exist."

I stared at the receiver, hating the distance that separated me from that attic, hating my own impatience with Lisa. "I'm sorry, sis. *Propia persona* means he represented himself in his criminal trial, which is why I was so sure they'd be there with the rest of his case files."

"I've looked through everything twice, Billy," Lisa was saying.

"I know, brat, but every trial lawyer has case files, even Dad."

"Unless," came Lisa's voice, "he destroyed them, before . . ."

Before he destroyed himself, I could have finished for her. But why would he do that?

"What about the Jed Sanborn file," I asked, "the earlier case he won by allegedly forging a key exhibit?"

"That's missing, too. Look, Billy, he didn't want to be remembered by either trial."

She had a point. I felt it all slipping away, but I couldn't give up. "How about general correspondence files, unfiled letters or documents, anything toward the end that mentioned Sanborn or Blackwell?"

"I didn't see anything like that."

"Or Judge Charles Ryan?"

"No."

I phrased the next thing as carefully as I could. "Would you be willing to take another go at it, Lisa? I know it's no fun up there, and I know you've been typically thorough, but—"

"Your style is improving, Atilla. I'd give you a six on that one."

"Did you factor in the degree of difficulty?"

"Now you're saying I'm difficult? Make that a four with a bullet heading south, but yeah, I'll give it another look."

"I love you, brat," I said, hoping to conceal my disappointment.

"Hugs, Billy."

Where could he have kept them? True, Dad was a lawyer who relied more on sharp, spontaneous wit than on tight organization and zealous trial preparation. I assumed this because he had strong opinions on organization like he did on most everything. I remember Ma ragging him one morning—I was nine or ten—about the way he was always starting projects, but rarely finishing them.

"Unless," she added, "the project at hand happens to be pouring yourself a stiff one."

"What are you talking about, woman?" he retorted in his typical style with a wink at me over her shoulder. "How about last night?" he added, as he gave her a kiss and a firm pat on the butt. "Seemed to me that little project was completed to your deep satisfaction."

"Shush, Joseph," she said, blushing as she secured the top button on his shirt and straightened his tie. "Here's exhibit A: Getting yourself dressed properly. Face it, dear, you're not an organized man."

"Ants are organized," he said, flashing me another wink and a smile. "But that doesn't keep them from getting stepped on."

I smiled back at him, for Ma was always at me, too, for not picking up my things and me and Dad had formed an unholy alliance on the issue that filled me with guilty pleasure. Lord knows I loved Ma and wanted her approval, but not like I needed Dad's.

"I'm not meaning you're to be sloppy in the conduct of your affairs, son," he told me after Ma had gone off to the kitchen. "I'm meaning it's a matter of priorities and moderation. Hell, one of the reasons James Joyce got himself thrown out of Oliver Saint John Gogarty's tower in Sandy Cove was because he wasn't keeping his things in order, and he damn well turned out all right. The important 'organization' is that of your *mind*, lad, and your *soul*—not your underpants."

"But how do I organize my soul, Dad? I don't even know where it is."

"Simple," he told me, smiling as he rested his warm hand on my shoulder. "Always follow the truth, no matter where it leads you, and be good to people in need. You'll see your soul shining back at you in their eyes."

He made it sound simple, and maybe it would have been if he'd stuck around.

I snapped out of my bleak reverie and called Betty to ask her out for Saturday night. All work and no play, I told myself. It would be our fourth date in as many weeks and we seemed to be moving cautiously toward something like a relationship. Betty was being careful, too, and I wondered if she was also trying to forget someone.

She asked if we could go to a tiny restaurant in the Muir Beach area called the Pelican Inn. I had been wanting to visit Inverness and Bolinas, so we made a day of it, even caught some late afternoon rays at Stinson Beach.

As I've mentioned, Betty had a radical streak, with her sunglasses (violet-tinted), tatoos (ankle and left breast) and buzz-cut hair. She was heavy into mysticism, too, but never laid any of her trips on me. She was a good listener, fascinated by everything I had done in my life. She enjoyed hearing about my youth in Enid, my dad, my plans to clear his name, even my prison experiences. I soon found myself opening up, in general terms, about my hopes for an unnamed prisoner at Soledad.

"He sounds like an evolved soul," she said. "But it also sounds as if you're taking a great risk. Professionally, I mean. This would be very unwise now with the moon in Scorpio."

"He risked his life to save me," I said, tuning out her astrological forecast, and she leaned close and kissed me, gently, lovingly, like a friend.

"I have a favor," she whispered, her lips touching my ear. We had spread a blanket out on the beach, and lay there watching the dying sun.

"Name it." I tried to turn to face her, but she held my head still so that I couldn't see her eyes. "Unless it involves getting a tattoo on my dick or going to your séance group."

"Just try . . . ," she said, ignoring my cynicism like she always did. I noticed a catch in her voice. "Try not to let me fall in love with you."

I said nothing. What do you say to something like that?

"And don't," she added, "even think about falling in love with me."

I was holding her hand, and gave it an ambiguous squeeze. The truth was, even though I knew next to nothing about Betty Perkins, I had been sort of trying to talk myself into falling in love her. But the main feeling I had for Betty was more like gratitude than love. I think she might have sensed this, because of the way she was still holding herself back sexually. But whatever happened between us, I knew I'd never forget her. Quirky as she was, Betty was providing a bridge for me to crawl across back into some kind of normal life, and I cared for her a lot.

Later that same day, at dinner, her own story finally began to come out. She had no family, and though she sometimes mentioned female friends she was doing things with, I had never met any of them other than Sandra dingbat at the bar that first day, and wasn't sure I even believed she had any real friends. She had been an office administrator for a small dot-com company in Silicon Valley until she developed Epstein-Barr—chronic fatigue syndrome—and, thanks to stock options and state disability, she would never have to work again. The problem was she would also never know when she'd be hit with devastating flulike symptoms and be confined to her bed. She complained a lot about her health, but how could I blame her, not having walked in her shoes.

One thing for sure, she always looked great, which she attributed to long naps every afternoon, tai chi, herbs with funny names like alba and sinensis, ginseng, and chai tea that smelled of mildewed oak bark, and "great sex every weekend."

She was right about the sex, though I was still slipping into fantasies of Dana, and she still seemed somewhat detached when we were doing it. I stayed over at her condo that night after dinner at the Pelican and we fucked in every room of her apartment except for her walk-in closet because that's where she kept her bicycle. Sunday morning, she made breakfast for me, including grits for her "Okie boyfriend," which I dutifully ate to please her. We took a walk all the way up to Coit Tower on Telegraph hill, which has got to be one of the most beautiful views in the world. She made it up to the plateau with only two stops for rest. I stood beside this pretty girl, her arm resting on my shoulder, watching sailboats bobbing around the Bay on quiet waters, presided over by a warming sun and a soft, white-flecked sky.

And I asked myself why I wasn't happy.

23

The next few days were the hardest months of my life, including the time I'd spent in prison. Ashton was out to break me, and he had a couple of partners helping him, mainly his flunky Wilcox in probate. Hale's hands were tied, but he helped indirectly by freeing me from all his assignments and even providing me with paralegal support. I was billing sixty hours a week, which meant I was working seventy-five, and keeping three paralegals and two secretaries on the run. I was running, too—running on empty. But despite my killer schedule, Betty Perkins and I added a weeknight at my place into our schedule, and I began spending the whole weekend at hers. I liked being in her Russian Hill apartment for a change. It was neat, orderly, and full of sunlight. I even got used to the crystals hanging everywhere, the "pyramid of energy" over her bed with it's magnetic mattress, and some of the strangest artwork I'd ever seen.

I began to look forward to those weekends, just Betty, me, her astrological charts, and my stack of office files. She didn't seem to mind that I was working most of the time. Fact is, she was usually too chronically fatigued to go out, which was fine with me. We did take in a George Jones concert at the Masonic one night. Old George was better than ever, not only somehow still alive, but apparently sober as well. Betty liked it so much we went a couple of weeks later up to Konecti Harbor to see Merle Haggard, who was without his keyboard man and backup lady and seemed pissed at the crowd giving him a bad time. It got a little nasty in fact, but Betty seemed to like that part. She also liked that it was an out-of-the-way place, concerned I guess that her ex-bosses would think ill of her, drawing disability, yet being out on the town.

Meanwhile, I kept accumulating documentation from the Enid County Courthouse. Betty was a great help with the correspondence and red tape, relieved to have something to do with her time.

I continued to worry about Darryl's case, but was too burnt out to come up with any ideas, and it was eating me up. I scared the hell out of Betty a few times, thrashing and shouting in my sleep, then waking up drowning in sweat, my skin cold as death, shouting things she couldn't understand. She'd soothe me, urge me to give up on Darryl before I worried myself into sickness.

My team contacts at S & S with Dana were hard on my heart, but I never let her see it. Once bitten, twice warned. Then one day after a meeting with Hale on a major IPO, she stopped me in the hallway on the way out.

"Billy, are you okay?"

"Why?" I said, feeling instantly defensive. "Did I say something wrong in there?"

She gave her head a quick shake and said, "You were perfect, as always. It's just that you look exhausted. I know what Ashton is up to, Billy, but you've got to ease up. Nobody can take what you're doing for long."

"I'm fine," I said, "but thanks anyways." I turned to walk away, but she touched me gently on the arm.

"Are you sure? Would you like to grab a cup of coffee or a drink after work? Maybe talking about it would help. I could get a sitter for Sarah."

Tired as I was, her invite set my heart to pumping. Vowing to be careful, I said okay, and two hours later we were at a little spot in Welden Place. She looked more beautiful than ever, and I realized she had applied some light makeup, even a pale lipstick. An optimist at heart, I took this as a good sign. This, at last, was a bona fide date.

After a drink and some small talk, she got around to asking me if I was really finished with the "Great Crusade."

I nodded, stung by her teasing tone. "The Christians have withdrawn," I said with a straight face.

"Thank God," she said, and told me that with the firm's one-year reviews coming up, the partners would have to acknowledge what I'd accomplished.

"How do you know what I've 'accomplished'?"

She shrugged. "A big bird told me."

I nodded. "He's a hell of a guy."

"So are you, Billy. I see that now, and I'm sorry I've been so . . . weird. I know I was slow to tell you things. I had my reasons as I've said, but I'd like to make it up to you. I could help with your projects if you need a hand, maybe ghostwrite memos or do some legal research, and you could bill the time for whatever I did."

I was stunned. For an associate to give away billable hours to another associate was like offering up a kidney.

"I couldn't let you do that," I said. "I don't mean to kick a gift horse in the mouth, but why this sudden burst of kindness?"

She laughed. "Better to be called a horse than a dog, I guess."

"I hear you ride 'em."

She looked stunned. "How did you—? Where did you hear that I ride?"

"A *little* bird—"

"Named Mace Rothschild? I know he lives in cyberspace, and he probably saw my name somewhere."

"So why the big secret? I can understand why you'd downplay your . . ."

"My . . . single mother status?"

"Sometime I'd like to finish my own sentence," I said, though I was relieved she had interrupted me. "Anyways, I'd figure the partners would think you being in the horsey set was the perfect S & S image. Don't most of them live down in Atherton and Woodside where all that stuff goes on?"

"You're assuming I do *dressage?*"

"Well, whatever that stuff is that goes on every four years on TV. Or maybe running down scared foxes. Hell, I don't know."

She threw her head back and laughed so loud people turned to look at her. "Billy, I'm nothing but a weekend barrel racer! I share a mare with two other cowgirls and I ride her on the circuit."

"Gait changes? Spins? Sliding stops? Okie riding?"

"*Western* riding, down and dirty. No English saddle in *my* tack room, podner. The reason I keep it under wraps is because Hale feels the partners would consider it behavior unbecoming a future lady partner at S & S."

"S & S seems to require that a whole lot of your life be kept under wraps."

She nodded, and gave me a pained smile, which made me feel uneasy, so I added, "I just can't see how Hale could think barrel racing makes a woman less a lady."

Dana laughed. "Maybe it's because Hale knows I'm not. The truth about me Billy, is that I grew up in a trailer court. My mother had boyfriends, and I never knew my father. I was working my way through my first year of law school waiting tables when I met Hale and Laura Lassiter."

Would Dana Mathews ever stop surprising me? I was stunned into silence, thinking about the girls at the Rose Queen, the way Steve Harmon and guys like him treated waitresses.

"Hale was an active alumnus and major fund-raiser at Boalt Hall. That's how we met. They have no children and informally adopted me, I suppose. Laura Lassiter taught me all I know about being a 'lady,' and Hale wangled me a scholarship, which freed me up to focus on my studies instead of survival. By the time I graduated, I had made Order of the Coif and had an offer here, all thanks to Hale and Laura."

I'll be damned. This girl had me going for sure. "Well, your secret's safe with me," I said, "assuming I can extort another date or two out of you."

She met my gaze. "Look, Billy, my barrel racing competition may get out some day, big deal. I'll take my chances. A chance I *won't* take is breaking the rigid taboo on office relationships." She paused, took a sip from her cosmopolitan. "Dating in the office would send me to the minors for sure if Ashton found out, especially if the man I dated was somebody he wasn't keen about in the first place."

"So what are we doing here?" I said, and reached across the table, ran a finger along the back of her hand. "Breaking up on our first date?" She didn't withdraw her hand, and every nerve ending in my fatigued body was suddenly dancing the funky chicken.

"I guess I'm giving in to that pushy, bullheaded, fire-walking perseverance you were warning me about. You seemed so down, I thought, maybe just this once."

"Yeah, I reckon I've been pushy at times, but I'm a little wary, too, Dana. Where I come from, a man doesn't test the depth of the river with both feet. Problem is, I haven't been able to get you out of my mind."

She moved her hand away and gave her head a dismissive shake. "Slow down, cowboy. Nothing has changed. We still work at the same firm, remember?"

"I won't tell if you won't."

"Be serious, Billy. Nothing remains secret long in a law firm. Besides, we're still not ready to deal with each other truthfully."

"What do you mean?"

"For starters, the Christians have *not* withdrawn. I'll bet this round of drinks that you're still digging up that old Synoptics can of worms."

She had read me like a dime western. Put me in mind of the way Emma Thompson saw through poor old Corin Redgrave in *In the Name of the Father.*

"Why do you say that?" I asked.

"I know where loyalty stands in your hierarchy of values, and while I respect that in you, I can't agree in this situation."

"This situation?"

"You're simply wrong the way you're going about it, Billy."

"You got a better way?"

She smiled. "You'll have to be the judge of that."

"I'm listening," I said.

I've always been a little slow to trust and accept a woman's caring, and I'd had plenty of reasons to doubt this one. It's also hard to draw a line between caution and paranoia when you're living a schizoid life like I was. I had been close to trusting Dana again, but now I could feel the sharp beak of suspicion breaking through my thin skin.

"You wouldn't have to admit to me or to anyone that you're still in the hunt. Just pull together what you have dug up so far. Then refer it out to a competent lawyer, a trial specialist. If you want my help, I know some good ones who might take your friend's case at base rates if I asked nicely. I could quietly pitch in, too, help keep costs down. Mr. Orton would be in the hands of an expert, and if Moncrief eventually blew up, it wouldn't be at you."

"Or at the firm," I said. "Or Hale. Is that why he choreographed this 'date' we're having here? Or was it Ashton?"

"Nobody knows I'm here. Nobody. And maybe I shouldn't be. Yes, I care about the firm. And Hale, too. I also care about you, Billy Strobe. A lot."

Maybe I was a sucker, but I believed her. Perhaps it was hearing her first real expression of affection for me. Or maybe the fact that her offer was generous *and* made sense. Anyways, I covered her hand again, and this time she didn't move it away.

"Well?" she said. "What do you think?"

"There's a problem, Dana." Did I dare mention the DNA?

"I don't care," she said, her eyes glistening with sincerity. "I said I'll help you, and I will."

"Hold on a minute, Dana. You said a while ago you wanted real truth in our relationship? Well, here's truth number one: I'm flat-out crazy about you."

She tilted her head, considering my words, considering me. Then I saw the invitation in her eyes and leaned toward her. She waited. Our lips came together as in slow motion, then held, softly at first, then harder. She made a little sound, and we were locked together, hungrily now, as if each of us were seeking the secret of survival from the mouth of the other.

I became vaguely aware of a presence next to us. The clearing of a throat.

"I'm sorry to interrupt," said our waiter, "but I'm going off for the night and wonder if I might clear your check."

"My God, Billy," Dana said, blinking her eyes playfully, "where did this bar come from?"

"And all these people," I added.

"And a restaurant, too," the waiter added with pride. "We've been here six years. So have you. Aren't you getting hungry?"

She was looking at me for the answer, so I ordered menus and a bottle of Veuve Clicquot.

That was a mistake. The waiter brought it too fast, and we drank it even faster, slipping off the subject, gabbing about Sarah, horses, people in the firm, what an asshole Ashton was, the power struggle at the top, all kinds of things.

Then she got serious. "Is there a 'truth number two'?" she said, and I nodded.

"To make Darryl's case," I said, "I have to find who really killed Deborah Hinton, and I can't expect any other lawyer to tackle that for me."

She looked at me in amazement. "Do you know *anything*," she said, "anything at all about the trial and appellate process? This is America, Billy. You don't have to be a detective to get a new trial. We'll just show his trial lawyer was a bungling dope fiend, or that you've got some new evidence, or that—"

"It's more complicated than the typical case. I told you, there's a problem."

"Truth number three?"

After the earlier two drinks, the euphoria of our kiss, the champagne on top of the drinks, and her renewed offer to help me, I decided she was ready. So I told her.

"*DNA?*" she said, her hand and the champagne glass frozen in space just short of her lips. "Orton's DNA was found on Deborah's *body?*"

I nodded. "Hair follicles."

"And you're still trying to help him get out of prison?"

"He's dying there, Dana. He'll be dead in six months or sooner."

She gave her head an angry shake. "This is the twenty-first century, Billy, and if he's dying it's because he has a conscience and is fed up with living. But I *knew* Deborah Hinton, and she *wasn't* tired of living."

I was wondering how I might have done this better. She was glaring at me as if *I* had killed Deborah Hinton.

"You're smart," she said, calming down a little. "And you're tough, and you've taken everything Ashton has thrown at you and never quit. But, you're also more than a little naive."

"I thought we were talking about Darryl Orton, not me."

"What I care about is you, Billy Strobe. I care about your loyalty, your passion, your guts, the way you look at Sarah, the way you look at me, the way . . . you *look*. Okay? There, I've said it, or most of it. But what you need to understand is that DNA is irrefutable proof of guilt and that the 'actual murderer' is already in prison. I also need you to know that apart from Ashton, you are building an incredible reputation at S & S. The only way you can fail is to persist in this fool's errand."

She took my hand again in both of hers. "You can have it all, Billy, or you can throw it away. Your choice."

"Dammit, woman," I said, upset myself now, but not letting go of her hands, "you could argue the tail off a dog. One minute you want to help and the next—"

"Deborah Hinton was a person I *worked* with, Billy. I knew her well! You've just told me you're helping the man whom you conclusively know to be her murderer!"

"He saved my life, for Christ's sake. I *owe* him, innocent *or* guilty."

"I'm trying to *tell* you who you owe, Billy Strobe. You owe yourself a decent life after everything you've been through. You owe *Hale Lassiter,* who has been like a father to you and who has put himself on the line for you. And yes, you owe the law firm that's paying you $125,000 a year to help find new clients, not lose old ones!"

"Whose bread I eat, his song I sing? Even if it's off-key?"

"Damn right. It's called loyalty, your number one value, remember?"

"Even if the lyrics are full of lies?"

"Everybody lies. Why didn't you tell me about the DNA before? Wasn't that a lie?"

I didn't answer.

"Let me guess. You didn't know, did you? He didn't tell you, am I right? You had to find out for yourself, because he knew if you knew the truth, you wouldn't try to help him. So he lied, too."

"You've got him all wrong. He doesn't even *want* my help; fact is, he fired me the last time I saw him."

"Then if you won't listen to me or to Hale or to whatever residuum of common sense you might possess, listen to your own client."

I shook my head. "He saved my life, so whether he wants help or not, I owe him."

"You owe him *nothing*. A precondition to any obligation you might have incurred to Darryl Orton for having saved your life was breached when he concealed a fact you concede to be material, thus excusing you from future performance."

"*Jesus,* Dana, do you ever stop being a lawyer?"

She stared at her clenched hands. "I can't believe you're risking the firm's best client, knowing Orton has *got* to be guilty."

"The firm again. Well, I'm more worried about a man losing his life than about a Montgomery Street law firm losing a client. Nobody buys me for $125,000 a year or any other amount," I told her. "Nobody!"

"So what does that make me?" she said. "A jurisprudential prostitute because I won't risk harm to a client by helping you free a proven murderer?"

She reached for her coat as the appetizer was arriving. I took some deep breaths and tried to shake off my frustration, keep some perspective. "Success at S & S is important to you, Dana. You've got a daughter to support. I understand you've got to be careful, but I don't. I can afford to take 'risks,' and Darryl Orton is one of the most important persons in my life."

She shook her head with impatience. "*You're* the most important person in your life, Billy, and I won't watch you kill your dreams this way."

"Dana," I said, giving in to my anger, "exactly what the hell do you know about my dreams?"

"I know you could end up running this firm someday if you wanted it badly enough. Hale has told me that. That's why it drives me crazy to see you risking it all for nothing. Even if you got Orton off, he'd be back within a year on three strikes, and you'd be searching titles for a law firm in Milpitas at a third of what you're now making."

Her words hit me like a kick in the groin. "And I reckon it would be strike three on you, Dana, if you were seen dating a paroled, storefront lawyer from Milpitas making a *tenth* of what you'll be making."

She pulled her arm out of my grasp and reached for her coat, not once looking at me. Then the tears came, angry tears, as she stormed out the door.

I watched her heading back in the direction of the office, watched as she disappeared up Grant Avenue. I had been unaware of the stares of everyone in the restaurant, but they looked away quick as I turned around and slumped into my chair.

I reached over and pulled her half-filled glass toward me, then put my lips around the red mark left on the rim and drained it.

24

Five minutes later, I paid the check and walked into a light mist that we locals called fog and visitors called rain. I couldn't face the office knowing Dana might still be there, so I headed back to my apartment, which I couldn't face either, knowing nobody would be there. It's strange, but I'd never really felt lonely, even in prison. Scared and miserable, but not lonely, not until I met Dana. Now I was lonely.

I paced my apartment while my frozen dinner thawed in the microwave, trying not to call her. What could I say to her?

When the phone rang, I ran for it—then restrained myself until it had rung twice.

It was Betty. She was lonely too, wondering if I'd come by and help her get rid of some lasagna she'd just made. I said okay, and after we'd eaten and fucked and showered, then fucked again, I was still lonely.

"You okay, killer?" she said, sunglasses and makeup back in place.

"Sure," I said.

"Things building up at the office?"

"The usual."

"How's it going with the prison guy?"

I gave her an update, which was more like a downdate, considering my lack of progress. Besides, it had been little more than an hour since my blowup with Dana on the same subject, and I didn't want to go back there.

"I'm sure you've done all you could," she said, nuzzling my shoulder.

"I haven't done shit."

"Are you still trying?"

"Sure," I said, "soon as I can think of something to try."

We sat in a suddenly awkward silence.

"What do you think of me, Billy?" she said, out of the blue, commencing to nuzzle me again, this time between my legs. That was Betty all over, skipping around subjects quicker than a rooster in a henhouse.

"I think you're wonderful, Betty. The best."

Her expression, despite the covered-up eyes, told me that wasn't the answer she was looking to get. But she suddenly let out a hearty laugh and agreed with me that she was wonderful.

"Let's have a hot brandy," she said. "What do you think about that?"

What I thought was that I was in trouble, and worse, I was dragging a perfectly decent person down with me. I knew now I was hopelessly in love with Dana, had taken to her like a sick cat to a warm brick from the day I laid eyes on her. Well, it wasn't meant to be, and now Betty Perkins was starting to love *me*, and I was letting it happen.

It was the sex we had just enjoyed that gave her away. Betty had always been sensual with me, but now she was *sexy*, holding nothing back, writhing on top of me, grinding her way into multiple orgasms, her body shuddering in complete abandon. She had even murmured the *L*-word the second time we made love.

Correction: Betty was making love; I was still fucking. Later, she offered to bake up something for dessert.

"I've got to go, Betty."

"Big day tomorrow?" she said, concealing her disappointment.

I started to give the perfunctory answer, then took her gently by the shoulders and told her the truth, nearly all of it.

She smiled wistfully, looked at me through misty eyes as big as robin's eggs. "It's okay," she said. "I always knew there was someone else."

"The someone else doesn't feel the same way about me."

She gave out an ironic laugh. "Then I know exactly how you feel," she said. She straightened her shoulders then, and added, "I don't say that to make you feel guilty. You're welcome here anytime, Billy. It's okay."

"I can't do that to you, Betty. You're too good a person."

She smiled and handed me my coat, brushing lint off the front. "You'll call when you're lonely enough, but it's fine. Really."

"I won't use you like that, Betty. I care for you too much."

"Don't worry, Billy," she said, meeting my eyes. "We're using each other."

I didn't know what to say.

"It's enough that you always make me laugh, and our sex is wonderful. I may not be strong physically, Billy Strobe, but my ego can bench-press problem boys like you. You're not the only one I'm seeing, you know. So don't look so glum."

I never knew when to believe Betty. I don't think I believed her now. I gave her a hug, then left, sorry I couldn't return her feelings, committed instead to a woman who disapproved of everything I stood for and who might even be going along with a coverup for Jason Moncrief that could cost Darryl his life.

I was wondering how things could get much worse, when the flu moved in and took over my depleted immune system. I had no thermometer, but knew I was burning up. Even my fingernails ached. Worse, I had overslept and had a meeting starting in forty-five minutes with Rex Ashton and a new client with an intellectual properties problem.

Stanton and Snow had a typically considerate illness policy for its associates. Like other progressive enterprises, they didn't want to expose employees to a sick person's microbes. But, *un*like other companies, they didn't tell you to stay home; they "allowed" you to work at the office—with your door closed—and to attend meetings via speaker phone. Even left lunch at your closed door. All you had to do was order from the cafeteria by 11:00 A.M. They brought in a doc if you wanted one.

All this so-called consideration was ringing a bell somewhere in my recent past, but truth is, I didn't mind. As much as I hated the place, I needed to be there. At least I needed to be somewhere. I guess Soledad had institutionalized me to the point where I needed regimentation in my life. Some radical I was turning out to be.

I took my car down the hill to work, which meant a twenty-eight-dollar parking fee, but I made it on time for a team meeting on the Dexter case, which was finally going to settle, terminating my only connection to Synoptics. After the meeting—which I dutifully attended in my own office via speaker phone—I took a handful of aspirin, then took inventory of my recent accomplishment, and it wasn't pretty. Getting sent to prison was bad enough, but then I'd diverted myself into hell's own halfway house, where I was making damn little progress on what had brought me here. Little wonder I was sick. It was my body acting in sympathy with my soul, and my damned moral compass, spinning out of control again.

I looked at my desk. Not a single square inch of mahogany veneer could be seen under the files, books, and documents scattered there. My once-great aspirations were bogged down in commercial paperwork; paperwork that did little but channel greed for the economic animals that foraged Montgomery Street, breaking up companies for fun and profit. To complicate things, the people I'd come prepared to hate and plot against, were—if you spared them the notion that one is what one does—decent folks. Rex Ashton excluded, of course.

My time at Soledad had not been pleasant either, but at least it was uncomplicated. I knew pretty much where I stood in prison: Billy

Fix-It, the jailhouse lawyer with all the answers. Nowadays, I wasn't even sure what the questions were. I was as confused as a pig trying to fuck a football.

I remembered once when I was a little kid of nine or ten, asking my dad how it was that only the innocent defendants came to him for representation. Joe Strobe won most all his cases, and I figured it must be because he only represented the ones who weren't guilty. Dad had laughed his croaky, whisky laugh and said, "They're all guilty as sin, son, but then, who among us isn't?"

Confused, I then asked the question no trial lawyer can get through a cocktail hour without having to deal with: "If you know they're guilty, how can you represent them?"

Joe had smiled and hit me gently on the shoulder. "Would you have your dad join up with the government to be certain every man down on his luck who robs a Seven-Eleven store gets the electric chair? No, I won't be doing that, lad. Remember son, this is America, not Red China. Everybody has constitutional rights, even the guys who go bad, hell, even Republicans. As a lawyer, you just do what you can for them."

So what could *I* do? I was behind on everything at the office, had two strikes against me at the firm, had run out of leads on Deborah's murder and even the semblance of creative thinking on the subject. And I was burning up with fever. Feeling guilty, too, for though I was sick, Darryl was dying—dying by inches. I decided to call Dr. Klinehart.

"Barney? I know you fired me, but I want one last favor, and I'll gladly pay twice your outrageous rates."

"Is this about the DNA guy?"

"This is for me, Barney. A favor, okay? Please humor me."

"What do you need?"

"I need you to go back to Deborah Hinton's parents and try again."

"They shined me on when I tried before. You're wasting more of your money."

"They were hurting and bitter, Barney, but that's months ago. Try them again. Tell them we think we know who knocked Deborah up, and we want to make her lover come forward."

"Let me write that down: 'knocked her up.' Yeah, that'll get 'em in a cooperative mood."

"Feel free to sugarcoat it with your own mastery of the King's English, Barney."

"For King's English I charge triple rates."

"I'm too sick to argue. Just do it."

Alone and lonely in my apartment that night, alternately freezing and sweating like a hog in heat, I heard the phone ring. Since it was by my bed, I answered, hoping it was someone I could hire to come kill me. It was Betty Perkins, who wanted to come save me. I didn't let on I was sick.

"Nothing's changed, Betty. I won't waste any more of your time or let you do it neither."

"Well, okay," she said, her voice heavy with disappointment, and then she slipped into a throaty whisper. "But if you decide you want me, handsome, just whistle. You know how to whistle, Billy?"

Sick as I was, I had to laugh, and for a split second I was tempted to let her come over.

"I need some time, Betty. Nothing's changed, and I'm underwater at the office right now, okay? But thanks for calling."

My fever didn't break that night, and when the alarm went off, I ignored it, took the phone off the hook, and slept all morning. I was feeling better by one o'clock, and called Barbara, my shared secretary.

"Mr. Wonderful is on the warpath, Billy," she said. She meant Rex Ashton. Barbara was in her fifties and disliked lawyers in general and Ashton in particular. She had survived at S & S despite her independent ways solely on the strength of her skills, which were amazing. She handled four of us associates and not one of us ever had grounds for complaint.

She told me I also had a message from a Mr. Klinehart.

"I put him through to your voice mail," she added. "You've got a few hundred messages; want to hear them?"

I told her no, I was coming down to the office.

I stumbled into my office, dizzy and aching, and flipped on my speaker phone so that I could listen to my messages and open mail at the same time. Klinehart was my eighth message. He sounded euphoric—and slightly drunk.

"Okay, pretty boy, it's Klinehart. Christ, it pains me to admit it, but you was right for once, and I was wrong. Deborah's parents opened up, and I got Darryl Orton's ticket to ride in my hot little hands. Meet me at my office at eight tonight? Okay?"

I played it again to be sure I'd heard it right, then quickly deleted the message and punched off the phone. My heart was pounding at one hundred beats per minute.

"Knock, knock," came a familiar voice, and I realized I had left the door wide open. *Shit!*

"Dana! Christ, you scared me. I'm supposed to be quarantined, but I forgot to close my door."

Had she heard Barney's message? What the hell was I doing on a speaker phone with the door open? Now I was up to 140 beats per minute. She didn't come through the door, just stood there looking sad. "I'd heard you had the flu, Billy, and wondered if I could handle anything for you while you were down."

My fevered brain was spinning out questions without answers. Wasn't she mad at me? Hadn't she walked out on me in that restaurant? Had I missed a reel in the disaster movie that had become my life? Should I ask her what she had just heard? Try to make a joke out of it?

"Everything's under control," I said, in a voice that sounded like it was coming out of a sewer. "But thanks."

"I won't say I told you so," she said, "but didn't I warn you about getting yourself run down?"

"As long as you don't say 'I told you so,' " I said, and she smiled and stood there almost awkwardly—a look I'd never seen on her.

"Sorry I ran off the other night," she said finally. "Nothing is ever settled that way. When you're feeling better, call me and we'll talk. Okay?"

"Sure," I said, feeling better already, though I was still wondering how much she had heard.

After Dana left, I put my head down on my desk, slept for an hour, and then got some work done. At 7:30, I swallowed some more aspirin and headed for Klinehart's Mission Street office. I was burning with fever, but also with anticipation. Barney never exaggerated, and I was sure he had the goods or the real killer. I felt my inside coat pocket to be sure I had my checkbook; Barney deserved double rates, and I could afford them now.

I reached his office near the corner of Castro and Mission Streets fifteen minutes early. It was windy and had started raining, surprisingly heavy for autumn, but good news for drought-fearing Californians. Unfortunately, I didn't have my raincoat and my umbrella got tore inside out by the time I'd locked my car door. My topcoat was soaked through, and I was shaking from the cold as I took the deteriorating stairs to the second floor and found the door with BARNARD KLINEHART, INVESTIGATIONS painted in black, old-fashioned lettering on the opaque glass door. He wasn't back yet, but the door was open, so I went in. A dull overhead light was on. I stripped off my soggy coat and took a seat in his tiny reception area.

How the hell could anyone work in a place like this? Even at night it was noisy from Mission Street traffic, people shouting at each other down on the sidewalk, and some guy on a saxophone butchering "Eleanor Rigby."

I picked up a day-old newspaper, but the light wasn't good enough so I put it down. My head was throbbing to the beat of the sax. *Ah, look at all those lonely people.* My clothes were damp from the sweats, and I was getting cold again, thanks in part to a draft coming from Barney's streetside office. I walked in to shut the window, and there was Barney, staring at me from behind his desk, a reddish-black half-inch hole in the dead center of his forehead. He was upright in his chair, his head tilted slightly back, a questioning look on his face, the first time I'd ever seen him appear surprised.

I moved toward him and reached out a trembling hand to feel his neck for a pulse. Nothing. His flesh was ice. When I withdrew my hand, he slumped forward onto his desk, and a smell came out of him. One eye stared vacantly off to one side. The sour taste of bile rose in my throat.

I tried to stay calm, but I'd never seen a dead man, not even in prison. I must have been in some sort of shock because all I could think about was getting out of there. I was an ex-con on parole at a fresh murder site.

I went over to the window, careful not to be seen, then took in three deep breaths of icy air and cleared my head. I walked back to the body. It had been what the movies called an execution-type murder, probably from close range with a small-caliber gun, maybe a .25 automatic, possibly a .38. The office had been ransacked, and his battered briefcase was nowhere in sight. The reception area hadn't been touched, so I reckoned they'd found what they came for.

I didn't call the police. Instead, I grabbed the newspaper I had been reading and used it to wipe the wooden armrest of the chair I'd been in and the window I had touched. I then wadded up the paper and stuffed it down my pants. My eyes were tearing up as I took a last look at the late Barnard Klinehart, put on my waterlogged coat, then half ran, half stumbled down the stairs to the sidewalk, where I lost myself in the crowd of all those lonely people.

I drove around town in circles for a while, mindlessly despondent, fighting off the recollection of Dana standing in the doorway of my office. How much of Klinehart's message had she heard? Could she have warned Moncrief? If so, I had better start fearing her instead of loving her.

And, what had Klinehart found out? What was it he was going to show me, and who had it now?

There was only one way to learn what he'd found, if it wasn't already too late. I popped some more aspirin and a half-roll of Tums, then pointed my car down 101 toward Foster City and 115 Spring Street, where Klinehart had told me Deborah Hinton's parents, the Breckenridges, lived.

And where I prayed to God they still lived.

25

There's something dangerously beautiful about a house burning at night. I'd seen one before when I was a kid growing up in Enid. Harris family, four houses down from us. Burnt out late one night under suspicious circumstances, being as how they were the only blacks in the neighborhood. Mrs. Harris was a local dance instructor, and Bobby Harris was two years ahead of me and the star halfback on our high school football team. Good folks. Everybody liked them. Well, I reckon not everybody did.

Anyways, here it was happening again. I saw the flames from blocks away and wondered whose it was. Getting closer, I saw a dozen or so neighbors who looked both worried and exhilarated, huddled around at a safe distance in the hazy night, watching the unleashed flames holding the black sky at bay. Unlucky for the firefighters, the rain that had soaked my clothes in San Francisco was nowhere in evidence this side of the Bay. I checked the address again. It was the Breckenridges' house, and when I asked a bystander, he pointed them out, huddled together on the lawn next door, inside the ring of onlookers, blankets pulled tight around their sagging shoulders to cover their sleeping garments. The woman was staring blankly at the scene and appeared to be in the grip of shock. Her husband was wildly waving his arms, pleading with a guy wearing a billed hat, probably the chief.

I was trembling all over, whether from the flu or wet clothes or finding Klinehart dead or the chill in the air, I couldn't tell. But I guess that's why I was drawn in closer to the burning building, close enough to feel the heat and taste the smoke in my mouth, fairly hypnotized by the radiance of the blazing structure. I was tasting fear, too, fear for the Breckenridges—who had lost a daughter, and now their home—but also fear of the unknown deadly forces my bungling efforts had unleashed.

I closed my eyes for a second against the sting of the smoke and the image of Barney's body as it had slumped forward, facedown, his heavy jowl spilled across the desktop. His death and the destruction of the house were clearly connected, so I tried to clear my head and read any signals the smoke might be sending me.

First, the destruction of the Breckenridges' home meant that whoever killed Barney did not find what he was looking for at his office. Second, because the arsonist had wanted the Breckenridges' house and its contents destroyed, but apparently not the people, he didn't care so much about getting possession of the goods as making sure nobody else did.

I flicked a piece of ash off my sleeve and backed off a few feet, thinking that since somebody was going to so much trouble to keep me from getting something I wanted, it would be nice to know what it was I wanted.

I became aware of the distant voices of firefighters—some on extension booms, others on the ground wrestling with hoses like gigantic unruly snakes—shouting frantic orders at each other I couldn't make out. A fine mist drifted down on my face as I looked up at the phosphorescent ribbons of water that shot into the sky from those hoses, then arced and disappeared into the fiery hole that just hours before had been the home of Harold and Rose Breckenridge.

I pushed my way up close to them and heard Harold Breckenridge say that an anonymous caller who had saved their lives was probably also the arsonist. Nobody paid me any mind.

"He *asked* you if you smelled smoke yet?" said the chief, a chubby, ruddy-faced man who had slid down his last pole many years ago. "Told you your house was on fire?"

"*Exactly* what he says," said Breckenridge. " 'So who's this?' I says to the guy, not believing him, but shaking my wife awake anyhow. 'What the hell are you talking about? I don't smell any smoke.' "

"And he wouldn't give his name?" said the chief.

"Hell, no, but then he says back to me, 'You'll smell plenty of smoke in a minute, Mr. Breckenridge'—*he knows my name, Chief!*—'then your house is going to turn into a volcano, and you'll be blowing smoke rings out your asshole. You got sixty seconds.' Then he hangs up on me just as I get my first whiff."

Of course they knew your name, I thought, feeling worse by the minute. They got it from Barney who got it from me.

Flames flashed from a window at the side of the house making a *whoosh*ing noise. Must have been a gas pipe exploding.

"We barely made it out, Chief," Breckenridge added, his voice hoarse and shaky and his eyes more teary from anger and despair than from the smoke. "Hell, didn't even have time to make a 911!" The distraught man paused, then threw up his hands in a gesture of utter despair and added, "Goddammit, Chief, our whole *lives* are in there!"

"We're doing all we can, sir," said the chief, sounding as calm as possible considering he had to yell over the sound of the voices of his men and a steady roaring sound I remembered now from the Harris fire—the sound of a house howling in pain, giving up its memories, fueling its own destruction.

"Like hell you are!" shouted Breckenridge, his features twisted in anger as he pointed at the house next to theirs where we were now all standing. "What the hell are those guys doing moving their damn hoses over here?"

With the patience of a surgeon delivering bad news, the chief explained to the dazed couple that their house was lost, that his duty at this point was to try to stop the spread. Breckenridge was about to protest when a huge tree in his backyard exploded in flames and for an eerie moment lit up the area over on Hester Street like a giant torch. The crowd went *ooooh* like it was the Fourth of July.

"Your *duty!*" screamed Rose Breckenridge, who broke her silence, but was then choked back into it from the smoke and the rage burning within her. She buried her face in Harold's sunken chest, and though I couldn't hear her sobs, her narrow shoulders were shuddering like all get out. The wind must have shifted then, because we all got a snoot full of smoke, which backed the whole crowd away with the efficiency of a SWAT team. The firefighters were all moving away from the Breckenridge house now, ladders down, hoses reeled in, grim-faced rescuers turned pallbearers. It was obvious to everyone that the house was a goner.

The chief offered more condolences, then started to walk away, but Breckenridge was fit to be tied and grabbed him by the arm.

"The son-of-a-bitch knew my name, Chief! He called me by *name!*"

Should I say something? I wondered. I felt like a ghost at a funeral, standing there, invisible, impotent.

The chief gently pulled out of Harold's grasp, told them he would take a statement from them later, and then lurched off toward one of the trucks. The Breckenridges stayed put, so I decided to move closer and come clean with them.

"Excuse me, folks," I said handing Harold Breckenridge my card. "I'm the lawyer who hired the investigator you visited with earlier today. Could I talk to you for a minute?"

They glared at me with expressions of astonishment that quickly turned to anger.

"I'm truly sorry about your loss, folks," I continued, hearing the inadequacy of my words and realizing I'd set an Olympic standard for bad timing. Rose unburied her head long enough to call me a bastard and a ghoul, while Harold reached out and jerked me toward him by my necktie. "Get away from me, you meddling son-of-a-bitch! Get the hell out of my sight!"

"Yes, sir," I said, "if you'd let go of my tie?"

He threw the tip of the tie at me in disgust, saying, "This all happened because of that damned investigator nosing around. Rose *told* me we shouldn't have cooperated. Now look at us."

I couldn't deny the connection of events, so I apologized again, then backed off and lost myself in the crowd as a squad of a half-dozen uniformed cops arrived and began pushing us off the front lawn into the street. I remembered reading that arsonists like to observe their handiwork, so I began scanning the crowd, looking for someone fully dressed like I was rather than in bathrobes or thrown-together clothing. Someone out of place. There were only two or three such people, and one of them looked a lot like that swarthy-looking character who had followed me home that night from Betty's. He was stocky, with thick black hair, and wore the same long dark raincoat.

I guess he'd been eyeballing me, too, because soon as he saw he'd been made, he started moving away from me. I started after him, pushing myself through the crowd. I shouted at a nearby cop, but he ignored me.

I was gaining on the guy, but he broke free from the cluster of people ahead and jumped into a waiting dark blue Range Rover that started to pull away before the swarthy guy could even close his door. I gave chase on foot, slamming the rear fenders of the SUV in frustration, probably looking like a crazy man.

I pulled up and bent over, hands on knees, hacking from the smoke in my lungs. I had me a good look at the retreating car, but there were no license plates. I'd have bet a year's wages there was a cell phone inside the four by four that had recently dialed Harold Breckenridge's number.

My head was throbbing with fatigue and guilt as I turned back toward the house and suddenly realized the crowd—including a cop in uniform—was now more interested in me—the nut case trying to run down a car on foot—than they were in the fire, which was commencing to burn itself out. Lucky for me, a loud *caroooommm* caught everybody's attention, and I looked up in time to see the roof crash into the gutted remains of the house and then disappear in a fresh eruption of flame followed by a mushroom of smoke. Pieces of the exterior walls flaked off in all directions; then all four sides of the house came down like dominoes as the house seemed to devour itself in a final, fiery swallow. The noise and heat backed the crowd away faster than the cops had, and I slipped away toward my car unnoticed.

My adrenaline began to fail me a half-block down the street, and I found a curb to sit on. I had witnessed two deaths in two hours, a man and a home, and I had caused them both; the Breckenridges were right as rain about that. I buried my face in my hands for a minute, and when I opened my eyes I saw that the heel on one of my shoes had come loose and that my best slacks looked like they been dragged through a grain harvester. I also noticed one of the cops giving me the once-over again, and I wondered if it was a good idea for an ex-con to be showing up at the scene of a murder and an arson the same night. If Barney kept an appointment book, my name would be the last one on his schedule. I tried to remember whether I had wiped my fingerprints off his throat after I had felt for a pulse. I didn't even know if you could leave fingerprints on flesh.

What made the whole thing even more agonizing was that the timing of these events pointed straight to Dana having overheard Klinehart's message, the one I had stupidly allowed to be broadcast on my speaker phone. Twice.

Who might *she* have told? Moncrief? Ashton? Qaddafi? Saddam Hussein? I knew I was probably overreacting, but wouldn't Ashton—desperate not to lose Synoptics—do whatever was necessary to protect his meal ticket, Jason Moncrief? It was common knowledge that losing the firms biggest client right now would not only be a disaster for the firm, but for Ashton's hopes of leading it.

But murder? That was still too big a bite to swallow—unless Ashton had been in the stock scam with Moncrief from the beginning and both of them were trying to cover the earlier murder of Deborah Hinton. I was speculating all over the damn place, but the net was getting wider in my mind, maybe even wide enough to include a woman I'd loved.

How far *did* this thing go? And who could I trust now with Barney gone? At least I knew the answer to that one.

I also knew I could no longer delay drafting Darryl's motion for new trial. I'd better go with what little I had while I was still alive to go at all.

I drove back to San Francisco, too tired to even turn the radio on. I stumbled into my apartment, saw that I had a call from Betty and another one from Mr. Bharani, asking me "please to get the hot water heater working again." I told my landlord when I moved in that I couldn't abide a cold-water shower, so he had somehow managed to turn me into the building super—unpaid, of course. I ignored both messages for once and fell on the couch. My ears were ringing, and I was still a little feverish, so I took three aspirin. The ringing started up again, only louder this time. It was the phone. I considered unplugging it, but grabbed it on the fourth ring.

"Hey, Billy, it's Lisa."

Her voice sent a shudder through me. A call from Lisa was as rare as the American eagle and usually not as pretty.

"What's happened? Is it Ma?"

"Relax, champ. I just called to tell you I've found confirmation that you were indeed the adopted one."

An old joke between us. I relaxed and said, "Which explains why I'm light-years smarter and prettier than you are."

She laughed. "Seriously, I finished up in the attic this morning and found a list of names stuck in Dad's college yearbook. Yellow lined paper, his awful handwriting, folded double in a sealed envelope. One of the names is Charles Ryan. Wasn't that the judge who killed himself?"

That got my pulse pounding with renewed hope. Ryan was Dad's friend who did everything but hold the jury in contempt after they'd convicted. "That's him. This might be our opening, Lisa. Who else is on it? How many names? Is Blackwell listed?"

"A couple of dozen people altogether, but no Blackwell."

"You're kidding."

"No Blackwell, no kidding."

"*Shit!* Is there any explanation as to what these folks have in common? Could they have been clients? That might explain Judge Ryan's loyalty to Dad."

"I've been through the files. Not one of them was a client. It's just names, Billy. No date, nothing. Mostly men, two women."

"Read them to me."

One or two of the names sounded vaguely familiar, but none were mentioned in the trial record of Dad's trial. I gave her fax instructions, and she promised to get it off to me in the morning. "Do you think it's important?"

"Probably not, but I'd still like to see it."

We visited about the usual stuff for a few minutes until my adrenaline rush wore off. I begged fatigue, sent my love, and hung up.

The phone rang again only seconds after I'd put it back in the cradle, and I figured Lisa had forgotten something.

"Yeah?" I said.

"Hi, Billy," came Betty's cheery voice. "First you won't see me, now you won't even return my calls?"

I told her I'd had my hands full.

"I'll bet you have, you rascal," she said, laughing sardonically, "which makes me even more jealous. Is she with you now?"

"I've had a long day, Betty, and I'm shaking off the end of a flu bug. I appreciate the call, but I'm alone and I aim to stay that way."

"Sorry, I'm coming over. I'm hungry, thirsty, and horny as a box of bunnies. Don't try to talk me out of it."

She hung up on me, which upped the odds against talking her out of it. Truth is, after the events of the past twenty-four hours, it would be refreshing to be with someone with no connection to Stanton and Snow. I was fed up with all of them and had damned sure had enough cops and robbers for one night. I tried not to think on the fact that whoever killed Barney had my address, too, and might assume that Barney had put whatever they were looking for in the mail to me. That was more likely, which meant Betty and I would probably be safe here at least for tonight. After that anything was possible.

Looking back, I guess I hadn't reckoned on the possibility of getting myself killed over a simple motion for new trial.

Betty showed up in twenty minutes with a veggie pizza, and after we'd eaten and had a glass or two of wine I let her seduce me. It started with a massage, her fingers all over my neck, back, and thighs. I was relaxed and half asleep when she rolled me over and went to work on my quads and stomach. Then her lips were working with her hands and it was as if five women were all over me, hands and mouths everywhere. I was so relaxed that when she took me into her mouth, I hadn't even been aware I was hard. Then, when she mounted me, I hardly knew I was inside her. The whole thing was like a dream, a wonderful dream—except that Dana wasn't in it.

Soon, I felt Betty's fingernails digging into my hips as she bucked and shuddered and groaned, triggering my own orgasm, more release than passion, but powerful and renewing.

Then she bent down and kissed me and padded off toward the bathroom. The last thing I remembered was a warm washcloth, then . . . nothing.

The next morning over coffee and toast, the weight of Barney's death and the fire came down on me again so hard I wasn't much company. Betty leaned over and kissed me lightly on the cheek. "Still got the bug?"

"I'm okay. Much better."

"What's on your mind, Billy? Tell mama."

I looked up at Betty's pretty face, looking so concerned. This was the woman I wished I could love, but experience had taught me that wishing don't make things true, especially where the heart is concerned. Still, it was great having a friend right now, and maybe opening up would be good. Shed some of my prison-bred no-trust attitude. So I did. Told her everything—everything but the part about Dana maybe overhearing my message from Barney. I also spared her mention of the swarthy-faced man at the fire scene who had followed me from her apartment house that first night.

"My God, Billy," she said after I'd finished up. "How could they have known about your investigator's discovery?" she asked.

"Go figure," I said stiffly.

She jumped to her feet and began clearing the dishes off the table. "You've got to move in with me, Billy. Today. Now. At least until things settle down."

"Thanks," I told her, taking her by the hand and pulling her back into a chair. "But I've already got one good person killed this week, and I don't expect things to settle down for a while."

After a few moments of silence, she said, "Why, Billy?"

"Why won't they be settling down?"

"No. Why are you putting your life in danger for this prisoner friend of yours?"

"We've been through that," I said, betraying impatience. "He's my friend."

"With friends like that, Billy, you don't need any enemies, though it sounds like you're courting them, too."

"I know it."

"Well, I'll bet that if you told this Orton person the truth about what's happening and asked him what you should do, he'd tell you to quit!"

I nodded. "He already has."

"Then why won't you?"

I shrugged, thinking here I go again, defending my actions. "Hell, Betty, I don't know. Maybe it's the way I was raised. My dad would never quit, no matter what, and I won't either."

Betty got up and began clearing the table again. She had obviously lost patience with me and loudly dumped the dishes in the sink, then leaned against it, stiff-armed, looking down and slowly shaking her head. Then she sighed and sat back down, lit a cigarette and blew smoke upward out of her lower lip. I sipped my coffee while Betty smoked in silence.

"I'm worried about you, Billy," she said finally. "I know how you feel about that other girl, but it doesn't change the feelings I have for you. So please stop this crazy quest before you get yourself killed. I'm begging you."

"I owe him," I said. "I told you before, Betty. I would have been killed a year ago if it wasn't for Darryl Orton."

Betty was quiet, but I could tell she wasn't persuaded or finished with me either. She stabbed her cigarette into her empty cereal bowl, then stared out my kitchen window, shaking her head again.

"Go on and speak your mind, Betty," I said, feeling a little impatient myself, yet sorry that I'd brought her down. "You always have. Just skip the airy-fairy stuff, okay?"

"What's that supposed to mean?"

"It means keep it simple for a simple man. Sometimes you'll go looking into the entrails of a hawk just to decide if it's a good day to buy garden tools. So tell me what's bothering you, and we can be done with it."

She couldn't help but smile at that, though it was one of those secret smiles women get on their faces sometimes that tell you something's going on inside their heads but not what it is. Anyways, any kind of smile was welcomed, considering I was acting like a bear with a sore foot. Still, she said nothing, just stared into a coffee cup cradled in both hands.

"And that's a cup, not a crystal ball," I added, "with coffee in it, not tea leaves."

She nodded and smiled again, then gazed at me with sad, swimming eyes that for some reason sent a chill down my backbone.

"Before this is over," she said at last, "you'll need a better reason for what you're doing than loyalty."

"What's a better reason than loyalty?"

She shook her head. "I don't know, but you'll have to find out if you insist on seeing this through."

Well, there goes Betty, I thought, being mystical again. Next, she'd be breaking out the tarot cards or throwing those magic sticks over her shoulder.

I started to apologize for waking up so grouchy, but she put a finger on my lips, leaned forward, and kissed me on the forehead. I realized she had been crying.

"Betty?"

But she jumped up, grabbed her backpack, and was out the door without another word. Before I could thank her for last night. Or ask her what planet she hailed from.

*   *   *

It was nearly seven o'clock when she left, and by ten, I had finished a draft of Darryl's motion for new trial, called in sick—though for the first time in days I wasn't—and headed for Soledad in my Ford Probe. The barrenness of the fall landscape as I drove through the fabled Salinas Valley put me in mind again of my first trip to Soledad, nearly two years ago. I pictured the pasty-faced guard with a mustache longer on one side than the other, saw Joey, the black kid sitting next to me who smelled like he had pissed his pants, remembered the Nazi skinhead across the aisle who stared at me the whole time. I shuddered, turned the car heater up a notch. Nothing like a little prison nostalgia to put my present anxieties in perspective. I kept reminding myself that though I was about to go inside, I could come back outside whenever I damn well felt like it.

It would be a quick trip, unless my client felt like talking to me, which he never did. In my pocket was a list of good criminal lawyers I had compiled and if Darryl really wanted me out of his hair, he would pick one and be done with me.

When I arrived at reception, they told me that Darryl had been confined to the infirmary and that no visitors were allowed. They also told me he would be transferred to solitary confinement as soon as he was physically able. Another fight in the yard.

Fucking Darryl, I said out loud to no one. I halfway felt like getting back in my car, but instead took my frustration out on the reception clerk.

"I'm filing a motion for new trial and need information that only my client can provide. He has a constitutional right to counsel, and I intend to see him. Now. Today."

"He's not fit to see visitors anyway," said the clerk, taking my card.

"I'll be the judge of that," I said, whipping out my pen and legal pad. "I'll be back in three hours with a court order, and I guarantee it will have your name on it"—I was writing furiously as I looked at his name tag—"*Mr. Adam G. Burns.*"

Burns, a short, scowling man in his fifties, had the wasted look of a man who had long ago buried his hopes. He stared sourly at my card as if he had been handed a speeding ticket.

In the end, we compromised on a five-minute visit that I knew I could stretch into ten. They searched me, found nothing but a Dixie Chicks CD I'd picked up for Darryl.

A CO came to escort me, who I recognized as a good-looking Eurasian woman we called Koby. She remembered me, too, and after some small talk, explained that Darryl had been returned to Soledad after three days in an outside hospital where he had been treated for kidney damage, two broken ribs, and a concussion, sustained from kicks after three Nuestra Familia gang members had put him on the ground.

"I may give him a kick or two myself," I said as we walked along a ten-foot fence, behind which a dozen prisoners listlessly roamed like dispirited animals in an abandoned zoo.

"Orton lucked out," she said, brushing against my arm as we walked, her seductively tapered eyes seeing me in a different light now, dressed in a blue suit and forty-dollar tie. Some female guards sort of "mothered" male prisoners, a few even married them, and Koby was wearing no rings. "He would have bought it for sure this time if the Brotherhood hadn't decided it was a good time to move on the NF. You could hear it all the way out here. They had to bust 'em up with fire hoses and stun bombs."

We had reached the entrance to the infirmary, and I thanked her for the company, gave her a lingering handshake. I needed some extra minutes with Darryl.

"You have time after, Billy, stop by and have a cup of coffee, okay?"

"Sure, Koby," I said, returning the squeeze her hand was giving me, "but take your time coming back, all right?"

She winked. I'd have at least twenty minutes.

I barely recognized Darryl. His skin was jaundiced and had shrunk against his cheekbones as if stretched across a snare drum. He looked like a mummy, his head, chest, and torso encased in bandages. His unbandaged eye was watery and unfocused as it sought to identify me. Even his hair seemed to be falling out. My breath caught in my throat as I tried to speak.

"Jesus, Darryl."

My anger at him drained into sympathy. He looked like the victim of a vehicular accident in which he had been the sole survivor. I pulled up a chair, careful not to tip the two hanging IV bottles attached by rubber tubing to his right wrist.

Darryl smiled weakly when he saw it was me. In his damaged condition, he had apparently forgot he was angry at me for my lapse of faith in him.

"Hi, Darryl," I whispered. The smell of antiseptic and adhesive tape filled my nostrils.

"Christ," he said, blinking his one eye, then squeezing it shut, "a fucking lawyer. So I musta died and went to hell."

Another smell hit me as he tried to shift positions. Stale urine. I'd raise hell with the male nurse as soon as I could find one. No aspect of prison life escaped the Department of Correction's stingy budget.

"You got it wrong, Darryl," I said, grabbing a clean towel and working it under his hips, despite his protests. "I'm your guardian angel."

"Ow!" Darryl grunted as I finished covering the damp stained area. "And I'm Winston fucking Churchill," he added gruffly.

"At least you've still got a sense of humor, such as it is."

"How the hell would you know? And ain't I mad at you? Didn't I fire you?"

"Must be the medication you're on, Darryl. Last time I saw you, why hell, you tried to kiss me."

I then started lecturing him on how nobody could keep taking this kind of punishment and he started giggling to himself, which was not like Darryl Orton at all. Something strong in one of those plastic bags.

"What's so funny?"

"This ain't nothin, kid," he said, and began telling me about his three years on the rodeo circuit: New Mexico, Colorado, Wyoming, and Texas. He told me how a bull had rolled on him one day in Cheyenne and crushed his upper leg so bad the local doc told him it should come off.

"I sent my buddy out for a tire casing"—Darryl pronounced it *tar-casin* so I didn't understand him at first—"then had him fill it with fresh cowshit. We strapped the thing on with baling wire, added fresh, warm dung once a day, and I was walkin next to normal in four months. Trick I learned from my daddy, who ranged the Pendleton and Cheyenne rodeo circuit with old Bob Crosby, King of the Cowboys."

"You're out of your head, Darryl."

"Hell I am. The dung made a natural poultice. My point is, them Messicans ain't nothin compared with ridin bulls and broncs."

Darryl's eyes were wild and overbright. The way he was gabbing, he might have been on uncut Peruvian marching powder.

"Did you ride again?"

"Couldn't. I'd broke my other leg twice before and was runnin outta legs. Besides, I weren't no 'Wild Horse' Bob Crosby, who lived on nothin but Mexican frijole beans and won the Roosevelt Trophy in 1928 with his leg and one arm in plaster casts. Not me, no way. Took a job as a mortician's assistant, hired by a distant cousin in Tulsa whose family stayed behind during the dust bowl movement west. I did all the heavy lifting plus cremations."

"I wouldn't have thought there was much interest in cremations in Oklahoma back then."

"Wrong, kid. We were doin plenty of shake 'n' bake, until I screwed up one day durin a lakeside memorial service."

"What happened?"

"Grievin family was in a semicircle around me, my back to the lake where the widow wanted me to scatter the ashes. Problem was soon as I started throwin the cremains into the lake, a bunch a' damn ducks come up thinkin it's feedin time. Et up every bit of the deceased right in front of the mourners. Widow went hysterical, and I went west lookin for a new job to support my music habit. Ended up at the TechnoCenter."

His face contorted, whether from pain or the thought of what had happened to him next I couldn't tell. He had never talked so much about his past, and I hoped to keep him going. But he switched gears and said, "Tell me what's goin on in the world of Billy Strobe, boy lawyer."

I opened up, too, even told him about my ups and downs with Dana Mathews—skipping my suspicions—which seemed to cheer him up a little. Later, when I realized I might be running out of time, I gave him the good news that I'd drafted his motion, and then the bad news about Klinehart and the Breckenridges' house. Another award for bad timing on my part, for he closed his good eye and began rolling his head from side to side, murmuring something about fearing friends with good intentions more than enemies with bad ones.

Then he lay still as a corpse. I put a hand to his throat to check his pulse—and experienced a shudder of remembrance. But this time I felt one, weak, but regular.

I let him rest a spell; then the eye popped open. It looked red and menacing and desperate.

"No . . . get out of it . . . you're . . . over your head, kid," he said, his words suddenly slurred. The uppers must be wearing off, or downers were kicking in.

"We're almost there, buddy," I said, but he kept rotating his head from side to side.

"How long you been singin that 'almost there' song? If there's anything galls me more than takin charity . . . it's takin charity that's worthless. Face it, kid, you're in the wrong line a' work. So get out of this thing while the gettin's good."

I shook my head, but realized he had closed his eye again. "We're bringing in the big guns," I said, "and here they are. Just pick a lawyer from this list, and I'll turn my files over the minute I get your new trial. Then I'm out of it, okay?"

He seemed to be coming alive again, alert enough to ask the one question I didn't want to answer. "Somebody must have knowed your investigator had come up with somethin worth gettin kilt over."

"I know it," I said. "Barney Klinehart *had* come up with something, but I don't know that we'll ever know what it was."

"That ain't my question. How did *they* know he'd come up with somethin?"

"They just knew," I said, lamely, "but there's a silver lining. I put all this in my affidavit in support of our motion for new trial. It's a sorry pass, Darryl, but these two tragedies are going to work in our favor."

But again, Darryl impatiently rolled his head from side to side, despite the discomfort it obviously caused him. "You *still* ain't answerin my question! *How did they know?*"

"I don't know," I lied, unwilling to admit to him my suspicions about the woman I'd been telling him about; unwilling to face them myself.

"Well, the things you don't know would fill from *A* to *Z* in the encyclopedia," he said, fully alert again. "So get your bony homesick ass out of this case in a hurry and maybe you'll be blessed with a long career of makin other people as miserable as you've made me."

"I plan on it."

Darryl seemed completely revitalized again, and raised himself up on one elbow. "Well, then, save us both more aggravation and quit wastin your valuable time and mine."

"You referring to your valuable time between breakfast and dinner, getting the shit beat out of you and watching Rabbit beat his pud in the upper bunk?" He was starting to get to me again.

"It's my time," he said, "and I'll do whatever the hell I want with it."

"Don't kid yourself, old man. You don't *have* time; you're *doing* time, the *State's* time. And you'll do exactly what *they* tell you to do with it as long as you're their guest. Look at you, for God's sake. You can't even take a leak without the help of a nurse. Can't brush your own teeth, can't do shit! Is this the way you want to live? Is this the 'valuable time' you don't want me to waste?"

He gave me a sullen look. "Get the hell out of here."

"You're getting challenged on your damn bench again, right?"

Darryl said nothing, just turned his head away.

"Will you explain to me," I said, as exasperated as he was, "why I am busting my ass trying to get you out of here when you don't care enough about yourself to even stay alive? Fighting over some dumb bench?"

"That *is* my way of staying alive," he whispered.

"No, Darryl, it's your way of salvaging your goddamn pride!"

Darryl gave his shoulders a weak shrug. "What's the point of stayin alive if you ain't got no pride? Call it whatever you want. It's what keeps me going day to day, hour to hour."

"Well, I *do* call it pride," I said, "and I'm telling you that you've got to swallow some of it before it turns your life conviction into a death sentence!"

He fixed his good eye on me for what seemed like a full minute, then damned if he didn't let out a window-rattling laugh.

"You keep this up, kid," he said, wincing from the effort, "and you're gonna hurt my pride."

I smiled despite myself, for I thought maybe that he had come to grips with something important, and so had I. Darryl was stuck in a typical prisoner's catch-22, where the one thing that makes life worth living is the one thing that's killing you. Like Dickens and drugs, like prisoners engaging in sex despite the threat of AIDS, like basking not only in the sun, but in the admiration Darryl got from owning "his bench." The catch was that to survive in a place like Soledad, prisoners had to find a reason to really want it, because once a con had placed little value on his own life, there were plenty of guys who'd gladly take it.

"Listen, Darryl, I think we can get you a new trial. Then I'm done with harassing you. I'll be out of your miserable life for good, okay?"

He shook his head vigorously and reached for a glass of water, which he proceeded to spill all over himself. "Shit!" he shouted. I grabbed another towel and tried to help him, but he swatted impotently at me with a paper napkin until I backed off.

"No, kid, *you* listen. If you were half as smart as you think you are, you'd have figured out by now that a new trial won't mean squat even if you get it. A jury would need more to acquit me than some unrelated murder and an unconnected fire over in some uninvolved county. Even I know that much. You're up against DNA, kid. Hard science. Isn't that what you told me the last time I fired you?"

"Something like that," I said.

"Well, it's a step I ain't willin to take. To get me off against DNA evidence, you'd have to not only prove somebody else killed that girl, but probably tell the jury who it was, give 'em somethin to hang their sombreros on. Din't I tell you that?"

I said nothing. He was right.

"Otherwise," he continued, "why would you expect twelve strangers to believe me when you didn't believe me yourself once you heard about my hair on that woman's body?"

I tried to meet his eyes—eye—but looked away. "I'm working on several leads."

Darryl shook his head and grimaced in disgust. "The last guy which tried to find a 'lead' is dead, and whatever 'leads' they didn't get from him has just gone up in smoke at the Breckenridges'. Ain't all of that true?"

"Okay, Darryl, but bear in mind that all this took place while you were locked up here. If I can connect Klinehart's death and the Breckenridge fire to Deborah Hinton's murder, that would make two out of three things you couldn't have done. Plus there's plenty of circumstantial evidence pointing to either Frank Hinton or Jason Moncrief, maybe enough to get past the DNA."

"Who's Moncrief?"

I told him, and explained how I intended to somehow get into Moncrief's company's files. This drew a disdainful snicker.

"Looky there, folks. Here comes the little mouse takin on the Big Cheese, walkin smack into a baited trap."

"I can handle myself," I said.

"Oh, really?" he said, giving me an irritating little smile. "Ever thought about the kind of pride that's gonna get *you* killed, Billy Strobe?"

He turned away from me, and I threw the list at his back and started out the door, thoroughly pissed. "Pick a lawyer," I said. "I'll come back when you're feeling more civil."

"I don't think so," he said in a tone so casual he might have been turning down a second cup of coffee. "I don't know how I got involved in all this, or how you did. But I do know I don't want nobody else kilt over it, even if it's you."

26

I got in early the next day, and waiting for me on my desk was Lisa's fax. The names, twenty-six in all, were in Dad's handwriting, but other than Judge Ryan, I couldn't recognize a one, though a couple seemed somewhat familiar.

I worked until 9:30, then hightailed it out to the Breckenridges' neighborhood and began canvassing the area, starting with the two houses adjacent to the charred remains of their home. I was struck by how small the bare foundation looked, with little left of the house but twisted bare pipes sticking up like scorched bones amidst the charred remains of smoke-scarred appliances, toilet tanks, a hot water heater, and assorted rubble. A pair of ten- or eleven-year-old kids poked with sticks at the detritus of a place where good people had once slept, screwed, fought, loved, read a morning paper over toast and coffee, watched TV, raised a kid, and then lost her as an adult. I felt somehow embarrassed to be looking at the rubble, as if caught staring at a naked corpse. I ran the kids off, though I'd be hard-pressed to explain why.

The neighborhood was a lot like the one I grew up in. Ma didn't like our house and was always on Dad to move to a bigger one in a better neighborhood. Dad would mumble something about we had a roof over our heads, which 62 percent of the world didn't have, and that would quiet her down for a while because Amy Strobe rarely said anything confrontational to Dad, except on Saturday nights when they both had a snootful, then watch out. The floodgates would open, and six days of frustration would come pouring out, Ma screaming like Bette Davis in one of those old horror movies and Dad giving it right back to her. My sister, Lisa—four years younger than me—would crawl into bed with me, and we'd lie there trembling, unable to make out the words.

Next morning, we'd sneak out early to see if Dad's packed suitcase was standing by the front door, and it was always there. Relieved, we'd creep back in bed until we heard Ma stirring around in the kitchen. Soon out would come Joe Strobe, grabbing a cup of coffee, joking around and patting Ma on her ass like nothing had happened. The suitcase would have vanished back into the closet.

After two hours of getting nowhere with the Breckenridges' neighbors, I concluded that Rose and Harold had either been recluses or the whole damn 'hood was tongue-tied with fear. Most people were nice, but a few doors were slammed in my face. If anybody knew where the Breckenridges had gone, they were keeping it to themselves.

Worried about attracting attention to myself, I approached the local fire department as a freelance newsman researching an article on seasonal fire dangers associated with candles in Halloween pumpkins and Christmas lights on drying trees. The guy at the counter bought my story—too bizarre to be contrived—but explained department policy prohibited giving out forwarding addresses in cases involving "possible arson."

I was stymied, so decided to call supernerd Mace Rothschild—Web whiz and retired computer hacker. When I asked him if the Internet could be used to find relocated people, he gave me his superior Ivy League chuckle.

"If they have settled in somewhere, it may take all of five minutes.

If you have ten, I can also steal their identities, transfer ownership of their automobiles over to you, and provide free access to all their credit cards."

I thanked him. "Their current address will do fine."

On my way back to the office, I wondered if Mace's Internet could also shed some light on Lisa's mystery list. Someone on that list other than Judge Ryan had seemed familiar, and it had been nagging at me for days. I stopped for gas and glanced at the list while waiting for my tank to fill. No lightbulb. Nothing.

But later, halfway across the San Mateo Bridge, listening to an old Willie Nelson tune, one name hit me square between the eyes.

Lowell Horan.

Horan had been the City Attorney in Enid, not the one who prosecuted Dad, but someone Dad had tried cases against over the years. That put me to thinking that since Charlie Ryan had been so favorable to Dad after the verdict, well, what if the list was like-minded folks who supported Dad's innocence? If so, twenty-six favorable people could pony up a hell of a lot of helpful information, especially if one of them was the City Attorney at the time Dad was convicted. A long shot, maybe, but the notion gave me a rush. Lisa's list could be the key to reopening Dad's case.

I decided I'd put *People vs. Joe Strobe* off long enough and would tell Lisa to track down some of the people listed and schedule interviews for me in Enid.

Back to my office, I had just hung up making flight reservations to Oklahoma and talking with Lisa when in walked Hale Lassiter, pale and grim-faced. He got right to the point without sitting down or so much as a howdy.

"Rex has reason to distrust the commitment you made to quit snooping around on your friend's case," he said, his tone uncharacteristically harsh. "I have doubts of my own. I want to hear the truth from you, Billy. Now."

I wished my office was big enough to pace in because I had a sudden hankering to do some pacing. Instead, I stayed put, trapped behind my desk, feeling my face go red as Hale's necktie. I was both ashamed at having been caught lying to such a good man and angry that Dana must have blabbed Klinehart's message to the whole damned partnership. On top of that, I was disappointed to have been caught. On probation already, this would kill me at S & S, and I hadn't yet made it back inside Synoptics.

"What I told you was true at the time," I said, after my mental pacing had led me nowhere. "At that point, I had stopped working with my investigator."

"A Mr. Klinehart, as I recall. I take it you started again?"

"Yes."

I studied Hale's expression, hoping it would reveal how much he knew, my devious intention being to admit only that much and nothing more.

"To do what?"

"To find Deborah's parents and talk to them. But nothing to do with Jason Moncrief or Synoptics."

"And did you or he talk to them?"

I realized I was being cross-examined by an expert who, for some reason, wasn't holding his cards close to his vest. He was almost telegraphing his intended direction, and I knew that what he wanted most of all was for me not to lie to him.

"I tried, but they wouldn't talk to me."

"I know," Hale said cooly. "They called me this morning to complain about you."

I was trying to figure out whether Hale also knew about Klinehart's murder when we were interrupted by Rex Ashton, who made his usual forceful, unbidden entry, then stood, hands on hips, looking from Hale to me and back to Hale again as if he'd caught us in some kind of unnatural relationship. My tiny office was suddenly jammed with senior partners and serious tension.

"Let me not waste any more words with you, Strobe," Ashton said, his features as rigid as an ice sculpture. "You're fired, and I want you out of here yesterday."

My stomach clutched at his words, but as Ashton turned to leave, Hale had grabbed his arm with enough force to spin the smaller man around and drop him into my client's chair.

"On whose authority?" Hale said, his voice hoarse and hot in Ashton's face.

"On the authority of the executive committee," said Ashton, betraying no anxiety. "Wilcox and I met an hour ago when we learned that Strobe's investigator was killed two nights ago. A Jewish chap named Klinehart. Fortunately, nobody has connected the investigator to Strobe or to S & S. So far. In any event, firing an associate is the prerogative of a majority vote of the executive committee under our bylaws, and two members qualify as a quorum as you well know."

Hale released Ashton's arm, but said nothing. What was there to say? I was screwed, and found myself wondering what would Joe Strobe do in a situation like this?

Hale had gone to the well too often for me and if I was going to get a last shot at getting inside Synoptics, plus keeping the flow of big money coming for Ma's rehab clinic, I'd have to save myself. Stay cool, *that's* what Dad would do and *think*.

I rose and extended my hand to Hale. "You've been more than fair with me, Hale," I said, as if Ashton wasn't there, "and I guarantee the press will hear about it."

"The press?" said Ashton, as a knowing smile crossed Hale's face.

I looked down at the still-seated senior partner. "It's funny, Mr. Ashton, but I still get calls from all those reporters who made such a fuss over you folks at S & S when you beat out all the other publicity grabbers who were trying to hire me. You'll be pleased to know, sir, that I haven't peeped about the way you've tried to railroad me out of here since the day I arrived. Nor have I shown any of them my time records or notes of commendation from other partners I've worked with here."

Ashton met this challenge without blinking, but I could see his shoulders begin to sag.

"Nor have I gone public with your personal vendetta against Mr. Lassiter—"

"Who," Ashton interrupted, "is going to believe such a preposterous claim?"

"Hard to say, Mr. Ashton. I guess you can take some solace in the fact that the associates who will confirm all this might want to remain anonymous, which may weaken the credibility of the exposé. On the other hand, my insights concerning the Hinton SEC investigation may spark some renewed interest in Synoptics and Jason Moncrief. Maybe even you, sir."

Ashton's shoulders sagged even more. His mouth began to move, but nothing came out. Ashen-faced, he looked up at Hale, but Hale just shrugged his shoulders.

Ashton turned toward me. "Are you blackmailing me, Strobe?"

"No sir," I said. "I think it's more like extortion."

Hale tried to hold back a smile. "It's extortion, Rex, definitely extortion."

"You bastards think this is *funny*?"

You would, too, I thought, if you had a mirror handy. But I restrained myself and said nothing more, not wanting to make things harder for me or for Hale.

The little man jumped to his feet, but Hale gently restrained him. "Rex, I think we'd better listen to Billy."

It took another twenty minutes to strike a deal and, as trial lawyers say about any good settlement, both sides were equally unhappy with it. The terms were simple: I would be allowed to finish drafting my motion for Darryl and to file it under the firm's masthead, but would delete any references to Synoptics, Moncrief, or both. That was giving Ashton the sleeves out of my vest, because if my first motion failed, I'd just quit the firm and bring another motion, using whatever I might later discover on Moncrief.

The only sticking point was the hearing on the motion.

"I don't want this tyro arguing a motion under the firm's banner," said Ashton to Hale, as if I wasn't even there.

Given the fact I couldn't argue the motion myself anyways, I decided to try to get the fox to throw the rabbit into the brier patch.

"Please, Mr. Ashton, I *need* to argue this motion. Maybe I could do it as part of the firm's pro bono poverty clinic." I knew Hale supervised this program and personally argued most of the important motions himself, unlike at other large firms where public service was seen mainly as a training device for compassionate but inexperienced young associates.

"Absolutely not," Ashton said, and I waited hopefully for the next shoe to drop. I didn't have to wait long.

"I'll argue it," said Hale.

"Well, fine," said Ashton, and it was done. It was hard to suppress a smile. Hale Lassiter arguing the case would be a huge plus for Darryl, given his skill and the high regard in which he was held by the appellate judges. Plus, I'd be off the hook once and for all.

I agreed and the details of the plan were worked out in Ashton's more spacious quarters. Within an hour, I had signed an agreement disclaiming any employee abuse to date, and barring me from complaining to the press in the event I should "at some later date" be discharged for "good cause," which would have to be supported by either the unanimous vote of the executive committee or a petition signed by no less than twenty partners. If terminated, I would receive two months' severance pay.

The important thing about this process was that it would take two to three months minimum for Ashton to marshal twenty votes to fire me, hopefully more than enough time for me to finish my investigation of Moncrief and Synoptics. In addition, the severance money I'd be paid would ensure Ma's stay at a top clinic while I found myself a new job.

Ashton insisted on one more thing. I was to have nothing further to do with Darryl Orton or his case once the motion for new trial was ruled upon. I hesitated only a second before agreeing. I planned to be gone from S & S after the motion was argued anyway. Besides, if I got lucky, Moncrief might have taken Darryl's place in prison by that time, which meant that Ashton might be gone even before I was.

*   *   *

It didn't take long—two hours at most—for Dana to hear about my new arrangement with the firm. I had been thinking about confronting her about overhearing Barney's message when she showed up in my doorway, smiling that perfect smile.

"Billy, this is wonderful!" she said, taking a seat across from my desk, her face a picture of glowing innocence. "Hale told me the good news. With him involved, the pressure will be off *you*. This will change *everything*."

"Not everything," I said coldly. "My investigator, Barney Kline-hart, is still dead and Deborah Hinton's parents are still burned out of their house. Or hadn't you heard?"

She seemed puzzled by my tone.

"I heard about the Klinehart murder, but I didn't know he was your investigator. And I've heard nothing about a fire at the Hintons' house. What are you getting at, Billy?"

I was fed up with dancing around with these clever folks at S & S, including Dana. "What I'm getting at is you overheard the message from Barney Klinehart when you were in my office two nights ago." I heard a sudden intake of air as she put the back of her hand to her mouth like I'd struck her. "I'm thinking you told somebody what you heard."

If Dana's response to my accusation was an act, then give the girl an Oscar. Her expression went from surprise to crimson anger, and the hand at her mouth had clenched itself into a fist of white-knuckle fury.

She said nothing, and I was relieved when she turned and strode toward the door. But then she stopped, turned slowly, and gave me another hard look and said, "You want to hear a good one, Billy? I know it's absurd, but I had clung to the notion that we could work things out."

"I'm sure you did," I said, picking up a file and opening it. "Then you remembered that the firm always comes first, right? After that, you opened your eyes and noticed I wasn't wearing a Brooks Brothers three-piece suit, walking a pair of prize-winning Irish wolfhounds toward my Mercedes SUV, right? Instead, you saw a man driving a '93 Ford to a professional dead-end in Milpitas."

"No," she said, arms folded tight against her chest. "What I saw was someone who lacked the ability to trust, something I can't stand in a man. Someone who persuades himself he's in love with me one minute and the next minute practically accuses me of a conspiracy to murder a man I didn't even know he was connected with."

Playacting or not, I began to feel a worm of doubt gnawing at my conviction. Had I overreacted again? Shooting from the hip like I sometimes did? Maybe shooting myself in the foot this time?

I walked around my desk and approached her. "Here's all I know for sure, Dana: My carelessness somehow caused a man's death as surely as if I'd pulled the trigger. I can't trust anybody now without a damn good reason, and you haven't given me one."

"No? Well here's one: How about the presumption of innocence you're always ranting about? Is that asking too much for someone you claimed to love?"

All this use of the past tense pierced my heart like a Soledad bonecrusher. "You *didn't* hear the message?"

"I heard words on your playback as I was walking toward your office. I couldn't understand them."

My brain was churning. "Listen, Dana," I said. "If I've been wrong about you, then I need *you* to trust *me*. And help me."

"You expect me to *help* you?"

"Why not? Think of it as helping me with this trust problem I've got."

She shook her head. "That's not helping you with your problem about trust, Billy. That's asking me to prove myself worthy of it. I think they call it 'enabling' these days."

I nodded, jammed my hands deep in my pockets, and said, "Well, maybe you're right."

When I saw her eyes soften, I added, "Just help me out here, Dana. Please. I know you'll think I'm crazy, but . . . well, I'm almost sure Jason Moncrief is involved in Deborah Hinton's murder. It may still be that Deborah's husband did it, but things are starting to point in Moncrief's direction, too."

Dana stiffened, and I swear her eyes went a darker shade of green as they flashed on me.

"Based on?" she said, her voice as cold and unyielding as before.

"Several things; I just need to come up with some hard proof."

"Do you even have any soft proof?"

"Call it medium-gauge," I said as I walked around behind her, shut the door, and lowered my voice. "Mildred Moon, Deborah's secretary, says Deborah and Moncrief spent a lot of time together. She thinks Frank Hinton thought they might be having an affair. Deborah was pregnant when she was murdered, which would have damn sure thrown a wrench in Moncrief's domestic tranquillity, plus which he could have been getting nervous she might blow the whistle on the insider scam I'm sure he engineered from the git-go. Or maybe she had taken her own profits without telling him, and he was going to teach her a lesson that somehow got out of control."

Dana folded her arms, unconvinced.

"Hell, Dana, I know it's frail, but Mildred Moon also told me he was coming into the building when she left work the night Deborah was murdered, though he later denied it to the police. Mildred says he asked if Deborah was still in her office."

She looked away. I moved in closer.

"On top of him lying to the police, throw in what you told me about Deborah and Moncrief making profits on the upswing in Synoptics stock. Do you think Deborah would have deferred that write-off without Moncrief's knowledge or approval? Mildred also saw him removing Deborah's computer soon after her body was discovered. And who other than Moncrief—the building's anchor tenant—would have the kind of clout to get his hands on, then destroy, the building log?"

"It's gone?"

"Disappeared, but *only* the week of Deborah's murder."

I waited, twenty, thirty or more seconds. Finally, Dana gave her head a quick shake and turned back to me. "No, Billy. Even if you were right on every point—which you're probably not—it's not enough to either free your friend or convict Jason, and you know it. If you have to act out this fantasy, pick on Frank Hinton, who at least had a motive, five hundred thousand of them. If Jason Moncrief were guilty, the truth would have come out long ago."

"Come on, Dana, be serious. With his money and power, Moncrief's a fox in the justice system's chicken house. Besides, as soon as the police found the weapon behind Darryl's locker, then tied in the DNA, it was all over."

"My, how surprising," said Dana.

"Dammit, it *is* surprising. I know Darryl Orton. The man is too smart to hide a murder weapon behind his own locker and he has too much decency to kill another human being, even a maniac named Ortez who nearly killed me in prison. Your infallible justice system convicted an innocent man, and alls I'm asking you to do is help me prove it."

Dana looked down at her clasped hands, and I sensed that I was wearing her down. "What could I possibly do that would help you," she said wearily, "assuming I wanted to?"

"I'm not long for this place, Dana," I said, taking a step toward her, so close I could smell jasmine in her hair. "All I've done by cutting the deal you heard about is to buy myself a little time."

"Time? For what?"

"I've got to see the files on the Securities Exchange Commission's investigation of Deborah, Moncrief, and Synoptics, all of them. The firm's files have been shredded, but there may be copies in the Synoptics closed file area, and you'd know where they would be."

She turned away from me and stared at her hands. I held my breath. When she spoke, it was like the words were being pulled out of her.

"I'll help you undertake this fool's errand, but if you do find something you think is significant, will you give me your word that you won't do anything stupid without letting Hale or me talk you out of it? Moncrief is our biggest *client*, Billy."

"I promise," I said, and I meant it. "I give you my word."

She lowered her head, exhaled loudly, eyes closed, but more in dismay than negation. Then she leaned forward and whispered so softly I had to lean in close to her, which in Dana's case I didn't mind doing even though I wasn't completely convinced about her yet.

"What you want to get into, Billy, is not like any other file room; it's a vault. It's where the firm's most confidential files are kept. It's fire- and burglar-proof with a combination security panel at the door with a ten-digit code for access."

"And you have access," I said.

She hesitated. "Rex, Hale, and I are the only ones in the firm."

I didn't say a word or move a muscle. She reached out and picked up some paper and a pen from my desk and started writing. I knew what she was doing and what it was costing her.

After she had written down the entry code, she told me that finding the vault would be my first challenge, then drew a crude map on the back side of the same sheet of paper. Then she got up without another word and walked out of my office.

I stared at the paper for a long time, my mind in turmoil. There was never any doubt but that I'd use it—and use it soon before Dana changed her mind—but I had to think of a way to protect her if I was caught. I also had to pick the best time to make my play. Breaking and entering Synoptics at night was beyond my expertise, so I decided I'd do it early the next morning, before all the top executives showed up.

Barbara, my attractive but sometimes pushy secretary, barged through the door without knocking and I shied like a stung colt, involuntarily crumpling the paper in my hand.

"A little too much caffeine today, big guy?"

"Trying to quit."

"Well, here's another little something from home," she said, and plunked down a package with a return address of the Enid County Clerk's office. I tore it open and saw the court docket and the exhibits from my father's trial, including the faked exhibit that both the client and Amos Blackwell had swore my dad admitted signing. I studied the signature carefully and had to admit that though disguised, the distinctive *A* and the unique way he made a *w* gave me a sudden headache. Of course, that's what Blackwell or the client would want somebody to think.

The clerk's file also showed that the jury had deliberated little more than an hour before convicting Dad of fraud and forgery, barely enough time to elect a foreperson. They had not been tortured by doubt.

I put the exhibits in my trial bag and headed for the thirty-ninth floor and to Mace Rothschild's new, windowed office to see if he had located the Breckenridges.

"It's been considerably more than ten minutes, Mace," I told him as I walked through his open door, "at least according to my monthly calendar."

Mace's tie was uncharacteristically loosened, his coat draped across one of his client chairs, his sleeves rolled up to his bony elbows.

"You look downright macho, Scarecrow," I added. "You on steroids again?"

"It's this damn hothouse they moved me into," he said, pointing to a window that looked east toward Oakland, just large enough to allow the morning sun to turn his office into a microwave oven set on high.

"As a law office," I observed, "this appears to be a good place to raise tropical plants."

He nodded agreement. "I'd raise hell if I wasn't so weak."

"Before you vaporize, would you mind locating the witnesses for my dad's case?"

"I'm sorry, cowboy, but your Breckenridges are going to have to settle in somewhere; you know, start some services, establish credit, develop some kind of pattern. They've vanished without a trace."

"Hale told me they just called him. Does that help?"

He cocked his head. "I might be able to do something with it, unless they used a pay phone. By the way, why did they call Hale if this is related to your dad's case in Oklahoma?"

Damn Scarecrow didn't miss a trick. "There's a simple explanation for that," I told him. "I've been lying to you."

"Oh. Well, as long as you're being truthful about it."

"It's true, swear to God. I lied through my teeth."

"Okay, I believe you. You're a liar. Does that mean this is an office case I could bill time to? I'm light this month."

I shook my head. "I'm lending a hand to some guy I met in prison, okay?"

Mace nodded. "Sure. I'll do what I can."

I returned to my apartment building around ten o'clock that night, brain-dead and wondering whether Darryl's motion had a hog's chance in hell of prevailing. No matter how many times I reworked the draft, I couldn't find a clear path around the DNA, three little letters that would comprise the beginning, middle, and end of the deputy attorney general's rebuttal. On the other hand, my hopes rested not on my inelegant prose, but on Hale's reputation and personal relationships he had with two of the three judges on the panel. I knew how the old-boy system operated, and I have to admit it felt comforting to know that for the first and probably last time in my career, I was on the winning side of it.

I stumbled bleary-eyed down the empty hallway of the third floor toward my apartment, wondering whether there was anything edible in my freezer. When I reached my door and started to stick my key in the lock, it swung open. I must have left it ajar when I rushed out this morning.

There was a light on in the kitchen. I must have left it on, too, when I rushed out this morning.

But sitting at my kitchen table was a very large, ugly man staring hard at me, who I definitely hadn't left sitting there when I rushed out this morning.

"Close it," he said, in a voice that sounded like a Sherman tank on loose gravel. I turned and looked longingly at the door, wishing to God I'd never walked through it. "Don't even think about it," he added.

Deborah Hinton, Barney Klinehart, and now my turn. I eyed the yellow hardwood block where my cheapo set of carving knives was stacked. Then I eyed the man, who gave his head a little shake that said don't even think about that either.

"You want to tell me who you are," I said, sounding surprisingly calm, "and what you're doing in my apartment?"

"You want to sit your ass down and shut the fuck up?" he said, then raised his knee and kicked his foot under the table, sending a chair flying toward me. I grabbed it, sat, and shut the fuck up.

"My name is Terrell Jaxon. That's spelled with an *x*. Like in *axe*."

Oh, shit. I took a closer look at my visitor. Terrell Jaxon (with an *x*) was beyond black. He was what Southern bigots called a *blue*. He was also a man of huge dimensions, with a head the size of a basketball and a brow like corrugated metal that smoothed out into polished ebony when it reached what had once been a hairline. Uncommonly small but intelligent eyes sparked like cinders when he spoke.

"I'm a homicide inspector," he continued, flipping open an ID wallet, "with the San Francisco Police Department."

My relief must have lit up the room, until he hit me with the rest.

"I'm talkin to possible suspects in the murder of one Barnard Klinehart. He worked for you, didn't he?"

"Sure he did," I said, and told myself to keep cool, no matter what. "Me and a few hundred other clients. I guess that narrows the field of suspects to a number you might be able to squeeze into the Giants' new ballpark."

He didn't smile. "You know somethin, Strobe? That's exactly what I thought at first, too. Then I found out that *one* of his clients was a paroled felon, can you imagine that? A paroled *felon*, who happened to get Klinehart's very last phone call before he was killed and who failed to come forward with this vital information. That's *you*, Mr. Strobe, and I think you would squeeze just fine in the back of my squad car."

27

Think, I told myself, staring into Terrell Jaxon's accusing, blood-shot eyes. What had I learned so far that could get this guy off my back? Well, first, if the cops had lifted any of my prints at Klinehart's office, Jaxon would have a warrant and would have flashed it right off. I'd already be in his squad car heading for the station. Which means they didn't have prints and couldn't put me in Barney's office that night.

On the other hand, he was right about how I should have come forward, which could constitute grounds for revoking my parole—particularly if he had bought himself some insurance by planting an ounce or two of coke in my apartment before I had arrived. Ex-cons are never really free.

On the *other*-other hand, he hadn't read me my rights, so I probably wasn't a formal suspect yet. I decided that to avoid becoming one, I should remain righteously indignant, yet show a willingness to cooperate.

I started the righteously indignant part by standing up so that I could look down on him. "Since you know so much about me, In-spector, you must know I'm a lawyer with a passing knowledge of the U.S. Constitution."

He widened his small eyes and covered his mouth with his fingers in mock fear. "A *law-yer*! You a real *law-yer*?"

"That's cute," I said, "but the fact is you're guilty of breaking and entering, and even if I had been here when you arrived, I don't see a warrant anywhere."

"True, all true, Mr. Ex-Felon Strobe. So there's your phone. You want my captain's direct line number?"

Was he bluffing?

"What do want from me, Detective?"

"Inspector. Inspector Terrell M. Jaxon—"

"With an *x*."

"Good to see you can be cute, too, Strobe. Look, I'd just like a little information; then I'll be on my way, okay? So come on and sit back down so we can visit a spell. Pretty please?"

Being by himself, I reckon Jaxon had to play both bad cop *and* good cop. But I welcomed the change and took a seat. He pulled a notebook out of the side pocket of his baggy sport coat and took me step-by-step from the first day I had met Barney Klinehart in my office. I told him everything except what he wanted to know, since that would have bought me a ride downtown. He was getting frustrated, ordered me not to leave the county pending his investigation.

"Hey, Inspector, I've got a job," I said. "Travel is part of it. Besides, Barney's last message said he had run out of leads and was off the case. That's the last thing I heard from him."

Jaxon raised his eyebrows, deepening the grooves that cut across his forehead. "Take a close look at my handsome face, Mr. Strobe, and see how surprised I gonna appear when you tell me you done erased that message."

"But it's the truth, sir. Really." And, for once, it was. "We get so many messages at the office, we have to—"

"Clean 'em off lickety-split. Sure you do."

Jaxon sparked his eyes at me, but I had become an accomplished liar and managed to meet his glare head-on, despite his annoying habit of rhythmically rapping fingernails on the table whenever he thought I was being evasive, which was pretty much all the time. Like the Chinese water torture, the mannerism made every minute seem like an hour. Suddenly, he stopped rapping and exploded to his feet in a way that caused his bountiful stomach to hit the table and push the other end of it into my lower rib cage and solar plexus, knocking the wind out of me.

"Why, ex*cuuuse* me, suh," he said, flashing me another wry smile. "I had wrote myself a reminder to get back on my Jenny Craig, but I guess I done *erased* it by mistake."

Bad cop was back.

"That's . . . all right, sir," I gasped, then pretended to lose my balance as I also rose to my feet, falling hard against the table, pushing the other side into his thighs, just above his knees. He didn't so much as wince, but it had to hurt.

"Excuse me, too, sir," I said, and he stiffened, but then flashed another droll smile at me. Neither of us had laid a hand on the other, yet each of us would be sore in the morning, and each had sent the other a message.

Then he sent me one more over his shoulder as he walked out, leaving my door open:

"I'll be watching you, Strobe."

Get in line, I thought, then set the dead bolt behind him.

I spent the next two weeks catching up on projects for Rex Ashton and working with Hale on the argument on Darryl's motion for new trial. He asked all the right questions, and I was starting to feel pretty good about our prospects, until I got home from work one evening with three days to go before the hearing and found a note in my mailbox, one of those cut and paste jobs.

DROP THE   or we'll   **client.**
                new trial   **drop your**

I shuddered when I read this, because I knew how easy it was to get somebody "dropped" in prison. The going rate at Soledad when I was there was a carton of cigarettes. It was also obvious that this guy wasn't a bluffer, whoever he was. He had killed at least twice before and wouldn't hesitate to kill again. On the other hand, the note also represented the best evidence I had so far pointing to Darryl's innocence, so I raced back to the office and prepared an addendum affidavit, attaching a copy of the note.

But what to do about Darryl? No point in telling him. Issuing a warning to that blindly courageous savant would be like taunting a bull with a red rose. He'd laugh at me or worse, tell me to go ahead and drop the motion since I'd been fired two or three times anyway.

Whoever sent the note wouldn't move on him until they learned whether or not I was going to comply with their demand. So he'd be safe until at least noon tomorrow. That left him exposed for two and a half days. I'd have to come up with something, but what? How could I stop a contract murder inside prison walls, operating as I was from the outside? On the other hand, how could I "drop it," now that I was so close?

It came to me after my second cup of coffee at six the next morning. The idea was far from perfect, but better than casting Darryl's fate

to a stranger with a fresh carton of Camels. So after a trip to my ATM
machine, I left a message to Barbara that I'd been called away on an
emergency, then headed toward Soledad. By11:30 A.M., I was seated in
the visitors area, not with Darryl, but with Tom Collins.

"You're looking good, Tom," I said, and I meant it. He looked not
a minute older than when I'd last seen him nearly a year ago, and he
still had his affable smile and the majestic presence and grace that a
few very tall men are endowed with. "Looking forward to Thanksgiv-
ing?" I said, knowing how Tom liked irony.

He laughed. "In here, we be more like the turkeys."

I asked about Dickens, and his eyes grew troubled.

"Dickens be dead, kid," he said, and reached into his pocket. "He
give me this the day before he OD'd. It's for you."

I unfolded the wrinkled scrap of paper. I could barely make out his
handwriting, and the sudden film of moisture covering my eyes didn't
help.

> My Dear Master Billy:
>
> "I longed for death but it cameth not." Until
> now. I'm free dear lad, finally free. God bless.
>
> Dickens.

In small letters scrawled below was carefully printed out: Job 3:21.
It was the clue he had given me months before. His escape plan.

Dickens had busted out.

"Sorry, kid, I know you liked the old man."

I nodded, folded the paper, and put it in my wallet, wondering why
I'd never told Dickens how much.

"Dickens was deep into Hinduism," I told Tom, "always talking
about 'Shiva the Destroyer, creator of the dance.' He'd be sharpening
a piece of rebar into a shank and say, 'Out of *destruction* comes *re-
creation*, Billy. *Renewal!*' "

"Who knows," said Tom Collins, "maybe the old fart be comin
back as a pope or sumpin."

I shook it off best I could while he brought me up to date on Darryl, Earring, Rabbit, and the current gang gossip.

"Is Darryl out of the infirmary?"

"He be outta the infirmary and in and outta the Hole and back in
the yard gettin his ass whupped and kickin some ass his own self, too.
Sure, he's okay. Till next time."

Till next time, I thought, frowning as I fingered Dickens's envelope
in my pocket; then I came to the point of my visit. After five minutes

of discussion, some of which got a little heated, I handed him an envelope containing fifty dollars, twenty-five for Tom and twenty-five for the heavy he would select to carry out the contract that I was issuing on Darryl Orton.

"Never thought I'd come to pimpin out a friend for twenty-five dollars," Tom said, "though I will say it's a hell of a lot of money and it *is* comin up on Christmas."

"And it's for a good cause. There's another twenty-five dollars after lunch for you when you tell me it's a done deal."

Tom nodded and started to walk away.

"Remember, Tom," I said. "I want him in solitary, not the infirmary. After he's been provoked into the fight, I don't want him seriously hurt."

"I *knows* what you want," he said, and then waved to take the hard edge off his tone. He still didn't much approve of the idea, but seventy-five dollars was big money inside; he'd keep most of the money himself, as he wouldn't really need to pay twenty-five dollars to get someone to provoke Darryl Orton. Nuestra Familia members did it every day for free.

I left the prison and drove into Salinas for lunch. I made some phone calls to cover my ass for disappearing at work, then headed south back to Soledad.

When Tom emerged from the sally port into the visitors area he gave me a thumbs-up, and as soon as he was seated, I counted out another twenty-five dollars and held it out to him.

"I can't take it," he said. "I've already done pocketed the whole fifty dollars. I got it took care of for two cartons of cigs."

"Take the money, Tom. Give it to Darryl next time you see him. Just don't tell him where it came from. Was he hurt?"

"Old Darryl, he get over it," said Tom, rising to his full six feet six inches. "Few stitches maybe. Had to hire two guys to make enough racket so's to be sure it wake up the COs. Darryl, he could put away one a' them so quick nobody notice, so I got me some spics to hit on him. The man ain't what he was, but he still a tough old motherfucker. Them boys earned their cigs."

"You sure he'll pull three days in the Hole?"

"He already there. Three days guaranteed. One of them Mexicans is in the infirmary for longer than that. Ain't nobody can touch a hair on Darryl's pretty head now."

"Good, he's losing it fast enough on his own."

Tom let out a laugh that lit up the drab visitors room, then took my hand and held it firmly for a moment, taking me in from above with those doleful, knowing eyes.

He nodded slowly and said, "You be some kind of lawyer, Billy."

"Thank you, Tom," I said, feeling a rush of pride, wishing Dad could have heard it.

Then he smiled and added, "Remind me never to hire you my own self. You got a mighty strange way of protectin your clients."

"Take care of yourself, old man," I said, smiling back at the master needler. "That's rough company in there."

"No rougher than what it sound like you into, kid. You best watch your white ass. I bet you got no Earring or Darryl Orton to protect you on the outside."

I nodded and watched him walk off.

The day of the hearing arrived, and Hale and I passed through the metal detector on the fourth floor of Earl Warren Building, which housed the District Court of Appeals where Darryl's fate would soon be decided.

I'm usually not all that impressed with buildings, but when we entered the appellate courtroom, I had to catch my breath. Hale explained that the structure had been retrofitted following the Loma Prieta earthquake. A thirty-foot-high coffered ceiling and lush oak paneling gave the room a look of majesty, but what knocked my socks off was a huge mural that ran forever across the long wall behind the elevated bench where the justices sat. Although the room reeked of traditional grandeur, it wasn't stuffy or dark like I'd expected, thanks to light-colored walls and a skylight in the ceiling high above us. The effect was to make the room seem much bigger than it was. It seemed a place more suited for celebration than argumentation.

Hale introduced me to the deputy attorney general who he'd be up against. He was a short, angular, sallow-faced guy in his mid-forties with close-cropped hair that looked like steel wool and grew down his forehead to within two inches of what appeared to be a single eyebrow. He saw me gawking at the mural and said, "It's a painting of the eastern Sierra Nevadas by Willard Dickson. Fabulous, isn't it?"

I wanted to ask him how he could stand at the podium facing such beauty and dare argue against a fellow human being's freedom.

"It's nice," I said, and we all walked forward up to the counsel tables. As we passed through the oak rail, I saw two bailiffs escorting Darryl into the courtroom from the side and felt a surge of relief that he had shown up. I'd urged Tom Collins to talk him into coming, but had placed the odds at no better than fifty-fifty.

Darryl was pale, with an angry wound above his left eye. The stitches were clearly infected, but at least he was alive and would stay that way. Whether we won or lost our motion, I'd prepped Hale to plead for protective custody outside of Soledad for Darryl, based on the threatening note I had attached to my affidavit. Ironically, the oozing wound and deathly pallor I had bought and paid for would maximize our prospects for winning at least that part of our motion.

Darryl spotted me and flashed me his crooked smile. He shuffled toward me as I approached him. I took his manacled hands in mine.

"Hello, Darryl. I'm glad you came."

"You're a hard man to fire," he said, and then scratched a three-day beard, making his chains rattle. "I guess I figured since I didn't pick a lawyer off that list, you'd have to argue my case your own self. Hell, I couldn't miss a show like that."

An alarm went off in my head. Should I have told him?

"Listen, Darryl. You've been in the Hole, so I couldn't tell you the good news. I got you a real trial lawyer, Hale Lassiter, the best in town!"

He shook his head brusquely and said, "I already got me a lawyer."

"Darryl, Mr. Lassiter's usual rate is seven hundred fifty dollars an hour! He's going to do it for *free*."

"Tell him I can afford a rate of seven hundred fifty dollars an hour, but he's just got to win my appeal in fourteen seconds."

"Be reasonable, Darryl—"

But he was already headed back toward the door to the holding cell.

"Where's he going?" Hale asked, and I tried to explain Darryl's pathological distrust of all lawyers.

Darryl stood quietly at the door to the holding cell, his back to us, the guard giving me a puzzled look.

"I hadn't told him you were making the argument," I admitted as the three judges filed in and took their seats. "I'm sorry, Hale. Maybe deep down I knew Darryl wouldn't come to court if I told him I wasn't going to do it myself."

"That's all right," Hale whispered. "His presence is not essential. Let him go."

Hale then walked up to a beautiful oak podium with a microphone mounted on top and began to speak but—

"Your Honors, sir," boomed a voice from the side door.

Christ, it was Darryl. He had turned toward the panel of justices.

"Excuse me, Your Honors," he shouted, "but see that dapper fellow there in front of the mike? Well he don't represent me, and I'd like to go back to my cell, if you don't mind. So you all can go right ahead with the next business on your schedule."

Hale resumed stating his appearance for the record and then said, "I apologize, Your Honors, but my client and I have not had the opportunity to meet. If we could have a moment—"

"Take all the moments you want," shouted Darryl, "but I ain't changin my mind. My lawyer is the young man sittin behind you, named Billy Strobe. He speaks for me or nobody does."

The senior judge—the bald-headed one in the middle—was patient, and tried to reason with Darryl, which anybody who knew Darryl could have told him was a waste of good time. Hale did his best, too, arguing every which way with both the chief judge and Darryl, but Darryl wouldn't bend.

"Mr. Lassiter is highly regarded by this court," the judge said to Darryl.

"Then you hire him, judge. I already got me a lawyer," Darryl said.

I walked over to the prisoner and said, "Dammit, Darryl, you know I can't talk with all these people in the courtroom. I'll let you down."

"Your dad would do it, right?"

"That was him. This is me!"

"Your Honors," Hale continued, more red-faced than I'd ever seen him, "this is outrageous. Mr. Orton's appearance isn't required for this hearing. If he hadn't shown up, we'd be well into it by this time."

The chief judge sighed sympathetically. "But he did show up, Mr. Lassiter, and he has a right to attend under the Constitution. He also has the right to his choice of counsel, misguided though it may be. No offense, Mr. Strobe."

"None taken, Your Honors," I said. "My . . . client is as m-misguided as anybody I've ever known—especially as regards this matter." I said the last words with a hard look at Darryl.

"Mr. Strobe simply isn't qualified, Your Honor!" said Hale, gripping the edges of the lectern. "He's a *first-year associate, a business lawyer.*"

Hale sounded like he was describing a crack-head or an axe murderer.

"He's assigned to the M & A and *probate* departments, Your Honors!"

Funny, but until I heard Hale's disdainful tone in explaining my job description, I hadn't realized how low I had sunk. The chief judge continued to be respectful of Hale, but it was clear his hands were tied. I'd never seen Hale so angry, which sort of surprised me.

The senior judge told the sheriff's deputies to seat the prisoner next to me. Darryl didn't resist, and came smiling toward me, rattling louder than a pair of armadillos copulating on sheet metal.

"The client being present," the senior judge said at last, "has every right to choice of counsel. Mr. Orton, please sit down."

Then, the judge turned his gaze on me and said three words that jabbed my gut with fear.

"Please proceed, Counsel."

"Dammit, Darryl," I whispered, "you *know* I can't do this."

"Know what your problem is, kid?"

"Hell, yes. It's you."

"Your problem is you growed up thinking your daddy was such hot shit you could never do anythin like he could do. Well, course you couldn't, you was just a kid when he died. Well, time you reckoned with the fact that he's dead and you're alive. At least you were when you walked in here, though I'm havin some doubts right now."

"Darryl, shut the fuck up and quit psychoanalyzing me. This is serious. Now, Hale can win you a—"

"So can you. My guess is you're taller now than your daddy ever was and smarter, too. You got to accept that and quit mumblin like a scared twelve-year-old. It's your turn now, Billy Strobe."

Meanwhile, Hale and the chief judge had an exchange I missed; then Hale stormed through the rail toward the main doors of the courtroom. Jesus, Mary, and Joseph—he was *leaving!*

"Hale!" I shouted, but he was gone. My heart was already ricocheting around my chest when I heard the judge say those damn words again.

"All right," he said, "please proceed, Counsel."

I sat, rigid as death, rooted to my chair, despite the judge raising his eyebrows at me and loudly clearing his throat. Twice.

Darryl squeezed my arm with bruising force, looked me in the eye with an intensity I'd seen only in the rec yard when he was protecting his bench. Then he said, "You know this story better than anyone in the courtroom, Billy Strobe; ain't nobody gonna gainsay you. If you're chickenshit about those three wore-out corpses up there, then stand up and tell *me* the story. Forget they're here."

"Fuck you, Darryl," I whispered. "You know I'm not chickenshit, but you've painted both of us into a corner."

"Didn't I just explain how it's all in your head?"

"Of *course* it's in my head, dammit, but that happens to be where the words get formed as well as where my damn mouth is! If you had accepted Mr. Lassiter—"

"Counsel!" said the senior judge. "For the last time, *proceed!"*

My heart was willing, but my feet were locked to the floor. I could have killed Darryl. How could I possibly argue a case in front of three appellate judges, a clerk, a bailiff, and two sheriff's deputies, plus another dozen lawyers behind the rail waiting their turn to argue their cases?

Darryl squeezed my arm even harder, pulled me close to him. "Now pay attention, Billy, I'm only gonna say this once. All that daddys ever amount to at the end is what they've left behind 'em. That's you, kid, and he's rootin for you. Show him you were payin attention."

I heard lawyers tittering behind me and one of the judges was shaking her head. I turned and looked at Darryl, and he gave his head a little encouraging shake. "It's just another step up the mountain, kid," he whispered. "You can do it. Just put one foot ahead of the other. One step at a time. Tell *me* the story, just you and me, okay?"

I don't know how, but I managed to rise on rubber legs and walk to the podium. I had no notes.

"Your Honors, I apologize for all this, but, well . . . like Mr. Lassiter said, I'm . . . no trial lawyer."

"Hell, kid, you don't sound any worsen the last one I had," said Darryl, to an outburst of laughter that was quickly squelched by the judge seated in the middle. The old con was trying to relax me.

"The prisoner will remain silent," said the senior judge, "or he will be removed. Continue, Counsel."

"Well, sirs, and madam," I said, but looking over at Darryl, at his open, encouraging face. "I think what I'd say . . . if I was prepared to . . . well, say it . . . is pretty much what I've already said in my brief."

The words were coming out of my mouth, at least, but by fits and starts, like a string of uncoupled freight cars.

"Counsel," said the senior judge, "are you waiving argument? If so, I wish you would make yourself more clear."

"I agree," said the deputy attorney general, "and if counsel is finished, I would like to be heard."

"Patience, Counselor," said the judge.

"Nice start, kid," Darryl said, in a stage whisper that brought more laughter. "At this rate, we might both get the death penalty."

Now he had the whole courtroom laughing, including me and the lady judge on the right.

"One more comment out of the prisoner," said the senior judge glaring at Darryl, "so much as a peep, and he will be removed from the courtroom."

Darryl nodded.

"What I meant, Your Honors," I said, again looking back at Darryl, "is that, well . . . if you have questions, I'll try to answer them."

"As a practical matter, Counsel," said the lady judge, "wouldn't a new trial just be wasting the taxpayers' time and money? Isn't the perfect DNA match dispositive of the matter?"

I have no idea how long I had not been breathing, but I realized that I'd better start again, seeing as how I knew the answer to that one.

"It might have been, ma'am," I said, taking in Darryl's encouraging smile, "but I don't reckon we'll ever know. It was never presented at trial, so its validity or lack of it was never tested on cross-examination."

Darryl beamed.

"But," she persisted, "the district attorney would be ready this time, if there were a new trial, would he not?"

Out of the corner of my eye I could see the attorney general nodding in agreement.

"Whether it came up at the first trial or not," she continued, "it's before us now. You're not really expecting us to un-ring that bell, are you?"

"No, ma'am. I'm telling you that 'the bell' hasn't been rung at all and if it has, you shouldn't be listening to it—not until the DNA issue has been tested on cross-examination. That's what the Constitution says, and that's what I say. So don't listen to it; don't even think about it."

I turned away from Darryl and saw three sets of hard, astonished eyes bearing down on me with the combined weight of at least seventy-five years of jurisprudential heavy lifting. It was so quiet in the courtroom, I could hear my own heart pounding. Behind the justices, the high Sierras had never looked so cold.

"What I mean is, Your Honors, I respectfully submit that it should not be considered by you at all."

Jesus, I was doing pretty well at this, though the judge to my left was shaking his head and scowling.

"Counsel, unless you're lip-reading cues from your client," he said, "would you mind looking at us once in a while?"

It's true, I'd been acting like nobody was around but Darryl, and it had worked. But now, though I was looking squarely at the judge, the words kept right on coming.

"Yes, Your Honor, but what *should* be considered, are the following facts: First, the defendant had inadequate counsel at his first nontrial, a lawyer who railroaded the defendant into a guilty plea, threatening Mr. Orton with his prior felony as a kid, something that could not even have been revealed to the jury unless Mr. Orton had taken the stand."

It was crazy, but I was sounding like a real lawyer.

"Second, my investigator, who had discovered evidence he believed would reveal Deborah Hinton's real killer, was murdered himself before he could turn it over to me." I wondered what Investigator Jaxon with an *x* would do if he ever heard I had said this.

The attorney general rose and said, "Speaking of things that shouldn't be considered, Your Honors—"

"Your opportunity will come, Counsel," said the senior judge. "Please sit."

"Third," I heard myself say in a voice blooming with new confidence, "there is no credible motive linking the defendant to Ms. Hinton. Fourth, the police, in their rush to judgment, dismissed the statement of an eyewitness to an argument between Ms. Hinton and her estranged husband only hours before she was murdered. Fifth, the logbook for the night of death showing who was in the TechnoCenter at the estimated time of the murder has mysteriously disappeared. That month, Your Honors, and *only* that month."

The words were coming so fast the court reporter had to ask me to slow down.

"Sixth, the home of Ms. Hinton's parents, probably containing crucial additional exculpatory evidence, was burned to the ground by an arsonist *within two hours of Mr. Klinehart's murder.* Seventh . . ."

The words kept rushing out of my mouth like a cavalry charge; there was no stopping them. I don't know how long I went on, but the judges eventually shut me up, and I felt Darryl shaking hands with me in full view of the judges and everybody else. The deputy attorney general, who had risen to commence his argument, couldn't be heard for the rattling of Darryl's chains and the laughter from the gallery.

"You done it, kid! You run right up that mountain."

As strong as I am, I couldn't get my right hand out of Darryl's grip. "Darryl, for Christ's sake!" I said, but his hand was like a vise.

"Please, Mr. Orton," said the senior judge with more patience than I expected.

It didn't take long for the deputy attorney general to get personal again, railing about how I'd made up half the stuff in my affidavit.

"Why," he intoned, "should we be surprised at this? Defense counsel and the chief affiant in support of appellant's motion are not only one and the very same person, he is an ex-felon and admitted longtime friend and fellow inmate of the prisoner!"

The bald senior judge, a plucky little guy with a red nose and veins breaking out all over his cheeks, furrowed his brow and made a disdainful clicking sound with his mouth. The AG smiled, thinking the judge was thinking ill of me, but I could see the old boy hadn't liked the AG calling another lawyer—even a rookie office lawyer—a liar in open court. I would later learn that judges never liked to see trial lawyers hold each other in public contempt; that was a perquisite of office reserved for judges only. So maybe I had at least one of the three in my corner.

When the arguments were over, the panel surprised everyone by retiring and conferring briefly in chambers. The bailiff said they did that sometimes when a prisoner was being held in temporary detention on the seventh floor over at the Hall of Justice.

"Hell," said Darryl, "they didn't have to rush on my account. The food's pretty good here. At least it's different."

The three judges returned to their seats ten minutes later to announce their decision.

"Mr. Strobe," said the woman judge, who I guess was in charge of the case. "You have given us not one piece of evidence that would support a jury verdict in favor of your client. Your affidavits, which consist of rank hearsay and are indeed subject to issues of credibility, were supplemented only by Ms. Moon's affidavit, which concerned an argument between the victim and her estranged husband. Rarely has this court been treated to so much supposition."

Darryl started humming "America the Beautiful." I kicked him under the table. I was frustrated by Darryl's behavior, even as I was cursing myself for having failed him. Hale might have made all the difference. The deputy attorney general was smiling openly.

"But interesting supposition it is," continued the judge, "and this court cannot turn its back on events subsequent to Mr. Orton's trial. Our written opinion will follow, but we hold today that the argument overheard by Ms. Moon just minutes or hours before Ms. Hinton's murder should have been presented to the jury. The fact should have been ascertained by defense counsel and failure to do so implies gross inadequacy of said counsel. We take judicial notice, incidentally, of the fact that Mr. Orton's defense counsel left the practice of law a year later in ill health.

"Furthermore, without the relevant pages of the TechnoCenter's logbook—missing under such peculiar circumstances as to defy coincidence—there is no evidence that the victim's estranged husband left the premises immediately after the altercation reported by Ms. Moon. Indeed, an inference can be drawn that he remained in her office and that the argument might well have turned violent.

"In conclusion, by a vote of two to one, we remand Mr. Orton's case to the Superior Court of the County of San Francisco for a new trial. Thank you, gentlemen."

I couldn't believe what I was hearing, Darryl smiled at me as the deputies took him by both arms and helped him to his feet. "Good job, kid," he said. "It weren't so hard now, was it?"

I'd seen that all-knowing smile before, and it hit me that Darryl never intended to actually walk out on his appeal. Beyond his general distrust of lawyers, he hated seeing me in a subservient, second-chair role. He had forced me to prove myself, and though Hale would have gotten the same result, it did feel good. *I had done it.*

As the judge called the next matter, I realized I had forgotten something.

"Your Honors, I'm much obliged for your consideration, but there's one more thing. You've seen the note I received three days ago and my affidavit. The only reason Mr. Orton is alive today to accept the benefits of your ruling is because he was attacked two days ago at Soledad and was locked up in solitary confinement until released this morning to attend this hearing. I urge this court to grant the prisoner protective custody pending trial."

"So ordered," said the senior judge. "You prepare the terms of such custody in a document and submit it to the deputy attorney general for approval. Meanwhile, the prisoner will be held here in San Francisco and an expedited trial date is hereby ordered."

How do I describe the feeling that swept up my spine, like cosmic waves of low-voltage electricity, warming and cooling me at the same time. I had never felt so . . . *whole*, like not even death could touch me at that moment. Darryl was right. Joe Strobe would like to have seen this, and I wished he could have. But even in this flush of victory, I remembered how he would quote Yeats after he had won a case: "In days of great joy, take comfort in the fact that disaster is just around the corner." It was true. The hardest work was still ahead.

The judge had been right: We didn't have a case to give to a jury, nothing but a half-full bag of suppositions. And though I had finessed the DNA for purposes of the hearing, the district attorney's office would be ready at the retrial with a full-blown presentation, employing the tried and true RFLP testing method.

Darryl had been right, too, a long time ago, when he predicted months before that the only thing that would trump the DNA at a retrial would be to expose the identity of Deborah Hinton's killer. So that's what I'd have to do, find her real murderer.

Even if it killed me.

28

"**I** behaved like a spoiled child," Hale told me the next morning, then congratulated me and went back to whipping himself. "My walking out of the courtroom was unforgivable," he said, "but the man simply infuriated me. In truth, Billy, I suppose I was embarrassed as well. I know those judges, two of them quite well."

"Darryl is a little . . . unusual," I said and apologized for my friend's behavior and my own success. "I know you'll be catching it from Ashton, since you handling the motion was part of the deal I made with him."

"Well, you won," he said, "which is, in the final analysis, the important element in all this."

"I was lucky as all get out, Hale. Your friends on the bench must have felt sorry for me, but I swear there was no mention of Moncrief or Synoptics."

Hale looked relieved, and I could tell he hadn't wanted to ask me. "I'll deal with Rex, as long as you'll now keep your end of the bargain and get out of the case."

"Sure, Hale," I said, hating myself for the expert liar I had become. "I'm finished with it as soon as I find Darryl a good trial lawyer to substitute in."

"And how long will that take?" Hale was a step ahead of me. "Do you want some help?"

"Thanks, Hale. Let me get back to you on that. You've seen how weird Darryl is."

"Let's say two weeks?"

"Sure. Two weeks."

Two weeks to get the goods on either Frank Hinton or Jason Moncrief.

Moncrief would be the toughest, so I decided to focus first on Hinton, take him head-on. My plan was to use my conversation with Suzy Threadgill to goad him into an admission, or at least a whopper of a lie, and tape the conversation. But how to get a recording device? Everything I knew about people wearing wires was from watching FBI movies.

Once again, I would have to count on Mace Rothschild, King of the Internet. I had recently read a freedom of speech case that involved specific instructions available to anyone on the Internet on how to build a nuclear device. Another Web site published a book on torture techniques and how to become a professional hit man. Surely there must be instructions on something as innocent as taping a conversation.

I found Mace in his office preparing to take a custodian of records deposition in a patent case. He looked appropriately bored. He also looked embarrassed about having failed to locate the Breckenridges and was happy to perform a service so mundane as ordering a wire for me on the Internet.

"Sure I'll help, but what the hell's going on? Business lawyer Billy going underground, sniffing out the violation of a septic tank ordinance? A mattress company's tags being torn off? Someone taking our client's antihistamines, then operating heavy machinery?"

It was getting awkward keeping Mace in the dark about the favors he was doing for me, but I convinced him he would be better off not knowing anything for the time being.

"Okay Billy, but when it's safe, I'd like to know what the hell I've been doing."

"Or, in the case of locating the Breckenridges," I said innocently, "not doing."

Two days later, Mace came to my apartment when the kit arrived and together, reading the instructions, we managed to tape the damn thing on me and test it out. An hour later, I found Frank Hinton's office in a small medical-dental complex in Orinda just west of Oakland and south of the Berkeley Hills. The low-rise building was new and not far from Highway 24. I parked my car and entered the reception area, where an elderly couple, a sloppily dressed teenager, and a mother and young child all grimly waited to be called.

I leaned in close to the chubby, blonde receptionist and told her I had to see the doctor. She said that he was with a patient and that it would be impossible anyway without an appointment.

"I understand, but maybe you could tell him I have important information about the murder of his wife?"

Her vacant eyes opened wide at that, and in less than four minutes, me and Frank Hinton, D.D.S., were sitting alone in his well-appointed office.

Hinton looked nothing like the man who had won the heart of a beauty like Deborah Hinton, and even less like a man with the where-withal to kill her. He was no more than five feet seven inches and one hundred twenty-five pounds. He had curly blond hair cut short, and wore a thin blond mustache under a long, narrow nose.

"Now what's this about Deborah?" he said after I had identified myself as a lawyer associated with Stanton and Snow.

"I think you killed her," I said, "and I think I can prove it."

My hope was to nuke him into panicking, but he didn't flinch, not so much as the flutter of an eyelid.

"No," he said, calmly, rising to his feet to dismiss me, "you can't. How do I know? Simple. Because I didn't kill my wife. Now get out."

The guy was cool. Physically, he looked like a shoe clerk, but I wondered if there might be more to him than met the eye. I began to suspect that his milky blue eyes and small stature belied a quiet inner strength that had somehow drawn Deborah to him—and, eventually, to her death. I hoped he was bluffing, because I could play that game, too.

"Well, then, Doctor," I said, also rising to my feet, "I'll see you at the station."

Hinton's shoulders came up along with his eyebrows. "What on earth is that supposed to mean? I've been through all this before with the police. They've got the guy who killed Deb. Perhaps you haven't heard. He's serving time in prison."

I gave my head an impatient, officious shake. "Not for long, sir. The case has been reopened. The suspect, Darryl Orton, has been granted a new trial. Here's a copy of the order. A new trial has been set for the last week in December."

He looked a little less sure of himself as he scanned the document.

"The court's ruling was based primarily on the testimony of Mildred Moon," I said. "Do you know who she is?"

Was that a muscle twitching in his jaw?

"Of course I do. She was Deborah's secretary."

"She was also a witness to a violent quarrel between you and Ms. Hinton in the very office where she was murdered a few hours later." I handed him a copy of the appellate court's written order containing reference to my affidavit, which he glanced at and then tossed on his desk.

"That's it?" he said, his features growing darker, but I couldn't tell if it was in anger or apprehension. "That's your proof?"

"There's more," I said, ready with my curve ball, "much more. Take your alibi—Suzy Threadgill? She's recanted. She will tell the jury she lied to the police. At your request."

"Suzy? Suzy said she would do that?"

Bull's-eye. Beads of sweat popped out on his forehead, and he sank back into his chair. I moved closer, unsure of the range of the taping device. "Ms. Threadgill doesn't have a whole lot of choices. She's going to be charged with lying to a police officer and obstructing justice."

Hinton turned pale, his cool evaporated. "My God," he said, rubbing his temples with surprisingly long fingers, which I could now easily imagine wrapped around a glass paperweight. "That was the last thing I intended."

I felt a rush and prayed the wire was working. But had I gotten enough out of him?

"It would be better for everyone if you told the complete truth, Doctor. I'm sure it would help get Ms. Threadgill off the hook."

"You're not in a position to guarantee that," he said.

"But I am, sir. You see, I represent the complaining witness—the party aggrieved by Ms. Threadgill's false statements—and I will assure you, in writing if you want, that if you tell me the truth now, he will not testify against Ms. Threadgill."

He paused to consider my words, then said, "Well, if she said that, I'll not dispute it. She's a good person."

"Then you'll admit you told her to lie for you?"

"I'll admit it to you. I won't admit it publicly until I hear it from Suzy's own lips."

My heart was thudding against my ribs, the dull drumbeat now recorded for posterity. If he hadn't been so scared himself, he would have seen my shirt hopping with each beat. But I had what I'd come for, and Darryl was as good as free. On the other hand, I had Hinton going with me now. I might as well shoot for the hat trick.

"Why," I said, "did you pick Suzy Threadgill? Was she your gal? Is that what riled Deborah? Why you fought? Why you killed her?"

Hinton shook his head and then broke out laughing. Then he stopped suddenly, and when he spoke, his voice was hoarse with despair, yet laced with amused disdain. "Where do they find hayseeds like you? Would you tell me that?"

I was caught off guard and mumbled something defensive like at least I wasn't a killer.

"Who said I was a killer?"

"You just admitted getting Threadgill to lie for you."

He shook his head some more, then slowly rose again from his chair, turned, and looked out at the garden courtyard that suburban dentists all seemed to have these days. Then his gaze moved to a credenza behind his desk.

"See that photograph over there? Those are my little girls. Deb and I were arguing over my visitation rights. That's what Mildred overheard."

"I can sympathize, Doctor, but men have killed their estranged wives over a lot less."

Christ, I was losing him. Had I asked that infamous 'one question too many' that trial lawyers are taught to avoid?

He smiled and placed his hands, palms down, on the desk in front of him. "Listen, Johnny One-Note, or whatever the hell your name is: I did *not* kill Deborah! Your silly little syllogism seems to go like this: I tried to protect myself by faking an alibi, ergo, I must be guilty of murder."

"What were you protecting yourself from if it wasn't murder?"

"Why don't you ask Suzy Threadgill?" he said, and threw his hands in the air with exasperation, then leaned forward, and said, "Oh, fuck it, would you like a blow job, Counselor?"

"Sir?"

"You heard me, blue eyes. I'm gay—queer as your uncle. A homo, okay? You happy now?"

I was anything but happy.

"After my 'violent argument' with Deborah, I went straight to Paul's apartment where, incidentally, I worked things out with Deb on the phone, as I always did."

"And Paul is—?"

"My real lover, not Suzy. Anyway, when I picked up a message from the police that Deb had been murdered and that they 'had a few questions,' I simply panicked. Everybody knew how much Deb and I fought and that we had just had one of our all-time office shoot-outs. That, plus the insurance money, would paint a bull's-eye right on my forehead."

"So you called Threadgill?"

"Next to Paul, Suzy is my best friend. Deborah's, too, actually. After Deb and I split over Paul, Suzy was always the one who would remind us the kids came first and somehow manage to calm us down.

"Anyway, as soon as I heard I was wanted for questioning, I knew I'd have to have help, and it couldn't be Paul. I called her, and she agreed to do it."

"Why not Paul? Why ask Suzy to lie if you were really with Paul?"

He sighed and slowly rotated his head from side to side. The man had aged ten years in ten minutes.

"How many gay dentists do you know?" he asked me rhetorically, then slapped the air in front of him. "Stupid question. You wouldn't know a gay if he had both fists up your ass. Let me reframe the question, Counselor. How many gay dentists do you know who could maintain their practice for ten minutes in our 'enlightened culture' once they were outed?"

"Are you HIV positive?"

"Hell, no—and neither is Paul—but that wouldn't matter. It wouldn't matter even if I posted our test results in the yellow pages!"

I felt my elation slipping away.

"That's not all," he continued. "My daughters are five and seven. I'm not ashamed of being gay; it's who I am and was always intended to be. But the girls need to be a little older before we have our talk about the birds and the bees."

I nodded.

"There's more. Paul is a Catholic priest."

"Jesus."

"No, just a priest. But the most decent man I've ever known. He knows he'll eventually have to leave the Church, but we want it to be on his terms, not because his partner outed him to avoid prosecution for a murder any sane person would know I couldn't have committed."

I was becoming one of those persons, though the 'sane' part was up for grabs. We sat in silence. A wall clock ticked. Water swirled in a room next to us, probably the hygienist. My head was starting to ache, and the tape was pulling the skin on my perspiring chest. This was turning out to be worse than a root canal.

"Sorry about the shock language a while ago," Hinton said at last. "It's not like me, but you can be very irritating."

"I've been told."

"Anyway, maybe you should meet Paul. He overheard me making up with Deb. He also knows that I loved her and couldn't kill a mosquito."

Well, he had killed my theory, and we both knew it.

"If you're conning me," I said, "I'll be back. But if you've been straight—"

He gave me a wry smile.

"Sorry," I said. "If you've been truthful, I've no need to tell anyone about this conversation. You've got my word on it."

We thanked each other for nothing, and I showed myself out.

I couldn't wait to get the wire off me. I'd lock up the tape in a safe place, but in my heart I knew I'd never need it.

I tried to shake off my disappointment as I headed for home, but reality was setting in. I was back down to one suspect, one very wealthy and powerful suspect.

What was it I had said about Jason Moncrief in that first team meeting with Hale, Ashton, and Dana when I was trying to make an impression? Something like, "Powerful guys like Jason Moncrief are used to getting away with murder."

I didn't sleep much that night, knowing I'd have to walk through the Synoptics building the next morning like I owned the place, find a room I'd never been in, open a vault I'd never seen, and then find a needle in a haystack of files. I had Dana's little map memorized and tried to visualize myself walking purposefully through a labyrinth of stairways, hallways, and rooms, straight to the vault. I had learned in prison that if you carried yourself a certain way, people left you alone.

"Sir?" said the sleepy-eyed receptionist as I strode resolutely through the heavy glass door within minutes of the eight-o'clock opening, then shot left down the hallway. She was putting her lipstick on, obviously not expecting visitors this early. "May I help you?"

"No thanks," I said, flashing my business card over my shoulder, "just getting my exhibits in order for the meeting later this morning. You have a nice day."

I think she said something else, but I was on my way, confident that she was back to applying her eye makeup by now.

As I continued down the hallway, I was surprised at the level of activity in the building. Most offices were already full of people talking on the phone or bent over keyboards. I walked with a confident gait, my head pointed straight ahead while my eyes scanned like radar in a 180-degree arc, hoping to avoid making a wrong turn.

Ah, there's the men's room, so get ready to take a right, then to the end of a short hallway and look for the large room that houses the middle management secretarial pool. Yep, there it is. Walk right through it. Ignore the stares, just keep going, maybe a casual smile or two. Good.

Now look for the employees' lounge that should be coming up on my right, and hot-damn, there it is. Go past it approximately ten yards and look for an unmarked door on the left and pass through it. Shit, two unmarked doors! Now what? Eeny, meeny . . .

I took the first one and strode confidently . . . right into a fucking broom closet. As I backed out and closed the door, a guy about my age wearing jeans and a SYNOPTICS RULES T-shirt sarcastically suggested I remove my neck tie before mopping down the hall.

"I do this every damn time," I said, laughing a bit too hard at his incredibly clever remark.

"I don't believe I've met you," he said, extending his hand.

I gave him a firm shake, hoping my palm was reasonably dry, and tried to process two issues at once: first, whether to identify myself

truthfully, and second, whether to walk right through the other unmarked door or keep going and circle back later for a second run.

"Dennis Friedrich," he said. "I'm head of marketing, and you are—?"

"Alan Green," I said. "I'm the new janitor."

He laughed, so I added, "And when I'm not scrubbing down the
hallways, I'm a security consultant working with Jason. I was on my
way down to check out the file vault."

"Having secured the broom closet?"

"That was just a mopping-up operation."

We were killing each other with blazing wit. But he seemed to buy
my story, so I reached out and opened the next unmarked door, hoping there wasn't a tiger behind it, and confidently strode through it. No
tiger.

A lady.

A stout, middle-aged lady, with gray hair tied in a bun, sitting at a
desk and looking as officious as a German train agent.

"Catch you later, Dennis," I said, closing the door behind me.

"Sure thing, Alan," he said, and I could have kissed him. The
woman's hard features softened, seeing I was on a first-name basis
with the head of marketing.

"How's it going?" I said and walked right past her, then took the
left-hand turn down the two flights of stairs as if I did it every day. I
heard her say something, but pretended I didn't and kept going.

Halfway down a long hallway was a door with a panel to the right
containing three rows of three keys, plus a zero. Numbered like a telephone. I was at the vault. Without even a glance back up the stairs I
entered the code into the security panel and . . . nothing!

I took a deep breath and looked at my watch. Only 8:15. It seemed
like I'd been in Synoptics for an hour or so. I wiped sweat from my
forehead with a trembling finger. Maybe I had missed a button or two.
I wiped my hands on the legs of my suit pants, took in another deep
breath, then let it out slowly. *Relax.* Try it again. My unexpected meeting with the marketing guy coming out of the broom closet had shaken
me.

Slower this time. That's it. I began again, carefully poking 8-3-7-5-
1-9-8-4-4-6, then the pound key and—*yes,* a quiet buzzing sound and
a click as the door opened to my touch.

I walked through the heavy steel, fireproof door and closed it behind me with another click that echoed ominously. I was in.

The room was cold enough to hang meat in, and about the size of
my bedroom, which is to say very small, about nine feet by twelve. The
ceilings were high, ten feet or so, and open file cabinets ran from the
floor to the top around the perimeter of the room. Each exposed file

had an identifying tab at its edge and could be pulled straight out. A library footstool was in the corner, the only furniture in the room—no table, no chair, not even a coat rack. Every square inch of wall space, except for light switches and a thermostat set at 58 degrees, was covered with files. This was not a reading room, or even a traditional file room.

Fortunately, the files were in alphabetical order, and I quickly found several on the Paul Dexter foreign corruption case Hale had settled a month earlier. I placed two of these files in the middle of the floor where I could retrieve them in a hurry. My backup.

Then I began looking for the Hinton-Moncrief investigation files and finally found a group of files marked SEC PRIVATE INVESTIGATIONS. I pulled several of them marked OCTOBER–NOVEMBER 1998, and raced through each, finding nothing that justified a high level of security. The first two were general correspondence files and deposition reports, from which it was clear that Hale Lassiter had been able to demonstrate to the SEC investigator's satisfaction that Synoptics' Corporation's books had been manipulated by CFO Deborah Hinton without Jason Moncrief's knowledge. She had apparently profited to the tune of over a quarter of a million bucks by selling approximately 15 percent of her company stock at the high point, a day before it fell, following an anonymous tip to the SEC that her write-off was improper. The anonymous tip, the first of two, triggered the informal investigation of Synoptics on October 11. Who had made that call, and why?

Next was a file of newspaper clippings that revealed the second tip, a leak to the press, this one detailing the SEC "private investigation." That's when the market in Synoptics stock crashed, following its brief but meteoric rise. Again, with Synoptics Corporation's high sensitivity concerning the confidential investigation, how could this have been exposed to the public? *Who was the deep throat here?*

Another sub-file marked HINTON, DEBORAH contained briefs to the SEC filed by Stanton and Snow, signed by Hale. Some of these tried to connect the CFO's flagrant violation of insider trading laws with her murder, arguing that the violence of her death supported the notion that it was probably the work of an outside co-conspirator in the stock scam. The possibility of a paid assassin was vaguely hinted at.

The final letter from the SEC's investigating officer ultimately concluded that Jason Moncrief had no knowledge of the deferred write-off that sent the stock soaring and that Ms. Hinton was the sole "inside perpetrator." The opinion was full of legalese, but concluded, as Dana had told me, that Moncrief couldn't have been so stupid as to have lent his support to a scheme when disclosure of his participation would not only have been possible, but also inevitable; plus he hadn't made all that much money for a guy already worth two billion dollars. The opinion closed with the following sentence:

> Of lesser weight in our determination, but worthy of brief mention, is the fact that Ms. Hinton's murder strongly suggests the likelihood that organized crime was involved, or at least an outside co-conspirator, who perhaps became angered at Ms. Hinton's private transaction.

I saw little logic in the Commission's decision, particularly the last line, which had been seized upon and adopted by the DA in Darryl's state court trial. The first assumptions about Moncrief being too smart to be stupid, though full of holes and far from exculpatory of Moncrief, at least bore the weight of logic. The last point did not, but Hale had done a good job of using Hinton's murder to somehow point to a conspirator outside the walls of the company. They say if you repeat something enough times, people will begin to believe it. The advertiser's credo. It seemed to have worked with the SEC.

None of this helped much, but I whispered the investigating officer's opinion into the small handheld tape recorder I'd brought with me.

My heart jumped when I heard a sound outside. Footsteps coming down the stairs? I knew I had been in the vault too long already, but I'd never get another shot like this. I quickly refiled the SEC Hinton-Moncrief files and grabbed the Dexter files off the floor. Then I stood, waiting, not moving a muscle. Ready with my bullshit story. After a few endless seconds, I heard the footsteps retreating down the hall.

This was my opportunity to get back up the stairs and out clean. I checked my watch—8:40. I should run for it. On the other hand . . .

No, I had to keep looking. All I'd confirmed so far were things that news articles and Dana had already made clear. I put Dexter's file back on the floor and dug out the last of the October–November SEC files. Something caught my eye—a sealed, buff-colored envelope, two-hole punched and clipped deep into file number L-600312. It was marked CONFIDENTIAL MULTI-TRADES INVESTORS FILE.

I carefully peeled open the envelope and here's what I saw:

Shareholder	Total Shares	Long	Sold	Short	Buy to Cover
Sheila Anderson	368,500	10-02-98	10-08-98	10-10-98	10-12-98
Jacob Bomberger	129,000	10-03-98	10-07-98	10-11-98	10-18-98
Jeffrey Casperson	50,000	10-02-98	10-04-98	NA	NA

All these Synoptics stock trades had been transacted about three weeks before Deborah Hinton's murder. All three had bought and sold huge blocks of Synoptics stock immediately after the fake quarterly earnings were reported based upon Deborah Hinton's fictitious Q-10 report, filed for the quarter ending September 30. Then, after presumably taking huge profits by purchasing Synoptics on margin, then selling, it appeared that two of them—Anderson and Bomberger—had, on or after October 10, then *shorted* Synoptics stock—betting the stock would go *down*—just before it crashed. Each gambled in early October that Synoptics stock would go up (which it did); then each had sold at the peak and shorted the stock, taking even greater profits than before when the stock tanked. What were the odds against someone legitimately being either that smart or that lucky?

My heart was racing again. There was a damn good chance I was looking at the name of Moncrief's outside conspirators and Hinton's and Klinehart's killers. I had found the third leg of a three-legged stool: Moncrief, Hinton, and now, Anderson and Bomberger.

I read the table into my recorder, replaced the list in the envelope, then did my best to reseal it. Then I went back to the As, hoping to find a file on Sheila Anderson and the other two main traders.

My heart raced again as I heard more footsteps coming down the stairs. This time they paused right outside the vault door, telling me my luck had run out. I stuck the recorder in my pocket and grabbed up the Dexter file again. My breathing had stopped along with the sound of the footsteps, and I heard what sounded like the hammer of a revolver being pulled back. No, it was the click of the security lock opening.

Slowly the door swung open, and there was the last person in the world I wanted to see: Jason Moncrief.

"Well, well," he said, flipping open a cell phone and punching in numbers I suspected were the internal Synoptics equivalent of 911. "Strobe, isn't it?"

29

"Yes, sir. I'm Billy Strobe. How are you, sir?"

"Curious is what I am, Strobe," he said, advancing into the room and snatching the file out of my hand. "Curious about what in the deuce you think you're doing in a restricted area without clearance."

I heard more footsteps behind him on the stairs and a woman's voice—the lady with the bun?—telling others to stand by.

"It's the new Thailand case, sir. I'm doing some background research, and I wanted to recapture some of the work I'd done on Paul Dexter's case. We can't find our Dexter files at S & S."

Moncrief scanned the file, sniffed, and handed it back to me, a good sign.

"Hale is handling the Thailand dispute," he said. "He's never mentioned that you're on it. You work with Rex Ashton and with Wilcox in probate, don't you?"

"I work for all three, sir, mainly Mr. Ashton. But I help out wherever I can."

He dialed another number. I saw heads bobbing in the partial door opening, security people trying to get a look at the terrorist.

"Hale Lassiter, please," he shouted into the phone. "Jason Moncrief here."

A dark presence filled my heart, weighed it down. My string had run out. The room suddenly seemed even smaller, a lot like the cell I'd soon be occupying on a parole violation.

"Oh, Christ," muttered Moncrief, "then give me Dana Mathews."

Bad as things were, they had just got worse. Now Dana's fat was in the fire, too.

"Dana!" boomed Moncrief's baritone, sounding deeper than ever in this echo chamber we were occupying. "Help me out here. You know that Strobe fellow that was on the Dexter case?"

He listened. I strained to hear. I prayed that she wouldn't try to defend me.

"Yes, that's him. He's not on the Thailand case, is he?"
Don't do it, Dana. I'm dead anyways when he talks to Hale.
"He is?"

Silence, then a weary smile, a change in tone—Moncrief, the tanned and elegant charmer.

"That's all right, dear. Not to worry your pretty head." I looked away, then returned the Dexter files to the appropriate cabinet and waited. "It's just that Mr. Strobe had Miss Hazelton quite edgy when she realized he wasn't on the list. Have Hale call me."

He snapped the cell phone shut. "I suppose I owe you an apology, Strobe. Ms. Mathews took full responsibility for failing to register you or informing you how to do it. Still, I'll be talking to Hale about this. Can't have my own lawyers going slack on security. Are you finished here?"

"I was wrapping up, sir," I said, guilt about Dana overwhelming any sense of relief at my own stay of execution. "And by the way, Ms. Mathews did tell me to check in with Miss Harrington, and I flat forgot."

"Don't lie to me, young man. I can spot a lie through a lead wall at fifty yards. In the first place, it's Miss Hazelton, not Harrington. In the second place, Ms. Mathews was quite clear that she had not informed you. So save your gallantry for your widows in Wilcox's probate department. That's really what you do mostly, isn't it?"

"It was, sir," I said, walking past Moncrief, Miss Hazelton, and two security guards, "but that's about to change."

The message awaiting me from Hale's secretary was no surprise, the summons I'd expected. But before I turned myself in, I had to talk to Dana, try to work out some kind of scheme to salvage her career.

But even before that, it turned out, I would talk to Mace. The Scarecrow was standing in my doorway, showing nothing but teeth.

"I've got them!" he said, and handed me a piece of paper as if it were a winning lottery ticket. "They're in a motel in Modesto."

"I assume there's more than one."

"There are twenty of them, plus nine hotels." He pointed a bony finger at the paper. "*That* one is the temporary abode of Rose and Harold Breckenridge. Their room and phone number are there, too, from the looks of their bills, they have electric heat, a kitchenette, one phone and no major appliances."

I looked at the address—930 Sycamore—and forced a half-smile, trying to show appreciation. "Thanks, Mighty Web Master. I owe you one."

"I'll settle for a little demonstrated affect," he said.

"I'd give it to you if I knew what it was."

"Emotional response, my man! Manifest joy! You know, whoopee, wow, Jesus, Mace, you're a fucking genius! That sort of thing."

"Whoopee, wow, et cetera," I deadpanned, then, as I brushed past him into the hallway, added, "I do appreciate it, buddy, really. I'm a little pressured right now."

"So am I, so listen up: first, my price is a quick drink at Aqua around six. Second," he added, pointing to the address, "I know you're under the gun, but though the Breckenridges are here today, they could be gone tomorrow. Don't sit on this."

"Done and done," I said, and headed straight for Dana's office. I put the Breckenridges' address in my wallet. If I could find what Barney found at the Breckenridges' and expose Moncrief in time, I might save not only Darryl, but Dana as well.

She was alone. I got ready to duck.

"Billy, thank God, are you all right?" she said, her face pale and strained. "Did I do okay?"

This was the last thing I expected from someone whose career I had just ruined.

"I'm fine," I said, "but Moncrief caught Hale unawares, and I'm afraid you're in trouble here, too."

"That isn't—"

"I'll tell Hale you lied because I threatened your kneecaps. Maybe he can—"

"Billy! It's *okay*. I caught Hale the minute he walked in. He covered for you, too."

I'm not sure how it happened—fatigue, tension overload, I suppose—but all of a sudden I had fallen into a chair, weeping like a child, my face in my hands. Then I felt her hands on my shoulders, gently stroking my hair. I lifted my head and looked up into those gentle eyes and knew I was in the presence of pure goodness. I put my arms around her hips and buried my face in her stomach. "It's okay," she kept whispering as she stroked my head. "It's okay."

It wasn't okay, and minutes later, while I waited for Hale to come out of his private bathroom, I wrestled with my emotions. I sat in the very chair I'd been in during that first interview with Hale a hundred years ago, and now I looked around his office for what would probably be the last time. I stared at the massive desk in front of me, not a file or a document in sight. Mr. Organization. I turned and looked at the gleaming glass and aluminum table in the conference wing where I'd attended my first team meeting and seen Dana for the first time.

I rose and went into Hale's conference area just as he entered carefully wiping his hands on a paper towel and discarding it in a wastebasket, an act I took symbolically and personally. He looked tired and at least seventy years old, and I hoped I wasn't fixing to cry again. I looked away as he crossed the room and took a seat beside me, at the glass table. I felt his eyes on me.

"I quit, Hale," I said, breaking the strained silence, "unless you want to fire me first. Your call."

He still didn't say anything.

"I appreciate everything you've done for me, sir. If there's anything else I can I do to minimize the damage I've done to you and Dana . . ."

"We're all right for the time being, Billy," he said. His voice was hoarse, and I could tell he was feeling emotional, too. "However, when Jason Moncrief and Rex get their heads together, there may not be much—"

I interrupted him. "Fire me, Hale. Dammit, fire me right now."

He looked away; then, after a full minute, I heard a barely audible voice say, "You're fired."

"Shoot, Hale, that wasn't so hard, was it?" I said, trying to lighten things up. It didn't work. "Firing" me would give Hale more cover with his partners than just accepting my resignation, but there was only one way to end the venomous threat Jason Moncrief posed to everyone: Dana, Hale, the Breckenridges, and, of course, Darryl. I had to expose the son-of-a-bitch.

I nodded. "Two weeks to clear up my matters?"

"Take as much time as you need," he said, managing a doleful smile.

We shook hands. I rose and walked out, leaving him sitting there, staring out the window.

As eager as I was to interview the Breckenridges, I was suddenly even more eager to get the hell away from S & S, away from San Francisco. I wanted to go home, and God knows Dad had sucked hind tit on my list of priorities long enough. Although I was a little concerned about the Breckenridges' breaking camp and Inspector Jaxon's order to stay put in the county, I called Lisa to confirm I was on my way to Enid. She told me she had been able to locate eight of the people on her mystery list. I told her to line up some of them for me to visit day after tomorrow.

Considering my new status at S & S, I didn't even ask permission to take Friday off. I just left a message for Mace that I couldn't buy him the drink I owed him, packed my bag, and headed for the airport.

I didn't reach Enid until an hour after sundown the next day, so Ma was already passed out in bed. On the plus side, Lisa looked even prettier than usual with the addition of a few pounds. But what was really shining through her pain and fatigue was pride of accomplishment. On short notice, she had been able to schedule interviews with Torville "Tor" Berenson, a retired local police sergeant; Lowell Horan, now retired from two decades as district attorney; and Karen Oates, a divorced ex-bartender.

"By the time you talk to them, I'll have lined up some others," she said, her eyes shining with excitement. "So, where's my Christmas bonus? I'd also like to discuss my benefits package, stock options, that sort of thing."

I laughed, both at her remark and at the unintended irony. I hadn't told her I was out of work myself.

"Good work, brat, but hold up for now. By the time I talk with this first group, I'll know what the people on this list have in common. Hell, maybe it's the roster for a city league baseball team or a list of campaign contributors, nothing to do with Dad's trial."

"So you're not optimistic?"

"Look, sis, it's a bit of a long shot, but the fact that Charlie Ryan is on this list means this could be a list of guys who have reason to think Dad was innocent. And if the city attorney himself is one of them, hell, we'd be home free. So I'm cautiously optimistic, but damned excited, too."

Her eyes were shining as we exchanged a high five.

Torville Berenson lived five miles north of town surrounded by oak trees, scrub brush, and dogs, some of them eyeing me hungrily as I arrived at his house at nine o'clock the next morning. Berenson's old ranch-style place was at the end of a private dirt road a hundred yards long. I parked in front of a garage that hadn't seen paint in my lifetime and figured I'd stay put until he called off a trio of rottweilers who looked bent on eating my rental car. Road dust I'd stirred up caught up with me, and I could taste the grit in my teeth.

"You Strobe?" a man shouted from behind a torn screen door.

"Yes, sir. You spoke with my sister."

He let out a sharp command, and damn if the unholy three didn't turn tail and trot right back toward him, heads lowered. He didn't invite me in, however, just walked out to the car and leaned against my door in a way that made it impossible to open.

"The boys are a little jumpy today. What can I do for you?"

I gave him my card, which he glanced at and stuck in the top pocket of his coveralls as I extended my hand through the window.

"Nice to meet you, Mr. Berenson."

He grudgingly extended a hand as hard and dry as petrified wood. "What can I do for you?" he said, in a tone that said make it quick.

I'd learned nothing at Golden State Law about conducting a potential witness interview from behind a steering wheel, especially a witness whose large bare biceps, shaved head, and girth brought back vivid memories of Earring and Ortez. What was puzzling me was that Lisa had said all three people on my schedule were friendly on the phone and looking forward to meeting me.

"I was wondering if you knew my dad."

"Sure, I remember your father," Tor said, then added, with a sneering half-smile that came off as mean-spirited as his words, "Hell, who doesn't remember the Irish Mouthpiece?"

"Were you acquaintances or friends?" I asked, hoping I'd misread him.

"He cross-examined me once. I knew his partner better. Amos Blackwell."

"So you weren't friends," I said, "with Joe Strobe?"

He coughed out a laugh that sounded like an epithet. "Hell, no— we weren't friends. He worked for the bad guys. I was one of the white hats."

I was beginning to picture him more in a white hood, but I stayed patient and tried to curb my growing disappointment. I leaned forward in the driver's seat, realized my back was damp—and it wasn't from the heat. What the hell was going on? Should I show him the list?

"Were you in any clubs or teams together?"

He shook his head, then fixed me with a hard look and said, "What gives, Strobe? This some kind of a joke?"

When I said I was intending to clear my father's name, the news registered on his face as a scowl of incredulity. Then I told him that I had come across a list that had his name on it and thought he might have some information that might help me.

He stood up straight and gave his huge round head a dismissive shake, saying, "You're barkin up a empty tree, son, and I got chores."

I noticed that two of the dogs had returned to stand like sentinels, one on each side of him, daring me to step outside.

"Hold on, sir, at least let me read you some of the names."

He turned, and I shouted at his back a dozen or so people on the list—Karen Oates, W. B. Lightfoot, Simon Peabody, Sam Somerville, and so on—but he just kept walking and shaking his head.

"Never heard of a one of 'em," he said over his shoulder. "Whatever the hell list you got there, son, you scratch my name off it and do it now."

"Could I read some more of them, sir?" He was on the porch now, the back screen door open. "Might jog your memory."

"I just told you, kid," he said, and spat off to one side. "I don't know a one of them. Hell, I was never even in Judge Ryan's court-room, not once."

He strode off, leaving the dogs, who eyed me without sympathy.

I was back on the other side of town, pulling up in front of Lowell Horan's plush two-story brick colonial when an icy chill accompanied the realization that of the several names I had read to Tor Berenson from the list, Judge Ryan's was not one of them.

Puzzled, I sat in my car and tried to clear my thoughts. Had Tor Berenson called someone after he heard I was coming?

No, there was probably a simple explanation. Lisa may have mentioned the list and told him the judge's name was on it. Or Berenson may have gotten a peek at it before he walked away.

The only thing clear at this point was that Torville Berenson was an asshole. Starting with him had probably just been a fluke. Time to move on.

Former City Attorney Lowell Horan, my three o'clock, presented a pleasant contrast to Berenson. A slight, smiling widower with a mustache a mile too big for his face, he welcomed me into his book-lined study, offered me a drink and a cigar, and listened with genuine sympathy as I told him what I was trying to do.

"He'd be proud of you, Billy," he said, smiling sadly. "I know I would be." He reached off to one side and produced a silver-framed photograph. "Here are my children."

The man and woman in the picture appeared to be about my age with another woman in her fifties sitting between them.

"A fine-looking family," I said. He smiled sadly and nodded, then urged me to tell him my story, which I did. We visited for nearly forty-five minutes—he seemed to like having me there—but I began to see that we were all the time veering off track, plus I was doing most of the talking.

"I don't want to put you in a conflict of interest with your office, Mr. Horan," I said, finished with cutting bait and determined to start fishing, "but as I mentioned, I've got reason to believe my father was framed. I'm hoping you might have some information that could help me prove it."

He gave me another sweet, sympathetic smile and lit a cigarette. "Although you do put me in a conflict of interest, Billy, it's irrelevant. At the risk of discouraging you, I simply have no information that could possibly help you, even if I were free to offer it. Despite being on opposite sides of the fence, I had great affection for your father and personally, I'd like nothing better than for you to succeed in your mission."

"Do you know anyone who might *not* want me to?"

He looked surprised. "Of course not. Justice should be served, even when delayed."

I told him about my list of names, which included his and Judge Ryan's, and asked him what the trial judge had thought about the verdict.

He chuckled at that. "Dear Charlie—rest his soul—he hated the verdict. He loved and, of course, shared your father's 'blood of the poets.' He and your dad would exchange quotations from Shaw, Wilde, Sullivan, Beckett, and the rest of them right in front of me during a motion or sentencing hearing!"

"Do you think Dad's conviction or his suicide was a factor in the judge's death?"

He shook his head violently, as if coming out of a coma. "Heavens, no, Billy. Charlie drank heavily and was in ill health. Rumor had him unhappy at home. On top of that, he was miscast as a judge. No, Billy, he had his own reasons for his self-imposed death sentence."

When the ancient grandfather clock sounded four chimes, I knew I was beat and that this lonely man would be happy to hear eight, nine, or ten chimes with us still sitting just as we were now, with me not learning a thing. I thanked him, bid him good-bye, and drove off, more baffled than before. The two men I had interviewed were from completely opposite sides of Enid's social strata: one poor, the other wealthy; one hostile, the other friendly. Yet, these unlikely bedfellows had two things in common: their names on a list and something they were covering up.

I bought some take-out Chinese—Ma's favorite—and was pleased to see her eat a small portion of chow mein and half a potsticker. She drank tea with her meal, and her hand was fair steady. Only the blotched skin and gin-flower smell gave her away.

Despite this, conversation was strained, given the fact Lisa and I didn't dare tell Ma what we were up to, plus which I didn't want to confess to being fired and knew I'd have to make up stuff about my work if we got into it. So we ate dinner in the living room and watched *Seinfeld* and *Frazier* reruns.

I was able to get in a private word with Lisa, who confirmed that yes, all three people had been very cordial on the phone, and no, she hadn't mentioned the list to Lowell Horan or Tor Berenson.

"What's going on, Billy?"

"Beats me. It's bizarre, but I'm hoping Karen Oates will clear things up."

At 8:15 P.M., I told Ma I was meeting a friend and headed for my meeting out on William Street with Karen Oates.

After Lowell Horan's elegant home, anything would have been a letdown, but Karen Oates's place was shocking. The wheels had been removed from a trailer house to create a studio shack that rested on railway ties. The back wall had been knocked out to expand the structure, using what appeared to be two-by-four wood framing covered by four-by-eight slabs of painted plywood. Scraps of assorted-size barn wood covered the exterior. A single window in the middle of the jury-rigged expansion was broken and covered with yellowed, opaque plastic.

"I'm afraid I've done wasted your time, Mr. Strobe," she said after I'd presented my card. "I ain't never met your daddy."

"Did my sister tell you why I wanted to talk with you?"

Oates nodded, nervously fingering a large bejeweled necklace. She had been pretty once. Her figure was still appealing, but too many years working in a smoke-filled bar had not been kind to her face. Lisa had said she was late forties, but she had the discouraged eyes of a person well past sixty and skin that was lined like a road map.

"Didn't you tell my sister you knew Joe Strobe and would be glad to meet any kin of his?"

She shrugged. "I was mistaken. Would you like a beer?"

"No. What I'd like is for you to tell me who called you after my sister did."

"Sir?"

"Who told you to shut up about the list?" I was getting tired of the game, and I guess it showed. She batted her painted eyes, fell into a chair, and reached for a cigarette.

She offered one to me. I declined, and she put one in her mouth and handed me the matches. I felt caught in a time warp. I lit her cigarette, then sat in the only other chair.

"What list?" she said, giving me a smile as fake as her jewelry. "Ain't nobody called."

"How about my father's partner, did you know him?"

"Depends," she said, getting up to get herself a beer out of a mini-refrigerator.

"Depends on what?" Was Karen Oates after money?

"Depends on what his name is. I ain't no mind reader, mister."

"Do you know Amos Blackwell?"

She shook her head, but the cigarette fluttered in suddenly trembling fingers. "I think you'd better leave now."

"He called you today, didn't he?"

"Din't I tell you I don't *know* him? And iff'n I don't know *him*, how could he know *me*? And seenin as how he *don't* know me, how could he be callin me up on the telephone?"

Satisfied with her syllogism, she sat back and took a pull on her beer bottle.

"All right, ma'am, I'll go, if you'll just tell me who you told about me coming to see you tonight."

"Nobody," she said earnestly. "I swear to God."

"And nobody called you?"

"No, sir . . . nobody. Really."

She wasn't swearing to God on that one, but it was clear I wasn't going to get anything out of her. I ran through the names on the list, since it was obviously no longer a secret that I had it, and this time her face registered what appeared to be a glazed and innocent deadpan. I got up to leave and in her relief, she apologized for any "confusion."

"The confusion is all mine," I said, "but not for long. I'll be seeing you again, Ms. Oates."

Lisa had waited up for me.

"The other thing these people have in common is silence," I told her. "Somebody got to them and put the lid on."

"Are they lying about Dad or each other? Or both?"

"Just about Dad. I think they may have been telling the truth about not knowing others on the list, other than Ryan and Horan."

"So where do we stand?"

"The list won't help us, at least for now. We've got to rely on our expert witnesses. That'll be our case. Let's get some sleep."

The next morning, I told Lisa not to worry, that I'd be back to Enid as soon as my experts finished their reports.

"Then what?" she asked.

"Two things: First, I'll either bang a confession out of Blackwell or file a fraud suit against him. After that, I'll take Ma for a six-month vacation at the best recovery clinic in Oklahoma City then transport you to San Francisco to serve a six-month sentence with your brother."

She smiled uneasily about both things, but said nothing.

After breakfast, I hugged her, kissed Ma good-bye, and headed for the airport, frustrated, but more determined than ever to break through the wall of silence protecting Amos Blackwell.

After a day in the office prioritizing the projects to be cleared from my desk before I could pick up my check and move out of S & S, I headed up 580 to Modesto, praying the Breckenridges were still there and that they wouldn't shoot me on sight. I drove up old Highway 99, then passed into the city center of Modesto under a giant archway that proclaimed WATER, WEALTH, CONTENTMENT, HEALTH.

Ironic that I'd end up at a place that had played such an important part in Darryl Orton's heritage, Modesto being one of the major resort destinations for the dust bowl Okies in the thirties and the place where he said his grandparents had made their first stop. The family later had moved on to Salinas when Darryl's dad, then eighteen, became the target of anti-Okie rednecks for dating the Modesto High Homecoming Queen.

I knew why water got top billing on the famous archway, because I had done a research job for one of Ashton's clients, a major canning company rightly accused by the EPA of dumping toxins into the Tuolomne River south of Modesto. Water was king in the Stanislaus Valley thanks to the Don Pedro Reservoir, nestled in the Sierra Nevada foothills, holding two million acre-feet of Tuolomne River water due east of the town. The Tuolomne flowed 150 miles from the highest mountain in the Yosemite National Forest, only to get corralled along the way by dams, then polluted by pesticides and industrial waste.

Even rivers got imprisoned and fed shit all day.

Harold Breckenridge's eyes got big as a pair of golf balls when he saw me in his doorway, but it didn't take long for his surprise to register as anger. He tried to slam the door on me, but I already had half of myself inside the tiny living room.

"Listen up, sir," I said, meeting his blazing eyes, "if I can find you, so can they."

"Let him in, Harold," came a woman's tired voice from behind him. "Things can't get any worse."

The man's head dropped, and he backed away from the door.

"We're tired of hiding," said Rose Breckenridge, her eyes suddenly filled with tears. "I'm halfway relieved you found us."

"Better me," I said, straightening the creases in my sport coat from the door scuffle, "than somebody else."

Harold grunted in resignation.

"She's right, sir," I said, "I'm your best chance of not getting burned out again or worse. If you'll give me whatever they think you've got, I'll make sure they know I have it so you can quit fretting every time there's a knock at the door. I also think I can get them put away so they can't hurt you anymore."

Harold threw up his hands in frustration. "That's what's so frustrating," he said. "We don't *have* any goddamn evidence or whatever. We gave it all to your investigator."

"Everything?"

"Every scrap, all of Deborah's papers. There wasn't much, but we wanted rid of it."

"Then can you tell me exactly what you gave him?"

Harold looked at his wife, and she nodded her assent. "Mainly some papers about stock transfers and things I couldn't make heads or tails out of," he said. "We found them hidden in the bottom of a shoe box in her closet. They were folded in half and covered with orange, store-type paper, then a pair of shoes on top of that."

"Deborah wore those shoes at her wedding when she married Frank," said Rose.

Another dead end. "Did the papers all have to do with stock transactions?"

"Mostly," said Harold, "although there were some memos from her boss, Jason Moncrief, full of legalese, plus what looked like a contract and some papers that appeared to be from her law firm."

"Were you ever interviewed by the police, sir?" I asked.

"Twice, by a little white guy and a big black one."

Small world, I thought, betting it was my friend Jaxon with an *x*.

"Looked like Mutt and Jeff," Rose said.

"Mutt wasn't a black man, Rose," Harold said.

"Of *course* he wasn't black, Harold. Jeff wasn't either, for that matter. Besides, Mutt was the *short* one and Jeff was a white man, tall and skinny as a pole lamp. Had a mustache, too. The police officer was a heavy man and had no hair at all, not even on his head. No resemblance."

This was a couple with a bad case of cabin fever.

"Who said Jeff was black in the first place? *Jesus*, woman!" said Harold.

"Excuse me, folks, but I'm a little short on time here? Did you show any of these documents to the police?"

"The police were just going through the motions with us," Harold said, with a final hard look at his wife. "Said they had their man already. Didn't ask for anything."

"Can you remember what was in the contracts? Were any names mentioned?"

Their faces looked blank as a pair of plates. "Any dates?" I said. "Locations?"

"One of the papers we gave your man looked like some kind of bank contract that mentioned a foreign country I'd never heard of it. Some island or other. Carolina Island? What the hell was it, Rose?"

Rose gave her head a quick shake and went off to the kitchen.

"Was it the Cayman Islands?" I asked.

Harold's eyes narrowed with concentration. "That sounds like it."

So they had used an offshore bank to launder the money used in the transactions or to inventory it once they were finished. No wonder Barney was excited; he had probably figured out every link in the scam's chain. Maybe more.

"What else did you give to Mr. Klinehart?"

"That's all I can think of."

I spent another fifteen or twenty minutes, but without learning much. The Breckenridges had forgotten their squabble and were sitting on the couch together. Harold rested a hand on top of Rose's and asked her if she'd make some coffee.

"Where in the world are my manners?" she exclaimed, and jumped to her feet. I accepted, seeing they were starved for company. The Breckenridges' self-imposed exile on top of the loss of everything important to them was obviously eating them up. Harold and I talked about how the Giants had folded in the play-offs and the 49ers' sorry rebuilding season. Even light subjects carried an edge of desperation.

Harold glanced toward the small kitchen and whispered, "What kind of trouble are we in, Mr. Strobe?"

"You'll be fine," I said. "Just stay put a little longer. You and Rose make a list of things I can do for you, people you want me to contact, whatever. I'll take care of it."

Rose entered with coffee.

"When," asked Harold, "do you think we can go back?"

"We miss our friends," said Rose, and her eyes went all teary again. "We want to go back to our neighborhood, build our house back like it was."

Harold and I exchanged a look. We both knew there would be no returning to "like it was."

"The insurance company is putting us up here," Harold said, "but we're having trouble getting them to settle up with us."

"Let me help you with that," I said, and took the information and a copy of their policy.

"Sorry we couldn't be more help to you," said Rose. "Won't you have another cup of coffee?"

"A half would be fine," I said, and we talked a while longer. They confirmed what Mildred Moon had said about Deborah being "high-strung" for several days before her murder. She had refused to discuss whatever was bothering her.

"Deborah was afraid of someone," Rose said. "Never seen her act the way she was. I think she was being threatened."

"Who do you think it was?"

They shook their heads.

"Do you think it was the night janitor the police arrested?"

More negative head shakes. "I think," Rose said, "it was her boyfriend. Debby was so secretive about him, I'm sure the man was already married. She was still technically married to Frank, of course, so the whole thing was a mess, what with the pregnancy and all."

"You knew Deborah was pregnant?"

"Not until . . . the autopsy," Harold said, and Rose commenced to crying so hard she had to leave the room. It was time to go.

Rose came back to say good-bye, and I thanked them for the coffee and wrote down the things they wanted me to do for them in the Bay Area. I assured them I'd call the minute I had any news and told them not to worry about the insurance, that I'd take care of that, too. I had started my car and backed halfway out of the common driveway when I saw Harold lumbering toward me along the sidewalk.

"I . . . don't know . . . if this is imp-important," he gasped, leaning his large forearms against my car top and peering down between them. "We made . . . a picture for him. Your man . . . thought it might be . . . a help."

"A picture?"

A minute later I was back in their apartment, and Rose was describing a gift she had seen Deborah wrapping. "It was for her secret beau."

"Her boyfriend?"

"It was his birthday, and she had bought this special sterling silver desk lighter for him. She was proud of it because she had helped design it."

"Rose is a good drawer," said Harold, his face still red from the exertion of running me down. "We gave a picture of it to the investigator."

"Could you do another one for me?" I asked.

Rose picked up a pencil and began drawing a fine replica of an oval cigarette table lighter.

"It had a diamond pavé base—something like *this*—around the base and . . . there was an emerald—a real one—stuck right here at the top . . . just *so*. And another one on the thing you pushed down to make it light, then a layer of green felt here on the bottom."

She finished her sketch with a flourish and handed it to me, smiling for the first time. I complimented her on the drawing and meant it. She blushed.

"I took art in high school."

"So that's what she gave him for his birthday?" I asked.

" 'For the man who has everything,' she told me. "I suppose that might have included a wife and kids."

How right you were, I thought, then folded the drawing once, put it in my inside coat pocket, and thanked them again for their help.

I glanced in the rearview as I took off and saw Harold in the doorway staring into the dust I had raised. He was wishing he was in the car with me, making his getaway.

I made it back to the office by 2:30 in the afternoon and asked Barbara to set up meetings with the three stockholders whose names I had found in the vault. Although I was eager to interview Mr. Bomberger, I was particularly interested in visiting with Sheila Anderson, whose speculations in Synoptics had, according to some rough calculations I'd done, probably garnered as much as $4.5 million by buying on margin before the stock soared and another $6 million or so by shorting the stock before it plummeted. I had seen her name somewhere else in the SEC investigation file, but hadn't realized how much money she had made. The investigators could find no Synoptics relationship, so couldn't charge her as an unlawful tippee. That would all change if I could prove that she and Jason Moncrief secretly knew each other. Another long shot.

Here's the scenario I was working on based on the information gleaned from the file vault: Jason Moncrief provided funding to his co-conspirator—Anderson, Bomberger, Casperson, or all three—and instructed him or her or them to buy Synoptics stock on margin, then told Deborah Hinton to defer a write-off that skewed the company's quarterly earnings dramatically upward, beating "street estimates" by fourteen cents a share. He then instructed his confederate or confederates to sell after the stock topped out, then to use the profits from that transaction to "short" huge amounts of Synoptics shares. Moncrief then placed the anonymous tip to the SEC about the improper deferral, putting the stock into a tailspin. While the SEC was hassling him and Deborah Hinton over nickels and dimes, Moncrief was making secret millions with his friends in crime.

The guy was smart. We could have used him in the Billionaire Boys Club II. But something went wrong along the way, and Deborah had to go.

My secretary, Barbara, scanned the names of the three major investors I'd given her. "Casperson?" she said. "Jeffrey Casperson? So *that's* where he went."

Casperson was the third-largest trader, listed on the schedule as currently living in Zurich.

"You *know* Jeffrey Casperson?" I said.

"Not really," Barbara said, "but he used to come in with Mr. Moncrief when he was in college. He must be in his early thirties by now. Everybody knows he's Jason Moncrief's stepson from a previous marriage."

Everyone, I thought, but me and the SEC.

"What was he doing in Zurich?"

"The way I understand it, Jason Moncrief's current wife didn't want Jeffrey or Jason's ex around. So Moncrief moved his ex and Jeffrey to Europe. Jeffrey took his mother's maiden name with Jason's blessing."

"Does Jason have kids by his second wife?"

"Another son," Barbara said. "Name's Richard, goes by Rick. He's a first-year law student at Stanford and, believe it or not, a really nice young man—except for the fact that he's going to be a lawyer."

Poor kid will probably have to come here, I thought. But more important, how had the SEC missed the connection? Maybe they hadn't. Someone smart as Hale might have convinced them that the stock transactions were merely a function of Moncrief's personal estate planning or compliance with the terms of his marital dissolution agreement. Or maybe it was just a happy coincidence that the stock went up dramatically after Jeffrey bought it, and unlike Anderson and Bomberger, Casperson had not shorted the stock before it collapsed.

"What do I tell these people you want with them?" Barbara asked.

"Tell them I'm a lawyer for Synoptics and have some important tax planning information for them."

She said she would take care of it, and I told her that I appreciated the good work she had done for me. When I added that I'd soon be moving on, she didn't feign surprise.

Hale entered a minute later. "I met with Rex and Wilcox this morning."

I nodded. "You going to come out of this okay, Hale?"

"I've still got a few friends here," Hale said, "and so have you. People who know how hard you worked and who know what's really going on."

"Hale," I said, "do *you* know what's really going on?"

"Hell, Billy, I know Rex has been out to—"

"Not about me, Hale, about who really killed Deborah Hinton."

Hale sighed and slowly rotated his large head from side to side. "I know you think it has something to do with the insider trading scheme that got Jason and Deborah in trouble for a while, but you're wrong to suspect Jason of being involved in Deborah's murder. Everybody knows that Jason valued Deborah. He liked her very much."

"Maybe too much?"

Hale barked out a laugh. "Billy, if a fanciful imagination makes for a great trial lawyer, you've been wasting your time on the business side of the office."

I didn't smile. "I've pretty much figured that out on my own."

"I'm sorry, Billy. That was insensitive, and I hope that you won't feel like your time here was wasted. And I do have some good news."

"I always try to stay open to the possibility."

"A law school classmate of mine heads one of the top firms on Wall Street. I've told him about you, and he wants you to interview with his firm. You'd be paid the same base salary, but with a guaranteed forty-thousand-dollar bonus and full credit for time you've spent here toward partnership. Frankly, Billy, it's a younger, more vital firm than ours, and you'd fit right in with them."

A square peg in a round hole came to mind. He told me to think about it, and I said thanks, I would.

I arrived at the Pacific Heights home of Jacob Bomberger and was greeted at the door by a middle-aged Asian nurse who escorted me into a sunlit room where Bomberger was waiting for me. He didn't look like much of a murderer. Jacob Bomberger was in his high eighties, wheelchair-bound and half-blind. He had granted full power of attorney to his stockbroker, and obviously neither knew nor cared what went on in his trading account. For all practical purposes, his portfolio was a blind trust. He had no recollection or understanding of even owning Synoptics stock.

I visited with him for a while because he was lonely and then asked him to introduce me on the phone to his stockbroker, a man appropriately named Harry Cash, a fifteen-year veteran at Montgomery Securities, an ethical, San Francisco–based brokerage house. Cash seemed happy to talk about one of his "best calls ever."

"Bomberger prefers not to be troubled with decisions," said Cash. "I'm sure he's told you that. He's a decent old guy, but I sometimes regret that those October Synoptics trades weren't made for someone who really needed the money or at least someone able to appreciate what I had done to get it."

"What was the basis for your timing?" I asked. "How did you know when to buy and when to sell?"

"If you were a potential client," he said, "I'd call it 'seasoned instinct.' The truth? Pure shithouse luck: one of those hunches that pays you back for years of rooting around in the muck of Wall Street."

" 'Even a blind hog comes up with an acorn,' " I said.

"That's me," he said, and laughed. "I wish I'd had the balls to have done it for myself."

I thanked him, said good-bye to Jacob Bomberger, who had dozed off, and got on my cell phone as soon as I hit the sidewalk. Barbara had reached Sheila Anderson, the largest Synoptics trader on the list, and had made an appointment for me at two o'clock the next day.

"Ms. Anderson says parking on Telegraph Hill is tough," Barbara said, "so you may leave your car in a private parking area off a back alley called Sierra Drive, then walk around to the front entry. Got it?"

I scarfed down a fast-food chicken sandwich for lunch as I drove up Sansome Street the next day, took a left on Broadway, then straight up Montgomery toward the West's largest phallic symbol, Coit Tower. I popped three anti-acids for dessert and was ready to go.

I found Sierra Drive, parked, and quickly walked around to the front entrance. Two o'clock on the dot. I was surprised at the relative modesty of the small, two-story, wood-frame building, considering the size of Anderson's stock transactions. Must be an eccentric or maybe it's the million-dollar view she had from the upper level.

But her name was on the lower flat, and somebody else lived in the upper. I began to worry that Ms. Anderson was going to be every bit as nutty as old Bomberger and I'd be out of leads again.

The building's outer door featured a huge Christmas wreath with holly berries and a matching red bow. It was wide open, which struck me as funny, it being one of those cold, crystalline days where I could see my breath. When I came to the inside door of her lower flat, it was also ajar and the key was in the lock. Must be a trusting neighborhood, though I figured she had probably arrived home just ahead of me, maybe lugging groceries.

I rang the bell and called her name a few times, but no answer. I went upstairs and rang the doorbell to the upper unit, but nobody answered there either. I returned to the downstairs hallway and rang Anderson's bell some more and knocked, too. Nothing.

Hell, she had to be in there, so I removed the key and nudged the door open and took two steps inside.

"Ms. Anderson? It's Billy Strobe. Our two o'clock appointment? Are you here?"

No reply. I looked around the living room, which was surprisingly sparse and modern in sharp contrast to the rococo facade of the outer building. The interior decoration was a little strange, too, with its pale pink ceiling, grape colored walls, and weird abstract art hanging everywhere. Not an old lady's house, unless she was a superhip old lady. Her coat had been tossed over a chair, and her purse was on a small dining room table. I called out again, louder this time. Could she be out emptying the garbage? Feeding a cat? Should I back the hell out of there before I embarrass myself or scare her to death? Or land myself back in prison on a burglary or trespass parole revocation?

The phone rang. I jumped. Five rings. Nobody answered. I was alone, uninvited, in a house belonging to someone I didn't know. Jaxon with an *x* would love this, and I knew I should turn tail and run.

But I was beginning to wonder if she was all right. What if she'd had a stroke? A fall. Needed help. I glanced into the kitchen off to my right to make sure the gas was off. A large picture of Buddha hung on the wall next to the oven. It was an electric range, and the only thing I smelled was a faint odor of musk and marijuana. She was hip, all right.

I was not feeling good about this, but my feet led me down a hallway—painted a darker purple—to an open door of a bedroom. What I saw there sent off an explosion in my head, and though my brain tried to reject what my eyes were seeing, on top of the bed in front of me was what looked to be a woman, completely covered by a thin bedspread. And the part that covered the head was blossoming red with blood.

I had found Sheila Anderson.

I heard a deep guttural sound, like an animal in pain, coming not from the body on the bed, but from deep inside my own heaving chest. I felt dizzy, and guess I had started to back away without knowing it, because I bumped against a dresser, my heart pounding in my throat. I took a few deep breaths and forced myself to the bedside, then slowly pulled the cover back, revealing the nude body and nearly severed head of a woman who wasn't Sheila Anderson at all.

It was *Betty Perkins.*

I threw the bedspread back over her head and covered my mouth with both hands. I vaguely recall staggering back toward the living room, bouncing off those purple walls, so shocked I didn't even hear the sirens at first. When I did hear them I knew I'd have to run—again—but I had to do something first, no matter what.

Back in the kitchen, I grabbed a thin dish towel, wrapped it around my trembling fingers so as not to leave prints, then carefully opened the purse I'd seen on the dining room table. I clumsily fished a wallet out of the purse, noticing that it was full of twenties and fifties. This had not been a simple robbery gone awry, but I reckon I knew that already.

My hands fumbled with the wallet and it fell to the floor. The sirens were getting close, but I had to see her driver's license. There it was. Oh, God, no! It was *Betty's* picture—though with longer hair and more traditional makeup and to the right, her name: SHEILA BETH ANDERSON. Oh, Betty, for Christ's sake, who the hell were you?

The sirens were nearly on top of me now, and I tossed the wallet and dishcloth on the floor and glanced out the front window. A patrol car was turning off Montgomery Street, so I raced to the rear of the house. The back door had a dead bolt, but it was also key-locked without a key and *shit*, nailed shut! Don't panic, try the window in the back laundry room. Nailed shut, too. She had been afraid for some time and had turned the place into a sealed vault.

I had only a few seconds and raced out her front door, pausing only to wipe my prints off the knob, and into the common hallway and up the stairs to the front door of the upper flat. I didn't even think, just threw my shoulder into it. The hinges held, but enough of the wood gave way that I could reach through and open the door. I cleared my prints again and ran to the back of the house, even as I heard the cops coming up the outer front stairs. I found a bedroom in back, opened a window—using my shirttail to wipe off my prints—and there it was, a rusted-out steel fire escape, not built to code I'd bet, but enough to lower me to within five feet of the ground. I dropped, then ran across a short backyard, vaulted a four-foot wire fence, and hopped into my car. While fumbling for my car keys I realized I had sliced my hand, probably on the fire escape. Bleeding like a stuck hog. How much of my DNA had I left on that jagged steel? Too late to worry about that now. I spun the car around and drove back down Sierra, then took the hard right onto Montgomery, nearly hitting a young Hispanic walking a dog. Terrific, ex-felon donates blood at another fresh murder scene, then nearly runs down a witness to be sure the guy was paying close attention. I could see him in the rearview, shaking his fist and shouting at me. His dog had broken loose and was chasing my car.

I could see someone else, too, someone burned into my memory for all time; a woman who had cared for me and maybe died because of me. Her name wasn't important, nor did I give a shit that she had dutifully called her murderer to warn him I was coming to see her. What mattered was that she had been young and full of life and now she would never see another sunset.

I had to stop this butcher before he killed again. That mattered, too, because I was sure to be next on his list.

I forced myself to slow down as I approached Green Street, stole a glance to my right, and saw the empty patrol car in front of Anderson's apartment house, then another one coming up the hill, siren and red lights blazing, two intense-looking cops inside, not giving me so much as a second glance. I stopped at a red light on Broadway and realized I was pounding on the steering wheel with both hands and crying, sobbing like a goddamn baby, scarred by another memory that would never heal.

*   *   *

Back in my apartment, I couldn't stop shaking. Nothing stronger than beer in the kitchen—and only one of those, which I chugalugged without effect. Probably good there wasn't more. I needed a clear head, plus when you're the offspring of not one, but two alcoholic parents, you think twice every time you take a drink.

I went into the bathroom and threw up the beer and my fast-food chicken sandwich. Had I really seen what I thought I saw?

I cleaned out the cut on my hand and bandaged it tight to stop the bleeding. I unloaded my wallet, keys, change, and another key I didn't recognize. Swell, I had pocketed the key to Anderson's apartment. Too tired to bury or otherwise dispose of it, Billy Fix-It took the lid off the water closet in the bathroom, then removed the float and worked it open at the seam. I then taped the key to the inside of the float, put the two pieces of copper back together, and reattached the float to the lever arm inside the tank. I replaced the lid, then flushed the toilet once to be sure everything worked normally.

I went into the kitchen and flipped the radio on, and within an hour learned that Sheila Anderson—"victim of a grisly murder discovered only minutes ago"—had been a former office manager at a dot-com called Headstarter, Inc., in Silicon Valley.

High tech was a small world, and I could picture Moncrief meeting Sheila Anderson at some function, she being attracted to his wealth and power, he to her youth and beauty, one thing leading to another, then . . .

Hell, I was speculating all over the damn place, but it *was* possible. Moncrief and Betty. Dear Betty, the first person I had come to trust, because she was totally unrelated to the craziness all around me. Dear Betty, hippy superspy, who had tried to get me to quit my "crazy quest" and get out of it. She should have listened to her own advice.

Ironic, I thought, how I had pictured myself as a Trojan horse inside Moncrief's fortress, when he had planted Sheila Anderson inside my very own bed.

Don't worry, Billy, we're using each other.

Fucking Moncrief knew everything I knew soon as I knew it. Monitoring my progress through his co-conspirator, until somewhere along the way Betty's lonely heart prevailed over Sheila's treacherous mind.

Then they both had to be eliminated.

Late that night, I found myself dialing Betty's phone number, wanting to hear her voice once more. I wasn't surprised to hear another electronic voice instead, reporting that the number was "no longer in service." I had no doubt that Betty's apartment over in Cow Hollow would be vacated now as well. After all, she had never existed.

30

Betty's problems were over, but mine were just beginning. As I nibbled on toast and cereal the next morning in my kitchen, I watched the Channel 4 news reporting that the police had the three numbers from the rear license plates and the color of a car seen leaving the scene of Sheila Anderson's murder. Cut to the witness.

"He was drivin fast, musta been inna a hella big rush to get someplace. Nearly clipped me. Hadn't jumped he woulda. White guy, twenties, fair skin, but dark hair, kinda long, combed straight back. Oh, sure, I'd know the dude if I see him again."

Cut to guess who? Yep, there was good old Terrell Jaxon, announcing that he'd like to question the driver of that car, and he'd appreciate it if he would present himself at headquarters. Not that he was under suspicion or anything.

It would be just a matter of time until Jaxon came calling again, and this time it would be with a murder arrest warrant. I pictured myself in a police lineup and decided it was time for a change.

"Take it off, Coco," I told her two hours later at the TechnoCenter, "take it all off."

"Fuck you," she said, signifying apparent disagreement with my request.

When I told her I was serious, she scowled. "Listen up, Billy Batshit"—which is what Coco insisted on always calling me—"that's not the NBA up there at Synoptics. I *know* those guys, and they would not like it one little bit. Neither would your boss, Mr. Lassiter."

"They'll have to learn to appreciate my inner beauty," I said, but she wouldn't smile.

"Forget about it," she said, head tilted critically, stroking the bead in her nose, checking out my head with the scrutiny of a surgeon. "You think a big-time client like Jason Moncrief is going to take you seriously looking like a Marine recruit? Besides, it's your best feature."

"Are you a barber or a career guidance counselor? Come on, Coco, just do it."

"No way. Some doctors won't do abortions. I don't shave heads. So let's get serious. A little off around the ears, Billy? Your usual?"

I finally got her to start cutting, but her heart wasn't in it.

I liked Coco, and we had become friends. When I was boning up on Synoptics gossip, we went out a couple of times, strictly buddies. She wasn't all that interested in men, she told me right off. I said fine, I ain't either, so let's go see a movie or something.

For all her bizarre looks, mannerisms, foul language, and pierced body parts, I quickly learned that Coco was as straitlaced as a nun. She had taught English Lit to freaked-out high school kids until she burned out and became a Republican. She served customers French champagne the day after Al Gore conceded. Given the slightest encouragement, she would rail against drugs and gangs and unwed mothers for the entire allotted half-hour haircut. Told me on her day off she listened to Rush Limbaugh! Working on her family values, she said, in case she ever decided she needed a family. Don't ask me how we got on so well.

She had heard I had won a new trial for Darryl Orton and asked about him.

"You knew Darryl?" I asked, surprised, forgetting that Coco knew everyone.

"Sure, I did," she said, the scissors clicking rhythmically to an old Donna Summer disco tune. "When he'd come on shift, he'd give me a free sweep, even clean my mirrors. Always had a smile and a good word. He was a musician, if you don't put too fine a point on it. Which is to say, he played country."

"I know it."

"Anyway, I'd give him a free cut in return whenever he wanted it." She looked at me in the mirror, shook her head in dismay, and said, "You want more off?"

I nodded. "I want the Marine recruit special."

"My God," she said, "you already don't even look like you anymore."

I smiled. "Keep going, Coco. Shorter."

"You have a nice-shaped head, Billy. I guess I'd be willing to shave it, which would at least be more hip than a crew. Nobody does crew nowadays."

"Crew's okay," I said.

A few minutes later I looked in the mirror and saw Coco and a plucked chicken looking back at me. She shrugged as if to say, you asked for it.

"How about dinner next week?" I said.

"You kidding? With you looking like that?"

I paid her and stared sadly at the soft mounds of dark hair on the floor. Coco reached for her broom and began sweeping my best feature into a dustpan.

"That should hold you for a while," she said. "If they ask who did it—"

"I'll deny it was you. Don't worry."

She smiled. "Dinner next week will be fine."

"We'll go to Oakland." I was halfway out the door when I heard a snapping sound as she shook out my plastic apron. I turned, looked at my hair drifting down, settling onto the floor like slivers of steel.

"Jesus, Mary, and Joseph!" I said.

"What's the matter, Billy? Change your mind? Want it back?"

I kept staring at the hair on the floor and on the plastic apron she was shaking out. Something had been nagging me. Free haircuts to Darryl. Moncrief a regular. *DNA from hair?* Could that be how he did it? Why not? Why the hell not?

If so, I had another major piece in place.

I took the elevator to the seventh floor of the Hall of Justice, flashed my state bar card and driver's license to a deputy, and within an hour of leaving Coco's was sitting across from Darryl Orton in a cold and claustrophobic visitors room.

Darryl's eyes widened as he took in my head. "Damn, kid, the Injuns got you."

"It's a long story. Listen, Darryl, I think I know how they framed you. So let's say I've figured out *how* they did it and *why* they did it. I also think I know *who* did it, but I can't prove it yet."

"Pardon my ignorance, kid, but I thought *who* was the important part."

I had hoped for a little more enthusiasm, but went ahead and explained everything I had learned: how Moncrief probably used two different women to work the insider scam, how Deborah violated the deal by buying stock of her own and focusing the SEC spotlight on Moncrief and his company, then how he got rid of her and created the perfect fall guy by grabbing some strands of Darryl's hair off an apron or the floor of Coco's salon right after Darryl left and then planting it on Deborah Hinton's body.

Darryl considered my words for a minute; then he said, "Ain't that a bit of a stretch?"

"How else could it have been done? You think some moonlighting tooth fairy crept into your trailer home and took a lock of your hair in your sleep? It's the only explanation that makes sense. Unless, of course, you did kill her."

"I think it was the moonlighting tooth fairy done it."

"Then, to make sure the cops knew whose DNA to check the hair against, he or she left the murder weapon in your locker."

Darryl considered what I'd said and then finally began to nod his head. "That's good, kid. That's damn good."

I smiled to acknowledge his rare compliment, then admitted it was still supposition at this point and that I was stuck.

"Stuck?"

"I don't know how to prove Moncrief did it. Coco doesn't remember Moncrief hanging around after one of your cuts. She doesn't say it didn't happen, she just doesn't remember him ever being around after you'd been in. That's where we are, pard. No way of proving it."

"You're stuck, Billy, because you're on overload. You're as jumpy as a horse before a thunderstorm. Remember that old song, 'She Got the Gold Mine and I Got the Shaft'?"

"You want to translate that for me?"

"You know what they say, kid: Follow the money. If you're right and Moncrief killed all these people—or had 'em killed—he did it for money, right? So follow the money trail while that stock was goin up and down. Take it one step at a time, remember?"

"I've been puzzling over the money angle, but the documents have disappeared."

He gave me a sympathetic look. "You look wore out, kid. You're doin great, but you'd better take a day or two off. Get a little rest. After that, start her all over."

"Start over?"

"You want to find what you're lookin for, no matter what it is, you start up the mountain one step at a time, retracin your steps ten times if you have to. It'll take a while, but you'll find what you missed the first time, and when you finally get to the top, you'll have your murderer. You'll recognize him by the big stack of money sittin next to him."

I nodded. "Maybe I will take a night off."

"Good," said Darryl, "and here's an idea. You said Moncrief used two women to make his scam work? Why not go to the one that's still alive and see what she'll tell you?"

I looked away. "She wouldn't be any help."

"Wouldn't hurt to try. Speakin' of women, you still in love with the queen of clean?"

I nodded. He frowned. "Those fancy ladies'll eat you alive, son. Find yourself a nice little Okie girl who'll appreciate you."

"I've gotten to know her, Darryl. She's a good and decent woman. I gave you the wrong impression."

He shrugged to say he doubted it, so I changed the subject.

"Food any better here, Darryl?"

"I miss the sunlight."

"Sitting on your bench."

"Okay, I'll admit I don't much miss gettin the shit kicked out of me. You miss your hair?"

"Not much. How about your roommate? I'm sure you're lonely for Rabbit."

"Rabbit? Shit, I bet that fool's still all the time flogging his Johnson to convince himself he ain't dead yet."

This was depressing me. "At least you'll stay alive here until we can get you out."

He agreed. I told him then that I'd been fired at Stanton and Snow, and he tightened his lips into a straight line and hunched up his shoulders.

"It's okay, Darryl. I got into Synoptics, which is why I went there in the first place. Plus, Hale Lassiter has set me up with a job in New York if I want it."

"Good pay?"

"More than I'm making here."

"You gonna take it?"

"I'm damn sure going to let them all think I am. And hell, who knows, maybe I will. I'd like to see this trial through first, plus I'm hard in love with Dana. It would be tough to leave without her."

"Well, if you're so damned set on her, take her with you."

I shook my head. "She doesn't know yet how much she loves me. Well, sometimes she does. Anyways, I'll be at the firm a couple more weeks, and maybe she'll wise up."

"Can't make a girl love you, kid."

"I know it."

"All you can do is keep stalkin her and hope she panics and gives in. She good-lookin?"

"The prettiest girl I've ever seen, and smart besides."

"Well, you can't have everything, especially in a mixed marriage."

"Mixed?"

"Didn't you just tell me she was smart and good-looking?"

"Fuck you, old man. You ever been married?"

His expression turned serious. "Twice," he said quietly. "No good at it. Only thing worse than marryin a jailbird is marryin a musician, and I was both."

"Would you do it again?"

"Maybe, or maybe to save you lawyers trouble, I'd find another woman I can't get along with and just start making monthly payments to her."

I laughed and put a hand on his shoulder. "We're going to get this done, Darryl. I feel it."

He nodded uncertainly, and commenced to smile, but it was like his face forgot what it was trying to do. "Look, kid, I ain't one to be pushy, but you're missin a bet if you don't try to git somethin outta that girl workin for Moncrief. You can't follow the money if you don't start somewheres. I don't understand why you ain't willin to—"

"She's *dead*, Darryl. She's fucking dead, *okay?*"

That shut him up, and after a minute or two I told him the whole story, how she'd been Moncrief's deep throat, how he'd arranged for her to hit on me at the firm's watering hole, and how when my secretary called to set up an appointment, she must have panicked and called Moncrief.

"I think Moncrief saw it as an opportunity to kill two birds with one stone. Silence the girl he had no more use for, and get my parole revoked by calling the cops the minute he saw me fixing to enter the place."

Darryl had nodded his head as I told him everything, and now he grabbed both his knees, then painfully rose out of his plastic chair. He walked around a beat-up table and bent down toward me, his eyes narrowed into slits as he leaned in close and poked a forefinger hard into my chest.

"You get the hell out of this damn case and do it *now!*" he said through clenched teeth. "In fact, you get the hell out of this damn town! You take that job in New York or whatever you have to do but *get out of it.*"

I reminded him how many times we'd been through this argument and that the only way the judge would release me from the case was if I formally substituted out.

"Then do it!" He commenced to pounding on the door. "Guard!"

"Well, thank you very much, Darryl! The problem is every time I try to get you to select a new lawyer, you back out on me!"

"Not this time. You pick any asshole lawyer you want, and I'll take him, her, or it. I swear it. I'll take the public fucking defender again if it will get you out of my hair once and for all. I'll take your grandma if you got one."

I agreed.

"*Guard!*" he shouted again, and this time the door opened.

"You've done enough, kid, okay?" he said, over his shoulder. "So get outta here and send me a real lawyer."

*   *   *

I thought about Darryl's words as I stepped off the elevator onto the main floor of the Hall of Justice, which, as ususal, was crowded with cops coming and going, their keys and gun belts jangling with every step. I'd never had a problem in elevators before, but my nerves were sparking now no matter where I was. I knew Jaxon must be closing in on me and if he didn't get me soon, Moncrief would send someone like that swarthy guy with the long raincoat who would. He couldn't afford to let me wander around with all I had learned, once he learned I'd learned it.

I was also tired and depressed about Betty, and the fact that nobody, not even my own client, wanted me to keep digging into this thing.

Before this is over, Billy, you'll need a better reason for what you're doing than loyalty.

Betty knew Moncrief would kill me if I got close, and now I was close.

31

Driving back to the office under suddenly clear skies, I knew that Darryl was right, as usual. I had to follow the money, and I'd been so shaken by Betty's death, I'd almost forgotten the documents the Breckenridges had given Barney. Moncrief wouldn't have bothered to burn out the Breckenridges' house if he didn't think Barney's papers were damned important or if his thugs had already found them in Barney's office. They were out there somewhere, and I had to find them.

I took Darryl's advice. I went back to the trailhead, the place where the documents got lost. What had Barney done with them? I had no hope of winning without them and not a clue as to how to find them. Nobody would believe that Moncrief had simply recovered a few hairs off Darryl's head from Coco's salon in order to orchestrate the most perfect frame-up in the annals of crime.

Unless . . . *unless* . . . What if I could turn the tables on him? Hoist him on his own banana. Could it be done? Why the hell not? *He* had done it, hadn't he?

But I couldn't do it alone. I'd need a smart investigator. Somebody with guts and not too sticky in the ethics department. So I followed Darryl's advice again and mentally retraced my steps all the way back to Soledad, and there, standing just a few feet up the mountain, was ol' don-Don Campora. He would know who I should hire.

The first Donald G. Campora listed in the Chicago directory turned out to be his son, and within an hour I had a call back from the don himself.

"So, kid, long time no hear. By the way, how's *your* hearing?"

"They just took a nick, don-Don, but then your boys tried to take more."

"I heard. Fucking bean-eaters, can't trust them to follow orders. No discipline."

I swallowed, said nothing.

"So bygones, Billy? Eye for an eye? Ear for an ear? Eh?"

"Sure," I said and told him what I needed: a sharp investigator in the Bay Area, the kind that got things done and didn't ask a whole lot of questions.

"That shouldn't be tough."

"And maybe one with some close ties to the local cops?"

"That's tougher. Let me make some calls. Give me your number."

"I'll be much obliged for this, don-Don."

"You have no idea," he said, and hung up, leaving me with a queasy churning in my stomach.

Twenty minutes later my phone rang.

"You call a girl named Mimi D'Angelo," came a voice like metal filings. East Coast accent? Maybe Chicago? "Trained in New York. I hear she's the best in the Bay Area, and she ain't no Sunday-school teacher neither, know what I mean? She don't miss nothing, but she knows when to look the other way, too. And she's connected locally, know what I mean?" I told him I knew what he meant.

"Tell her hello for Sal Carrerra in L.A. He's the one who gimme her name."

"Yes, sir. I'll tell her. Thank you."

The voice didn't offer his name, and I didn't ask it.

"Aw, fagehabowit," he said.

I left a message for Mimi D'Angelo, uneasy to be putting even my nose under the Mafia's tent, but knowing I had to take the chance. I was still staring at the phone in my cramped, fluorescent-hued, solitary office, when Dana said knock, knock, and entered my office. The room brightened with her presence, at least until she got a look at my new hairstyle.

"My God, Billy! What happened to your head? I've read nothing about a Sioux uprising."

My hand went involuntarily to my head as I laughed for the first time since I'd found Sheila's body.

"Whatever look you were going for," she added, "you missed."

"I was despondent over getting you in trouble with my bungling at Synoptics," I said, "so I put my head into the front end of an International Harvester."

"Well, since you wouldn't want to be seen in public again, and given the fact that you're about to join the ranks of the unemployed, you could probably use a home-cooked meal."

"The answer is yes. When and where?"

"Tonight. Seven-thirty. Here's my address. Bring a bottle of red and earplugs if you're not used to being around a two-and-a-half-year-old."

My phone rang, and I considered ignoring it, but had left my number on D'Angelo's pager.

"It's a Ms. D'Angelo," said Barbara, "though it sounds more like a Mr."

"I'll take it," I said, then I covered the mouthpiece and said, "I've got to take this, but I'll be there and I'll bring *two* bottles so we won't need the earplugs."

She smiled and left.

"Thanks for calling," I said, and told her how I had heard about her.

"Sal already called me," came the husky voice, another East Coaster. "He says I'm to do whatever you ask and do it quick. He tells me I don't ask no questions, something I'm very experienced at not doing. So what can I do for ya, Mr. Strobe?"

"Start by calling me Billy, okay? First, I need you to run down a car that was owned by an investigator named Barnard Klinehart."

"I heard of him. Too bad. A good man."

"I know it. Anyways, when you find the car, I need to get custody of it."

"You want I should steal it or buy it?"

"Let's buy it. Then we'll tear it apart and see if we can find what I'm looking for."

"No problem," she said. "That's it?"

"I want to give you the rest face-to-face."

"I get it," she said, her voice dropping to a conspiratorial whisper. "Walls have ears. Bugs on the phone. Loose lips sink ships. Love it, man. When you want I should come up?"

Was she making fun of me? Being sarcastic, or was she just nuts?

"Not here. Where's your office?"

She gave me her address and we agreed to meet at 5:00 P.M.

*   *   *

The office of Mimi D'Angelo, Investigations, made Klinehart's dump look like the suite I'd had at the Four Seasons in New York. It was located in a converted warehouse about ten minutes south of the financial district, about a mile off Third Street in an industrial area. I checked and rechecked the address she had given me, then entered the ancient block wall building through a large door made of steel. I had first taken it to be an emergency exit, but it turned out to be the main entrance. The rear door, a couple of hundred yards away, was identical, but locked.

Once inside, I started clockwise down an endless, poorly lighted corridor, my footsteps echoing off the unpainted walls. On the way, I got to the end, turned right, and walked another hundred yards, looking for 42B. I passed cubicles not much bigger than my cell at Soledad, many with open doors to attract air. People inside looked at me with hungry smiles and welcoming eyes, hoping I'd come to give them the contract that would allow them to go public, retire to New Zealand, and live on a fifty-six-foot yacht. Some had small signs over their doors: ALGARVE.COM, CHAMPAGNE TOURS, GALVIN PRESS, AARDVARK EDITING, MONKEYBUZZ.COM, and so on down the cold, narrow corridor.

Some of the work spaces seemed much bigger, and live music could be heard pounding through the walls. Rehearsal studios. The door to 42B was closed. I knocked—no answer. I waited. I would never walk through a door uninvited again.

At 5:15 I saw a small figure coming toward me, snapping the fingers of one hand, carrying a large Styrofoam carton in the other.

"Sweetboy!" she shouted at me. "Can-you-dig-it? *Yesss!*"

Sweetboy? Christ, I had told her to use my first name, but . . . *sweetboy?*

"That you, Strobe, or are you a prince looking to try a shoe on me?" she shouted down the corridor, then over her shoulder shouted, "Sweetboy, *oh, my soul,* and bless your *gi-gan-tic* nigger asses!"

She didn't offer a hand as she approached me, which was fine by me, but immediately went to work fumbling with a key to her cubicle while explaining that Sweetboy was a R & B group that was rehearsing up the hall in 37A.

"Fucked the bass player, which was stupid," she said, shaking her head sadly as if she had realized her mistake at that very moment. She walked around her desk and shoved some papers aside to make room for her food carton.

"Have a seat, Strobe. Mind if I eat?" she added as she attacked a huge portion of large noodles. "Chow fun," she said. "The best. Got it at Lazio's Deli up the street."

"That sounds chancy."

"I know. The lead guitar player or singer won't look twice at you once you fuck the bass player."

"I meant buying Chinese at an Italian deli."

"Oh. See, Lazio, he got this Chink cook. Smuggled the poor fucker in, so now he's working off his passage. No English. Guy can cook, though."

Mimi D'Angelo was oddly attractive if you wore earplugs. Nice body, full black hair a bit out of control, brown eyes, incongruently fair skin, and surprisingly delicate features except for a mouth so wide it looked like one of her chop sticks had wedged in her jaw. She was dressed in jeans, sweatshirt, and platform sandals that got her up to about five feet four inches. When I tried to imagine her on the witness stand, my problems with Darryl in a courtroom seemed minor by comparison.

"So what can I do for ya?" she said as she attacked her food with a thrashing enthusiasm that reminded me of an Explorer segment on TV where a school of piranha had caught a wounded bird in a stream.

"Mind if I close—?"

"Close the door?" she said. "Be my guest. Oh, boy," she added, her eyes sparkling. "Now the secret stuff."

I explained what I wanted her to do. It didn't take long, because of her maddening habit of finishing my sentences for me. Her impatient quickness was frustrating, but also reassuring. I was beginning to see that although Mimi D'Angelo was loud, sarcastic, and nuts as a bunny, she was also damn smart and probably ate Number 10 roofing nails for breakfast. On top of that, she confirmed that she still had a "very close friend" in the homicide department of the SFPD.

After she had heard me out, Mimi rose and walked the eight or nine feet to the door of her cubicle. She jerked it open, peered up and down the bleak corridor, and then closed it again.

"Lemme get this straight," she said. "You want me to get this guy's hair, then break into a closed-off crime scene, plant the hair around the victim's bed, then get my cop buddy on the job to find it and take it to the FBI lab is what you're sayin?"

"That's right. I'll make it easy for you to get Moncrief's hair, and you won't have to break in to 'plant it.' I have a key."

"He has a key," Mimi D'Angelo said to the wall. "Lemme ask you somethin, Mr. Strobe. Did you take your medicine this morning?"

I smiled at her. "It will work."

"I've been wondrin all afternoon, why me?" she said, pushing aside her half-empty container and chopsticks. "I'm, you know, normally eighty-sixed by you Montgomery Street white-shoes. Now I guess I know why me."

"Sal vouched for you. Says you can get a job done."

"No matter what's required to get it done, right? Told you my fucked reputation was richly deserved, right?"

"I'm counting on it," I said.

I explained that I hoped to turn the tables on Moncrief by framing him exactly the way he had framed Darryl Orton.

Mimi picked a half-eaten potsticker from the abandoned carton and eyed it thoughtfully while pivoting slowly from side to side in an antique swivel chair that squeaked irritatingly with each rotation. "So when the defense lawyer springs the DNA on this guy Moncrief at trial," she said, "he browns his shorts, drops to his knees, and prays forgiveness for his sins." She popped the morsel in her mouth, which did nothing to slow the words coming out of the same place she had put the food into. "And your guy walks into the sunlight, right?"

"I'm hoping Moncrief will at least panic and take the Fifth. That would damn sure raise a reasonable doubt in the minds of the jury about Darryl Orton."

She shook her head. "You'da done nothin but raise a doubt concernin a murder Orton ain't even charged with. So let's get back to that medicine you forgot to take today."

"That joke is getting old, Mimi. You want to do this or not? Maybe Sal or the don can come up with someone who needs the work."

I wasn't bluffing. Time was running short, and with everyone—including my own client—against me, I needed full dedication even if I had to pay through the nose for it. I was whoring for commitment.

She smiled, a huge smile like the kind that kids cut in a jack-o'-lantern. "Hey, simmer down, okay? I was just checkin your *cojones.* I'm all ears."

"All right then—here's the deal. I think I can connect the two murders. So if the jury thinks—even for a few minutes—that Moncrief did the second one, they'll think he might have done the first one, too."

"How are you gonna do that?"

"You're going to do it."

"Me? Maybe I'm the one who forgot to take my medicine. I missed that part."

I explained about Barney getting killed and the Breckenridges getting torched, and documents that might tie Sheila Anderson to the scam initiated by Deborah Hinton. The connection. She nodded.

"If you ain't got the documents, maybe it's 'cause the bad guys do."

"If they had them," I continued, "they wouldn't have burned down the Breckenridges' house. I'm hoping that whatever they wanted is stashed somewhere in Barney's car, which he practically lived—"

"Lived in, right? Didn't have snazzy digs like mine, huh?" she said with a wink.

"No, and Barney was a very careful guy. I doubt he'd leave a batch of smoking-gun documents sitting around in his office. Sure, it's a long—"

"Long shot. Okay, okay, if it rolls on wheels, I'll find it. It'll take a few days longer if it's been stamped into a cubic foot of compressed steel, in which case you'da had trouble reading the fine print anyway. Right? What I wanna know is how I'm s'posed to get this guy's DNA."

"A friend of mine cuts his hair. I got a look at her appointment book, and he's scheduled in day after tomorrow. Two o'clock. Here's a newspaper photo of Moncrief. You walk in to make an appointment while he's paying and they're busy. Grab some hair off the floor or the plastic apron. Maybe buy some shampoo or something while you're at it, then bullshit your way out the door."

I was worried about offending her, but I had to ask one more question. "Are you familiar with evidentiary rules on how to collect evidence and identify it for court?"

"Did Noah know how to build a fuckin boat? By the way, it's called 'protecting the chain of evidence.' "

"I stand corrected."

"Now, when's the trial?"

"December twenty-ninth."

"The *twenty-ninth*?"

"I'm told they start trials on Fridays now. Don't ask me why."

She got out her calendar and made a note, a ministerial act that somehow reassured me.

"What else?" she asked.

I felt morally obligated to warn her about the danger she might find herself in, and she said the only danger she feared was not getting paid. She demanded thirty-five hundred up front, then a hundred dollars an hour plus expenses.

"Isn't that a little steep?"

"I charge double my usual rate for committing felonies, especially when my previous colleague, Mr. Barnard Klinehart, is currently at rest with a half-ton of dirt and dogshit on top a' him."

I shrugged, and wrote the biggest check I'd ever written, which she casually tossed in her desk drawer without looking at it. "Okay, we're in business," she said. "I'll be ready on Thursday, though I'm still curious about how I get into Anderson's pad to plant the hair. You said something about a key? That would help because I charge triple rates for second story."

I gave her the key I'd taken out of the copper float at my apartment, happy to be rid of it. She said she'd be in touch and call me the minute she found Klinehart's car. We shook hands. Her grip was firm and left a remembrance of Lazio's Deli on my hand for the rest of the evening. I started my trek back to the parking lot, absorbing a deafening earful of Sweetboy as I passed 37A.

Dana greeted me with a hug that was either warmly fraternal or hopefully, a prelude to something more. Either way, just the sight of her after my interlude in the warehouse was downright cleansing.

"Welcome to our humble home," she said, and I heard little footsteps headed our way. Sarah Mathews gave me a shy look and disappeared behind her mother's skirt. I placed my wine bottles on the floor and kneeled down to smile and get a closer look at the cutest damn kid I'd ever seen. She had dark, naturally curly hair like her mother's, and huge pale blue eyes. So there was some blue-eyed bastard walking around I'd kill on sight if I knew who he was.

Sarah didn't smile back, in fact she made a face at me, which was a little embarrassing. Dana asked her if she wanted to say hello to Mommy's friend Billy. She shook her head and wrapped her lips around a finger.

"Want to shake hands?" I said, and extended a finger.

She shook her head again and withdrew behind her mother's legs. "Who are you?" she said.

"My name's Billy. You saw me at work one day."

"*Mean* people at work," she said, and ran off.

"I've not been around children much," I told Dana, "except for my kid sister, who I hated and picked on because she was smarter and cuter than me. Looks like I'm being paid back here."

"Give her time," Dana said. "She doesn't see many humanoids of the male persuasion."

"Okay," I said, "but meanwhile, I'm prepared to bribe my way into her heart if I have to."

I held out a small toy chicken that clucked when squeezed. Sarah must have heard it, because she came running back, hands high in the air. She stopped abruptly, eyed the toy, eyed me, then cast her dancing blue eyes up to Mommy, saw the encouragement there, and reached out a tiny hand and took it. "Thank you," she said, and toddled off with her clucking chicken.

"The old trick bag again," she said.

"She's a cute kid, Dana."

"The evening's young," Dana warned. "Withhold your verdict till the trial is over."

She led the way back to the kitchen, past a small Christmas tree on a table in the corner of the living room that was decorated with hand-drawn ornaments cut out of cardboard: scribbled drawings of cats, dogs, trees, and flowers.

Dana's apartment—condo actually—was much more spacious than mine and built at least thirty years later. She had decorated it in a modern style without sacrificing warmth. Her furniture and pillows were in earth colors, brown tones blended with autumn yellows and meadow greens, creating an atmosphere of pure light and comfort. Some miniature plastic horses on the sofa's end table created a jarring note, as did an antique saddle draped over a sawhorse near the hearth of a small fireplace, over which hung an impressionistic oil painting of two horses and a distant moon that must have set Dana back a month's salary.

On a small table next to a rocking chair was a framed photo of Sarah perched on a Shetland pony, caught by the camera in an uncertain smile, and one of Dana on horseback, racing around a barrel at an alarming angle, her hair trailing in full flight behind her, her eyes wide and alive.

By the time we had finished a glass of wine in the kitchen, Sarah was flirting with me and a Caesar salad was ready to be served. I coaxed the child into sitting beside me and once there, she was on my lap, asking questions, pulling on my nose and probing my mouth and eyes with a finger, like I was some sort of curiosity just in from Mars. She grabbed an eyebrow and announced, "Eyebrella!"

"She's being a pest now. Shoo her away when you've had enough."

When Sarah knocked over my glass of wine with her foot, I was amazed at Dana's response. Without a word, she bent at my feet and did her best to minimize the damage. "Watch those little feet, honey," she said, and gave each foot a kiss.

"I love you, Mommy," said Sarah, with a look of concern, which set me to thinking what a great way to apologize for an accident, one for which no blame had been laid. What would it be like to be loved that way, by a woman like that? I sent up a prayer that maybe I'd find out.

After dinner, I sat and listened to music while Dana read a story to Sarah in bed. I made a quick trip to the bathroom and sneaked a look into Dana's bedroom on the way back. Some say women are more nosy than men, but they're wrong, at least when it comes to curiosity about women. I've always wanted to know what makes them tick. I want to know everything, not just what they look like beneath their clothes, though that's near the top of the list, but how they get dressed in the morning, how they smell, what their bathrooms look like, clues to the eternal mystery.

Her dresser was full of trophies and a wall was covered with medals, mostly blue or red, plus more photos of Dana on her horse, many with Sarah.

Then I heard the door softly close, and I hightailed it back to the living room. I had planned to confess my snooping, but when she entered the room it was like neither one of us could wait another second. She was in my arms, the full length of her hard lean body pressed firmly against me, our mouths jammed together so hard I tasted blood with no idea whose it was. Her tongue passed through my lips and I circled it with mine. She thrust her hips into me with an urgency that matched my own and in a rapid-fire series of desperate clumsy motions, I opened her blouse and lifted her bra up and over her small breasts and took a hard nipple into my mouth. We collapsed onto her couch, me on top of her, panting like an animal, feeling a hand under my shirt, another on my fly, then my own right hand frantically ripping at my belt, pulling my chinos down and her skirt up in one motion, parting her panties to one side with no finesse whatsoever, praying she wouldn't stop me, then relieved as my hand met no resistance, only flowing lava as I guided myself inside the only woman I would ever love.

Later, over a hot brandy, and after I'd located my wristwatch on the floor of the living room under a sofa, we joked about my elegant foreplay and her demure resistance. But underlying the humor and barely dormant passion was a warm and comfortable feeling I hoped would hold up under the battering that lay ahead of us.

"Guess I should of got myself fired a long time ago."

That turned her serious. "Are you going to take the New York job?"

I shrugged. "Maybe, but I'm not going there alone."

She didn't bite. "It sounds like a good opportunity, but there are other firms here in town. . . ."

"I think me *leaving* town is part of the deal—you know, out of Dodge by sundown?"

"Part of what deal?"

"I figure it's a deal where Hale might land on his feet despite having hired an ex-con who almost lost their biggest client for them; a deal that involves appeasing Jason Moncrief."

"Do you still seriously believe that Jason is involved somehow in Deborah's murder?"

I wanted to tell her everything. Trust was no longer an issue, but her own personal safety was.

"I know it; I just can't prove it. Yet. I'm . . . under way with something that I hope will work out before I have to leave for New York."

She frowned, shifted one leg under the other. "You told me that if I got you into the vault, you would tell Hale what you found before you did anything rash. Why won't you let him help you?"

"First, because there's nothing he can do. Second, because my bungling has already served him up on a skewer, with Ashton happily turning the crank. I've done everything to Hale so far but stick a glazed apple in his mouth. You don't want me to hurt him even more, do you?"

"Of course not. But Hale is still the big dog in our firm and can take care of himself."

How easy the words rolled off her lips: *Our firm.* Darryl's wise-ass warning about a mixed marriage intruded for a minute, but I shut it out.

"Isn't it true," I said, "that Hale's standing as the firm's leader would plummet if Synoptics took its business elsewhere?"

"Not unless he caused it. What you're missing is that Ashton would suffer more than anyone. Seventy percent of Rex's billings come from Synoptics. Trust me, Billy. Hale dislikes Moncrief nearly as much as he does Rex Ashton. If Moncrief was what you think he is, Hale would help you expose him."

Damn, the woman was making sense again.

"I suspect," she continued, seeing I was paying attention, "that Hale knows things about Jason he's never told me or anyone else. Put your cards together with his, Billy. You might have a full house."

"What if I told you that Rex Ashton might be a joint-tenant with Moncrief in that house."

She blinked at that. "Are you saying Ashton might be implicated in the insider trading *and* protecting Moncrief on the two murders?"

"Three."

"*What?*"

I told her everything I knew about the murder of stockholder Sheila Anderson, skipping the part about Betty Perkins and my being sought by police as a suspect in the murder. She turned the appropriate shade of pale and said, "This is getting crazy and frightening, Billy. But it still doesn't connect Ashton."

"Maybe, but he's been the one trying to get rid of me and halt my efforts to reopen Darryl's case. I think the man would do anything to keep Synoptics money flowing into the firm."

"Even protect Moncrief from exposure for a murder? I don't think so."

"Unless he was involved in the stock scam at the beginning."

She shook her head. "Yet another stretch. But *if* you're right about Moncrief, you could be in danger."

"I know it."

She came to me then and kissed me gently, then kissed me again, but less gently, and soon, for the second time, our passion ignited, fusing our bodies into one.

She made some coffee after, and we reluctantly returned to what we had been talking about.

"Okay," I said, "I'll talk to Hale."

I then asked her flat-out whether she would join me if I had to leave town. Her smile vanished, and she lowered her gaze.

"I'll go right after I testify," I said, "if you'll come with me."

She took my hand. Our eyes met and held. "I can't leave San Francisco, Billy, but I don't want to lose you, either. Can't we talk to Hale about taking you back?"

"I never fit in at S & S. You know and I know it."

"But you were doing so well."

I decided to tell her why I had selected Stanton and Snow in the first place, told her everything.

"So they thought they had recruited me," I said when I was finished. "Hell, I recruited them. But it's not where I belong."

"Where do you belong?"

"Maybe a storefront south of Mission. Maybe in the Tenderloin where Cecil Williams's church is—something worthwhile. I don't know yet. I've got to deal with Moncrief first, get Darryl a lawyer, and clear my Dad's name."

"Something worthwhile? It looks like you're the one questioning *my* values now," she said.

"I always have," I said smiling. "That doesn't mean I'd have a problem sharing the seven-figure salary of a Montgomery Street heavyweight."

She smiled back, and I realized we had taken the first step toward a future together.

I slept on Dana's advice—in my own bed, unfortunately—and decided she was right. The DNA stunt Mimi D'Angelo and I were going to use to trap Moncrief was little more than a parlor trick with long odds. But with Hale's help, maybe even his testimony, the odds would swing in Darryl's favor. It could work for Hale, too, if Dana was right that he wouldn't mind if Moncrief, and then Ashton, disappeared plumb off the face of the earth. Whether he would help me or not, I knew now he at least wouldn't try to stop me.

I made an appointment with Hale at eleven o'clock the next day and caught an elevator to the penthouse a few minutes early. I marched into his office with my meager proofs and paranoid suspicions well organized. I was surprised to look out his wall of windows and see that what had started out as crisp and clear fall day had turned into a torrential hailstorm.

"*Billy,*" said Hale, swiveling toward me, "what happened to your head? Never mind. Good news. I spoke with Vic James in New York this morning. They want you to come out next week—their nickel—and go through a few *pro forma* interviews, then travel to Southhampton for a small gathering to meet the heavy lifters in the firm. They're very excited about you joining the firm."

I tried to return his enthusiasm. He couldn't have been more proud if he'd been my own father. To get me a tentative offer without even meeting the partners meant that Hale had put himself on the line for me. Again. "That's great, Hale, really. But—"

"They've even lined up an apartment for you with a view of the Hudson. They are willing to pay the first six months' rent as a part of your relocation expenses."

"You must either have put a gun to James's head or you've got photos of him running around naked in a herd of sheep. But listen, Hale—"

"Anyway, I'm glad you came in, Billy. I know it's only eleven, but let's go over to Aqua, have a little bubbly to celebrate, then an early lunch."

"In this weather?" The sound of hail clattering against the windows was unnerving.

"I'll have my car pick us up," he said hitting an intercom button.

"Jesus, Hale, slow down a minute." But he was handing me an expensive looking cigar. The only thing I hate more than the smell of a cigar is the taste of one, but I took the damn thing, bit off the end, and leaned forward as Hale reached in a drawer and held out a lighter for me.

A sterling silver lighter with a diamond pavé base and two emeralds, one on top and one embedded in the activating lever.

32

I leaned forward, staring dumbly into the flame that danced on the wick held steadily in front of me. That sterling silver lighter might as well have been the pearl handle of a gun.

"Billy, you're white as a sheet. Are you all right?"

It wasn't a gun, of course, and there was no explosion except the one in my head.

I mumbled an apology—something about having had a touch of the flu.

"In that case, a cigar is the last thing you need, Billy. Save it for later. Get some rest. We can celebrate and talk about your case tomorrow."

"It can wait," I said, and the next thing I knew I was in the hallway outside Hale's office, the scorched tip of the unlit cigar clutched in my hand and a painful hole smoldering in my heart.

Nobody bugged me for the next couple of hours, which was good. Gave me a chance to pull myself together, try to figure out what to do. At 2:15 P.M., Mimi D'Angelo called to say everything was cool. She had got in and out of Sheila's apartment with no problem, then anonymously alerted SFPD homicide to vacuum the place again and gave her homicide cop-buddy a heads-up at SFPD. She asked me what she should do with the key to Sheila's place.

"Hold on to it for now," I told her. "Also put another sample of Moncrief's hair in an envelope with a memo setting down everything you've done. Make a duplicate envelope for the new trial lawyer I retain to try the case for Darryl; then seal both and lock them up somewhere."

"New trial lawyer? What kinda experienced mouth you expect's gonna volunteer to substitute inna wingy bowl a bullshit stew like you been brewing up here?"

I was getting so I could understand Mimi, which scared me a little. "Someone as wingy as we are," I said. "I was hoping you might have some ideas."

She was quiet so long I thought she'd hung up.

"Mimi? You there?"

"Simmer down! I'm thinkin! Okay, try Douglas Beckwith. He's good, and he's got guts."

"We can assure him complete deniability."

"Somethin which, by the by, we ain't got any of."

"I know it."

"I gotta ask my mama sometime how I got to be such a kook magnet. Anythin else?"

"Keep after Barney's car," I said, and added that I needed credit reports with assets status on Moncrief, Ashton, and Hale Lassiter, going back ten years.

"I'm on it," she said. "Meantime, don't squat with your spurs on, cowboy, okay?"

She clicked off, leaving me alone with my thoughts, which had lately become sorry company.

Hale. Mr. Straight. Deborah Hinton's mysterious lover and probable killer. Jesus. Had I been I wrong in assuming that Deborah's mysterious boyfriend was also her killer? Possibly. Was even asking myself the question a lame effort at rationalizing away Hale's guilt? Probably. Had I just set up an innocent man for the murder of Sheila Anderson? Definitely.

I told Barbara I had to run an errand and left the building. I needed to clear my head, get some air, maybe conclude some new way to swing Darryl's jury to a defense verdict. But all I concluded was that time was running out and I'd have to stick with my frame-up of Moncrief. I'd hire a lawyer, then show him how to demonstrate to the jury how easy DNA could be planted, using Moncrief as his laboratory rat. It was dirty, but Darryl's lawyer would quickly admit the truth as soon as Moncrief left the stand and the jury had learned its lesson about the vulnerability of DNA evidence. Better to let an arrogant asshole like Moncrief take a twenty-minute hit to his vanity and reputation than to let Darryl permanently rot in Soledad.

The demonstration could be explosive, but it wouldn't be the first time reasonable doubt grew out of pure theatrical confusion. Ask Johnnie Cochran. But I wondered if Dad would have approved, and felt the heat of his condemnation blossoming in my face.

At 4:00 P.M., the phone rang again. Hale's voice, sounding friendly, even content, like a cat purring with a canary in his mouth.

"I've just spoken to Victor James, Billy. He wants to confirm dates with you for those interviews in New York." The man was in a hurry to get me out of town. "As I said, it's a mere formality, but necessary.

It would be best if you made arrangements to leave as soon as possible."

With the benefit of my new knowledge, Hale's last few words came across as a warning, maybe even a threat. Had he figured out what I'd figured out? If so, maybe I should get out of town before I got a visit from the swarthy guy I'd chased at the fire scene. Or from Jaxon with an *x*. I would laugh at the irony of contrasts if I wasn't so anxious: a lawyer, former criminal, being pursued by both cops *and* robbers.

I was going to need every nickel to admit Ma into the detox clinic and to pay Darryl's lawyer's retainer and expenses, so I was relieved to learn the firm would take care of my flight to New York and that for a few extra bucks of my own, I could get a layover in Oklahoma. I called home from my apartment.

"How's it going, brat?"

"About the same. Some days I'm the windshield; usually, I'm the bug. I'd be better if I heard you were soon to be gracing us with your estimable presence."

"Coming soon to your neighborhood. Just made my airline reservations. How's the Momster?"

"Have you lost your watch? It's six-fifteen p.m. out here."

"Okay, so she's drunk."

"Totally shit-faced, but ensconced in the relative safety of her bed, where I doubt she can hurt herself."

"Good. Well, not good, but at least we can talk. Call Bridgedale Serenity in Oklahoma City. It's one of the best detox clinics in the country. Get them going on the paperwork. I've got the money for the first three months, and by the time that's up I'll have another job to keep it going."

"Another job?"

"I'm getting downsized out of S & S, but it's all right. I may take another job in New York."

"Oh."

Ever since we were little kids I've been able to tell what Lisa was thinking. And what she was thinking was, What about me?

"Yeah," I said, "Maybe New York instead of San Francisco. But like I said, once we get Ma set, you're coming with me."

"What about that girl you were hot for, Dana somebody?"

"Her travel plans are . . . up in the air presently."

"She caught you messing around, huh?"

"What makes you think that?"

She chuckled. "You're a guy. The good Lord gave guys a brain and a penis, but only enough blood to run one of them at a time."

"Funny. Are you coming to stay with me or not?"

"To New York?"

"Wherever I end up."

I swear I could hear her smiling, but all she said was, "We'll talk about it."

Early the next morning, I scheduled a night meeting in Oklahoma City with an ex-FBI forensic expert in Okie City named Mark Lowenthal at Material Analysis, Inc., one of the top independent labs in the region, according to Mace. After studying the exhibits, I had sent Lowenthal some original documents for ink analysis to confirm that the forged signature that had convicted Dad had been written with a fountain pen. Joe Strobe never used a fountain pen in his life, always a cheap ballpoint. Lowenthal said he'd have no problem telling which was used, maybe even be able to ID the brand of pen and ink, despite the nearly fourteen years that had passed.

Next, I called Dana and asked her to meet me for dinner. She said she'd never be able to get a sitter at this late date but I told her it was important. She agreed to try, and twenty minutes later told me it was on. It was the first date with Dana I wasn't looking forward to.

Then I called Douglas Beckwith, who sounded expensive, but agreed to take Darryl's case, subject to reviewing the file and meeting with him. Now I'd have to pay someone to hit Darryl with a zookeeper's tranquillizer dart; calm the savage beast long enough to pass muster with Beckwith.

Housekeeping matters completed, I went to work cleaning up a probate matter for Wilcox, another thrill-packed hour researching the impact of a poorly drawn testamentary trust on an heir with too much money to begin with. At least it kept my mind off Hale for a while.

It was almost 6:30 when I left the Western Bank Building and headed down Montgomery Street across Market toward Hawthorne Place, where Dana said she would meet me at seven. It wasn't raining, and I figured the walk would clear my head, maybe clarify what I should tell her and what I shouldn't.

But the walk didn't clarify anything, and the instant she made the180-degree turn from the front entrance of the restaurant into the small private alcove I had reserved, I knew I would have to tell her everything. She looked gorgeous, her dark hair parted in the middle, her large, jade-green eyes—maybe set a tad too far apart if you were desperate to find a flaw—glowing with surprise as she realized we were all alone in a cozy niche in San Francisco's busiest restaurant.

"How did you arrange *this,* Mr. Fix-It?"

"My dazzling personality and half a year's salary."

The waiter appeared with my Wild Turkey on the rocks and I persuaded her to join me. She ordered a cosmopolitan.

"So what are we celebrating?"

"We're mourning," I said, "not celebrating." I reached across the
table and took her hand, told her I loved her and asked her to hear me
out completely before she said anything. She agreed, but her smile had
faded.

"There are some things I've known and haven't told you, and some
things I've recently learned myself. I think it's time to tell you all of it."

She nodded apprehensively.

"First, I figured several days ago how Deborah Hinton's real killer
framed Darryl. I've been sure the killer was Jason Moncrief, but was
stumped on Darryl's DNA. Then I learned that Coco Lewis over at
the TechnoCenter Building routinely gave Darryl free haircuts in exchange for him showing up early most nights and cleaning up her
place for free. I figured out that Moncrief had picked up a few strands
of Darryl's hair off the floor or his apron as soon as Darryl was out
the door, then planted them on Deborah's body. It was simple, but
brilliant.

"So when I saw how it was done to Darryl, I decided to turn the tables on Moncrief and see where it took me. I figured he'd be called as
a witness in Darryl's retrial like he was the first time, and we'd pin
Sheila's murder on him right there on the stand in front of the jury. If
nothing else, he'd know that *we* knew how he did it and maybe he'd
panic and somehow incriminate himself, or at least take the Fifth. Even
if he didn't, it would be a graphic demonstration how Darryl might
have been framed, so—"

"Hold your horses, cowboy," said Dana, who had been looking
skyward as if praying for restraint. "In the first place, your ambitious
stunt would never work, for which, incidentally, you should be grateful, because you would probably be disbarred if you had succeeded. In
the second place, you don't have solid proof that Moncrief killed *anybody*, and certainly not Deborah Hinton, who is the relevant victim
here, *not* Sheila Anderson. In the third place, Jason is much too cool
to panic over a gambit like that, and in the fourth place, you'd never
find a reputable lawyer who would even try it."

"Thanks for hearing me out completely before going to the fifth
place."

"Sorry, but—"

"I've already got a 'reputable lawyer' I'm sure you've heard of—
Doug Beckwith—subject to his meeting with Darryl."

"I know him," murmured Dana. "He pushes the ethical envelope,
but never breaks it."

"That's why I got him. He's damn good, too. Best record in the city."

"Nobody's good enough to pull this off, even if the judge gave him leeway to do it, which he won't."

"You agreed to hear me out, dammit," I said.

"I'll try, but—"

"So I hired an investigator with SFPD contacts and had her plant some of Moncrief's hair in Sheila's room—"

"Billy!"

"She then called a friend at SFPD who nudged the cops into a final search of the premises. They found the hair, but of course don't know whose it is. Yet."

Dana was frowning in obvious disapproval. "How, may I ask, did your investigator get into a cordoned-off crime scene?"

"I told you about finding her body; well, I kept Sheila Anderson's key that day by mistake."

"Okay, so the police have Jason's hair but don't know it."

"Right. Then I had my private investigator mark and seal several strands of Moncrief's hair taken from the apron Moncrief wore at Coco's. She sent it anonymously to the inspector in charge of the case—a guy named Terrell Jaxon—along with a note saying she had reason to suspect the hair came from the head of Sheila's killer. Jaxon had it sent to the FBI crime lab and guess what?"

Dana's eyes were blazing—whether in astonishment or anger I wasn't sure. "It will be a perfect DNA match," she said, her voice a stunned, subdued monotone, "with the hair they'd found at the murder scene." She started to say something else, but the waiter appeared with her cosmo and saved me. She leaned back, eyes closed, her pulse visibly beating in her throat, while the waiter took forever setting her drink down, tidying up the table.

"Why?" she said the minute he was gone. I could tell she wasn't going to hear me out, and felt my shoulder muscles tightening. "Why are you doing this, Billy? The DA might not even call Jason as a witness."

"He was on the DA's witness list last time and presumably will be again. Remember? Moncrief makes the DA's case on motive—that Deborah Hinton was a victim of her own co-conspirator. Darryl was cast as an assassin hired by the co-conspirator."

Dana nodded. She remembered.

"So on cross-examination of Moncrief, Beckwith shows that he killed Sheila, then brings out his profits on the earlier scam. Then Beckwith puts me on and we use the prosecution's own insider trading scam to tie the murders of Sheila and Barney Klinehart to the one Darryl was accused of but couldn't have committed because he was in prison! Reasonable doubt all over the place."

Dana took the first sip of her cosmo, and it was a big one. I picked up my Wild Turkey rocks and joined her.

"Why are you telling me this, Billy?"

I took another sip of my drink, a bigger one.

"Because everything I've done was a waste of time and everything I've told you is wrong. Just as I got Moncrief perfectly positioned for the perfect frame-up, I learned he was not Deborah's murderer."

"Of course he wasn't," Dana said, "but what kind of Damascus Road experience brought *you* to this belated conversion?"

I ignored her irony, but couldn't ignore what my next words were about to do to her. And to us. I flashed to a Sunday morning in Enid— Dad was home—a bird hit our window in front. It was a wren, Dad told me. I was only eight or so, but to this day, the moment has the clarity of oxygen: holding the tiny thing in my hand, probing its fragile softness with my thumb, it's vulnerability, feeling the runaway heartbeat and, in my awkward, indifferent youth, an awareness of the ease with which I could crush it, end its life.

"It was Hale, Dana. Hale killed Deborah."

How do I describe the expression on Dana's suddenly bloodless face. Anger? Confusion? Disdain? All of the above? I didn't get a good look, because the remains of her drink splashed into my face, blinding me. By the time I was able to open my eyes, and wipe my face with a napkin, she was on her feet, coat and purse in hand, brushing past me. I reached out and grabbed her by the arm.

"Not this time, Dana. You said you'd hear me out, and dammit, you will."

She looked down at me with an expression of raw fury I didn't think she had in her. She pulled herself out of my grasp, her full lips drawn in a hard line. "I've heard enough out of you," she said, "to last me a long time."

"You agreed to hear it all."

She stared at me for another beat or two, and I said, "You've got nothing to lose but another five minutes. Then do whatever you want with what I've told you. But try to remember how much Hale means to me, too, okay?"

She jammed her hands deep into her blazer pockets and stared out through the window into the street, where a skateboarder wove her way through stopped traffic. Restaurant smells and bar sounds drifted in, ice clinking, the drone of a mixer, laughter. After a half-minute, her shoulders heaved as she took in a deep breath and exhaled, then she slowly turned and sat back down. She stared at me across a table ten miles wide, arms folded, jaw set. I would have to do this just right.

"It's like this, Dana. Hale, for all his success, is not a rich man. Sure he lives well, but I had my investigator check out his assets yesterday, and it turns out he lost most of his money in 1996 in some goofy hotel computer venture."

Dana flashed me a bitter smile. "Not a rich man? It may interest you to know, Detective Clouseau, that Hale and Ashton each came up with five million dollars to bail the firm out of trouble *just a year ago*. I call that rich."

"That's exactly my point. Where did that money come from all of a sudden? Hale's entire estate a month before that loan was valued at less than a million dollars. Not that I couldn't live on that right comfortable, but it's a far piece from five million. The time period we're talking about here is right after Sheila Anderson made her killing short-selling Synoptics stock."

Dana gave her head a quick, impatient shake. "What's that got to do with Deborah's death? Plus, you're forgetting that Hale didn't even *know* Deborah!"

"How do you know that?"

"Because I asked him if he wanted to go to her funeral with me, and he said he had only run into her once at some seminar."

"Then you have to ask yourself why he lied to you. He was Deborah's lover."

"Oh, God, Billy," Dana said, and slammed her clenched fists on the table, drawing a glance from our waiter. I turned him away with a hard glance. "Where in the world do you get these crazy notions?"

I quickly laid out the whole story about my trip to Modesto, where the Breckenridges were hiding, the drawing of the unique, custom-made lighter Deborah had given her secret boyfriend, everything.

"I saw that identical lighter in his office yesterday," I said.

It didn't surprise me that Dana came up with all the bullshit responses you'd expect from a good trial lawyer defending a good friend. It could have been a bad drawing, it could have been a similar but not identical lighter, it could even have been something she had designed for Jason or somebody else who didn't want it around after her death and who passed it on to Hale, and so on.

I straightened my shoulders, because this time it was Dana tromping on thin ice. I took the drawing out of my pocket.

"The lighter I saw, eight inches in front of my face, was custom-made and identical to this picture right down to the diamond pavé base and emeralds embedded in the top *and* on the igniter lever. Deborah told her parents it was custom-designed, one of a kind."

I handed her the drawing. "It's a copy. Take it; then go see it for yourself. Prove me wrong, Dana—I'd like nothing better."

She was silent. I held my breath.

More silence. She stared out the window at the sidewalk where a beggar had approached a young couple.

"Do you want to hear the rest of it?"

"Does it matter?"

"It does to me. It's not only Hale who was short on money. My investigator found that Rex Ashton's wealth was tied up in real estate. He didn't have anything like five million dollars in liquid funds before the bailout loan, either. After making the loan, he still had all his real estate. So where did he get *his* one-half share of the total ten-million-dollar bailout loan to the firm? Do you want to guess the total amount of Sheila's profits from her transactions?"

"You wouldn't be telling me this if it were not damn close to ten million dollars."

"Ten-point-three million. They probably gave Anderson the three hundred thousand. It's possible both Hale *and* Ashton were in on the scam *and* the murders. It's common knowledge that the Young Turks—a dozen junior partners—were on the warpath and looking for scalp not long before I showed up. Good lawyers were leaving the firm and taking key clients. You also know about the loss of the International Outback case, and with it, the firm's outlay of seven-point-five million in time and cash advances.

"I've heard from several sources, and you can confirm it, Dana, that this loss was the last straw for Stanton and Snow's bank, and they called the firm's line of credit. A revolt was imminent, and the only way that Hale and Ashton could salvage their positions and maybe the firm itself was by a tremendous infusion of cash. I'll put my money on Ashton as the guy who conceived the bailout idea and then took charge after Deborah's death."

"Then why are you trying to hang Deborah's death on Hale?"

"Because it was his libido that was threatening to unravel their perfect scam. Picture it, Dana: Hale and Deborah were lovers. She turns up pregnant and starts making waves. They're halfway into the insider caper, and it's coming apart. One thing stands in their way of saving their careers, their firm, their future financial security, even their freedom. *One person.*"

"If you're so sure of all this," Dana asked, "why haven't you taken it to the police."

I twirled my empty glass in my fingers, thinking this would be a good time for the waiter to appear.

"That's something else I haven't got around to burdening you with."

She was already shaking her head, but having swallowed the whale, I knew I couldn't choke on the tail. It hurt to see how pale she was, but I had to keep going.

"I may soon be a suspect myself," I said.

"Why? Because you found Sheila's body?"

"I'm an ex-con, Dana," I said, "plus someone saw me leave in my car."

"My friend, the desperado," she said, "Billy the Kid."

My heart quickened with hope. "Besides, even if I went to the cops, they'd think I was crazy—like you did."

"Like I do, Billy. Like I always have."

"Okay, but what's making me crazy now is that even if I could get the cops to start a new investigation, honored citizen Lassiter would simply come up with something like, 'I had helped her with a personal legal matter, and she sent me the gift in gratitude.' Of course, Hale would know that you and I would realize he's lying, but what good would that do Darryl?"

Dana put her hands, palms down, on the table surrounding her empty glass. "Billy, I need to know what you intend to do."

"I'm not sure. I've got to get to Oklahoma soon. My mother's real sick and I'm going to have to put her into a clinic. I'm way overdue closing up a half-dozen projects at S & S. Darryl's expedited trial date is on December the twenty-ninth, about two weeks away. I have everything in place to pin Sheila's murder on a jerk who's probably guilty of every imaginable crime against nature except for the one I've framed him for. Did I mention I'm also expected in New York next week?"

Dana rested her forehead on her hand in mock exhaustion. "That's all?"

"The firm is so short-handed I've been told to stay on until I finish all my projects."

"I could help you with some of them," Dana said.

I tentatively touched her hand. "I'm hoping you'll help me prove a case against Hale and Ashton."

A shadow of despair crossed Dana's eyes as she looked up at me, and I knew it was hopeless before she said a word.

"You can't even think about hurting Hale, Billy. You were wrong about suspecting Moncrief to be the murderer, and now you're wrong about Hale. You simply can't destroy a man's career on the basis of a cigarette lighter. Have you asked him about any of this?"

I shook my head. "That wouldn't be smart," I said. "I think Hale is trying to save me from Ashton by shipping me off to New York. If I challenge Hale now, he'd have to turn the dogs loose."

"The only thing loose, Billy, is your logic." The color was back in her face, and her perfect teeth were clenched. "You've *got* to give him a chance to answer your suspicions before you embarrass him and yourself with a misfired gambit like the one you were going to pull on Moncrief."

I felt heat behind my eyes, spreading out to my cheeks and ears. I was about to respond when the waiter came back to take our dinner orders.

"The drink," Dana told him, rising, "fully satisfied me."

I left some bills on the table and followed her out the door, plenty angry myself now. "Is this the way you always resolve arguments? Toss a drink, defend a killer, then walk out the door?"

We were standing outside in a wet and heavy fog. Her eyes were wet, too—tears of anger, disappointment, and despair. She said something about being sorry and needing some space, and we went our separate ways, me headed on foot to my apartment, she waiting for the valet to fetch her car. I was already across Mission Street, wishing I'd worn my topcoat, when I heard a car pull up behind me.

"Get in," she said, and I did.

We rode in silence, not a word, not even the radio. I didn't ask her where we were going. She drove out across Market Street and hung a left up Sutter, past Union Square, pushing her Accord to make the timed lights all the way to Van Ness. She turned left at Tommy's Joynt and headed west out Geary through Japan Town, then cut over to Fell and into the Haight-Ashbury. I was beginning to wonder if she remembered I was in the car.

As we drove through Golden Gate Park, we hit fog so thick you could barely see the old windmill as we turned north onto Ocean Beach. We drove along the Pacific Ocean, passed the Cliff House and Seal Rock, then headed up into Lincoln Park toward Lands End. She finally stopped the car at the Palace of the Legion of Honor.

She parked and turned off the lights, and we sat there, silently staring ahead through the ghostly moonlight toward the slate-gray Pacific Ocean. Then she was talking, but in so low a voice it might have come from another car.

"This is hard for me, Billy, so please don't interrupt. It's your turn to keep quiet. So not a word, okay? Don't even look at me."

I nodded, and she continued speaking in a quaking voice that sounded more like a hurt or frightened child than the strong woman I knew and loved. I strained to hear her.

"When Hale saw what lengths Rex was going to in order to wear you down, he asked me to get to know you, help him watch your back."

I turned my head away, and the passenger side window fogged with anxiety and betrayed hope. "To pretend to like me?" I murmured.

She exhaled impatiently. "I pretended for no more than an hour into our first 'date.' All my feelings about you, both good and bad, have been real since then."

I let it go, but I had an inkling what was coming, and it wasn't good. I said, "You overheard Barney's message, didn't you." It was not a question.

She put the back of her hand to her lips, then let her head fall against the driver's-side window.

"And you told Hale everything Barney said."

She turned toward me, grasping the steering wheel as if we were careening out of control down a mountain road, which is pretty much what was happening. Her face in the fog-filtered moonlight was deathly pale, disembodied, and I could see tracks of tears on her cheeks.

She nodded her head, then looked back out across the Pacific Ocean, glowing fluorescent in the hazy moonlight. "I was worried about you, Billy. It sounded as if you were in some kind of trouble. Getting in over your head. I thought perhaps Hale could—"

"Help me? Is *that* what you thought? Christ Almighty, Dana, we—you with your blind loyalty to Hale, and me, with my gross negligence—*we* killed Barney Klinehart as surely as Hale did."

"Or somebody Hale told, or somebody completely unrelated to what I told Hale, a burglar, a nut, a random killing! It doesn't have to be Hale! I had to tell you this, Billy, but it doesn't mean I think Hale is involved."

I opened the car door.

"There's more," she said so softly I didn't hear her at first. There was a warning intensity in her voice that told me that if there was *more*, I'd best hear it. Know the odds, I thought, and closed the door. Her skin now looked even more unhealthy under the glow in the overhead streetlight. The stress was making her physically ill, and I found myself torn between sympathy and anger.

"This may or may not explain my 'blind loyalty,' Billy, but you've got a right to know the rest. When I'm finished, I'll take you home, and it will be up to you to decide if you ever want to see me again."

"I'm listening. Get on with it."

She nodded, put her lips in a straight line. Her expression was like a bronco rider fixing to enter the arena. "Hale Lassiter . . ."

"Go *on*."

"Hale is . . . Sarah's father."

It took a second or two for her words to break through my resistance, but then something that felt like a bazooka shell exploded in my stomach, and I had to squeeze my eyes shut from the pain. There was a rush of bile into my mouth, and I felt like I was going to throw up. Dana couldn't meet my eyes.

"You know most of it already," she continued, though I could barely hear her for the noise in my brain. "How Hale and Laura took an interest in me, helped me, took trailer-trash Dana Mathews off the street, put shoes on her feet, gave her a new life. I'd never had a real father, and Hale had become my guardian angel. The night I passed the bar exam, the three of us went out to dinner and celebrated. We came back to the Lassiters' house and had some more drinks. Everybody drank too much, and Hale had to take Laura to bed. Then, he and I had another drink or two and—"

"He took *you* to bed."

"For the first, last, and only time. We couldn't believe the bad luck, but there it was. Hale knew I was a Catholic, and finally accepted that I was going to keep the baby. He agreed to get me into the firm and help out with expenses."

I've never come close to hitting a woman, but my fury was hard to control. I knew that it was Hale I wanted to hit. "So that's why you're in such a pucker whenever you have to bring Sarah to work."

"If that means I'm anxious, yes. Hale asked me to keep Sarah away from the office."

"He took advantage of you, Dana, and now you're both an embarrassment to him. How does it feel to be swept under one of Stanton and Snow's fine Persian rugs?"

"Wasn't I taking advantage of him, too? He was making it possible for me to get through school and to have the money to make Sarah a good home."

"There's a word," I said bitterly, "for that kind of arrangement."

She looked like she was about to say something, but I threw the car door open again, felt the blast of night air as it penetrated my damp shirt.

"Please, Billy . . ."

I had both feet on the ground, but felt no more grounded than the leaves blowing across the pavement around my knees. I slammed the door shut, saw my breath fogging the air, felt my heart jackrabbiting in my chest as I ran off into the fog.

Dana knew better than to follow me this time.

I slept in the next morning. After leaving Dana, I had got myself good and lost in the Presidio and wandered for three hours in a heavy drizzle until I saw the lights of Lombard. It was after midnight and I had worked my way nearly up to Van Ness—my progress slowed by a stop for a pair of Wild Turkeys on the rocks—when a cab finally stopped for me. I had briefly considered getting seriously drunk—a genetic response to stress—but the stakes were now too high to indulge myself in a binge of self-pity. So I went to bed and stared at the cracks in my ceiling for hours, spotting a water stain in the shape of a human skull I'd never noticed. Sleep turned out to be harder to find that night than a cab had been.

I got up around eight, showered and shaved, and made myself some coffee to go along with milk that was only three days over the limit printed at the top of the carton. I dressed and headed for the Hall of Justice.

Darryl flashed me a wry grin as he was shown into the tiny visitor's room on the sixth floor. "Well, damned if it ain't my mouthpiece, looking and smelling only slightly worse than the other deadbeats I've been with this morning."

"You prefer the guests at Soledad?"

"My roommate here thinks Taco Bell is a Mexican phone company." He took a close look at me. "You just break out of intensive care? You look like you'd have to improve to die."

"I was celebrating," I said, then brought him up to date, skipping my problems with Dana. "I've retained Douglas Beckwith to substitute in for me, subject to his meeting you. Top-flight lawyer. He'll be up here later this morning. I'm here to tell you to be nice."

"Sweetness and light."

I looked around at the scratched-up walls. "You okay in here?"

"Sure, though I still miss the sunlight. Did you know that as far back as 1609 a guy named Kepler figured out the way planets revolve around the sun?"

"So they let you bring your encyclopedia, and you're up to the *K*s?"

"Nearly finished with 'em. How's things with your girlfriend?"

"Fine," I lied, and got down to business. I told him what I'd found out about Hale, the cigarette lighter, and what Mimi D'Angelo and I had done to set up Moncrief. "I'm considering going ahead with the Moncrief stunt anyway, but just as a demonstration of how your DNA could have been planted."

"Even though Mr. Lassiter did the deed? Sounds like somethin Perry Mason's evil twin would do."

"Thanks, Darryl. Like I don't feel bad enough about it already."

"Sorry, kid, but I reckon you'll get over it. Your daddy didn't win all those cases by worryin about hurtin people's feelings, or their reputations neither."

"It's true that Dad fought the government tooth and nail, though he never would've done anything this unethical."

"Moncrief'll get over it. So what else you got?"

"What do you mean, what else?"

"I mean where's the beef? The tooth-and-nail part. Our defense. Far's I can see, you got the scam rigged on the wrong man—Moncrief—and nothing but a cigarette lighter on the right man, Hale Lassiter. Is that your case?"

I shrugged. "I'm still working on some angles, and I've got an investigator tracking down documents that could help."

Darryl looked disappointed, but let it go. "Well, you best watch your ass. This Lassiter fella could be dangerous, now that he knows you know he killed the Hinton girl."

"He doesn't know I know."

"Hell he doesn't. He shows you the lighter the victim gives him and all of a sudden it turns up missing? He knows it's you what took it."

I felt a rush of heat up my spine and a dampness spreading across my back. Darryl assumed I'd been smart enough to have corralled the damn lighter, which, of course, I hadn't.

"Don't worry about me," I said, "I'm getting out of town for a few days."

"Good, you look a damn mess. Taking the girl? Dana?"

"Truth be told, Darryl, things aren't going so good in that department."

"Caught you messin around?"

"Jesus, what's with you people?"

"What people? Only me here far as I can see."

"Never mind. My sister said the same thing. Anyways, I'm going to New York."

"Good," he said. "You're lookin a little overwrought, and your breath smells like a Mexican spittoon. Get some rest, and while you're there, do me a big favor?"

"Sure, Darryl. What?"

"*Stay* there."

"You'd die of a broken heart."

"Sure, just like your other pet did."

"Seriously, I've got to be a witness at your trial, but I do plan on making myself scarce until I go on the stand. Maybe spend Christmas with my family. While I'm gone, you charm Beckwith into thinking you're normal, and I guarantee you've seen the last of me as a lawyer."

"Maybe there is a God after all," he said.

I stood, palms damp, heart pounding, at the parking garage, second-level entry to the Western Bank Building. I had decided to wait until midnight before beginning my assault on the offices of Stanton and Snow. I reached down to make sure my Walgreens rubber gloves were still in my pocket.

Unlike the TechnoCenter where Deborah was killed, the Western Bank Building's security system was a joke. The computerized entry log was on the main floor, but it could be bypassed by simply entering on the second parking level entrance. The door there was locked at night after seven, but we all had keys. I'd be in and out with no record of my ever being in. I'd just have to avoid being seen by the usual late-night people: the "grinders"— drudges hanging by a thread—and the "minders"—associates with no life but S & S, who competently performed the work brought in by the "finders"— partners whose finely honed skills embraced low-handicap golf and the fine art of schmoozing at the Bohemian and Pacific Union Clubs.

I lucked into an empty elevator that swept me all the way to the penthouse—no stops, no people, no sweat. I stepped out into the subdued lighting of the lobby and glided soundlessly to Hale's corner office, a foot-long crowbar tucked up my left sleeve. If the drawers were locked, they'd have to be popped open. Billy Fix-It, second-story man.

There's Hale's door, no light spilling out beneath. Good. Slip on the rubber gloves. Turn the knob, ease it open, don't hesitate, walk right through. Close the door, best leave the lights turned off, plenty of light bleeding in from the full moon. Walk straight to his desk. That's it. In and out in twenty seconds max unless the drawers are locked, then one minute max. Whoa, never heard that clock before, sounds like Big Ben.

Try the top center drawer where Hale took the lighter from, flip the penlight on. Notes on three-by-five cards, a bottle of aspirin, some antiacids, pair of scissors, a manicure kit, pencils, ballpoints, a ruler, spare mini-tapes, paper clips, a stapler. Shit, no lighter.

Okay, open the smaller drawers on either side, maybe it came out of one of them. All drawers unlocked, won't need the bar. Good. Easy does it. Shit, nothing on the left but yellow legal pads, smaller note pads, Post-its, more pencils, and a quartz clock with FROM YOUR PART-NERS—1988. *This ain't working.*

Slide open the smaller drawers on the other side. Oh, man, nothing but a large appointment book, a dictionary, and a thesaurus.

What's that? Footsteps? Oh, Christ, coming this way. No time to move away from the desk, best duck under it. The door's opening! A cone of light sweeping the room, halting for a second on the desk and Hale's empty chair. Can he see me? The beam now covering the conference area. He's in the room! Coming closer. Ten feet, five, my hand closing around the crowbar. No, don't even think about doing that.

He's turning, and as quickly as it came on, the light snaps off. The door closing. It must have been Emil, the night security guy making his rounds, going through the motions, footsteps going the other way.

Take a deep breath, take another one, wipe the forehead. Finish and clear out of here. It's got to be in one of the bigger drawers at the bottom of each side, but the first one is full of nothing but files. My heart still whacking against my rib cage. Only one more shot, the one on the right. Has to be it . . .

Pull it open, shoot the light into it.

Empty.

Looking back, I knew I was beat right then and there, but what the hell, since I was inside, I went into the conference area, opening drawers under the bar and the medicine cabinets in Hale's private bathroom, scanning all surfaces in both rooms. Nothing. I returned to the desk and frantically rummaged through the top drawer again, taking out some of the larger items like the stapler and note cards, thinking it *had* to be in there somewheres.

But there was no lighter, which meant two things. First, that my proof against Hale had gone from frail down to squat. Second, that Hale had seen through my "flu attack." Had he also known I had tracked down the Breckenridges? Had he located them, too? Talked to them about the lighter? If so, he'd know I'd have to come for it.

I closed the drawers and moved back to the door, which I opened cautiously. No one in sight. Good. I ripped off my gloves, stuck them back in my pocket, started toward the elevator. Oh, Christ, my crowbar! I raced back, retrieved it off the floor, stuck it back up my sleeve, then moved quickly down the hall again and into the elevator, jamming my fingers into buttons that read 2 and CLOSE DOOR. I tried to control my breathing and prayed nobody would get on the elevator. The doors finally closed, but opened again at the twenty-third floor, and my heart pumped out a last spurt of adrenaline as I waited, but it was a night secretary I had never used and who probably wouldn't recognize me.

"Getting late out," I said, then coughed so I could cover my face.

"You got that right," she said, and exited at nineteen. I made it down to the second floor and moved swiftly into my car, taking little consolation from the fact that I hadn't been caught in the act of accomplishing absolutely nothing. Worse, a new germ of distrust was gnawing into my gut. Had Dana warned Hale that I might be coming for the evidence that could hang him?

33

I had to know, so I drove straight to Dana's apartment, pushed the buzzer, and soon heard her sleepy voice.

"Who is it?"

"It's me."

"Billy? It's nearly one in the morning."

Her tone was as cold as the outside air temperature. "Dana, it's a little awkward standing out here talking to a speaker. Buzz me in, for God's sake."

The door buzzed, and I walked through it, then up to Dana's third-floor condo. The door was already ajar, and she opened it as I approached.

"Taking another one of your midnight walks?"

I didn't smile. "Did you tell him?"

"Hale? About your suspicions? No, why would you say that?"

The innocence in her face derailed me, as usual.

"I went to get the lighter tonight. To his office. It's gone. I thought you might have said something—"

She gave me a motherly smile and took my icy hands in hers. "Shh," she whispered. "You'll wake Sarah."

"Just give me an answer," I whispered, "so's I'll know once and for all where I stand with you."

"You stand very tall, Billy Strobe, despite being . . . misguided at times. But you must understand that I would never do anything to put either Hale *or* you at risk. I swear to you I haven't said a word to him. Now come into the kitchen and let me fix you some hot tea."

I followed her into a small kitchen, less anxious, though not convinced, and still upset at the things she had told me the night before.

Her kitchen was like a hospital, as orderly as her office, not a thing out of place. She removed two spotless, clear-glass coffee cups from a cupboard and began boiling water. Didn't she have a microwave? How did she survive? She put two pieces of bread in the toaster.

"I think you missed a crumb there," I said, my paranoia beginning to yield to her warmth.

She smiled and shook her head. "Comes from growing up in a shoe box. Let things get ahead of you in a small space and—"

"Your house starts to look as messy as my office."

"Frightening."

She had me smiling, even relaxing a little. But my interrogation was delayed, not forgotten.

"You say anything to anybody else? About the lighter?"

Dana looked me square in the eye. "Not a peep. Sit there at the counter, and quit shaking. Herbal or regular?"

"Hot."

"I'll give you comfrey. You look like you could use some sleep."

My suspicion was in retreat, leaving nothing but a desperate hope that she might take me to bed. The woman owned me.

"I reckon this thing's wearing me into a state of paranoia. Without that lighter, I have no case against Hale."

"I know. Can we spend Christmas together? Sarah would like that."

"Hale must have caught on," I said, not to be distracted. "I took his office apart. It's gone."

"It's gone," she said, softly, soothingly, "because I took it."

The words took a second to register. "*You?* You took it?"

The teapot whistle answered me.

"I've put it where it's absolutely safe."

I felt dizzy as I took the cup from her. This roller-coaster ride with Dana was flat-out wearing me down. "I can only assume you got it for me as a Christmas present," I said. "The problem is I need it right now."

"Call me the Grinch, but the lighter is out of play."

"Don't mess with me on this, Dana."

"I know I've disappointed you, Billy, but you'll thank me someday. That lighter has too much potential for mischief; it's something that could cause irreparable harm if you did something foolish with it—to *both* you and Hale."

I sat staring at her as she calmly busied herself taking out butter to put on some toast that was popping up.

"Lemon?" she added.

"*Jesus,* Dana, you are the queen of rationalization. Do you realize you're protecting a murderer? You've made yourself an accessory."

"I have raspberry or apricot. The apricot is homemade."

"Don't do this, Dana."

She turned from the counter, holding a piece of toast in her hand as if it were a law brief that should explain everything. "I'm not an accessory to anything, or to any*one* either, including you and Hale. What I'm doing is protecting an innocent man's good name from someone I love who admits he suffers from bouts of paranoia, and who was about to ruin his own career."

"And you wonder," I said darkly, "why I have a problem with trust."

"As someone who knows how much I owe the Lassiters and who values loyalty the way you do, I hoped you would understand. Don't you see? You think Darryl Orton is innocent although he's pleaded guilty, and I think Hale is innocent although you're convinced he's guilty, purely because you think you've connected him to Deborah."

I felt like shaking her by the shoulders. Instead, I took a second to sip my tea, burning my tongue in the process.

"What you're saying is that we're both blinded by loyalty."

"No. I'm saying you think that I am, and I think that you are."

I stood up and leaned across the counter toward her. "All right, then, let's look at what I *really* think. I think Hale was a hell of a lot more than 'connected' to Deborah. He was *physically* connected to her *and* lied to you about it, and dammit, Dana, you'd better start asking yourself why. He's also 'connected' to the sum of five million dollars, exactly half the amount that resulted from the scam initiated by the very same Deborah Hinton and exactly the sum lent to the firm at a time when his net worth was less than a million."

Dana didn't say anything.

"But then you knew all that," I added, feeling plenty warm now, "when you decided to protect him and condemn Darryl Orton to life in prison."

Her eyebrows lifted, indicating surprise at the fury of my outburst, and I tried to modulate some of the anger out of my voice.

"That's not all I think, Dana, and it's not all you know. You know that only three people in the entire free world were aware that Barney Klinehart had the goods on Deborah's murderer: you, Hale, and me. Okay? Well, I know I didn't kill Barney, and I don't think you did either."

She turned away from me.

"I realize I'm just a lowly business lawyer with a head full of 'loose logic,' as you recently put it, but I'm going to go out on a limb here and say that three minus two leaves one."

"Or," said Dana, "somebody the 'one' might have told. Or somebody who *Barney* might have told. It's not as cut and dried as you're making it out to be."

This wasn't working, and I was beginning to wonder how I might have done it better. How Dad would have done it.

"I want that lighter, Dana. This goes beyond loyalty now."

"Which is what?"

"I'm not sure. Maybe something to do with what kind of person I am. Or need to become."

"So what are you going to do? Tear Sarah's room apart? I assure you it's not here."

We sat in silence for a minute; then I shoved my cup away and grabbed my coat.

"Don't go, Billy. Look, I'm sorry you're in this situation—"

"This *situation*? The situation I'm in is one you created, so I don't want your tea *or* your sympathy. Just tell your friend Hale he and his buddies will have to kill me to stop me, because I'm gonna beat all of them."

I heard her cry out my name as I stormed out of the kitchen, though I managed to gather myself by the time I reached the door so's not to slam it.

The phone was ringing as I let myself in my apartment.

"Yes?"

"It's me," she said. "Please don't hang up."

I felt like Charlie Brown, fixing to kick the damn football again, but I told her go on, I was listening.

"I've been thinking about what you said before. You have your DNA thing with Moncrief in place. Why won't that suffice?"

"Because after Beckwith finishes with the DNA demonstration on Moncrief and admits that's all it was and that Moncrief didn't really kill Sheila Anderson, he's got nothing else."

"What if it's not merely a 'demonstration.' Why not carry it all the way through until after the verdict comes in. Show Moncrief's DNA on Sheila; then use the financials to establish Moncrief's profits, tying him into the scam *and* Deborah. The circumstantial connection might provide reasonable doubt as to Darryl Orton. Isn't that what you want?"

"That's what I want," I said, feeling irritated about being urged in the direction of something I'd been drifting toward myself.

"Merely use all the arguments you made to me before."

"None of which seemed to persuade you at the time."

"I didn't know about your little DNA demonstration with Moncrief then—and the possibility of . . . expanding it."

"Interesting," I said coldly. "All this from a true believer in the justice system, the stickler for decorum and practicing strictly by the rules."

"Don't tell me the possibility of waiting until *after* the verdict before exonerating Moncrief hadn't occurred to you."

I admitted it had. "But waiting until the verdict to reveal our little DNA hoax would ruin him, Dana. I was ready to do it when I was sure he had killed Deborah. But now . . . to carry it all the way through the verdict, knowing he didn't really do it?"

I could feel her exasperation through the phone line.

"Number one, Billy, you don't *know* he didn't do it. More importantly, Moncrief would never be charged. Beckwith can back off the minute the jury verdict is recorded and blame you for misleading him. You'll take some heat, sure, but once Orton is freed, he can't be tried again no matter what. Double jeopardy. He's out for good, and Moncrief can walk away and get over it."

"Walk away into a world of innuendo, rumor, and suspicion, his reputation in shreds."

"Reputation? Could it get any worse? He's not a nice man, Billy, and he's hurt a lot of people. Think of it as a form of rough justice. Remember what you said to me once? You told me that if I wanted the legal system to really work, I should be prepared to cheat on it when necessary, break its rules, and laugh at its weaknesses."

"So you were listening to me."

"Listening," she said, "not necessarily agreeing. You also said trial lawyers operating in our system should breathe life into the holes that reality had poked in it, by using ingenuity, guts, and some other things I can't remember. All right, Mr. Strobe, let's see some ingenuity and guts and those other things I can't remember."

Her voice sounded like it was strained through wire mesh. This whole notion went against her grain to the point where you could almost hear her pain. What she wouldn't do for that fucking Hale. The girl was nuttier on loyalty than I was.

"I know you've thought of all this, Billy, but if you want to try to free Orton by coming down on Moncrief instead of Hale, I'll help you any way I can."

I wondered if I could read a concession into her words, some growing suspicions about Hale.

"But if I do go after Hale?"

A longer silence, a silence like the endless seconds before an executioner's blade falls.

"Please, just consider what I've said," she said at last. "Good night, Billy."

Half-awake around seven the next morning I was thinking about Dana, needing her, wishing she was next to me. Despite all the things that were working against us, I was still a goner over the girl. Everything about her excited me—the way she dealt with little Sarah, her apparent skill and strength on a horse, how she touched me, made me laugh, even the way her mind worked in team meetings. Just thinking about her made me hard.

But her evasion of my final question last night on the phone, though gently spoken, had come through loud and clear as a threat. She might as well have said it right out loud: Go after Hale and we're finished.

I decided to take a drive and headed for Sausalito. I needed time to think, and I've always drawn inspiration from crossing the San Francisco Bay, driving over the Golden Gate Bridge, with its art nouveau design and night shadow lighting. I'd read that folks in the mid-thirties considered it to be impossible to build. But they did it, despite the high winds, blinding fog, and the unprecedented distance between Fort Point on the San Francisco side and the Marin Headlands. The miracle would claim the lives of eleven workmen during construction, their bodies washed out into the Pacific, human sacrifices to convenience and progress.

Moncrief came to mind. Did I dare tell Beckwith he was about to sacrifice an innocent man? No, he'd back out. More lies; lies had become the building blocks of Darryl's bridge to freedom.

The morning fog was still blanketing the headlands at the north end but had faded into wisps of torn cotton by the time it hit the Golden Gate. To the east, the sun had slashed through low stratus clouds that were bleeding fiery red over Oakland. I cranked down the windows and cranked up the chorus on a Silverhound tune called "Forget Me Not." The words hit me particularly hard given recent events.

Your note just said, "Forget me not,"
Oh Lord, I wish I could
But it's clear the words I could not say,
Were clearly understood

The note just said, "Forget me not,"
As if I ever could
You started a fire in my cold heart,
Then you put it out for good.

I took the Alexander turnoff past busloads of Japanese tourists flooding across to the lookout on my right, making Fuji Film's day. I briefly considered driving to Muir Woods or over to Stinson Beach, but instead turned back to my apartment to begin packing for my Great Escape. If Hale Lassiter wanted to save my life, I'd give him every opportunity to do it. Since he was still being nice to me, he probably hasn't even missed the lighter that Dana had filched, him having quit smoking regular early this year.

I had painful mixed feelings about Hale getting away with murder, even if I had come to love the son-of-a-bitch like a father. I had no such mixed feelings about Ashton, but I also had no evidence against him other than the circumstantial five-million-dollar loan. But one thing that was becoming clear was that without any hard evidence against Hale or Ashton, I'd have to turn Beckwith loose on poor old Moncrief. I didn't feel good about it. I hoped that Dad would look down and agree that sometimes you had to be a little unjust in order to remedy a greater injustice.

So I'd let Moncrief take the fall and then deal with it. I was uncomfortable fooling Beckwith, but I'd have to allow him to think that Moncrief really was guilty if I was going to expect him to do the deed. Mimi knew better, so I'd tell her our DNA stunt was still only a momentary demonstration to show how Darryl was framed. That would keep both of them relatively in the clear with the judge, who could do what he wanted with me. When it was over, nobody would know the real truth but me, Dana, and, of course, Hale himself. Hale would keep his mouth shut, of course; Darryl would be free; Moncrief would never be formally charged; and Dana would love me forever for leaving Hale out of it.

Let sleeping dogs lie. Right? What the hell was so wrong about cutting some slack to a basically decent guy who did a bad thing and screwing a bad guy who'd probably never done a good thing in his life? Your natural law and rough justice police at work, filling gaps in a system that had, after all, allowed Jason Moncrief to get away clean with blatant illegal insider trading. I had no doubt that stepson Casperson had kicked back most if not all of his profits to big daddy. And only God knows what other sins—other than being arrogant and obnoxious—the man had gotten away with in his fifty-plus years on earth.

It would be, as Dana said, rough justice—damn rough—but what would be the loss to society? Jason Moncrief wasn't fit to carry Hale Lassiter's briefcase. Dana and I would take Moncrief down together and, eventually, forgive each other for what we had done.

Wouldn't we?

Leaning against the door back at my apartment was a FedEx envelope from Mark Lowenthal at Material Analysis in Oklahoma City. I'd been pushing him so I would have his opinion before my trip home. I held my breath as I ripped the package open in the hallway, then skipped through the technical crap to the last paragraph.

In conclusion, we have compared samples of the writing of the purported signatory, Joseph Strobe, with the allegedly forged signature at issue. While certain similarities with the Strobe sample appear in the subject signature, these similarities appear belabored and contrived, as distinguished from Mr. Strobe's natural hand. In our opinion, the subject signature was not written by him.

We also conclude that the signature on the subject forged document was written with a fountain pen of high quality and a fine-grade point, possibly a Waterman or Mont Blanc. The forgery was definitely not accomplished with a ballpoint pen.

I exhaled with relief and allowed myself a pat on the back. The fact that Dad never owned or wrote with anything but a ballpoint should have been hammered on at trial, along with the news that Blackwell had an old Waterman set on his desk. Facts I would soon hammer into the cadaverous skull of Amos Blackwell, then into the collective heads of an Enid jury.

I finished packing for Oklahoma and New York, then walked down to the office, hoping I wouldn't see Hale. It had occurred to me that if he did miss his lighter, he might assume I had taken it. At least I knew he didn't keep a gun in his office.

"Hi, Billy," said Barbara cheerily as I walked past her cubicle. "The papers are ready in the Holzapple matter. Oh, yes, Mr. Lassiter would like to see you."

Of course, he could always carry a gun with him.

But, Hale was still all smiles as he looked up and saw me in the doorway.

"Good to see you, son! I understand from Vic James that you're New York bound."

"Yes, sir. Leaving tomorrow. Then, if everything works out, I'll be back in a few days to close things out here and pack my bags."

Hale turned serious, his eyebrows angled in distress, his blue eyes convincingly downcast. He wore the expression of a man growing weary of life.

"You'll be missed, Billy."

I forced a smile and a modest shrug of my shoulders. Maybe the reason I was so convincing was because I was actually beginning to consider moving to New York. Not before the trial was over, and not with Wulff and James. Maybe find a public interest firm there. Get back on track, a fresh start, talk Dana into going with me. I'd grown weary of the confusion here in San Francisco, where nothing was the way it seemed. One thing about prison, the ground rules were clear; a man knew where he stood. It didn't shake out that way here in the City, where your best friend and mentor turns out to be your worst enemy and where the first girl you had come to trust, dear Betty Perkins, had been planted by your best friend to betray you. No thanks.

That which nourishes me is killing me.

It hit me that when I pulled the sheet back that day, the tattoo, including the black rose on her left breast, was still there—the only thing about her that hadn't been fake. Aside from Dana, come to think on it, nothing was real in this damn town except death. Deborah Hinton, Barney Klinehart, and Betty Perkins. All dead. There could be more killing, too, if I wasn't careful.

Anyways, whether I stayed or moved on to New York, the important thing now was that everybody must think I was leaving. Out of the way. No threat.

"Thank you, sir," I told Hale, "but considering all the trouble I've caused, you'll be well rid of me." Bad choice of words.

"I assume you've decided to accept the offer from Wulff and James?"

"I'd be crazy not to."

"Yes," said Hale, "you would be." Was that a message?

I heard a gentle knock on Hale's open door and saw the shock in Hale's eyes at the same time. I turned, and there was Dana, and at her side was little Sarah.

"Forgive my interruption," she said, smiling a tight smile, "but there's no school today, and I'm showing off my daughter around the office. Can you say hello to Mr. Lassiter and Mr. Strobe, Sarah?"

"Hewo," she said, and I wanted to grab them both up in my arms. Hale recovered his poise, and I almost felt sorry for him as he played out his role of avuncular boss greeting employee and child, though his eyes were full of pain.

"Well, aren't you a sweetheart," he said, taking her little hand. Dana smiled sweetly at us and said they'd have to be on their way, many people to see. How I adored her in that instant.

Alone in the room with Hale again, we each played it safe, commented on how cute the child was, then picked up where we'd left off. I told him I'd brought Doug Beckwith in to handle Darryl's retrial.

"Good," Hale said, nodding thoughtfully. "I've heard he's an able advocate."

I was pleased, because to someone of Hale's professional pedigree, "able advocate" was high praise. Still, it bothered me that I still looked to him for approval.

We sat in silence for a minute; then Hale, who seemed to have recovered from the shock of Dana's boldness, reached out his hand and said, "Whatever you decide, whatever happens, I want you to know you've been like a son to me, Billy, and I'll miss you."

Whatever happens.

I shook his hand, mumbled a similar sentiment, and walked out.

Douglas Beckwith's secretary escorted me into his large office, offered me coffee, and promised he'd join me in a minute. I took in his furnishings, which were modern and uncluttered, two stark hardback client chairs designed to discourage long meetings, a credenza with monitor and phone controls behind a garish, kidney-shaped glass-topped desk that would probably curve around Beckwith's body like it was tailored to him. Nothing on top of it but pens and pencils, not a file in sight. An optimist would see tidy organization; a pessimist might wonder if the guy had anything to do.

A Dartmouth undergrad diploma hung on an elegant, koa-paneled wall between his Yale law degree and a photograph, presumably of himself, standing in full dress whites on the bow of a submarine with twenty or thirty other navy types, all in a state of rigorous salute. Next to that picture was Beckwith again with a Junior League–looking woman and three kids, blond like his wife and appropriately cute.

As promised, Beckwith appeared a minute later, wearing a gray linen shirt, a blue blazer with buttons that probably signified something rich, and a smile that could charm a verdict out of a jury of morticians. It was a $7,500 smile, actually, the amount of the retainer check I'd handed his secretary.

Doug Beckwith didn't look like your typical criminal defense lawyer, if such things can be generalized about. My own lawyer two years ago was a young public defender with a face pale as cocaine named Adam-something who wore a sparse beard, stringy blond hair to his shoulders, and an expression of impending doom. Every movement he made was as if he had almost forgotten to make it in time.

Now here was Beckwith, tall, blue-eyed, clean shaved, the picture of youthful enthusiasm and rectitude, looking more like a Montgomery Street corporate lawyer than I did. He slipped behind his tailor-made desk and it struck me that his appearance reflected his furnishings like some owners begin resembling their dogs. Beckwith and Darryl would get on together about as good as George W. and Al Gore had on election night.

"You're with Stanton and Snow, I understand."

I admitted the allegation, technically true, as I was still winding things up at the firm.

"Damned fine outfit," he added.

I nodded, and, after the formality of a quick mating dance, we got down to business. He had read the file, including the clerk's record and trial transcript on Darryl's first trial, and my own ponderous memo covering Barney, the Breckenridges, my findings from the Synoptics vault, and my theory about Moncrief's insider trading and how I expected the hair that was being analyzed by the FBI lab would match hair recently found by police at Sheila Anderson's murder site.

"You realize," he said, "that the DNA testing will have to be the PCA protocol, not the more definitive RFLP test, which takes weeks."

"Is the PCA method accepted by the courts?"

"Oh, yes. It's thoroughly reliable. We're talking about one in a thousand, perhaps, instead of one in a million."

"One in a thousand sounds good to me."

"You realize that you'll have to bear the costs of this testing?"

"Yes, sir."

"Is there anything else I need to know at the outset?"

"It's all in the file," I managed to say, though my throat was suddenly dry as canvas.

"All right, let me be honest," he said, tilting back in a high-backed wood and black leather bucket chair that needed only a shoulder harness to qualify for intergalactic space travel. "The case is fascinating, but full of *if*s."

"I know it."

"Heavy reliance on circumstance and innuendo, with no new evidence disproving the DNA match on your client."

"I know it."

"Plus it's coming to trial in less than two weeks."

"Right again."

"It's a tough case, with precious little time for preparation, exacerbated by the proximity of the holidays."

"No way around that, either."

Beckwith furrowed his unlined brow and stared intently at his gold leaf ceiling, as if the key to Darryl's defense might be written there.

"So, first, Mr. Strobe, I need you to appreciate that this is going to be a costly endeavor."

I nodded, hoping this guy was not as big a dandy in court as he was outside of one.

"Second, we might well not prevail. I don't mind telling you, Strobe, that I'm frankly a bit surprised you even got a new trial granted."

"No more surprised than me," I said, getting a little impatient and wondering if he was trying to wriggle off the hook.

"So," he said, spreading his hands, "what would you suggest we do?"

"You're the lawyer," I said, "I do wills and contracts."

"Well," he said, nimbly rising to his feet, "I'd say our only hope for success in saving Orton is success in pointing the finger at Moncrief."

This was more like it. The horse was heading straight to the finish line.

"And the only way we can do that," he continued, "is if the DNA tests presently under way present a good match on the Sheila Anderson murder."

"It'll match."

"I hope so, but then we come to the problem of tying Sheila's death to Deborah Hinton's, so that we can raise the inference that Moncrief murdered them both."

"It's a problem," I said.

"The Casperson connection might help, but it's frail."

"Don't forget Moncrief's own profits," I said, "and how pissed he must have been when he found out Deborah had gotten greedy, exposing both of them to an SEC investigation."

"True," he said, beginning to pace, talking to himself more than to me. "*If* I can convince the jury that Moncrief murdered Sheila, then make a plausible connection between him and *both* women, then tie them and Moncrief to the insider scam, the jury could very well find a reasonable doubt as to Darryl Orton, who was in prison when Anderson was killed."

I nodded and said, "Deborah faked the books, logically with Moncrief's approval and knowledge. He knows everything that goes on at Synoptics. I can testify to that; so will the woman who worked on his trial matters. Name's Dana Mathews. Anyways, it'll be clear that Deborah wouldn't dare do something like that without his approval."

"And also," interrupted Beckwith, "because he had his stepson buy Synoptics on the European exchange."

"You got it," I said, encouraged that he had read the file.

"Had Casperson ever bought stock before?"

"Never. Not once. I checked the stock register."

He smiled. "That's good. Circumstantial, but quite good. All of a sudden, for the first time in his life, and mere days before the company stock's biggest percentage dollar gain in history, Son-of-Moncrief gets an itch to buy Synoptics shares on the European market."

"Moncrief must have had Sheila Anderson buy stock, too," I added. "He probably knew her from high-tech conferences. Then, when it was time to sell it at the top and short the stock, he had her do that, too, then killed her like he had Deborah Hinton, and pocketed the ten million Anderson had made for him."

"It would work if we could tie him directly to the ten million, but we can't."

"I'm working on it," I said, "but we don't have the burden of proving everything, do we?"

"Theoretically, we don't have to prove *anything*. But jurors don't like unanswered questions, so in a practical sense, we do have a burden. If we can't convince the jury that someone other than Orton killed Deborah, we'll have a difficult time overcoming Orton's DNA on her body, the murder weapon with her blood on it behind his locker, and the new money in his bank account."

"I'll keep trying to track the scam proceeds." The papers, the fucking papers! What I wouldn't give for a gander at Barney's papers.

Beckwith said, "It's a bloody shame we just missed a Christmas verdict."

"A Christmas verdict?"

"We try to get our hardest criminal cases set two or three weeks before Christmas. People are in a charitable mood. It's common knowledge."

Not common to me, but it made sense. "We're in the week after Christmas," I said, "that help any?"

"Not the same. People are feeling overweight, hung over, their trees are drying up, they're realizing how much money they spent. The good citizens are no longer feeling warm and fuzzy."

"Oh."

"We'll do what we can. Does Moncrief have other children?"

"One with his present wife. Kid named Rick, second-year law student at Harvard or Yale. Other than that, I hear he's a good kid."

Beckwith displayed his perfect teeth to show me he could take a joke.

"Any stock?"

"Sorry, not a share."

Beckwith drummed on the desk with a pencil, an expression of either concern or deep thought on his pink face. "Let's sum up here. *If* the DNA on Sheila turns out to be Moncrief's *and* we find that Moncrief was the recipient of Anderson's profits, we would win."

"Don't worry about the DNA," I said.

"You're that confident that Moncrief is a murderer."

"I have no doubt that the DNA will match," I said.

I felt him measuring me, so I added, "Of course, the proof of the pudding will be in the FBI's lab report."

"Ironic, isn't it," he said. "Counting on DNA evidence to rebut DNA evidence?"

"Ironic," I repeated. "Yes, sir, that's what it is."

I returned to my apartment and called Mimi D'Angelo to tell her I had met with Beckwith.

"Seen him in court once," she said. "He'd be a hunk if he'd take the broomstick outta his ass."

"Yeah, he's strung a little tight, but his record is good."

"Is he willing to pull off your demonstration stunt?"

"I didn't exactly tell him it was a demonstration."

"Excuse me?"

The lies were piling up on me, and I couldn't bring myself to lie to Mimi about how I had lied to Beckwith. "I figure if he's going to convince the jury that Moncrief killed Sheila, he'd have to believe it himself."

"You let him think Moncrief's the real killer?"

"That's what he thinks."

She paused, and I could hear a match strike, then toxic wind blowing into the receiver at the other end. "Well, it's your call, but you know it'll ruin Moncrief's name in this city."

"I'll have him clear it up, right after the demonstration."

"Sure," she said, and I heard the reproach in her tone. "Unring the bell, right?"

"Like you said, it's my call. We're taking on the power of the government here, Mimi, and the Lord only helps those who help themselves. Don't worry—we're on the side of the angels."

"Yeah? Well in your case, there may be the devil to pay."

I hung up, then snapped my suitcase shut, called a cab, and within two hours was winging it toward Oklahoma City and a night meeting at my airport hotel with handwriting expert Mark Lowenthal. I felt like I was trying to hold a nuclear reactor together with Scotch tape and baling wire.

34

"**I**'ve missed you, brat," I said, putting my arms around Lisa the next day. I took in her face, too worn for someone her age, but still pretty. I put down the gift boxes I was carrying, and she took my coat. I glanced around the living room with that strange sense of comfort I always felt coming home again, even under the worst of circumstances. There was a small, overdecorated Christmas tree by the fireplace with a sad collection of small packages underneath.

"Ma asleep?"

"She won't come out of her bedroom. I made the mistake of telling her you were coming to take her to Oklahoma City tomorrow, and she figured out the rest."

"Is she drinking?"

"Does a bear shit in the woods?"

"Jesus, Lisa, I thought you were going to make sure she—"

"Don't start the blame game with me, Billy. It would take a busload of Pinkertons to keep that woman from alcohol, and I'm only half a person on double Prozac, plus thanks to that specialist you hired from San Francisco, something call mixantrone."

"My sister the junkie."

"And now Ma's on a hunger strike. Said it worked for Gandhi and Martin Luther King and that she's as much a prisoner of fate and prejudice as they were."

Her imitation of Ma was perfect and would have been funny if it wasn't so damn sad. "When did she start the hunger strike?"

"Today. After lunch."

Lisa then led me into her own bedroom and proudly displayed the log and filing system she had created of the exhibits I had copied her with on Dad's trial, including the new expert's report. She had also broken down the testimony of key witnesses at the trial, raising questions as to how they might have been cross-examined by a more objective—and sober—defense attorney.

"Good job, sis," I said, then told her about my late-night meeting with Mark Lowenthal at my motel after I had landed the night before. "He says Dad didn't forge the document *and* he'll make a good witness."

"Excellent," she said. "Now what?"

It was great to see Lisa so caught up in the case. There was a light in her eyes I'd hadn't seen in years.

"I'm taking on Amos Blackwell again this afternoon," I told her, "then I'll drive Ma down to the clinic in the morning. I have to be in New York by tomorrow night."

Things were piling up on me, so I ran a schedule through my head to make sure it could all happen. Lisa said something, but . . .

"Well?" said Lisa.

"Sorry, sis, what did you say? I was lost in thought."

"That's because it's such unfamiliar territory, Billy. I asked if you will stop over on the way back from New York. Spend Christmas with us? I could take the bus down to the city, maybe spring Ma from Serenity for dinner?"

"Got to get back to San Francisco."

"That's bullshit, Billy."

"I've got a trial starting right after Christmas. Plus I'm on the firm's nonrefundable air ticket, so lighten up, okay?" I didn't mention my plan to spend Christmas with Dana.

I heard the reprimand in her silence, saw it in her expression.

"Look, Lisa, I'm lucky I was able to stop over at all, and I'm sorry that—"

"Don't pay any attention to me," she said, "I'm just being bitchy because you brought all those presents, and Ma and I haven't finished our shopping yet."

"Don't even think about it."

She went over to the tree and tossed me a package with an envelope attached. "Well, I got you a subscription to *Sports Illustrated* and a shirt you're going to hate."

"I'll love it, brat."

"I thought the swimsuit edition might fill the void in your love life."

"I'm sure it'll help."

I wanted to tell her about how things were with Dana, but decided against adding another layer of confusion. Instead, I asked her if she had thought about joining up with me after I got Ma settled at the clinic. She was evasive.

"I've been thinking," I said, "we could sell the house and use the money to get you a place in San Francisco or New York. Then Ma could move in when she—"

That was all it took to get Amy Strobe out of the bedroom. "I heard that, you son-of-a-bitch!"

"Yes, I *am* your son, Ma."

"Always the clever comeback, our Billy," she said in a hoarse, mocking voice, "quick like his old man. Well, here's *my* comeback: I'll sell this house, Billy Strobe, over *your* dead body!"

She stood swaying in the doorway in nothing but her bathrobe and one slipper. Her hair was matted and hung in strings around her puffy face. Her nose and cheeks were covered with broken capillaries and despite her anger, the eyes that stared at me were dull and lifeless. Her legendary beauty had deserted her and with it, the last shreds of confidence and self-respect. But despite her best efforts to do herself in, Amy Strobe was a survivor, and she intended to make her stand in the home she had lived in for thirty years. I expected it and respected it.

I walked over and put my arms around her. It was like hugging a broken ladder. Her arms hung loosely at her sides and the smell of gin oozed from her mouth, her nose, even her pores.

"A prisoner does not always cotton to the warden," Ma said, backing away and trying unsuccessfully to button the top of her robe. You should know that much from your own tarnished past and wasted future. Indeed, it's the duty of every prisoner to attempt to escape."

"That's prisoners of war, Ma."

"Well, I've been at war my entire adult life."

"That's a long time not to have any peace. Which is why you've got to let us help you."

"Help from a jailbird? That'd be the halt leading the blind. I'll take my chances here on the battlefield."

"Go ahead, Ma, say whatever you want. It won't work. We'll never quit on you."

"*Don't give up on me, baby . . . ,*" she started singing, her voice cracking but still right on pitch.

I kept talking. "I promise you'll like this place, Ma. Give it a week. If you don't, we'll bring you back, and won't ever bug you again. As soon as you're well, you can move back in with Lisa in San Francisco or New York, wherever we end up. We'll all be together. Remember how you liked San Francisco?"

She turned and stared out the large living room window. She wore the expression of a person who had let her past slip too far away. "San Francisco," she repeated dreamily. "Cable cars. The Top of the Mark. I was pretty then, wasn't I, Billy?"

She had visited San Francisco with her parents, before she met Joe. I wasn't sure which trip she was referring to.

"You're still pretty, Ma. Just give it a chance, okay? Give us a chance to help you come back to us."

Her lips tightened into a straight line, and she shook her head. I could see I was losing her.

"I don't need any help from you, Billy Strobe. Lisa and I are doing fine, aren't we, dear?" Before Lisa could answer the rhetorical question, Ma added, "At least neither of us has been convicted of a felony yet."

With that parting shot, she retreated to her room and firmly shut the door.

Frustrated from the confrontation, I gave Lisa a hug and headed for my appointment with Amos Blackwell.

We had picked a neutral site, an Enid institution downtown called the Famous Restaurant. Dad used to take us all to dinner at least once a month and sometimes to brunch after Mass on Sundays. My plan was to confront Blackwell with my expert's report, then try to force a confession, maybe even a financial settlement for a trust fund for Lisa. Blackwell's alternative would be a civil suit for fraud and criminal charges for perjury for lying about Joe's involvement in the faked exhibit. Convicted or not, he'd be faced with bells that would be hard to unring in this small town.

Blackwell had arranged a booth with relative privacy, but with enough people around to protect against a repeat of our last confrontation. The Famous was one of those clean, noisy, sprawling, brightly lit American restaurants where you could still get a good meal at a fair price. This one had an open kitchen full of efficient Chinese cooks in white outfits with little white hats on their heads. The place still served everything—except Chinese food.

Blackwell was waiting for me in a dull red Naugahyde-covered booth. He spotted me and slid out of his side and up on his feet with surprising quickness for a man his height. He smiled his cadaver smile and extended his hand. I took it and matched his firm grip, disappointed that his hand was dry and warmer than mine. He seemed thoroughly at ease, and though his face held a smile, his eyes didn't bother to conceal his dislike for me.

The waitress poured coffee for us both; then Amos waved her away with an imperial movement of his wrist.

"I assume, Billy," he said, after the usual niceties, inquiries about my work, my mother, and sister, "that you didn't ask for this meeting to apologize for the last one. So given the fact that we're both busy, why don't you tell me your agenda?"

I slid across the booth and leaned into him so close I could smell his cologne.

"Sure," I said. "No problem. Your testimony convicted my dad. You swore under oath that you saw him forge a signature."

"And I *did* see it. On a letter that allowed Joe to win Jed Sanborn's case."

"Well, I have the top expert in the state ready to testify it wasn't Joe's handwriting."

"Of *course*, it wasn't Joe's *typical* handwriting. He was trying to make it look like the plaintiff's signature, for God's sake."

I waved him off. "My expert took that into account. He will testify that somebody was trying to make it look like Joe was attempting to make it look like the plaintiff's signature—a forgery of a forgery. I think it was you or the client who forged the signature and that you both lied under oath. The judge knew the verdict was wrong, too, as evidenced by his aggressive polling of the jury, his light sentence, and his subsequent depression and suicide."

The last zinger was a bluff, of course, but I was learning that the art of litigation was a battle where words spoken firmly seemed to carry their own truth and where factual gaps could be filled by clever bluffsmanship. I held back on Dad's ballpoint fixation and the Waterman pen part of the opinion as a clincher for after I had Blackwell on the ropes.

His expression was not so much surprise or anger, but more like the puzzled look of a man trying to place who I was. Then he smiled and shook his head dolefully. "Where in the hell do you get these ideas, punk? Hanging around other prisoners? Too much exposure to all those fruits and nuts living in 'Frisco now that you're out?"

"You're about to learn plenty about exposure, Mr. Blackwell. I'm going to sue you."

He laughed out loud, a single, sharp report, like a car's backfire. Or maybe more like a door slamming shut. I felt heat rising in my face, but stayed calm.

"Go ahead and sue," he said, reaching for his coat. "Anything else you got to say, punk?"

"Two things. Despite the promise I made to myself before I came in here, if you call me punk once more, I'm going to pull you out of this booth and wipe that patronizing smile off your face."

"Good. Then I'll have a countersuit for assault and battery. What's the other thing?"

"The other thing is that win, lose, or hung jury, I'm going to make sure my lawsuit will ruin you in this town."

He sighed and carefully laid his coat back down and signaled the waitress to pour us both more coffee. I took this as a good sign. He stirred in two heaping teaspoons of sugar and raised the cup to his lips with a hand as steady as an Olympic sharpshooter—*not* a good sign. He sipped, then put the cup down and reached into a brown folder under his coat, his eyes never leaving mine. He removed five sheets of paper, each imprinted with copies of canceled checks, front and back. He tossed them in front of me, and I saw the name JOSEPH STROBE printed on the left and Sequoia National Bank, Joe's bank, printed at the top.

"What's this supposed to be?" I asked. "Exemplars of my father's handwriting? I've got plenty of those already."

"I doubt you've got any of these."

I scanned the first page quickly, checks in amounts ranging between $500 and $3,500, paper-clipped together, all to the same payee.

Charles Ryan, the judge who had sat on Dad's case.

"Your father wasn't very careful for a man skilled in the whys and wherefores of criminal behavior," Blackwell said. "There's more where these came from."

I stared at the checks, my brain circling the revelation like a desperate pilot running low on fuel. There had to be an answer, an explanation, a place to land.

"You want to know why that judge killed himself?" Blackwell asked rhetorically. The bastard was giving me a fatherly, patronizing look.

"I'll tell you anyway. Because your father was threatening to expose him, pure and simple. I couldn't talk him out of it. See, Judge Ryan had been on the take from Joe for years. He had agreed to overrule the jury if they came in against Joe in his trial, which of course, they did. But when Ryan couldn't nudge a single juror into recanting his vote, he had to let it stand; the proof had been so damn clear and overwhelming against Joe that Charlie knew he'd be in front of the Judicial Commission lickety split if he threw out the verdict."

I tossed the pages back across the table and met the triumphant gaze in his milky eyes.

"And I suppose you had nothing to do with the forged exhibit?" I said. "Didn't know a thing about it?"

"Of course I knew about it. I was in it up to my ears," he said, palms up, eyebrows angled; look, no secrets. "So was the client, our biggest client, Jed Sanborn. We knew everything about it. But it was Joe's idea out of the chute, and it was Joe who faked the signature of the deceased right in my office, exactly as I said at trial, pure and simple. Sat there and used my own fountain pen, with Jed Sanborn sitting there with me watching him, going along with him all the way."

"That could send you to jail."

"Not a chance," he said, offering me a wry smile. "You've got an expert, have you? Well, so did the DA, as you know. After your last two visits to our fair city, I got a whiff of which way the wind was blowing, and I retained another expert. Both say it's Joe's writing, deliberately disguised, but clearly his. What I'm saying, Billy, is bring your damn suit, and I'll blow the whistle on things that will make that pissy-assed little forgery by Joe look like Donald Duck getting a parking ticket."

He tossed a pair of reports in front of me. The one on top was from a major lab in Dallas.

"Want to know why Joe really killed himself?" Blackwell continued, the avuncular pose gone now as he took in my stony expression. "Well, hell, I'll tell you why. Joe was understandably pissed off at the judge for taking his money then reneging on the deal, and, like I said, he threatened to expose Charles Ryan. That was a mistake. Charlie told him to go to hell, said he couldn't sleep at night anymore and was going to the U.S. Attorney in Oklahoma City to make a clean breast of everything. He was going to name names, other people your dad had bribed and extorted."

"You're lying!" I said, trading fake smiles with Blackwell as I clutched at a straw of hope. "The feds wouldn't have jurisdiction, and Judge Ryan would know it! *He'd have gone to the local district attorney.*"

Blackwell blew air out of sunken cheeks, clucked his tongue, and sorted through the pages of copied checks in front of him. The overall impression was that of a teacher patiently arranging colored blocks for a retarded child.

"Take a look . . . *sir,*" he said, sliding the packet toward me, "at the second group of checks."

"Made out to Lowell Horan," I said, my heart sinking. "So what?"

"He *was* the 'local district attorney.' "

He paused for a few seconds to make sure that one had sunk in, then added, "Those copies are for you, and you can check all this out, talk to some of the folks he paid off, scared off, or pissed off if you want. Meanwhile, I'd suggest . . ."

He kept talking, but I barely heard him for the roaring that had commenced in my head. It sounded like steam building up in a chamber, and the chamber was my head. The pressure was so strong I thought my eyes might pop out. A waitress approached and asked me if I was okay. I mumbled something, and she walked away. I took a sip of water from a twitching glass. I quickly scanned the other pages. Saw checks made out to other names all too familiar: Sam Somerville, Karen Oates, W. B. Lightfoot, Torville Berenson . . .

The list.

"Your dad was a fascinating man," Blackwell was saying. "A true exponent of dialectic materialism. A socialist in spirit, a radical in concept, and a crook at heart. He was a good lawyer, too, a damn brilliant lawyer, but that wasn't enough, not for *your* dad. Joe wanted *insurance* for his clients, so he used and abused the system in order to beat the system. Manipulated the holy hell out of it: threats, bribes, extortion—hell, Billy, you name it. It started with the little things all defense lawyers do, but by the time of his death, he'd stop at nothing. In Joe Strobe's world, there was never a means that could not be justified by whatever end he had in mind that day."

I tried to meet the old man's eyes, but his face seemed blurred and all out of proportion. The pain in my forehead felt like I'd been hit with an ice pick, and my heart was pounding against my rib cage so hard my eyes were jiggling. All my energy went into concealing my growing despair from this calm, grinning jackal.

"And here you sit—ex-con Billy Strobe, fruit of your father's loins—accusing *me* of a crime. Haven't you heard, young Strobe, that the apple never falls far from the tree?"

I gave him a look that caused him to flinch, but his words kept coming.

"You might as well know it all, kid. It turned out that not even Charlie Ryan's Irish Catholic guilt could trump your father's. See, Joe knew that if he did himself in first, then Ryan wouldn't have to take that trip to Oklahoma City. Joe's dirty laundry would never be hung out where it could be seen.

"He was right, of course. Who'd there be to blow the whistle? Someone who'd taken his money? Not a chance. The client? Hell, no— he'd go to jail, too. Your mother, the pillar of propriety and decorum, who knew everything but couldn't get him to stop? Hell, no—she's never even let on to you or Lisa, has she?"

He paused a beat, took another sip from his coffee. "I didn't think so," he said. "Brave woman, keeping that locked up inside her all these years."

I wanted to yell at him to stop, but my brain had shut down; it had caved in on itself, trying to bury the pain there, and I couldn't speak.

"That leaves me," he continued. "Would *I* tell? Of course not. My hands were soiled, too. I'd have been some kind of fool not to have figured out what my own partner was up to all those months before he died. Not even a Joe Strobe wins *every* case, and there was no case he wouldn't take on and no case he couldn't win. Defend a murder case with an eyewitness? Adios eyewitness, and *buen viaje*. Vehicular manslaughter while drunk? Goodness me, whatever could have happened to those blood test results? Smoking gun in his client's hand? No problem, the hard-hearted DA suddenly goes soft and agrees the damn thing must have gone off accidentally. 'We're taking on the damn government, Amos,' he'd say. 'We're on the side of the angels,' he'd say, and yes, Billy, I'd look the other way.

"Don't say it, Billy, I'll say it myself: I was equally guilty. In my weakness, I fed at the trough of your father's iniquity."

As he spoke, his shoulders convulsed suddenly, and his chalky face betrayed a look of pure self-loathing. Through blurred eyes, I could see that Amos Blackwell had come here with an agenda, too, needing not so much to defend his actions, but to purge his conscience, expiate his own guilt.

"So that's what I was guilty of," he continued, "nothing more, but God help me, nothing less. Charlie Ryan couldn't live with his guilt, but I will, for better or for worse, and there's not a damn thing you or I or anyone else can do about it."

I was vaguely aware that Blackwell had got to his feet, put a five-dollar bill on the table, and walked away.

35

I drove the rented Ford back home so slow people were honking at me. My headache was worse, and keeping a car on my side of the road was about all I could handle. I'd looked at the checks again when I got to the parking lot at the Famous Restaurant and there was no doubting it was my dad's distinctively bad handwriting, written with a ballpoint pen. In small letters on the back of each check, Blackwell or someone had written down the function of each payee: cop, DA, judge, witness, whatever.

On the side of the angels.

Only one person could straighten this out, make it go away. I reckon the reason I was driving home so slow was because I knew she couldn't.

I walked through the front door and must have looked like yester-day's dinner because Lisa asked me right off if I was okay. I ignored her and went straight to Ma's door and started pounding on it. She didn't respond, and I turned the knob.

"Billy, what's wrong? She's out cold, and she keeps her door locked."

I put a shoulder to it, and the hollow-core door gave way like cardboard.

"*Billy!*" shouted Lisa. "What in the hell—?"

Ma was wide awake, sitting on her bed with her back against the headboard, arms wrapped around knees against her chest. She looked at me through eyes that knew all they needed to know about pain and disappointment. But now those eyes betrayed fear, too, not of me but of what I'd found out. She knew where I'd been.

I threw the copies of the checks at her. She didn't stir as they fluttered about the room, just kept staring at me.

"He told you everything," she whispered finally, her once-fine head rotating slowly on sagging shoulders. "The damn fool told you everything."

I grabbed her by the shoulders. *"Told me what?"* I shouted at her. *"What did he tell me?"*

She kept turning her head from side to side, and I was shaking her, screaming at her like a crazy person, which I was. I felt Lisa's weak hands around my neck, pulling at my face, an ear, a finger in my eye. I pushed Lisa away, heard her shouting at me, heard myself still shouting at Ma.

Then Amy Strobe collapsed in a ball on the bed, me beside her, crying my damn eyes out I don't know how long. Lisa gathered up the checks, crying, too. Ma had her back to me, and when I tried to turn her toward me, her shoulder was hard and unyielding. She wasn't crying, just staring at the wall.

"Why," she whispered at last, in a low hoarse voice, "*why* couldn't you just leave him be?"

I had no words to answer her, so turned the question around. "Why did you stay with him?"

She didn't answer for a time, then slowly turned toward me.

"He wasn't always like that, Billy. It happened to him slowly, in bits and pieces, like water wearing down a rock. First, hints to clients on what to say to get off, which he told me everybody did. Then he began writing scripts for them, even helping them to find 'friendly witnesses' to support the story. He claimed he was merely 'leveling the playing field' because the system was loaded against his clients. He'd say, 'The government plants evidence, why shouldn't the citizens be able to even things up?' He believed in what he was doing, at least he did at first."

I reached out and touched her hand. "He used to tell me how unfair the justice system was," I said. "That's why he didn't respect it."

She shook her head. "That wasn't it. He didn't respect the justice system because it was so easy for him to corrupt. Toward the end, he was buying judges, cops, even prosecutors. He told me once, 'You put the criminal justice system in a box, give it a good shake, then tip it upside down and all that falls out are people who want more than what they've got.' It was 'people' he manipulated, and it was those same people he feared."

"Feared?"

"He used to say that in any system, there are always people who can't be bought and people who will sell you out. 'One or the other will get me someday,' he said one night when he was even drunker than usual. He was right about that, just didn't figure the Judas would be his own partner; then, of course, Charlie Ryan."

"But you stayed."

"What was I going to do? Be the one to sell him out? Besides, we were never a month's rent ahead of the game. The law practice profits—such as they were—all went to judges and to buying off witnesses. Was I supposed to take a job, work at the five and dime just to make enough to pay the baby-sitters I'd need during the day for you two? I had no skills, Billy, only a degree."

She put her head in her hands, rubbing her temples with long, thin index fingers. "Yes, I stayed," she said, her voice heavy with regret.

"Did you love him, Mama?" came Lisa's voice from behind me.

Ma's expression softened; her eyes narrowed as if trying to remember where she had put something.

"For a long, long time. He kept promising that as soon as we had enough to get you kids through college, he'd stop what he was doing. I wanted to believe him, but deep down I began to realize it had nothing to do with money. Your father was a crook and a coward, but he never made a dime off his misdeeds. Some of the clients he cheated to help couldn't even afford to pay his fee, let alone the bribe money. Robin Hood is how he saw himself, and how I saw him, too, in our early days together. I loved him then; yes, I loved him for a long time."

She raised her swollen eyes to mine, as if to catch a glimpse of his youth, and maybe her own. "It was never money, Billy, it was power. He was playing God, he was, more powerful than any judge or politician, and drinking all day to hide from himself. But not even God can hide from himself."

She shocked herself with that one and did a quick sign of the cross. I thought she was finished, but she wasn't.

"The more he won, the more he was terrified of losing. Toward the end, he never took a bit of pleasure in winning, just relief he hadn't lost. And by then, the drink had such a hold on him, he was afraid he couldn't win without . . ."

"Setting things up," I said, my voice harsh, my throat dry as gravel, my last scraps of hope fragmenting like that coyote in the cartoons.

She looked up at me, and suddenly tears filled her eyes, the first I could remember seeing since Dad died. She put her arms around my neck, and I felt her body shuddering against me.

"At the end," she sobbed into my shoulder, "I'd come to hate him as much as he hated himself, but no, I couldn't muster the courage to leave."

"How about now, Ma?" I whispered. "Can you leave him now?"

She considered my words, then nodded slightly. I slid off the bed, got to my feet, and turned to Lisa, who was still quietly crying behind us.

"Help Ma get dressed, okay? I'm taking her to Oklahoma City. Now."

Lisa nodded, and I walked back out through the shattered wood door.

I gave Ma a final hug in her room at Serenity. It wasn't much bigger than my cell at Soledad, but it was private, and she had her own bathroom. She didn't complain, but asked our guide, a gentle, pony-tailed male nurse named Michael, if she could have something from her home—her nightstand, or perhaps a small dresser and some photographs, things of her own.

"That would be fine," he said.

"I'll arrange it tomorrow," I said. Michael smiled sympathetically, but the glance we exchanged told me she wouldn't even know who she was by tomorrow.

"I love you, Ma," I whispered, holding her trembling body tight against me. "You're going to be fine."

She nodded her head in a way that struck me as both brave and unpersuaded.

"You are, too, Billy," she said, stepping back from me, her voice a harsh whisper. "I know that finding out the truth about your father has been hard on you, but he was fond of saying knowledge was power, even when it was *unwanted* knowledge."

I nodded, though no more persuasively than she had nodded to me.

"My father was fond of saying a lot of things. Right now, I don't know if a single one of them was true."

"Shush, Billy," she said. "You'll heal. You've always been good at fixing things."

"This is something broke beyond fixing, Ma."

She shook her head. "I'm sure you thought the same about me yesterday, but just look at how you've sweet-talked me into this godforsaken loony bin.

"No offense," she added to Michael, who smiled and shrugged his shoulders.

I smiled, too, embarrassed that my self-indulgent despair had put poor Ma in the role of consoler. I assured her I'd snap out of it by morning. She seemed to accept the lie and kissed me on the cheek. I then lowered her into a sitting position on her small bed, told her good-bye, shook hands with Michael, and began to answer my desperate need to be clear of the place.

"William!" she shouted as I reached the door. I turned, and she beckoned me back to her side.

"Yes, Ma?"

Her breathing was coming hard now, but I let her talk. "You've spent the first part of your life trying to live up to your father. Now that you know the truth, don't waste the rest of your life trying to live it down."

"I'll forget about him in time, Ma."

She gave out an ironic chuckle. "Joe Strobe is not a man easily forgotten," she said, then met my eyes with a laser intensity as she added, "Instead of trying to forget him, why not be *better* than him?"

I nodded, started to get up, but her poor claw of a hand squeezed my wrist with surprising strength. She wanted something more of me.

"I promise," I said, and she smiled as she released me. I walked out past Michael, then hurried down the hall and into the cold, fresh air.

I don't cotton much to drinking on airplanes. Man's organs'll dry out fast enough at 37,000 feet without the aid of methyl alcohol, but I had a few on the way to JFK anyways. Reckon I was trying to blot out all that had happened the day before, which, of course, didn't work. If I'd learned anything from the day's revelations, it was that alcohol only makes bad situations worse.

Something else was bothering me. If it was "the drink" that had dulled Joe Strobe's conscience toward the end, what was my excuse for what I was about to do to Jason Moncrief? Every time I tried to answer that one, my head went all smoky, like it was cluttered with smoldering ashes.

I checked into my New York hotel room in the early afternoon, still trying to make sense of things. My only consolation was the fact that Ma, freed of her punishing burden of silence, had gone so serenely into Serenity.

As for Lisa, she was reacting unpredictably to what I'd discovered.

She said she felt a "lifetime of ambiguity" was behind her and told me that the truth—and mitoxantrone—was going to set her free.

When I asked her if she'd come live with me, she said she'd like to move to Denver, maybe, or somewhere in northern California. Get her own apartment.

"Ma has a new home for now; I suppose I'll eventually need one, too," she said, but I told her I'd feel better if we'd stick together.

"You don't think I'm strong enough to be on my own," she protested, "but I will be, you'll see. I think I've been using my poor health as an excuse for not being able to help Mother more. Well, she's gone off to get well, and maybe now I'll do the same."

Though she was starting to sound like a shrink, I believed her. I even envied her, because the truth-will-set-you-free solution wasn't panning out for me at all. As I got closer to New York and a new set of lies, I felt as shackled as I did that day on the bus heading for Soledad. Though I was getting good at deception, I still hated it, and here I was headed for Broadway, cast in a new role in front of a fresh audience, with a new pocketful of lies. And not even sure who I was anymore.

Still, I've got to admit it was nice to be met at the arrival gate by a driver holding up a sign with my name on it. Even insisted on carrying my briefcase and carry-on bag. Tossed me and the bags in a Town Car and carted me off to the Mark Hotel, to a room with a bathroom three times the size of my entire cell at Soledad.

After two days of shaking hands and two tons of verbal bullshit, I had dinner with Vic James and Brian Schlinkert, the firm's presiding partner. When Schlinkert asked me if I was accepting their offer, I said yes, and we all shook hands. I had come to like Vic and felt bad about being two-faced with him, but I knew it would be back to Hale within hours that I'd soon be out of the way.

As I sat waiting for my flight to be called, I felt like I hadn't really been in New York. Sure, my body had been going through a set of smiling, robotic motions, the kind I was getting too damn good at, but I'd left my heart in San Francisco and my soul in Enid, Oklahoma, rotting in a felon's casket.

I called Dana to tell her how much I missed her, and she said the same. She invited me for Christmas again, and I said yes, sure. She asked if anything was wrong, and I kept denying it. How do you explain to somebody in a long-distance phone conversation that the star you've navigated by all your life has fallen from the heavens? So I steered the conversation to the good news about Ma going to the clinic, and she was happy to hear it.

"By the way," she said, "Hale talked to Brian Schlinkert this afternoon. You made a good impression."

I told Dana she should take the Wulff and James job instead of me. I could get on with a public service firm, and we'd live happily ever after in New York, far from Bad Memories Land.

She didn't think so; didn't think Hale could handle losing both his favorite people at once. It bothered me that she was acting like nothing had changed at all. Like nothing was about to change a hell of a lot more.

36

Dana picked me up at the airport seven hours later, and I told her more about the New York trip, but kept dodging the Enid news. When we got to dinner, she pressed me, and her eyes filled with tears when I told her about Amos Blackwell's accusations and Ma's corroborating confession.

"She was protecting you all those years."

I nodded. "It was like she was sneaking food to someone in the attic, someone she didn't even much like, keeping the main part of the fantasy alive, something for her children to hold on to."

"I'm sure your father did a great deal of good, Billy."

"For some bad people. Truth is, Dana, he was a phony."

"At least you knew him."

"Not really, and maybe you were lucky not to know yours."

She gave up trying to talk me out of my misery and reached over and took one of my hands in hers.

I renewed the notion of us both going to New York.

"I don't think I can, Billy."

"Well," I said, "I don't want to stay around here."

"Why not? Moncrief may be the top dog at Synoptics now, but after the trial, the board of directors may vote him out. They are publicity-shy to a man. If Moncrief's gone, Ashton will lose his clout, and that leaves Hale."

"That leaves Hale," I said, almost to myself.

She squeezed my hand, and I took in her sympathetic eyes, her beautiful mouth, a nose so small and well formed you didn't notice it unless you were heavy into noses, which I never was.

"You know I don't belong at S & S, darlin," I said, "with or without Ashton. I'm not sure I belong anywhere right now, but at Stanton and Snow I've felt like the ape in that Tarzan movie they brought back to civilization, and all he could do was grunt and try to learn it's not nice to shit on the imported rugs."

She smiled and shook her head. "A firm like S & S makes a monkey out of all of us at times. Remember, you're talking to trailer-trash Dana here. But Montgomery Street is just another system, and you're picking up the rules of survival faster than you think."

I'm not sure why that came across to me as a negative. I shrugged and said, "I've only quit shitting on the imported rugs. Besides, you're the one who believes in systems, not me. Fact is, I don't believe in much of anything presently. That bullshit propaganda about those astronauts walking on the moon? A U.S. Supreme Court above politics? That crap about the Earth being round?"

Dana smiled and touched my cheek. "You're just a man who thought he had all the answers and found out nobody does."

"Maybe, but I'm also an ex-con, sired by a crook."

She smiled, tilted her head. "Some kind of genetic monster, right?"

I felt heat in my chest, rising into my face. "You think I was dragged kicking and screaming into the Billionaire Boys Club II? Or how about the little Christmas present I'm about to give Moncrief? How many canons of ethics will that one break?"

"Billy, you're shouting."

I lowered my voice, but not my intensity. "How many lawyers do you know who would frame an innocent man to spare a guilty one?"

"You're doing it to spare Darryl Orton, not Hale."

"Whatever, they disbar lawyers for less, even where I come from. But what the hell, I'll pull it off without breaking a sweat. Why? Because I'm a fucking chip off the old block!"

The fingers of her free hand fluttered the air with impatience. "You can't really believe . . ."

"I don't know what to believe anymore," I said. "I've built my life around a man who never existed, a guy playing God with a corrupt system."

"The system is fallible, Billy, but it can survive a battering now and then."

"Like the one *we're* fixing to give it?"

That shut her down. I knew she saw then I was having serious second thoughts about sparing Hale and screwing Moncrief, and that was scaring her. So we changed the subject, I apologized for raising my voice, and we even managed to have a few laughs at dinner. But there was something between us now.

After dinner I told her I was tired, and she dropped me off at my apartment. I took Sarah's rabbit out of a shopping bag, asked her to wrap it for me. Dana was touched, but after we kissed good night, there was an unspoken awkwardness.

Neither of us had mentioned the fact that it was four days before Christmas and we hadn't made any specific plans.

She drove off into the night, the exhaust from her car leaving ghostly swirls in the cold air. As my eyes followed her car, they fell on another vehicle parked on the other side of the street. It was a dark colored Range Rover, like the one I'd chased the night of the Breckenridges' fire, and there were men huddled in front, maybe in back, too. I felt cold all of a sudden, cold with fear. I managed to stare at them to let them know I knew they were there, then turned and hurried inside.

I grabbed my mail—the usual number of bills and solicitations from credit card and long-distance phone companies—and hustled inside my apartment. There was a note from Darryl saying he was suspicious of Beckwith, convinced he was being set up again by a lawyer. I crumpled it up and threw it against the wall, then, since I couldn't call the cops, I called Mimi D'Angelo.

"It's Billy. Can you get me a gun?"

"You on a cell phone?"

"No. Can you?"

"Use a gun, go to prison."

"Cute, Mimi, but I'm expecting company."

"Grab a pencil, hotshot, 'cause this may be too complicated for your mind to remember. Ready? 9-1-1."

"Dammit Mimi, can you or can't you? There are guys parked out front who must think I've got the Klinehart documents. What does that tell you?"

"That I should have stuck with something safe, like driving a cab in the Bronx?"

"What it tells you, Mimi, is that the papers we need are still out there, maybe in Barney's car which you keep on not finding. Now how about the gun?"

"How soon is this particular item required?"

"Tonight. Now."

Silence.

"Can't that soon, but I'll do the best I can."

"Don't come to the front. Drive into the alley behind my apartment house. Toss it up onto the low roof covering the trash bins in back and call me on your cell."

"Shall I wear a mask and my Avenger decoder signet ring?"

"A black cape will do."

"Exciting," she said.

"Yeah," I said. "Exciting."

"Oh, yeah, some good news," she said. "I *am* closing in on the car, thank you. It was sold out of probate. Trouble is there ain't nothin in the inventory but a flashlight, first aid kit, tire iron and jack, some pens, and some diet pills."

"Useless."

"Yeah, I hear he was still fat when he was dropped."

"I mean the inventory. Dammit, Mimi, the papers have got to be in that car. Where's it at?"

"In Union City, south of Oakland."

"Will the guy sell it?"

"On the phone he wants thirty eight hundred dollars. I'll get him down. Blue book's thirty-two fifty."

"Do the best you can, but buy it. Park it somewhere quiet, and we'll go tear it apart."

"Cool."

"Mimi?"

"Yeah?"

"You be careful, okay?"

She chuckled. "That's a good one comin from a guy under siege lookin to score hardware."

I awoke the next morning, grateful to be alive. The Range Rover was still there, blue—definitely the one at the burning Breckenridge house. So considering what these guys were capable of, I decided I'd better stay put in my apartment, hole up until necessity forced me outside. I told Dana to cover for me at the office, then instructed Barbara that if anyone asked for me I was home packing boxes for the movers. She reminded me the office was closing at noon.

"Closing?"

"Hellowww? Earth to Billy. It's the Friday before Christmas." She sang a few lines from "Here Comes Santa Claus." "What and how much did *you* have to drink last night?"

I thanked her for the reminder, and she rattled off several messages, including one that shot electric needles up my neck into the back of my head.

"A young-sounding female cop called. Wants to make an appointment for you to bring your car in. Something to do with a murder investigation."

So Jaxon was getting warm. "When?"

"Soon as possible. She emphasized that it was routine. You're one of five other drivers being asked to cooperate."

I took in a breath, told Barbara to phone the cop back and tell her I was in New York City for the holidays, but due back right after the first, and I'd come in right after I landed. She agreed, and I signed off. The net was closing on me, but the trial would soon be under way, and after my testimony was in, I'd face the music.

I spent the day sleeping, reading, and talking on the phone—a half-dozen calls on projects for various partners, a message to Mimi asking where "the item" was, two brief conversations with Dana, four long ones with Doug Beckwith, and one with Mace, checking whether anyone was cruising around my office.

"Are you in trouble, Billy?" he asked, and I could picture his thin face dark with worry.

"No, what makes you think so?"

"People are talking, that's all. They're concerned that if a hot ticket like you can get fired, who's next? They think maybe you're back in some kind of trouble with the law. Are you?"

"I'm fine, Mace," I lied. "We've been through this. It was a square-peg-round-hole situation at S & S."

"Peg? Hole? A sex scandal, huh? I thought so."

"When do you fly home, Mace?"

"Red eye tonight."

"Happy Hanukkah."

"Shalom, big guy."

Necessity forced me out of my lair the next day. I had rationed the last two pieces of bread and cheese in the house throughout the day and was starving. The Rover was still out front, so I waited until it was dark, then raced down the back fire escape, jogged across the small yard, checked the trash bin roof (no gun), climbed over the six-foot solid wooden fence, and dropped down into the back alley. There was a mom-and-pop grocery store three blocks away that would have everything I needed.

Twenty minutes later I walked out with three frozen chicken pasta dinners, a loaf of bread, assorted fresh fruit, a hunk of Monterey Jack cheese, some cereal, milk, four ready-made sandwiches, and an expensive bottle of Sequoia Grove Cabernet. Hell, it was almost Christmas.

Ever cautious, I circled back to my apartment the long way, up Taylor to Pine Street, then east three blocks until I was sure I wasn't being followed, then back up Bush Street and a right turn that led me to the opposite end of the alley I'd left from.

The fog had rolled in, shielding the crescent moon's dim glow, giving new meaning to the words "dark alley." The street light would give me less than thirty feet of courage, then I'd be on my own in semi-darkness without a flashlight. I'd considered entering from the front of the apartment house on Bush Street, but had spotted the glow of a cigarette in the driver's side of the Range Rover on my pass up Taylor. There was nobody in the passenger seat or in back, which could be good news—meaning he was alone—or very bad news—meaning he had company and they were out covering both ends of the alley.

Cars were randomly parked along the left side of the alley, so I started up the right side and in five seconds was swallowed up in darkness. Christ, it was quiet. Then, about fifty feet into the alley, something moved directly off to my left. A rustling sound. In the dark my ears seemed hypersensitive, but I heard nothing more except for a dog somewhere in the next block and a TV from the house behind me. I decided that whatever it was had taken off, probably either a cat or a raccoon.

I continued on for another ten feet when I heard something else behind me, and this time it was the unmistakable sound of footsteps. And *shit*, they were closing hard on me. I spun around, and there he was, the swarthy man, boldly walking toward me with what looked to be the outline of a smile on his face and a cop's nightstick in his hand. A thin ray of hope: Could he be a plainclothes?

No. Cops rarely emerge from behind cars or a bank of trash cans or run from the scene of an arson fire, and plainclothes don't carry clubs. They also ID themselves. This was one of the bad guys.

In the semidarkness, he looked bigger than I remembered him, though I still had plenty of height and reach on him. But the adrenaline rush that lit up my bloodstream didn't obscure the more important difference between us, which was that he held a club in his hand, while I was wielding a bag of groceries.

As he came to within five feet of me, he bent his knees slightly and began slapping the club against the palm of his left hand. I considered dropping the groceries and running for it, but I figured there had to be at least one of them at the other end of the alley where they had expected me. I'd have to get past him, back to the street where I'd just come from, then run for it.

"You wanna do this hard or easy?" he said with a heavy East Coast accent, a Pesci voice surprisingly high-pitched.

"Do what?" I said. "Who are you?" As I backpedaled away from him, I reached into my bag of groceries and frantically groped with my right hand for the neck of the wine bottle. My fingers closed around it just as he raised the hand holding the nightstick. I let the rest of the groceries fall to the ground and went into a wrestler's crouch, holding the bottle over my head, my left hand extended in front of me.

He laughed at me. "Red or white," he said, "I can't tell in this light."

"Come any closer you're going to find out," I said. He chuckled again at my bravado and suddenly my face was stung by shattered glass and I was holding the neck of a broken bottle in my bleeding hand. I felt the cool, sticky cabernet running down my face and neck, and my eyes were burning from wine or glass or both. Jesus. I swear the guy had hardly moved. The baton had been a blur. This man was a professional.

"I was curious, dat's all," he said, not even breathing hard. "It's a red. A very nice color on you, incidentally."

All I could think about was that the bottle could have been my head. I shuffled sideways—but he did, too. I was quick—but he was, too.

I extended my arm straight out with the broken bottle, pointing it at his face. I decided I would feint a thrust to his head, then try to dart around him and make for the street. He was probably carrying a gun, but that was a chance I'd have to take. I began moving my head and shoulders from side to side like an Egyptian dancer, holding his eyes with mine, the broken glass circling the outline of his face.

"Street fighta, heh? That's cute, Billy, dat's real cute."

I took the first blow from the nightstick on my right shoulder, but managed to duck under and smash him in the gut with my left fist. It was like hitting a tractor tire. I tried to come down on him with the jagged remains of the bottle in my right hand, but he easily danced out of the way, graceful for a stocky man. Before I could recover my balance, he delivered a glancing blow to the left side of my head that set my ear to ringing and impaired my balance. At the same time, I felt a slashing shot to my rib cage. It must have been a backhand. The damn club was a blur, like two guys were on me.

"Wheh aw dey?" he said, but I was breathing too hard to answer even if I'd wanted to. Besides, I was thinking survival, not twenty questions.

It finally dawned on me that I was in a populated neighborhood, and I began shouting dumb things like, "Call 911!" and "Need help!" all the time crouched and looking for an opening back into the street. I noticed lights popping on in a couple of houses and figured if I could somehow survive for another few minutes, I'd hear sirens.

"*Wheh awda goddam papehs?*" he said.

"I don't have them," I gasped, then jabbed the glass toward his head as menacingly as I could. He easily sidestepped my wild lunge, passed the baton into his left hand and launched it toward my head. I blocked the blow with my right arm, felt a sharp pain below the elbow, and heard something pop I knew wasn't the nightstick. I was down to one arm and Jesus, here came the club again. I managed to move my head out of the way and took another hit to the right shoulder that would have fragmented my skull. The pain shot down into my disabled right arm, nearly knocking me out. My attempt to thrust the broken bottle into his stomach missed by six inches, partly because my hand had gone weak.

I decided it was time to take my chances up the alley, since the only parts of my body still working were my legs. But Swarthy Man took care of that next, with a horizontal shot as if he was swinging a baseball bat at a sinker. It caught me in the left knee and knocked me off my feet.

I scrambled up and staggered backwards, but he was at me again, expertly flipping the baton from hand to hand, feinting to his left, then right, then left again while my throbbing head lolled back and forth on my neck like a drunk, trying to stay focused on him. Then he stood upright and turned, and I thought he was finished with me. I straightened, too, but he suddenly spun around and sent his foot crashing into the right side of my head.

I was back on the ground.

"Last chance, Billy-boy," he said. *"Wheh's da fuckin documents?"*

"I haven't got them," I muttered, my voice weak and hoarse as I struggled back to my feet. As I rose, I remembered that night in the laundry at Soledad and grabbed up some dirt in my left hand.

That's when I vaguely heard the beautiful music of sirens, lots of sirens, though maybe too late for me, for the kick-blow had me dizzy, nauseated, and disoriented. I was ready to try something different, so when he raised his arm again and I saw the baton come flying toward me, instead of backing off as I'd been doing, I threw the dirt at his eyes, heard him gasp with surprise, and propelled myself forward, under his wild thrust. Hands gouging at his eyes, he stumbled toward me, and we toppled to the ground with him on top. He had dropped the club, so I rolled out from under him and picked it up. He was still down, so I raised the baton and started to come down with it, but noticed that he was still on the ground, in a sitting position, paying me no attention, one eye popped wide open in amazement.

"You . . . son-of-a-bitch," he said, not looking at me, "you stupid shithead . . ."

He was staring down at his stomach, holding what appeared to be the neck of the wine bottle. I watched as he grabbed it with both hands and pulled six inches of glass shard out of his stomach. But as the glass came out, so did blood, spurting like a broken fuel line, and now his face was as red and sticky as mine. He looked up at me then, batting his eyes from the dirt, and realized I had his baton.

I reached down and grabbed him by the front of his shirt. "Who," I said, "are you working for?"

He gave me a strange, ugly smile. "You don't need . . . to club me, asshole . . . dumb fuck . . . You awready fuckin killed me."

I looked down at him and could barely make out in the darkness that the hands pressed against his stomach were awash in blood, blood everywhere, flowing onto the dirt floor of the alley.

The sirens were getting close, no more than a block away.

"Don't give up," I said, and pulled his shirt out of his belt to get a look at his wound. He tried to push me away, but I took off my coat and pulled my T-shirt off, then pressed it into the wound. "Hold on, they're here in less than a minute. They'll get you to a hospital. Pull the shirt hard against you, okay? Both hands. *Pressure*, that's the way."

"Fuck you . . . kid . . . fucking dumb-shit asshole . . ."

"Don't talk," I said, "except for telling me who hired you. *Tell me who hired you.*"

He was fading fast. "Hold on," I shouted into his ear.

"Too late," he whispered.

"No, you'll make it, unless I pull my shirt out of that hole in your gut."

"You don't . . . have the . . ."

I gave the shirt a little jerk, but couldn't really pull it.

"Was it Hale Lassiter?"

He was losing consciousness fast. "Who?"

The sound of the sirens was on top of us now, and when I saw the beam of the first car's headlights bouncing up the street, I knew I had to run for it. I snatched up my jacket and limped away as fast as I could, my right arm hanging limply at my side. I was halfway down the alley when the cruiser, lights blazing, entered the alley from the same direction I had. They stopped to help the fallen assailant, so I was able to run the last thirty feet to the rear of my apartment house. Swarthy Man must have indicated my route, because the last thing I saw as I made it over the fence was the cop's spotlight shooting up the alley where I had been two seconds before.

I lay on the other side of the fence, facedown, panting into the damp ground, trying to keep myself conscious. Lights were coming on everywhere, and I knew I had to make it back inside my apartment before people started coming out.

But I had to check one more thing first. I reached up onto the roof covering the bank of trash cans, and, bless Mimi's brazen heart, my fingers closed around the barrel of a gun. Next to it was a box of shells.

I shoved the prizes into my pockets and lurched across the backyard. My head, arm, and shoulder were killing me, but there was no time to think about that. There would be police, an investigation, and I didn't need any more attention from the police right now.

I made it in the back door and to my apartment, grateful that Mrs. Alvarez across the hall was listening to her TV through the headphones I had set her up with last month. But then I saw that my door was partly open. Not again, I thought, though even Jaxon would be a welcome change from a friend of Swarthy Man. I flipped the switch on the overhead light but nothing happened. I closed and dead-bolted the door in the dark, then stumbled around the room until I found a floor lamp. Nobody there.

The place had been trashed, totally torn apart, the couch cushions slashed, drawers pulled out and emptied onto the floor, books pulled off shelves, refrigerator contents splattered across the kitchen floor. Even the ceiling light had been pulled down and lay shattered on the ancient oval rug in the center of the room. I killed the floor light. If the police did a door-to-door, I wasn't going to be home.

In the dark, I saw my message light blinking. It was Mimi about the gun. And Dana. Call me.

"It's me," I whispered twenty minutes later, after I'd cleaned myself up, put on a shirt, and wrapped some ice around my right arm that didn't appear to be broken, thank God.

"I was worried about you," Dana said. "I thought you were going to keep yourself under lock and key."

"Hunger prevailed. Had a visitor while I was out."

"Why are you whispering?"

I told her everything. Almost everything.

"Billy, they might have killed you if you had walked in on them!"

"If they wanted me dead," I said, "they wouldn't have sent a man with a stick. He didn't kill me because they hadn't yet found what they came for."

I listened to the uncomfortable silence as the implication of what I had said burrowed into its unwanted host. Not that Dana was slow. Nobody was quicker at conceptualizing complex issues than Dana Mathews, and nobody could make it look easier. I've read that Joe DiMaggio could make playing center field look easy because he got a jump on the ball before it even left the bat. That was Dana. Her problem was not what it meant, but how to deal with it, with me.

Then she said it. "All right, Billy, I'll return the lighter. I'm so sorry."

"It's documents, not the lighter they're looking for. Hale hasn't even missed it. But if you're really sorry, give it to *me*."

"We've been through that Billy, and—"

"I'm sure now that Ashton's in it, too, Dana."

"Why do you think that?"

"Because I think Hale is trying to save my life by shipping me off to New York, and I don't think the guy who attacked me even knew who Hale was. That leaves Ashton, the other guy who lent five million dollars to Stanton and Snow. Hale and Ashton are in it together."

"But Hale *hates* Ashton, and Ashton would do *anything* to keep Synoptics money coming in. Maybe Ashton's protecting Moncrief, and *they* are in it together."

"Well, I've got nothing on Ashton."

"Or on Hale either," she said. "So aren't we back to Moncrief?"

Suddenly I was angry. My body ached, and I felt a covey of flushed quail whirring around in my chest.

"I've nothing on Hale because you won't give it to me," I shouted into the phone, then slammed it down and it fell out of the cradle and I grabbed it and slammed it down again.

She waited twenty minutes for me to cool down before calling me back. "What are we going to do?" she said. I could tell she'd been crying.

"Well, while you decide whose side you're on, I'm getting out of Dodge before they kill me."

"Now? Tonight? I'll come take you to the airport."

"No. I'm staying put tonight. When I do go into the office, I'll tell Hale I was burgled over the weekend and let it be known I'm leaving for New York for good before the trial starts. Maybe they'll let me go."

"Why do you think they will let you—"

"Because I'll be confirming that I'm leaving town, that I'm no longer a danger to them."

"But your testimony—"

"I'll go to the airport on Friday and go through the motions of checking in—just in case they're checking up—then hop another cab and double back into town for my testimony. The flight will leave without me just as the trial is starting. It's all set with Beckwith. He'll put me on first. Once my story is public, there's no more need for them to get me out of the way. It will be too late."

"I'm coming over."

"No way. They've got this place watched front and back. If they come back again tonight, it'll be nasty."

"You going to hit them over the head with a briefcase?"

"I've got company."

"What?"

"Couple of guys named Smith and Wesson."

"You've got a *gun*? My God, Billy, you've got to get out of there."

"I know it. As soon as daylight comes, I'll lose them and check into a flea-bite hotel somewhere in the Tenderloin where neither Ashton nor the cops can find me."

"Come over here, Billy; they won't look for you here."

"They might follow me. I won't take that chance."

Silence.

"Sorry about Christmas," I said. "Got you a couple of dumb blouses in New York."

"And I have a sweater for you. We'll have our Christmas later."

"Later."

"How bad is your apartment?"

"I think the photographers from *Architectural Digest* and *House Beautiful* will be sorely disappointed."

I listened to a few seconds of silence, then, "I love you, Billy, and I'm sorry about . . . everything."

"I love you too, Dana. It's tough times."

"Yes," she said. "Tough times."

I opened the last Sierra Nevada ale in my fridge and sat in the dark staring at the door I don't know how long until I heard a pounding on it and across the hall at the same time. Must be two of them, canvassing the neighborhood.

"Police. Open the door please."

More pounding, then Mrs. Alvarez's voice from across the hall. I crept closer to my door, put my ear to it.

"Did you hear anything, ma'am?"

"Hear anything?"

"A man's been killed, ma'am. Did you hear anything?"

I could hear her door opening and the frustration of two tired cops dealing with a deaf woman with earphones on her head.

"Who was he?" she shouted.

"Man had no ID. We're working on it."

"He's *dead*?" she repeated.

Silence—the cops probably nodding.

"Oh, my," she said, and I could picture her doing signs of the cross, one after the other, as she murmured a prayer for the faithful departed.

I swung away from the voices and fell onto my slashed-up sofa.

*   *   *

I'm not sure how long I lay there. I know I got up after the cops had left, set the dead bolt and chain, and checked my .38. It felt comfortable in my hand, like an old friend. I spun the cylinders, saw a shell in each chamber. I took the safety off, wondering what it would be like to be free of the turmoil I had brought down on myself and others. Not that I had any intention of shooting myself, but in those awful hours, I did begin to understand why people—even sane people—did it. Things got out of balance to where the fear of dying was overwhelmed by the pain of living. I cocked the hammer; then I eased it back down, turned the lights back out, and angled the couch so that it faced the door.

And waited for daylight to come.

37

I woke up still alive, but not much grateful about it. It was 7:25 A.M., and sunlight was already seeping through the cheap curtains covering my single living room window, filling the room with a dull light. The knowledge of what I had done the previous night was there, too, right where it had been before sleep had granted me a temporary parole. Other visions crept in through my half-open eyelids, the tore-up cushions underneath me, my stuff thrown every which way.

Suddenly awake, I wanted to scream out loud, but held it in. My right arm was a dismal rainbow of dark colors. It hurt like hell, but the physical pain was an almost welcome distraction from my dark thoughts. I stood up, but felt dizzy, then nauseated, and barely made it to the bathroom in time. When I was finished, I dropped to my knees and vomited again, and then again, and sat on the bathroom floor with my back against the tub. Out in the hall and on the second floor above me, I could hear doors opening and closing, footsteps, the sounds of a new day.

The gun!

I staggered back into the living room, and there it was on the floor where it had fallen when I fell asleep. I picked it up and put the safety on.

The effort had made me dizzy again, so I sat myself down on the remains of the sofa and took inventory of my current situation. Put simple, I'd set in motion the deaths of Barney Klinehart and Sheila Anderson, just killed a man with my own hands, the cops were closing in on me, and Darryl's trial was commencing in six days, the same day I was expected in New York. Add to that, a body that felt like it had come out second best in a bear fight.

Part of me felt like curling up on that ratty couch and sleeping for about 190 hours, but deep down I knew that nobody was going to put my world back together but me.

I made some coffee, then took a shower and dressed as best I could with my aching right arm all bruised and swollen. The nightstick had maybe dented it, but since I could move my fingers, I figured it wasn't too serious. My face looked like a mile or two of bad road. I wrote a check for Mr. Bharani to cover the cost of fixing or replacing his furniture in case he got nosy, then tossed some clothes and toilet articles into a small bag. I hung my most sincere suit—a navy blue number with thin white vertical lines—a white shirt, and tie on a hanger for court on Friday.

When I was ready, I called a cab, knowing I wouldn't dare try to start my car in the back. I tucked the Smith and Wesson behind me under my belt and told the cabby I'd give him a fifty for taking me ten blocks if he could first lose the Range Rover up the street.

Twenty-five blocks, four alleys, and two blown red lights later, my driver said, "We're clean," and entered San Francisco's Tenderloin District, passed Cecil Williams's Glide Memorial Church on Ellis, turned, cruised by a small park that appeared to be fenced and shut down at night to discourage the free marketing of drugs, then pulled up in front of a broken building on Eddy Street's poverty row with a sign in front that proclaimed it to be the Premier Hotel. The owner had to have a sense of humor.

I glanced around as a wino in worse shape than me tried to clean the taxi's windshield and spotted a pair of hookers near the front entrance. An eclectic mix of tenants eyed me furtively from the small lobby through a street-side window. Patrons of the Premier were probably more often delivered in police vans than taxicabs.

On the plus side, the Premier offered a bargain rate of twenty-eight dollars a night, and was the last place on earth somebody would look for a Montgomery Street lawyer. The clerk accepted my false name without so much as a wink or a request for a credit card. On the counter was a cluster of small, slightly brown-crusted apples in an unraveling basket.

Entering my room on the third floor, I saw why no credit card imprint was necessary. There were no services to charge: no honor bar, TV, room service, or even an in-room phone. But it was bigger than my cell in Shasta B at Soledad, and it was all mine.

After I'd rested for a few minutes in my shoe box of a room on a swaybacked twin bed with a tick mattress and no box springs, I went to a mirror and surveyed the damage. My left leg was badly bruised from Swarthy's final blow, and my right arm was throbbing in sympathetic rhythm with my head. A deep cut under my hairline showed no sign of infection, but the bump surrounding it was the size of a lemon. A bruise was blossoming on the other side of my face. I cleaned up the cut as best I could, then fell back onto—actually into—the mattress, and, despite the powerful smell of must and mildew from the pillow, and aching flash intrusions from Dana, Joe Strobe, Hale, Moncrief, and Swarthy Man, I managed to fall into a deep sleep.

I slept on and off throughout the day and the next night, too. I finally got up around noon on Monday and saw that the fog was still holding the sun at bay. When I realized it was Christmas morning, I started crying and couldn't stop.

I pulled myself together and made some instant coffee with a plug-in water heater I'd brought along. I breathed in the familiar smell as I ate another apple from the check-in counter. I had to break it up into small pieces to get it in my swollen mouth. Feeling better, I used my cell phone to leave a Christmas greeting on Dana's home answering machine. She and Sarah must have been at Mass. I told her I'd call her in a day or two and not to worry.

I went downstairs to rustle up a *Chronicle* and saw it there on page three of the late edition:

ASSASSIN FOUND SLAIN

The article said that the victim was Carlo Mastrani, aka Carl Hansen, age thirty-six, identified through FBI fingerprints. He was wanted by the FBI and three states for racketeering, kidnapping, and murder. Other than that, the police were mum, and I was relieved to see that the no-comment was issued by an inspector other than Jaxon. I probably should have been relieved to know that Swarthy Man was no great loss to society, but I wasn't.

It being Christmas, I decided to chance the outside and, after grabbing a muffin for breakfast, walked over to Glide Memorial to catch a Christmas service. I stood in back of the jammed church and prayed for forgiveness for what I'd done to Carlo Mastrani and for all my other fuckups. When I began to get dizzy, I hurried back to my room and slipped into another deep sleep.

Next thing I knew, it was Tuesday, and I'd gotten through my second worst Christmas in a row.

I had some coffee, checked my cuts and bruises again, and realized I'd have to lie low and heal up. I then faced my office voice mail, using my cell phone. Messages were lined up from Beckwith, Mimi, Mace, Dana, Lassiter, Ashton, and others, all in various stages of angst at not having talked to me. My first call was to Barbara, who, as usual, wanted to know where I was.

"Everybody's been looking for you. I heard Mr. Lassiter got so worried he sent someone to your apartment!"

He sent someone, all right, I felt like saying, but what I said was, "I'm fine, Barbara, but I won't be in for a few days. Fell off a porch and landed on my arm. Nothing serious, but it's doctor day."

"Will you be all right?" she said, sounding genuinely worried.

"It's okay. I'll be back in Thursday, then on to New York the following day. Pass that on to anybody looking for me."

My next call was to Beckwith to be sure everything was set for Friday.

"Christ, Strobe, I've been calling you. I've got *wonderful* news!"

Before I could apologize for being out of touch he babbled on. "It's the DNA! Ms. D'Angelo just delivered me a copy of the FBI lab report: a perfect match with Moncrief's. The son-of-a-bitch really killed her. You were right all along!"

"That's good news, Doug."

"Good? It's great! This case may be winnable now. Billy? *Strobe*—are you there?"

"Yes, Doug, I'm here. Sorry, my battery must be dying."

"Well? What do you think?"

My hand had gone cold on the phone. "I think—"

"Are you hearing me, man? We've got a *match*, for God's sake. I can destroy the bastard with this information."

"I'm sure you will," I said.

"You're not coming down with something, are you, Billy? I'm going to need you as a witness, you know."

"No, I'm fine. A little tired, that's all. I'll be ready. Still putting me on first?"

"You're my lead-off. Meet me at eight o'clock at Department 26. I may need some help with the client. He said he's been told by someone there that I'd been 'got to.' You may need to calm him down. He doesn't seem to trust me."

I said I'd talk to him.

"While on the subject of trust, are you aware that this D'Angelo character doesn't have the best rep in town? Who recommended her?"

"I don't recall," I said.

"Well, *entre nous,* Billy, this whole thing's a little . . . well, offbeat to say the least. Quite frankly, if you weren't at S & S, I'm not sure I'd be doing this."

I mumbled something reassuring.

"Anyway, not to worry about your testimony," he continued. "I'm going to take you through the things in your memo that aren't blatant hearsay. I'll give you a quick final prep in the morning, okay?"

"Sure," I said, thinking I should mention that I looked more like an injured auto accident plaintiff than a defense witness. Instead, I programmed more enthusiasm into my voice. "Eight sharp, Doug. Friday."

"Perfect, but keep after those documents. We're going to kill that fucking Moncrief on Friday, but we still need to connect him to the Hinton murder. Okay?"

"Sure thing," I said, then went into my bathroom and threw up again.

I wanted to call Dana, hear her voice. I knew she'd be worried, but if I called her, I'd end up begging for the lighter again and she'd say no and I'd get pissed off and there we'd be. Instead, I put a message on her voice mail at her office, telling her I was safe, that I loved her, and that I'd see her soon.

Next, I kept my departure charade alive by calling Vic James in New York to say I'd be flying out on Friday. I knew it would get back to Hale.

I hung out in my room all day, reading and fighting depression. When loneliness became unbearable, I'd dial up Dana's voice mail message just to hear her voice: *Hello, this is Dana Mathews. I'm away from my desk right now, so please leave a message.*

I must have played the damn thing ten times during the longest day of my life.

By Wednesday afternoon, I was starting to get into the rhythm of doing nothing, and it wasn't so bad. It was a little like prison, long boring hours interrupted by interludes of high anxiety. I had walked after lunch among the pimps, whores, addicts, and regular folks down on their luck, enjoying the anonymity, checking out spots where I could rent office space for next to nothing, but mainly keeping to myself. I read, listened to street music, stayed out of the way. I called Beckwith several times to see if he had any questions. Dana left worried messages on my office machine, and I left reassuring messages back.

When Thursday arrived, I visited Darryl at the Hall of Justice.

"Good to see you, kid, though you ain't as pretty as you once was," he said, looking a little jumpy. "Get crosswise with your girl again?"

"Sure," I said, "that's it."

"How's things look otherwise?"

"Everything's fine," I said. "You ready to deal with life on the outside?"

He smiled and nodded furiously. "Sounds like you got your daddy's confidence. I hope this Beckwith's got your daddy's skill."

"Don't talk to me about Joe Strobe," I said, and it all came pouring out. Somewhere during my rambling tirade I told him how I'd figured out that *The Verdict* had been Joe Strobe's favorite movie because the movie depicted a vulnerable system easily manipulated: a trial judge bought and paid for by James Mason's big firm, a defense lawyer breaking into a mailbox for evidence (a federal felony), and slipping money to a mortician for allowing him to solicit bereaved widows (a violation of the canon of ethics and grounds for disbarment). And we all sat there loving it, the whole damn country.

"How the hell you find out about your daddy, kid?"

I explained what had happened in Enid, and he told me he was sorry, that he was sure a lot of good had come out of my dad's work anyways. I apologized for burdening him with my problems and reviewed what Beckwith had told me was going to happen in court.

"You sure about this Beckwith fella?" Darryl said.

"Sure as rain," I said. "You've got nothing to worry about."

It was unlike Darryl to be so nervous, and I figured it was the anxiety that is often the price of true hope. Darryl Orton was sensing the possibility of freedom.

An hour later, I boldly strode into the lobby of the Western Bank Building, with hardly a limp, then up to the top floor, knowing my presence would be reported to Hale. I looked okay, except for the scab on my head that my hair was still too short to cover. My arm was feeling almost normal.

Daniel back in the lion's den.

Mace Rothschild spotted me first. "You look bruised but rested," he said, in a slightly accusatory tone. Looking rested at S & S was a misdemeanor, probably grounds for discharge.

"Just came in to say good-bye, Scarecrow. I took that job in Manhattan."

"You bastard," he said, making a face. "Moving to God's country,

leaving me here in the untamed West to deal with all these cultural sav-
ages?"

"Think of my leaving as one less savage," I said, returning his
handshake. "Come visit me, Scarecrow, okay?"

"How did you get that cut on your head?"

"Fell off my back porch."

"And your arm? When we shook hands, you winced."

"Tried to break my fall."

Mace gave me a raised eyebrow look to remind me he hadn't come
into town on the last load of lox and bagels.

"Does your apartment house even have a back porch?" He didn't
wait for my next lie. "Never mind, masked man. E-mail me your home
phone when you get settled in New York, and I'll be on your doorstep
before you know it."

"You'll have it. You've been a good friend, Mace."

He self-consciously put his thin arms around me, and I hugged him
back. "Take care, big guy," he said, then hurried out.

The tom-toms were working, and Hale asked me to stop by. I put
the last of my things in a briefcase and headed for his office.

"Billy! What happened to your head?"

"Some guy mugged me on my way back from the grocery store last
week," I said, watching his face closely. "Tried to kill me actually."

"That can't be, Billy!" Hale said, his expression both confused and
angry. "It . . . it just-can't-*be!*"

Hale had completely lost his poker face, revealing too much surprise to be faking it. So it *was* Ashton, and Ashton probably wasn't
telling Hale what he was doing.

"Yeah, they tore my place apart. Guess they thought I had money
hidden somewhere."

"It's not safe anywhere anymore," Hale said, the trial lawyer back
in control. "I've been calling you at your place every day, even sent a
messenger. Are you all right?"

"Sure. I've been cleaning up details around town."

"And now you're cleaning out your desk?"

"Yep, I leave tomorrow on the nine a.m. to JFK."

Hale didn't seem surprised. He and Ashton had probably checked.
I had made it easy for them by buying a ticket through the firm's ticket
agent.

"That's good," he said, "though you must know your friend's new
trial starts tomorrow. Jason's been subpoenaed again by the DA."

"The conspiracy theory."

"I know, it's ridiculous. Moncrief wants me there in case the judge

lets your Mr. Beckwith go crazy, though frankly I wouldn't mind seeing Moncrief's fine feathers ruffled a bit."

"You may get to see that, Hale."

"Well, if Beckwith is as competent as he usually is, he'll point the
finger at the guy who made money on the scam and perhaps stir up
some reasonable doubt as to your friend."

Where was Hale going with this? Be careful, Billy.

"And you're supposed to protect Moncrief so that doesn't happen?
That sounds like fun."

He shook his head wearily. "Whose bread I eat, his song I sing. On
the other hand, Billy, as you've figured out over the months you've
been here, Jason Moncrief is not one of my favorite people. In point of
fact, the man is rude, amoral, cheats in his business dealings, treats his
people like dirt, and deserves whatever Beckwith does to him."

"Other than that—"

"I think he's swell."

I smiled and picked up my briefcase, ready to leave. "Well, Mr.
Orton is in good hands, and I'm out of it, as you know."

"Then may I assume," he said casually, rising to his feet, "that you
will be returning my cigarette lighter, Billy?"

My breath left me in an audible rush, and I felt a lump of molten
lead suddenly hardening in my gut. Hale was calling me out, here and
now. Well, why not? If he thought I had his damn lighter, maybe this
was as good a time as any.

"Sure I will," I said. "When you're ready to admit the truth about
Deborah's murder."

"The truth?" he said, then clasped both hands behind his back,
turned, and stared out the window. It was raining, as bleak outside as
it had suddenly become in Hale's office. "The 'truth,' Billy, is that I've
been your protector since the minute you began nosing around in this
thing. The 'truth' is that I'm still trying to save your life."

"My *life*?" Warning bells were going off in my head. I knew this
was a time for caution, but I was tired and angry and . . .

"Yes, Billy. We've been on the same side here on the Orton matter—"

"The only 'side' I'm on is Darryl Orton's."

"Which is precisely why you need protection. Listen to me, son.
When you began learning things, Rex and I made a deal. I would not
blow the whistle on what he'd done, and he would leave you alone.
Why do you think I contrived to send you away to New York? Got you
that job?"

"Because Ashton was reneging on your deal to 'leave me alone'?"

"I couldn't be sure. That's why I was so angry the day Orton
wouldn't let me argue his new trial motion. Rex and I had agreed that

I would argue the motion in a way that would ensure that we'd lose it, which would have put an end to your efforts as well as your danger. Little did that damn fool Orton know that by pushing you into arguing his appeal, he had pushed himself into a new trial and put you back at risk! Your unexpected victory raised the stakes for everyone, and I knew I'd have to get you out of town to protect you from Rex."

Out of town. It hit me then that I'd better be smart if I was to even get out of this building alive.

"Who's going to protect *you*, Hale? Have you thought about that? Ashton has proved himself capable of eliminating loose ends."

"Don't worry about me, Billy. He knows I'm too much a coward to come forward to the police, and too smart not to have made arrangements for things to come to light in the event of my death."

"Why are you telling me all this, Hale?"

"Because there's a way we can all walk away, even Orton. But I need your help. Sit down for a moment. Please."

"Let me guess," I said, as we sat side by side in client chairs in front of his desk. "You don't want me to give Beckwith the lighter, right? And you want me to instruct him to burn Moncrief instead of you?"

"You're correct as usual, Billy. To the head of the class."

"What would Rex Ashton think if he heard you suggesting that we crucify his buddy Moncrief?"

"He suggested it, Billy."

"What?"

"He despises Jason Moncrief."

"I don't buy it, Hale. Moncrief is Ashton's meal ticket."

"That's just it. Moncrief never lets him forget it. Rex Ashton is the smartest man I've ever met, Billy. It galls him that he has devoted his life to solving the problems of men he considers intellectually inferior, all of whom could buy and sell him. It's made him bitter, Billy, very bitter."

"That's crazy."

"Not entirely. I sometimes share his resentment, though it embarrasses me to admit it. Rex feels, with some justification, that lawyers from Montgomery Street to Wall Street are often little more than indentured servants to thoroughly undistinguished men—'entrepreneurs'—who often possess little more than a gift for making money. These ordinary merchants skirt the edges, then when they get in trouble, depend on smart, skilled professionals to pull their fat out of the fire. They openly label us their 'plumbers' and pay us an hourly rate while we watch their stock options shoot up into the hundreds of millions. I fear it has sent Rex over the edge."

"So he's willing to kill the golden goose?"

"If it will save himself and the firm, yes. Perhaps I need to step back a bit and explain how we reached this sorry pass."

"I'm listening," I said, though my brain was spinning and my legs had gone weak. I realized with a shudder of despair that I had naively held out hope that Hale would have an explanation for the lighter. I knew better now, but listened as he told me his story.

"The ship was sinking, Billy, one of the oldest and best firms on the West Coast, with me at the helm. The bank was calling the firm's loans, good partners and associates began leaving the firm and taking clients with them. Rex and I had lost our shirts in that damned hotel computer venture. Everything was coming apart. Then Rex came up with the bailout idea."

"You're referring," I said, "to the insider trading scam?"

"Have it your way," he said, managing a wry smile, "you're an expert in that particular field yourself, as I recall. At all events, my main part in the 'scam' would be to persuade Deborah to defer the write-off. I would also provide an absurdly optimistic legal opinion for the Synoptics quarterly report regarding a case against Microsoft for allegedly stealing proprietary secrets. We would indirectly acquire Synoptics stock through a nominee on margin, the shares would soar; then we would short the stock and save Stanton and Snow with loans from our ill-gotten profits. Rex and I would live out our miserable lives in relative comfort on the monthly loan repayments from the firm.

"I told Rex the idea was ludicrous, of course, but on reflection, it appeared to be an easy way out for everybody. And it *was* easy—until we began to run into problems. The SEC began snooping around, owing to Jason's regrettable and quite coincidental acquisition of stock and Deborah's own secret transactions, feathering her own nest without our knowledge."

"A nest," I said quietly, "for the unborn child you had fathered?"

He winced, turned away from me, fingers interlocked behind his head like a prisoner. He looked out the window again. "I can't expect you to understand, Billy. I'm not sure I do myself. What you don't know is that Laura suffers from clinical depression, literally surviving on pharmaceuticals, crying one minute, screaming at me the next. God knows I love her, but she's been . . . incredibly difficult to live with the past few years.

"Anyway, Deb and Rex had worked together for some time, and he introduced us. Deb was bored in her marriage, and I was in agony in mine, and well, it just . . . happened."

Ashton the matchmaker. The man could have manipulated Machiavelli out of his vineyards.

"I kept trying to break it off, but Deborah had fallen in love, and I was weak. I suppose we had also become bonded somewhat by the exigencies of our unsavory little business enterprise. It was stressful, of course. I was living a double life well beyond my means, and Laura was getting suspicious. Next came the snooping by the SEC, then the bombshell: Deb announced that she was pregnant."

"This seems to be a pattern in your life, Hale," I said, watching him carefully.

His head snapped around as if I'd hit him in the face. "She *told* you?"

I nodded. "I know about Sarah."

"Oh, God, Billy," he said, leaning and sinking into his chair, "what you must think of me."

"Never mind what I think," I said, laying my briefcase on his desk. "What happened next?"

Hale clamped his eyes shut, pushing one painful memory out, only to invite another back in. "Deb insisted on having the child. Ultimately, she even threatened to expose everything if I didn't divorce Laura and *marry* her. Then, as if things were not dicey enough, Jason, hearing that his stepson had made large profits on the run-up—also coincidental—panicked, and told me he was going to give Deborah up to the SEC to save the company and himself. That's when Rex and I panicked, too. Things were piling up."

I leaned toward him. "Deborah had to go."

He nodded sadly.

"And you were elected?"

He shook his head as if dodging bees. "Don't be absurd, Billy! I had no idea that Rex planned to . . ."

He squeezed his eyes shut against the memory forcing its way out, while I sat, transfixed, wishing to God I was wired like I'd been with Frank Hinton.

"That he planned to kill her?" I said.

"He told me we needed to reason together, the three of us, so we scheduled a meeting. She was getting paranoid by then and insisted the meeting be held in her office at Synoptics. Rex immediately incited a fight between Deb and me—he knew she was pregnant—then I became angry at Rex and . . . well, it became a melee, sheer bedlam, Deborah threatening me and at one point reaching for the phone to call 911 to 'blow the whistle on all of us.' She might have been bluffing, I don't know. Anyway, I grabbed the phone and nearly struck her with it."

He paused, seemingly out of breath, reliving the incident.

"Then Rex *did* strike her. His fist came out of nowhere, from behind me. She fell backwards, hit her head on the edge of a file cabinet. I watched in horror then as Rex finished her with the paperweight."

"Did he also . . ."

"Rape her?" Hale shook his head again. "I left, but I'm quite sure necrophilia is not among Rex's pathologies. Based on the autopsy, however, I suspect that he used means intended to make rape appear to be a possible motive."

"It appears he thought of everything."

Hale nodded, and said, "When he took out the little plastic bag with your friend's hair, I knew his plan had been to goad me into killing Deborah, then to do it himself if I didn't."

"But you said nothing afterward. You went along."

He stared into his hands. "He threatened to tell Laura everything, even about Dana, which would have killed Laura. I can't have her hurt more, Billy. She above everyone here is innocent."

He looked away from me, but not before I saw his eyes were wet with tears.

"Rex knows everything about Dana," Hale said, his voice gravelly with despair. "There was a time when he and I were friends."

"How did Sheila Anderson get involved?"

"Rex brought Sheila into the picture because she had no association with Synoptics or our firm—thus couldn't be deemed an inside trader—and because she was brainy, yet brash enough to go for the brass ring. Neither Deborah nor Sheila knew about the other."

I tried to steady myself, use my head. I'd be no good to Darryl if I didn't get out of this building in one piece.

"I take it you won't put all this on the record, Hale?"

"You know I can't do that. I was there. I'd be admitting my own complicity."

"As an accomplice?"

He turned toward me, his face a mask of despair. "No, of course not. As an accessory after the fact. You must believe I had no knowledge of what Rex was going to do."

He pressed his face into his hands for what seemed like several minutes, as if everything would be gone when he uncovered his eyes. Despite myself, a small part of my heart went out to this man I had loved and admired.

"But her death was convenient for you, wasn't it," I said, pleased with the coldness I heard in my voice, "what with the pregnancy and all?"

"Convenient," he murmured, nibbling at the knuckles of his clenched fingers, his lips trembling. This was a man at the end of his tether. My self-proclaimed protector could barely deal with his own conscience.

"So who killed Sheila, and why? And Barney Klinehart?"

He managed a deathly grin. "You did, Billy, in a way. You see, we thought our problems were resolved, with Deborah dead and Orton off in prison somewhere. Then you came along. Later, for what it's worth, when we saw you were getting close, I considered giving it all up, as I said before, admitting everything. Rex told me to relax, that Sheila would go underground and, as 'Betty Perkins,' would keep an eye on you, perhaps even succeed in discouraging your 'fool's errand.' "

I felt a rush of anger at Ashton for having lured Betty into his deadly game.

"Rex told me to relax again after he had Klinehart killed—he used a professional assassin I knew only as Carl and never met—then reassured me again after Sheila's murder. Good old Rex, the king of rationalization, always grinning his little fox smile and telling me to stay calm.

"It was intolerable, yet I tolerated it. Whenever he had somebody killed, I would *want* to do the right thing, believe me, Billy, but Rex would convince me it was *really* over this time and that we were safe. Then he'd remind me that revealing the truth wouldn't bring the victim back, and that the firm would never survive a scandal such as would doubtlessly ensue. Hundreds of people out of work, et cetera. I was easily persuaded, I admit it."

"And now, Hale, it's you telling *me* to relax," I said, "that nothing good can come of *me* telling the truth."

"But it's true, Billy, can't you see? Everybody can still walk away. Alive."

"Sounds like a threat."

"You can't win, Billy. I'll continue to help all I can, but Rex has things arranged for you to take the fall on Sheila and even Klinehart if you don't play it his way. Believe me, he can do it."

"And he wants me to instruct Beckwith to hang Moncrief."

"Yes, and he wants me to help Beckwith do it. Look, Billy, I can't force you to give me the lighter, but if Beckwith uses it, I won't protect you. I've held Rex off this long by persuading him you're no longer a risk."

Play it cool, Okie, I thought. Back off and live to see another day.

"Well, like you say, I'm no longer a risk. I'm leaving town, remember?"

"Good, but I still need you to give me that lighter and your assurance that you'll instruct Beckwith to burn Moncrief."

"Just curious, but does your buddy Rex know you got a little sloppy with Deb's lighter, Hale?"

He was cool, I'll give him that much. Stood there holding my challenging gaze, not batting an eye.

"He doesn't know, does he." It wasn't a question.

Hale looked away then, and I knew something else. "And you're afraid of him, too, aren't you."

"This isn't getting us anywhere," Hale said. "The important thing is that we both walk away from this in one piece, Billy. That's why I've told you all this."

I rose, buttoned my jacket, and swung my briefcase off his desk. "Forget about the lighter; it's my protection. But like I said, I *am* walking away in one piece, all the way to New York City."

Hale's eyes narrowed with suspicion, and I knew I'd have to give him more. "But since you're more curious than a Quaker bridegroom on his wedding night, Hale, I'll be honest with you. Beckwith is going to try to do exactly what Ashton wants. He'll go after Moncrief. It's all set. I've framed Moncrief for Sheila's murder as effectively as Ashton framed Darryl Orton for Deborah's."

Hale smiled with obvious relief and looked like he was going to extend his hand, then thought better of it. "Thank you, Billy. You needn't tell Beckwith, of course, but trust me to sit on my hands when he goes after Moncrief, at least until it becomes too obvious. Then, when the moment seems right, I'll suggest to Jason in front of the jury that he take the Fifth. If that doesn't create a reasonable doubt, nothing will."

"It should work," I said, "though I'd rather you help Beckwith nab Ashton than an innocent man."

"Take it from me as his lawyer, Billy, Moncrief's hardly an innocent man. He's a polluter, always on the edge of the law; he sexually harasses his female employees with impunity and he reneges on contracts at the slightest whim. Anyway, he'll never be formally accused, Orton will walk—*and so will you and I.* Nobody loses, everybody wins."

That sounded like the kind of cold comfort Hale kept getting from Ashton.

"Especially you, Hale," I said, choking down the bile rising in my throat. "You always win, don't you, one way or another? You witness a murder, what the hell, she was getting too serious about motherhood. Find out about two additional murders? Shit happens. Seduce a young girl? Get her a good job."

"That was below the belt, Billy."

I leaned in close to him, trembling with rage, heartbreak—shit, you name it. "Your whole life settled below the belt the night you took advantage of a girl barely out of her teens."

Hale looked as pale as his shirt. "Billy—"

"Just don't go seeing yourself as superior to that 'polluting, sex harassing' Moncrief, okay? I'll sic Beckwith on him not to help you, but because it's the best way to get Darryl off."

I spun and headed for the door, but ran straight into the devil himself. Coincidence? Maybe.

"So, Strobe," said Rex Ashton, resplendent in a navy double-breasted suit that barely contained his puffed-out chest. "Stalking greener pastures in the East, are we?"

I met his direct gaze and sardonic smile with my own. "Maybe a pasture with a little less horseshit for me to step in."

"Well, at least you've kept your sense of humor, vulgar though it may be."

Hale moved in, mediating between us right to the bitter end, perhaps reminding me who I was talking to. "Billy's leaving us for New York tomorrow morning, Rex. You might surprise both of us by extending a modicum of civility. Nobody has worked harder for this firm than Billy."

"Tomorrow? Isn't your name on the defense witness list, Strobe?"

"Vic James and Brian Schlinkert want me in New York for an orientation retreat in the Hamptons Sunday morning. Doug Beckwith decided all I could contribute to the case was hearsay, so I'm gone."

Ashton could not restrain his pleasure, even managed a smile. "Well, then, Hale, we must do the decent thing by the lad and send him out in style."

Hale nodded. "I should have thought of it myself."

"My driver will pick you up at your apartment, Strobe," said Ashton. "He'll have plenty of time to get back and take Jason to court."

"That's really not necessary, Mr. Ashton," I said, hearing too much urgency in my voice, "I can take a cab—"

"Nonsense," Ashton said. "Look, Strobe, we never hit it off, but that happens in the best of families. I wish you luck, and rest assured you'll be picked up at, say, seven a.m. sharp? Give you plenty of time to relax at the airport."

I started to make excuses, but realized I was being tested.

"Besides," Ashton added with a wry chuckle, "our reputation with the Wulff and James firm would suffer if we failed to deliver the *corpus* on schedule. Arrange for him to get into the Red Carpet Club, Hale."

"Of course," said Hale, "and I'll send my own car and driver, Rex. You needn't bother."

I guess that was meant to reassure me, and I reckon it did somewhat, though I decided to buy some protection anyways, considering the importance of being on time for the start of Darryl's trial, and the obvious box they were trying to put me in.

"Thank you, Hale, and I'll be sure plenty of folks around here know about your and Mr. Ashton's generosity." Not even Ashton would be brash enough to try something with the world knowing I was in his care.

Hale gave me a knowing smile, and I thanked them both and walked out. With a little luck on traffic, I'd have time to circle back by cab and make it to court well before the trial started.

I checked in with Mimi on my cell phone as soon as I got onto the street. She had purchased Klinehart's automobile. She'd been driving around in it for a couple of days, unable to reach me.

"What kind of shape is it in?"

"I'll put it this way: The blue book value varies with how much gas is innit."

"That good?"

"Yeah, and gas don't stay innit long. It's a gas-hog Buick, a lil bit shorter 'n a aircraft carrier."

I told her to grab a wrench set and some heavy duty cutlery, then to pick me up out front of the Premier.

"Sure," she said, "though I may have to sell it on the way over for gas money."

An hour later, we were under the Golden Gate Bridge, just off the road leading to Fort Point, ready to tear up Barney's old car. Though the sky was clear and the sun was as high as it got this time of year, I could feel moisture in the air from the hard wind whipping the Bay a hundred yards away. The air temperature was only about fifty-five degrees, but the dampness and wind-chill factor pulled it down to somewhere in the thirties. I heard sounds I first thought were gulls or cormorants, but it was distant laughter, probably kids poaching in the old fort.

Mimi opened a canvas pouch and laid out an amazing variety of cutlery. I selected a curved blade with a handle she said was used in a cutting shed for halving Cling peaches and gouging out the pit. The blade was like ice to the touch.

Mimi went to work under the hood, while I spent the next ten minutes mutilating the front and backseats, dashboards, side panels, firewall, and floorboards of the once-proud Buick. "Nothing," I shouted. "Let's try the trunk."

"There was no key to the trunk," Mimi said. "I guess we're screwed, huh?"

Before I could spit out a four-letter word I saw a broad smile behind the steel crowbar she was holding.

I had the trunk open in minutes. Other than a few tools, it was clean. "Check the wheel well," Mimi said, and I pulled out the tire. Nothing.

I caught the glint of sunlight off a windshield and looked up to see a patrol car cruising toward the fort. Probably got a report about street people hanging out there.

"Okay," she said, "you might as well rip open the spare while I go to work underneath."

I started cutting up the tire and found a section that was easily pried off. My heart pounded with hope and . . . *there it was,* inside the casing: a sheaf of papers wrapped in plastic.

I ripped open the plastic and found several sets of documents on various matters, each clipped together separately, Klinehart's confidential filing system for hot docs. I knew ours would be there and toward the bottom I found what I'd hoped for, about twelve typed pages.

I told her to get the front seat reassembled enough to get me back to the Premier. While she did that I scanned the pages which, though some were more confusing than enlightening, clearly revealed stock purchases and short sales by one "Sheila Anderson, an unmarried woman," plus trade confirmation documents from an off-shore brokerage house and records showing fund transfers from Sheila to a numbered account in the Grand Cayman Islands "for the benefit of 'Project Salvation.' " The total sum was $10.3 million. Betty Perkins had been very rich for a very short period of time.

"Are they important?" Mimi said over my shoulder.

"Enough to kill for."

"But what's it all mean?"

"It means I could get my old bosses thrown in prison for trading on the inside knowledge of a client."

"Talkin about the big dogs at Stanton and Snow? That's a laugh."

"Yeah? What's the punch line?"

"They'll spend eighteen months in a bird sanctuary, with lunch boxes after tennis catered by Wolfgang Puck."

"It's something."

"Yeah, but how's that going to help your friend Orton?"

"I'm not sure yet," I admitted. "It ties Anderson to the scam."

"Well, alls it does for me as a juror is detract attention from Jason Moncrief as a guy who's supposed to be goin around killin people. And once I quit thinkin about Moncrief, I go back to thinkin about a guy named Orton whose DNA was found on Deborah Hinton."

"Glad you're not a juror."

"Yeah, well I'm glad you ain't my lawyer. First place, Beckwith can't even get this shit in evidence. Papers in the trunk of a car? Give me a fucking break."

She was right from the standpoint of admissibility. But I was sure that a trial lawyer as sharp as Beckwith could use them to bluff his way into reasonable doubt.

I glanced up and saw that one of the cops had got back in the patrol car.

"Let's get out of here," I said, jumping behind the wheel. "What we're doing here might look a little strange to a cop with time on his hands."

She followed my gaze. "What we're doin here *is* strange, cowboy, so gitty-up. Just don't blame me if you get a spring up your ass."

"Quick," I said, "give me the key."

"I *did* give you the key."

"The hell you did. *Shit.*"

The second cop had finished talking to a bearded guy at the entrance to the fort and was back behind the wheel.

"Hiding under the dash ain't gonna help us much, Billy."

I had found the wires, but the engine didn't catch the first time. *Damn.*

"They're back in the car, Billy. Fuck a duck, they're movin! We don't leave quick, we got some explainin to do."

The engine caught. "Close your door, Mimi, we're moving."

I drove away slowly to avoid suspicion, and the patrol car veered off toward the St. Francis Yacht Club. I exhaled and ran my shirtsleeve across my damp forehead.

"That's the fastest hot-wire I've seen in twenty years in the business," Mimi said. "Was that the beef you was busted on?"

I shook my head. "First time I've ever tried it. A guy named Rabbit at Soledad, compulsive car thief and masturbator, all he talked about was hot-wiring cars."

"I'm glad you paid attention."

"I've got a knack for fixing things. Also for screwing things up. Are you okay?"

"I think I got a spring up my ass."

38

At 6:30 A.M. I packed a bag and paid a week in advance at the Premier, then cabbed to my apartment building. I didn't even bother going in; I waited for Hale's car out front. The Range Rover was gone.

Hale's Town Car was prompt and by ten past seven I was in the backseat headed toward the airport with a burly driver I'd recently seen around the office at the wheel, and an even burlier companion with a pockmarked face only partially covered by a badly trimmed black beard. He was introduced to me as a "driver trainee" for Mr. Ashton. I thought it strange that a trainee would be wearing a loud plaid sport coat and wraparound Ferrari shades. Had Ashton and Hale expected I'd offer resistance? Or did they have some trip in mind other than to the airport despite my "insurance." I had left my gun in the room, knowing it wouldn't make it through the Hall of Justice metal detector, but I had a fully charged cell phone at the ready and decided to use it to buy another policy.

I punched in Dana's home number, hoping she hadn't left yet. She picked up.

"Dana?" I said in a loud voice, "Hi, it's me. I'm in Hale's Lincoln Town Car. . . . Yep, off to New York, *two* drivers no *less* . . . Hale and Rex Ashton arranged it as a going-away present. . . . Be sure to tell all our friends at the firm how generous they were to make sure I arrived at the airport on time, okay?"

I saw my burly friends in front exchange a look, then lowered my voice and said, "I might have a problem here, Dana. Listen carefully. You've got to go to court before eight o'clock and tell Beckwith I might be a little late. Give him my cell phone number in case he needs it. Okay? Will you do it?"

Burly Number Two with a beard was leaning back, trying to hear me, and Burly Number One adjusted his rearview like he was trying to read my lips. Both were scowling.

"Of course," Dana said, "and . . . be careful, Billy."

We hit heavy traffic getting out of town, and Burly One took his sweet time. It was 7:50 by the time Burly Two was lifting my bag out of the trunk of the Lincoln. My cell rang. It was Beckwith, and he was seething.

"Our goddamn client won't come out of the holding cell. One of his fellow prisoners has convinced him I've been 'bought and paid for.' "

"Darryl's a little paranoid about lawyers, but—"

"Dammit, man, this is precisely why I insisted you be present this morning! If you're not here to deal with him by nine o'clock, I'm filing a MacKenzie motion to *withdraw*! I've got a reputation in this town."

"I'll be there," I whispered, though I was beginning to feel things slip away. "Tell Darryl you talked to me, and I told you they've bought off his fellow prisoner, not you."

"He won't believe I'm even in communication with you. The man acts as if I'm Satan!"

"Tell him to stay cool like our buddy Tom Collins. Remember that name. Then tell him I said we're almost to the top of the mountain. Got it?"

I clicked off and thanked the guys for the ride and reached for my carry-on bag, but Burly Two snatched it up. Burly One put a sign on the dash and said, "We're told to make sure you get safely on board, sir."

Ashton and Hale were two steps ahead of me as usual. I waited in line and by the time I got my boarding pass and bag checked it was 8:10 A.M. Jury selection would start in about an hour and these bozos were going to walk me all the way to the gate and then watch me get onto the plane.

A dull ache in my head blossomed into something like a migraine when Burly One tried to grab my briefcase with the original set of the Klinehart papers. I held on to it, but things were really getting dicey. I had to get away.

I took stock of my assets and decided the only weapons I had to support my escape were a cell phone, a briefcase, and a coat. I palmed the cell and hit redial, hoping Dana would answer, then listen in.

"Look guys," I said in a loud voice. "I'm a grown-up; I can get to the gate all by myself."

"Don't be difficult, sir," said Burly One, continuing to grab at my briefcase.

"Get away from my goddamn briefcase," I snarled, securing it with my undamaged left hand. "Do I have to call a cop?"

"That would not be advisable, sir."

"What are you going to do? Murder me right here in front of a hundred witnesses?"

"If necessary, we have the means to kill you instantly, sir. Trust me on that."

A cold wave of electricity shot up my spine as they forced me onto the moving sidewalk. It was clear there was no reasoning with these thugs. I had to act.

"Were those Hale's orders or Ashton's?"

"We asked you not make this difficult, sir," said Burly One.

"I wouldn't think of it," I said and then came up with an elbow to his chin and threw my coat over Burly Two's head. By the time he tossed it off I had hopped over the rail and was running back toward the street. These guys were hobbled by their bulk, and I figured I'd beat them back to the Town Car and if the keys were in it, I'd be dancing in tall cotton. A long shot, but . . .

I glanced back. Burly One had made it over the rail and was slowly moving toward me. The other was trying to muscle his way backwards on the moving sidewalk, knocking people aside like they were ten pins. I was back on the street well ahead of them and into the driver's seat of the Lincoln.

No keys. I checked the visor and under the seat. Nothing. I looked under the dash. Protected. Shit.

A cab stopped to let people out. I jumped in.

"Sorry, mac, I can't pick up here."

"How about for a hundred dollars."

He shook his head. "Not for a thousand. They'd cancel my ticket. Sorry."

Burly One came bursting into the sunlight, shielding his eyes. He looked toward the Town Car, saw the door I had left open. He squinted in both directions.

"You own this taxi?" I asked the driver.

"Yeah, but it's no good to me if they take away my medallion."

"I understand, but I've got a situation here. My wife's in labor. I know you can't pick me up, but I'd like to rent your car for two, three hours." Another lie, but one I'd make good to the guy. "Here's my VISA card for security; oh, hell, take the whole damn wallet except for my driver's license. There's three hundred in cash there and it's yours for three hours' use of your cab. I'll be right back here after that, okay? I'll pay you a hundred for every hour I'm late. Deal?"

Burly One was running toward me.

"You've got yourself a car, Mac," he said, after checking my photo on the driver's license. He hit the OFF DUTY light and removed his medallion. "But be gentle, okay?"

"As the rain," I said, moving into his seat.

Burly One saw me slamming the door, so he turned and ran back toward the Town Car. Burly Two was coming out onto the sidewalk.

I gunned the cab toward the freeway, then put the phone to my ear, but if I'd made contact, it had been lost. I hit redial again and Dana answered. Her voice sounded tired, even distant.

"Hello, Billy."

"Did you hear it?"

"Part of it; enough of it. Are you all right?"

"I got away from them and I'm heading for court in a cab. Did you see Beckwith?"

"Briefly," she said, her tone flat and cold, "also, the police. They're waiting for you in court, Billy. You *and* your car have been positively made leaving the scene of Sheila's murder with the cops in pursuit. They're using Darryl's trial as bait, sure you'll show up. They have a warrant for your arrest for Anderson's murder. Rex explained that they also have her diary, which had wonderful things to say about your skill in bed."

"Don't listen to him, Dana, I can explain—"

"This is all wonderful, Billy. According to you, Hale murdered Deborah. According to Rex and the police, you murdered Sheila. Speaks well for me, doesn't it? The two men I love most, both alleged killers? Well, I'm not sure about Hale, Billy, but the police are quite sure about you, given the fact you and the victim were lovers. *Lovers,* Billy. It's all insane!"

Tell me about it, I thought. Here I was trying to explain sleeping with a woman who never existed while being chased at ninety miles an hour by hoods as I raced toward my own arrest by the cops. I didn't know where to begin.

"I can explain everything, Dana. You know I couldn't kill anybody, and you're Darryl's only hope now."

Even over the whine of the engine I thought I could hear her breathing on the other end, almost feel her heart pounding through the line.

"I know how you feel about Hale," I said, "but you've got to choose. This isn't just about Darryl Orton anymore. I've had two friends killed by Hale and Ashton. Now they're trying to kill *me.*"

Nothing.

"Dana, you've got to go to Darryl. Tell him who you are and that I'm coming in. Tell him he's got to trust Beckwith, then tell Beckwith to stall as long as he can."

I looked in my rearview and saw a black Lincoln weaving through traffic a dozen cars back.

"After that, meet me on the second floor of the Hall of Justice and *bring the goddamn lighter.*"

Dana's voice began to break up, and the problem wasn't in the hardware. "Billy, I can't meet you *or* Darryl at court! I've got a deposition with Rex Ashton starting in five minutes in a huge case . . . Oh, *hello*, Rex, is everybody here?"

The receiver went dead. How much had Ashton heard? Probably enough to know what I was up to.

A car was lumbering along in the fast lane at sixty, so I had to thread the needle across two lanes to keep up my speed, then weave my way back into the fast lane. I couldn't see the Lincoln, but I knew he must be gaining on me. I glanced in the rearview. Yep, there he was—three cars back and closing fast.

I decided to let him think I was going off on 280 at the junction coming up ahead, then shoot across two lanes at the last second back onto 101 and hope he wouldn't be able to make it. I'd have to cut it close for it to work. I shot to my right in front of several cars into the 280 exit lanes, then saw Burly One following hard on my tail. It would have to be the last minute . . . hold it, hold it, hold it, *now!*

I was shouting now, shouting at no one and everyone, demanding, yelling, and cursing like hell wouldn't have it, screaming out loud as I cramped the wheel to the left and went into a barely controlled skid, swerving back onto 101, horns honking everywhere. I made it, but *shit*, so did the Lincoln, though I saw a trail of sparks as his right side slammed against the concrete junction divider. Burly Two would need a clean pair of shorts. Maybe I would, too, because the Town Car was gaining on me again.

We raced all the way toward the end of the freeway, weaving between cars, threading the needle over and over. Burly One was a hell of a driver, but I still had two car lengths on him and was almost within view of the Hall of Justice. That's when I slowed to eighty-five and hit the beginning of the final sweeping curve down to Bryant Street.

I realized I had slowed too little and too late, and a new chill of fear shot through me as I felt my back wheels start to slide out of control, pulling me as if by a giant hand toward the edge of the ramp, eighty feet above the ground.

39

The Hall of Justice is a stark, gray building located on Bryant Street, right as you come off the 101 freeway exit. I was halfway through the curve, my speed down to seventy, when I slammed against the ramp railing and somehow wrestled the cab back under control. But slowing down allowed the Lincoln to pull up beside me and now he was ramming the side of the cab. For a horrible second or two I thought we were locked together and both going over the ramp, but he must have realized the same thing, because he backed off, at least I thought he had, until I saw him beside me again, on my left, and *holy shit*, there was Burly Two, leveling a shotgun no more than six feet from my face. We were on Bryant now, side by side, and a hundred feet from the entry stairs to the Hall. I instinctively ducked as the gun went off, but hit my brakes, too—which locked—and took the cab into another side skid. The Lincoln, slower to react, shot past me.

The stench of burning rubber stung my nose, but I stopped within ten yards of the entrance to the Hall. I was going to owe that cabbie a new car.

I grabbed my briefcase, abandoned the taxi in the middle of the street, and raced up the outside steps, mindful of the amazed stares of onlookers, fortunately none of them cops. I then put on the most casual look I could muster as I entered the interior. I glanced at my watch. It was 9:10 A.M. The jury might already be in the box, *voir dire* under way.

"Late for court," I gasped to the guards at the metal detector, managing a wan smile. I raced to the front jail elevators and, as I frantically pressed the UP elevator button, I prayed the Burly Brothers would be packing guns and that at least one of them was too dumb to remember it. Sure enough, I heard the buzzer go off at the metal detector, and all they could do was watch helplessly as the guards frisked them and my elevator doors closed.

Department 26 is on the third floor of the Hall of Justice, but I took a wild chance and stopped at the second floor. Dana would be right at the doors if she had come. I said a quick prayer as the doors opened. Nobody.

I started to punch the third-floor button but remembered just in time that Jaxon was waiting for me there, so I punched 7, the jail floor instead. I held my breath as the 3 flashed, but the car kept on moving. When the doors opened again on the seventh floor, I stepped off and flashed the deputy my state bar card and driver's license.

"I'm here to meet with my client, Darryl Orton," I said. "He's starting trial this morning."

The deputy, even younger than me, seemed confused, which is what I'd hoped for. "He's gone down, sir. We took him down an hour ago."

"You *what?*" I said, feigning surprise and outrage. I produced a docket sheet showing Darryl's trial date, time, and department, and my name along with Beckwith's as counsel of record. Contrary to my commitment to Ashton, I had never formally withdrawn.

"Standing orders, sir. He's either in court by now or in the holding cell on the third floor."

"Are you making it impossible for me to meet with my client prior to trial?" I said, imitating Rex Ashton's most imperious manner.

"Well, no . . . I mean—"

"Where's the back elevator to the holding cell adjacent to Department 26?" I said, taking advantage of his confusion. "I'll try to catch him before he goes in."

A minute later I was stepping off the elevator into a small room occupied by a deputy and Darryl Orton in an orange jumpsuit. He looked genuinely frightened, probably for the first time in his life, but angry, too.

"I got the word from a guy inside, Billy. Beckwith's settin' me up; he's been paid by someone."

"By *me*, you asshole," I shouted at him. "Beckwith's as straight arrow as they come." I then turned back to the deputy. "Open the door. We're going into the courtroom."

"He won't go," said the deputy, jerking his head toward Darryl.

"The hell he won't," I said, and pulled Darryl to his feet by the front of his jumpsuit, ignoring the pain that shot up my right shoulder.

"I guess I'll go," Darryl said, his eyebrows raised in surprise.

As we entered, Judge John Hernandez was thanking the jury for their attendance.

"Your Honor!" I said in an unnaturally loud voice. "Mr. Orton is here."

The judge scowled at me and said, "That's nice, and who might you be?"

"I'm a lawyer and a friend of the defendant, Your Honor."

"Well, sir, this is not a case of better late than never. The defendant refused to appear when summoned. I have accepted Mr. Beckwith's withdrawal from the case on a Mackenzie motion, in consideration of accusations and physical threats issued by his client. He was patient, as we all have been, but he has left the courtroom."

As the judge rose, I frantically scanned the gallery, its battered oak benches only sparsely filed with reporters, courtroom regulars, and street folks looking to get warm. No Beckwith. Without representation, the case would be kicked over two weeks to a public defender who would never buy into the Moncrief DNA stunt.

"As I was saying, members of the jury . . ."

"I'm also Mr. Orton's lawyer," I shouted.

The judge, a large man with thick black hair and intelligent eyes peering from beneath eyebrows like untrimmed hedges, appraised me with hard eyes. "Just who are you, sir?"

"Like he said, this here's my lawyer," said Darryl, in a voice even louder than mine had been. "Name's Billy Strobe."

"That's, uh, true, Your Honor," I said, feeling my old stage fright lurking in the wings. "You'll . . . see my name . . . on the pleadings there."

This was terrible. I'd never seen a complete trial outside a movie theater, other than my own.

The judge glanced at the deputy district attorney. "Ms. McCutcheon?"

I glanced at her, too. According to Beckwith, Norma McCutcheon was one of the best they had at the SFDA's office and had been the deputy DA at Darryl's first aborted trial. She was willowy and striking with fiery red hair worn short. Beckwith had said she knew how to play the game hard without appearing "overly aggressive" or "shrill," the labels often attached to tough female prosecutors, especially after the OJ debacle. I could see the jury would like her.

"Trial counsel for the defendant has been excused," she said, clicking her briefcase shut and heading for the rail, "and I have other matters awaiting me upstairs."

"Judge?" I managed say, "Mr. Beckwith was just one of Mr. Orton's lawyers. I'm the other one. I apologize for being late. I was hit by a car on the way here."

"You certainly look like it. Are you prepared to proceed on behalf of the defense?" the judge said with a resigned expression.

"W-well, sir," I said, breaking a sweat, "yes, yes, I reckon I am."

Ms. McCutcheon looked exasperated, but turned back to her end of counsel table and sat down. I heard some laughter behind me from the handful of folks back there.

Judge Hernandez scowled at the sparse gallery, then glanced downward for a minute, scanning the pleadings under his dark hedgerows, then turned toward the jury and said, "It appears that we have a trial after all, members of the jury. All right, counsel, state your appearances and let's proceed with jury selection."

But someone was moving behind me, someone very large. I turned, and there was Inspector Jaxon with an x at the bailiff's desk, whispering to him. Where had he come from?

"One moment, please, counsel," said the judge, as the bailiff approached the bench. He muttered something to the judge I couldn't hear, who then said something to his clerk and called a brief recess.

"Remain seated, members of the jury," the judge said. "I'll see counsel and the defendant in chambers. You, too, Inspector Jaxon."

I followed Norma McCutcheon into chambers, wondering if I should demand a real trial lawyer to represent me as well as Darryl.

"It's all right to leave your briefcase in the courtroom, Mr. Strobe," Norma McCutcheon said. I nodded my thanks, but a man had died for those documents, and they were staying with me.

Inside the judge's cramped chambers, I was stunned at the number of books, not just law books either. Two huge bookcases were filled with volumes on world affairs, race relations, sports, politics, and philosophy, plus several novels by folks I mostly hadn't heard of. There were not enough chairs for all of us inside the judge's chambers, so he stood behind his plain oak desk, looming above everybody, even me and Jaxon.

"Now, what's this all about?" said the judge to Jaxon.

Jaxon introduced himself and presented his credentials in a professional, matter-of-fact manner. "I have a warrant here for the arrest of William Joseph Strobe, Your Honor. He is a suspect in the murder of a woman named Sheila Anderson. He may also be charged with the murder of one Bernard Klinehart, once our investigation has been completed."

I felt a rivulet of perspiration running down my left temple. The only thing necessary to make the irony perfect would be for him to charge me with the murder of Deborah Hinton. I took a deep breath, trying to calm myself. I realized the judge was looking at me, and I heard myself mouthing the most defensive cliché in the book: "There must be some mistake, Your Honor."

"There ain't no mistake about it, Judge," said Jaxon. "We got an eyewitness to Strobe's escape from the murder site and other evidence supporting probable cause. You'll see that the warrant has been signed by Judge Coates. I'm takin him in with me right now." Jaxon turned toward me. "Put your hands behind your back, sir. You have the right to—"

"Your Honor," I said, jerking a hand out of Jaxon's grasp and putting it back on the handle of my briefcase. "May I say something?"

"You may if you wish, though Inspector Jaxon was about to warn you that anything you say may be used as evidence against you."

"That's okay by me, Judge," I said. "All I want to do is make a comment, then ask a question."

"Go ahead."

"My comment is that Mr. Orton deserves a trial no matter what this inspector may think of me. If you give him a trial, the jury will see that Mr. Orton didn't murder Deborah Hinton and that I didn't murder Sheila Anderson or anybody else."

The judge looked perplexed. "I can only hope your question is more lucid than your comment."

"My question, Judge, is this: Are we in Judge Coates's courtroom, Inspector Jaxon's courtroom, or *your* courtroom?"

The judge's bushy eyebrows shot up, and he folded his arms across his broad chest. "This is *my* courtroom, Mr. Strobe, and your insinuation is impertinent. You do, however, make a point."

"If you wanted, Judge," I added, "you could order that I be taken into custody at all times court was in recess. I've got no pressing business elsewhere."

The judge unfolded his arms and stared thoughtfully at the backs of his hands for a second or two as if considering a manicure or checking his liver spots, then turned to Jaxon and said, "Mr. Strobe is, at the moment, under my jurisdiction, Inspector. He'll be going nowhere until this trial is finished."

I couldn't resist a small smile at Jaxon as he began to sputter a protest, but the judge assured him that an extra bailiff would be brought in to ensure my continuing presence in the courtroom.

"I'll have a few of my own men in the courtroom," said Jaxon, narrowing his eyes and aiming them at me. "He tries to leave the courtroom, he don't get far. Fact, nothin would pleasure me more than to see him try."

Without being excused, Jaxon stormed out of the chambers, speaking into his radio as he left. My gaze trailed him out through the open door, and came to rest on Hale Lassiter out in the gallery. If he was surprised to see me here, he didn't show it.

"This started out as a rather boring day," the judge said, giving Norma McCutcheon and me each a wry smile. "Let's get that jury selected."

I reentered the courtroom and noticed that to Hale's left was a lean-looking young man, a duplicate of Jason Moncrief but with none of the world-weary smugness, the surgically induced youthfulness. He was seated between Hale and his father, taking me in the way I was him. Rick Moncrief, future lawyer and proud kid come to see his daddy testify. Why did his presence make me feel uneasy?

I remembered the time Dad had taken me to watch his closing argument in a murder case, how proud I'd been that day, staying close to him so people would see us together and know I was his kid. He had let me carry his old briefcase and introduced me to a friend as his junior partner. I was ten. Rick Moncrief was much older than that, but men don't grow out of the habit of identifying with their dads, for better or for worse.

The judge's voice interrupted my thoughts. "Please proceed, Counsel."

I had never picked a jury, but figured it couldn't be too hard. I just hoped that when I opened my mouth, something would come out.

40

I made it through jury selection by trying to recall how the lawyers had done it in my own trial and by turning the DA's questions upside down. I watched Norma McCutcheon real close, and if I thought she wanted a particular juror, I'd kicked him or her off. Heck of a way to practice law, but the fact was, I really *was* practicing.

Norma was a little sneaky sometimes. It was like she was bent on arguing her case from the git-go.

"Mrs. Bruce," McCutcheon said when she came to Juror Number Four, a white-faced, thirtyish woman with thick glasses. "Do you recognize the defendant from television or newspaper stories reporting on this terrible tragedy? Have you seen any photos of this defendant? There was a great deal of dramatic coverage of this crime because of its violent nature."

"I'm not sure. I suppose it's possible."

"Well, despite what you might have seen and heard concerning this particularly vicious killing,"—McCutcheon allowed herself a shudder here—"neither Mr. Strobe nor I want emotions to govern your verdict.

Do you think you can still be fair and objective as you hear the evidence?"

"Well, I'm not even sure I saw or heard anything, but yes, I think I can be fair."

"Mrs. Bruce," I said, when it was my turn, "it sounds to me like as if this here prosecutor doesn't give a hoot in hell whether or not you can be fair to my client and act without 'emotion.' Fact is, she was just now trying to light a match under your emotions, using words like 'terrible tragedy' and 'vicious killing.' I don't know Ms. McCutcheon, but she must want you to think from the git-go that this was the crime of the century and that Darryl here is Public Enemy Number One. Well, I'm here to tell you that's not the way it is."

"Your Honor," said McCutcheon, "is there a question in there somewhere? This is supposed to be *voir dire,* not argument."

"Yes, Counsel, your question, please."

"Okay, here's my question, ma'am. Do I look to you like the kind of lawyer a defendant would hire if he was guilty of the crime of a century? Do I look like some kind of dream team to you?"

"Your *Honor.*"

Judge Hernandez called us up to the bench for a side bar. I was so damn nervous I walked to the wrong side, of course, then quickly joined Norma over on the side opposite the jury. The judge gave Norma McCutcheon a kindly smile. "Mr. Strobe has not yet mastered the fine art of camouflaging improper argument with a question."

"That's quite obvious," said McCutcheon.

"Nor," continued the judge with a wink, "how to object when he hears it done well by a master."

McCutcheon turned red, and the judge turned to me. "I like to let lawyers try their cases in my courtroom, leave them alone when I can. So if you don't object when she goes too far, I probably won't do it for you. Understand?"

"Yes, sir," I said, gratefully. This judge was beginning to remind me of Joseph Welch in *Anatomy of a Murder:* smart, humorous, tough as nails. I later learned John Hernandez was the most feared and respected judge on the San Francisco Superior Court.

"I'm aware, sir, that you aren't taught practical jury trial technique in law school, unless you were fortunate and attended one of the few institutions that did provide hands-on experience."

"My institution offered plenty of hands-on experience, Your Honor," I said, "but none in trial practice." Darryl chuckled, but the judge didn't hear him.

"That's always been the problem with our law schools, Mr. Strobe.

Well, we will make allowances, but we have our limits. Now step back and put your argument in the form of a proper question."

We returned to our seats.

"What I'm wondering, Mrs. Bruce," I said, "is whether after all that stuff you just heard about dramatic coverage and a vicious killing, you can follow the law, listen to the evidence, and be fair to a man who the *law* presumes to be innocent no matter what this prosecutor says she saw on the TV."

Norma started to object, but Mrs. Bruce smiled and said, "Why, yes, I'm sure I can."

We both behaved after that, and things went pretty smoothly. I knew from watching my dad and every law movie ever made that I had a bunch of juror vetoes called peremptory challenges. I didn't have to explain to anybody why I was bouncing a juror. I used them to get rid of a convenience store manager, a guy who seemed mad at the world, and a couple of Republicans.

After about an hour of visiting with the citizens and exercising most of her challenges, Norma McCutcheon accepted the jury, and I figured I'd better do the same so the twelve people in the box wouldn't think I had something to hide. Maybe I didn't have a Henry Fonda on my jury like the original production of *Twelve Angry Men,* but I had a pretty good bunch, including two African Americans, a writer for a liberal magazine, and a Native American union man. I didn't figure these folks to be rabid fans of the government, but I was a long way from hoping to achieve an unanimous verdict, which is what it would take to get Darryl off.

The jury was sworn, and the judge told the deputy DA she could proceed with her opening statement, which was brief because it didn't need to be otherwise. She hit on the slay-for-pay theory, casting Darryl in the role of cold-blooded assassin for hire, then talked about that thousand dollars showing up in Darryl's bank account, the murder weapon found behind his locker, and, of course, the DNA match. Her voice was gentle but engaging, her manner smooth and conversational, feminine but not sexy.

"In summary, members of the jury," she said, "the People will provide you with everything but an actual film of Mr. Orton crushing Deborah Hinton's skull, more proof than you could ask for. We will ask, in return, that you act on the overwhelming evidence and find Mr. Orton guilty of premeditated murder."

Every eye was on her, including mine, but when she sat down, the jury's gaze turned to me. The expressions on their faces seemed to be asking whether a trial was really necessary. I pictured one of them rising and saying, "We have a verdict, Your Honor."

Had I come all this way to have Darryl's fate in the hands of a scared-shitless rookie? Shifting nervously in my seat, I realized the back of my shirt was already soaked through.

The judge's resonant voice mercifully interrupted my bleak speculations. "Do you wish to make your opening statement at the present, or reserve it, Mr. Strobe?"

I took that to mean I could make it later if I wanted to, but Darryl was jabbing me in the ribs. "Get up, kid," he whispered, too loud, as usual. "She done good. You got to turn 'em around before they get too set in their damn ways."

"What the hell can I say?" I whispered back. "Most of what she told them was true but for the part about you being a paid assassin."

"Well, I'm the client," said Darryl, delivering an even more painful jab, "and the client wants you on your feet."

For an instant, my anger at Darryl overcame my terror and I felt like getting up and giving them a variation on what Joe Pesci said in his opening in *My Cousin Vinny*: "Everything she just said about Darryl? It's all bullshit."

No, I'd try for a Gregory Peck look instead, trying to reflect the candor and trustworthiness of an Atticus Finch. But when I tried to stand up, I felt like I was held together by taut wire that might break and send pieces of me flying all over creation. Unlike Norma McCutcheon, who glided toward the jury like she was on roller skates, I felt all herky-jerky, like a guy with ski boots on, like Frankenstein's monster. Then I caught myself wiping my hands on my pant legs.

Forget Atticus Finch, I thought. Just pick out a juror that most resembles Darryl Orton—like number five there, the PG&E troubleshooter whose hobby was ham radios—and tell him the story like you were sitting around the mess hall at Soledad talking to Darryl.

"Members of the jury. I'm . . . not a trial lawyer. If that's not clear by now, it surely soon will be. Truth is, I'm actually not much of any kind of a lawyer. Been researching contracts and writing wills for less than a year.

"But sir, uh, folks . . . well, this is a case even *I* can win, because this here man didn't kill anybody, and the evidence will prove it. I'm much obliged for your attention. Thank you."

I sat down and was greeted by another sharp nudge in my side. "Dammit, kid," he whispered, "our evidence don't have to 'prove' me innocent! It's up to the prosecution to prove me *guilty*!"

He was right, of course, but I was mainly relieved that words had come out of my mouth when they were supposed to. "I'll get better," I told him, "and quit punching me."

The first witness was the crime lab guy who found strands of Darryl's hair on the body of Deborah Hinton. When it came my turn to cross-examine him, I said, "No questions," and readied myself for another poke in my bruised ribs. Same when the DNA expert reported a perfect match with hair taken from the head of the defendant.

"No questions, Your Honor."

Darryl rolled his eyes right in front of the jury, and I gave him a poke back. That's when the judge called counsel back to side bar.

"It's not my job to conduct the defense of your client, Mr. Strobe, but I must tell you that the jury will have no choice but to find him guilty if you don't start doing something."

"I reckon I couldn't blame them, Judge," I said, "but it'll be a spell yet before the last dog is hung."

The judge looked perplexed, but told us to step back and called the morning recess. We had been at it for only an hour and a half, and I was already wore out. My stomach was aching in sympathy with my aching head, and when I glanced over at Norma McCutcheon, she gave me a doleful look. Even the prosecutor was feeling sorry for me.

I turned around and saw Moncrief giving the jury a big smile as they walked by him. He was looking pleased as a dog with a bone. Dana and Hale were right: the son-of-a-bitch hadn't killed anybody, but he damn sure deserved any comeuppance he got.

I began to picture what I'd do when it came my turn with Moncrief, how I would first establish Sheila Anderson's death, then turn toward the witness, glance narrowed-eyed at the jury, and in a firm, but quiet voice say, *and you murdered her, didn't you, Mr. Moncrief,* which would cause Norma McCutcheon to scream out an objection and cause the jurors to look at each other as if to check their own hearing while Moncrief would stare slack-jawed at me as if I'd accused him of murder, and when it sank in that I had, he'd manage a denial and a ridiculing smile that would quickly fade when I asked him to explain then how the SFPD had found strands of his hair in the bed where Sheila Anderson had been viciously murdered, and right there, yes, right at that moment would be the beginning of the end of the spotless reputation of Jason Daniel Moncrief, whose lips would move soundlessly as he'd look in vain to the judge for deliverance, but instead, there would be Hale advising him to take the Fifth, and if Moncrief hesitated, I would close in again—Henry Fonda taking on Ward Bond in *Young Mister Lincoln,* George C. Scott, coldly relentless in *Anatomy of a Murder*—cruel and pitiless I'd be, a wolf with glistening teeth sunk into the goat's throat, tasting blood, squeezing the last drop of innuendo out of the man's darkest moment, forcing him to utter the magic words *on the grounds that it might incriminate me* before I'd allow him to stumble, a broken man, from the witness stand, seeing only his son's back, as the devastated young man stormed from the courtroom.

I felt Darryl tugging my arm and snapped out of my heroic reverie. "Don't mean to be pushy," he asked, "but you ever gonna do anything?"

I tried to explain to Darryl that *(a)* there was nothing I could do to these witnesses, because it *was* his hair, so of course it was a perfect match, and *(b)* I wanted the jury to fully *believe* in DNA for now, to ensure the success of painting Moncrief as Sheila's murderer when it was our turn.

I then walked into the corridor to stretch and calm myself down, which was not easy, being trailed by a pair of deputy marshals. What I saw there took me by surprise, stung me somehow. Moncrief, trotting awkwardly down the hall, looking anything but dignified, trying to catch up with his son. Rick Moncrief, leaner than his dad but otherwise a carbon copy, turned and brightened when he saw his father; then the pair of them walked down the corridor, their arms locked together in a quaint sort of old-world intimacy. Moncrief was laughing at something the kid had said.

Like a stalker, I found myself drawn to their mutual affection. Was it envy? Nostalgia? They didn't see me in the crowded area, but I plainly heard Moncrief say something like, "Did *I* say that?" Whatever the exact words, the kid blushed with pleasure and gave his dad's arm an extra squeeze.

I felt a rush of feelings up into my face I couldn't explain. I didn't know what they were talking about, but it didn't matter. I spun around and stormed back into court.

I sat down next to Darryl, my thoughts whirling inside my head like freshly sharpened spurs. Neither the judge nor the court attachés had come out yet.

"I've got a problem, Darryl."

"I've noticed."

"I mean I'm not feeling good about, you know, the thing with Moncrief."

In as few words as possible, I reviewed my dilemma to Darryl: that I had identified the true guilty parties to Deborah's murder—not Moncrief, but Hale and Rex Ashton—but if I went after them instead of the innocent guy who I'd already set up with DNA, I'd probably lose the case. In the interest of full disclosure, I told him I'd also lose the woman I loved, but that wasn't his problem, nor was it the main problem.

Darryl sat quietly, taking it all in, and then gave me a sympathetic look. "I think you're spread a little thin right now, kid," he said. "Maybe we oughta try for a postponement."

His words hurt me. I was looking for some support, and he was pulling the rug out. "Hell, Darryl, I'm okay; I just needed you to know—"

"You *ain't* okay. Fact is, ever since you got that bad news about your daddy in Enid, you've been looking more confused than a raccoon tryin to ride a motorcycle."

The clerk, then the court reporter strolled into the courtroom. The judge wouldn't be far behind.

"Dammit, Darryl, this has nothing to do with—"

Darryl shook his head and held up his hand to stop me. "I learned a powerful lesson from my own daddy that fits you to a tee, Billy, and you oughta pay attention: People that get their lives busted up over somethin when they're kids tend to get stuck there and feel they got to go back and fix things. You look to me like someone tryin to fix too many things at once."

"We're going to do okay, *okay*? I just—"

"Bullshit, okay! You got the cops stalkin you all over the courthouse, a judge losin patience because you ain't asked squat on cross-examination, and a jury that's lookin at us like we're a pair a' bugs under a rock. I think it's time I pull an appendix attack and we start over later when things are a little more—"

The judge walked in and summoned the jury. I started to get up, I had to clear my head, but Darryl grabbed my arm and said, "Simple question, kid. Does Moncrief deserve bein wrecked?"

"He's not a good man."

"But you are. Ain't *that* the real problem?"

The jury began filing in. Darryl pulled me down close to him. "Let me tell you one more thing, kid; then the sermon's over and the singin can begin. You're gonna have plenty a' other girls, and plenty a' other clients, too, other 'n me. But that guy inside your skin? You're stuck with him, Billy. My advice is do what *you* think is right. You do that, and you won't lose nothin; at least nothin that can't be replaced."

I reached down and put my hand on his arm, looked into his intelligent eyes, and knew only one thing for sure at that moment: I would not let this good man go back to die in Soledad.

"Call your next witness, Ms. McCutcheon," Judge Hernandez said.

The prosecution's next witness was Jason Moncrief, and as he confidently strode to the stand and took the oath, my heart started bouncing around inside my chest. I didn't want to steal another look at Moncrief's son, but couldn't help it. Damn kid was smiling at his dad like he had been elected president of the U.S. of A. Why in the hell did his damn son have to be here?

Moncrief testified, as he had done before in a deposition, how he had discovered during the course of an SEC investigation that Deborah Hinton had improperly deferred a multimillion dollar write-off so as to artificially rocket the company's earnings.

"The company's internal investigation" he said, "aided by information obtained during a private investigation by the Securities and Exchange Commission, disclosed that Ms. Hinton was an 'inside' co-conspirator in an illegal 16b fraud."

"And why," asked McCutcheon, "did the Commission's investigation conclude that Ms. Hinton had an outside co-conspirator?"

"Two reasons. First, her salary could not justify the huge amounts she had invested before the stock shot up, and second, her large profits had been professionally laundered and never appeared in her checking account. Ergo, she must have had someone on the outside funding her and handling the money."

"Was that money ever found, Mr. Moncrief?"

"No, other than the thousand dollars that mysteriously showed up in the defendant's bank account."

"That's unfair, Your Honor!" I said.

"Un*fair*?" said Judge Hernandez.

"I mean, I object."

"That's better, Mr. Strobe. This may come as a surprise, but those twelve people over to your right are the ones who get to decide what's fair or unfair."

"Yes, sir." I knew I was redder than a split pomegranate. Goddamn Beckwith. I wondered if I should apologize to the jury, but the judge was at me again.

"Now, Mr. Strobe, perhaps you would like to state your grounds for objection; you know, for the record?"

"Well, Judge, for one thing, there's no evidence connecting the two things."

"So you're suggesting there is a lack of foundation?"

"Lack of foundation, yes, sir. Thank you, sir. Plus which the man shouldn't get to sit there and give his opinion about things he hasn't proved."

The judge smiled. He seemed to be taking some pleasure at my expense and so was the jury, to look at them.

"There now, Mr. Strobe, see how easy it is? Opinion and conclusion and assuming facts not in evidence."

"Yes, sir, I'd like to add those, too. For the record."

"And after all this trouble I've put you to, I suppose you want his answer stricken?"

More titters from the gallery.

"Works for me, Judge. I mean, thank you, Your Honor. I move to strike it."

The judge exhaled with relief and said, "It may go out."

I was beginning to see why John Hernandez had the best reputation on the San Francisco Superior Court bench. He wasn't going to make it easy for me, but he was going to protect Darryl from my inexperience—and keep his sense of humor in the bargain.

"Might I *continue?*" asked McCutcheon.

"I wish you would," said the judge.

"What kind of employee was Ms. Hinton?" asked McCutcheon.

"Until this incident," he said, "Deborah was a devoted employee. She was known to work late practically every weeknight. Her co-conspirator obviously knew this and found the right man for the job, someone who also was there every night."

I objected again and was amazed when the judge not only sustained my objection, but told the jury to disregard the testimony, then admonished the witness not to volunteer his conclusions. But the bell continued to ring with Moncrief's implication.

"Your witness," said Norma, offering me a half-smile that might have been either malevolent or sympathetic.

Showtime. I got to my feet, but stayed behind counsel table. "Now Deborah wasn't the only one to profit from her improper deferral, was she, sir?"

Moncrief raised his brow a tad and said, "I know of no one else who did—unlawfully, that is—with advance knowledge. The SEC so found."

"I didn't say *unlawfully,* sir, and I move to strike what the witness claims the SEC found, Your Honor."

"Sustained. The jury will disregard it. Answer the question, Mr. Moncrief."

Moncrief's eyes narrowed, and he sat silent for at least twenty long seconds. Then he turned and looked straight at the judge. "Your Honor, this is patently absurd. I came in here as a citizen to testify against a murderer, not to be badgered by one of my own lawyers."

John Hernandez's eyebrows lifted in surprise, and he stared at Moncrief for a second or two, like he was a spoiled kid acting up.

"You're not being badgered, sir. You're being cross-examined by someone who apparently thinks he's the defendant's lawyer, not yours. Please answer the question."

Moncrief was fuming, his jaw working from side to side, not used to being pushed around by anyone, let alone a rookie like me and a superior court judge who took an entire year to earn what Moncrief's stock options generated on a single good day on the NASDAQ market. I realized that even a good judge like Hernandez was as territorial as a stellar jay when it came to who controlled Department 26.

"You personally made more money on the rise than Deborah Hinton did," I said. "Correct?"

"Yes, but *I* had no advance information. She obviously did."

"I didn't ask you that, but since you raised it, are you saying you paid no attention to what your CFO was doing?"

"I can't be everywhere, Mr. Strobe."

"Your outside law firm is Stanton and Snow, correct?"

"Yes."

"And you know I was a lawyer there?"

"Yes. I thought you still were."

"Well, I'm not. Now, if I told you that you had a reputation as a hands-on chief executive officer, would you agree it was well-founded?"

"I suppose so."

"Would Ms. Hinton as chief financial officer normally have checked with you before deferring such a large write-off?"

Another grudging agreement.

"But you expect us to believe she didn't do it this time?"

"Objection, argumentative."

"Sustained."

What the hell was that all about? Guys like Jimmy Stewart, George C. Scott, and Raul Julia always got away with tougher questions than that. I kept going. "Who else made substantial profits on the temporary upswing of stock?"

"I don't know."

I popped open my briefcase, removed the table of major investors, then walked up and started to hand it to him. I never made it, for the clerk snatched it from my hand and gave me a look that would break a windshield. I backpedaled as if I'd walked onto hot coals, then remembered Glenn Ford in a great movie called *Trial,* and said, "Sorry, Your Honor. May I have permission to approach the witness?"

"Granted, but you'll have to get that exhibit marked first."

I drew a blank. "Right," I said, and took it back from the clerk. I stared at the document for several seconds, my mind a blank. "I'm afraid I don't know how to do that, Judge."

Snickers from the gallery, even from a couple of jurors.

"Describe the document," John Hernandez said, with a firmness that suggested his patience was exhausted, "then ask to have it marked for identification."

With the courtroom mystics completed, the clerk returned the document, now marked DEFENDANT'S EXHIBIT A, and I again asked permission to approach the witness. The judge gave me an indulgent nod and said, "Permission granted."

McCutcheon piped up. "Objection. Counsel has not shared this document with the prosecution, Your Honor."

"I just got it myself, Judge."

"What was the source of the documents?"

"Found it in the trunk of a dead man's car, Your Honor. But if it's not an accurate copy, I reckon Jason Moncrief is the man to say so."

"Did he," ask Norma McCutcheon, "just say he obtained this exhibit from the—?"

"Yes, Counsel, I'm afraid that's exactly what he said. But I'll overrule the objection for the present time."

"Does this document," I asked, "refresh your recollection that there were others who profited from Ms. Hinton's improper deferral?"

Moncrief carefully studied the table of major investors through narrowed eyes behind which I could almost hear the gears moving. Finally, he nodded in the affirmative.

"And one of them, Jeffrey Casperson, is known to you, isn't that a fact?"

Moncrief shifted in his chair, the first betrayal of discomfort. I moved closer.

"Yes," he said finally, and I moved in close to him.

"Do you deny he made a large sum of money on the uptick in stock caused by Hinton's deferral?"

"No, but—"

"And he's your *son*, isn't he?"

I took another step toward him. He crossed his legs. His eyes were burning into me with a menace barely under control. "Stepson. My blood heir is Richard—Rick—Moncrief, here in court today."

I followed Moncrief's gaze and saw that young Rick Moncrief had gone pale and was no longer smiling. Did the poor kid even know he had a half brother?

"How about Sheila Anderson. She made millions buying, selling, then shorting the stock, didn't she?"

"Yes."

"And you knew her, too, didn't you?"

"No."

That was stupid. How had I forgotten the way George C. Scott in

Anatomy of a Murder lost his case by asking one question too many—one he didn't know the answer to—pushing Kathryn Grant into revealing that Quill was not her lover, but her father?

"Ms. Anderson was murdered, wasn't she?"

"I've heard or read that she was murdered."

This was it.

I took a deep breath to steady myself, for I knew my next question would shock the courtroom into a stunned silence that would ferment into an explosion of surprise, confusion, denial, and, perhaps, with luck, reasonable doubt. Once I asked him if he had murdered Sheila Anderson in cold blood, then proceeded to prove he not only "knew her," but had been in her bed, there would be no turning back for me or him. I looked into his unsuspecting eyes and realized the man had no idea of the power I held over him. I also knew this was no time for sentiment; my friend's very freedom was at stake.

But as hard as I tried, I couldn't see the enemy in those eyes; I saw a human being, a father, a man with strengths and weaknesses. I knew about fathers with weaknesses.

I walked up closer to him. He waited. Just say it, Billy, for Christ's sake, just say it!

"Mr. Strobe?" I heard the judge say, but the sound of his voice came out of a hazy place full of echoes, echoes of the past. I heard Darryl clear his throat and glanced over at him.

Kill him, kill the motherfucker!

But Darryl was sitting there, quietly staring at me. In fact, everybody was staring at me, and I felt like that confused ten-year-old kid back at the Red Hen Café in Enid, Oklahoma.

Just say it, just say it, son! Three words, that's all you have to say!

I felt dizzy, like as if my head was going to split open across the top. Jesus, what was happening to me?

Just say it, son!

"What is justice?" I heard myself murmur, and saw a quizzical expression on Moncrief's face. I said it again, louder this time. "What is justice?"

"Pardon me, Counsel?" Moncrief said.

I gave my head a hard shake.

"I said, Your Honor . . . that I have no more questions at this time."

The judge told Moncrief he was excused for now, and the arrogant bastard walked off the stand and through the rail as erect and unsmiling as a palace sentinel, pausing only to give me a look somewhere between bewilderment and disdain.

I heard the judge say, "Call your next witness, Ms. McCutcheon."

I stood frozen to the spot where I'd had been, unmoving, devastated.

"The People rest, Your Honor," I heard her say.

"Very well," said the judge. "I see it is nearly 12:30, so I'll declare the noon recess. The jury will return at 1:45, at which time the defense will present its case."

I was conscious of the jury filing past me; then I turned, reluctant to face my client, having failed to destroy Moncrief—bullshit "having failed"—having not even *tried*. But it wasn't what I had failed to do that was the real source of my despair, but what I knew I would now *have* to do.

I looked over Darryl's head and met the worried eyes of Hale Lassiter.

Given the fact that I was still technically under house arrest, Darryl and I were escorted to a prisoner's conference room on the seventh floor, where we were locked up and given lunch.

"So, Counselor," Darryl said as he attacked his bologna-and-cheese sandwich. "What's *our* case gonna be?"

"I've got some witnesses," I said, sounding defensive.

"I see you decided against your DNA stunt?"

"Change of plans."

"Yeah, well, I reckon I'd better be changing my plans, too, about adjusting to the outside, for instance?"

I didn't know what to say. I felt like those wires holding me together were snapping.

"Hey, it don't matter," he added. "Really. Ever hear that old country song, 'I Started Out with Nothin and I Still Have It All?' Hell, kid, that's me."

Darryl wasn't fooling himself or me neither. I knew he wanted his freedom now—as much as I needed him to have it.

We sat in silence.

"So what are you going to ask me when I testify?"

"I'm not putting you on, Darryl. Not smart to parade your prior felony."

"I can deal with it."

"That's what John Derek said to Humphrey Bogart in *Knock on Any Door*, and John ended up in the electric chair."

"No, he ended up with Bo Derek. Pardon my nosiness, but how the hell do you expect to win this thing?"

"I'll have to go after Hale Lassiter."

"What I figured," he said, then grunted something I couldn't understand.

"What?" I said.

"I said one of the things I like about you is you keep remindin me

of me when I was young and too dumb to scratch my own ass with a
fist full of broken glass."

"Meaning?"

"Meaning that on the rare occasion when I had done the right thing
in life, I'd get all upset when I realized I was the one that was goin to
have to pay the cost of it. Nothin good comes easy, kid. There ain't no
free lunch, even for good deeds."

We sat in silence for a few minutes. I was too devastated to make
small talk.

"You gonna eat that?" Darryl said. He was pointing at my sandwich.

"It's yours," I said, and rapped on the door. "I need some time
alone, pard. Don't worry. We'll be okay."

"You'll come up with something, right?"

"I'm working on it."

But I wasn't fooling either one of us. Having abandoned the prov-
able lie, I'd now have to take on the unprovable truth.

"Look kid, I meant what I said. I'm ready to go back if I have to."

I met Darryl Orton's gentle eyes and saw that he was sincere. Had
he ever really expected to be free again? Or was he simply forgiving my
vacillation, my incompetence. Either way, his generosity of spirit—and
the staggering weight of my responsibility to him—flooded me with
fresh adrenaline and deepened my resolve.

I didn't trust myself to answer him right then, so I nodded and
walked out to where a deputy was waiting to take me to a holding cell
until time for court to resume.

41

"Let the record show the jury has returned to the courtroom and
is seated," said John Hernandez at exactly 1:45 p.m. "I'll ask
the bailiff to remove anyone not respecting the sanctity of these pro-
ceedings."

I realized a crowd had gathered. Every seat was taken, and a dozen people stood in back. Most were well dressed, probably lawyers who had heard something was developing in Department 26.

Darryl tugged at my sleeve, and I jerked it away. I knew what he wanted to do, but nothing could be gained by his testimony. Besides, I knew what had to be done, what had always had to be done.

What I had to do.

"I call . . . Mr. Hale Lassiter to the stand," I said, my voice cracking in midsentence.

I didn't look behind me, but it was obvious there was no movement. I almost hoped he had left, though I knew Moncrief would not let him leave until he, Moncrief, had been excused by the judge.

The bailiff rose and said, "Hale Lassiter?"

I turned then and saw him rise to his feet and move resolutely, as erect as the nineteen-year-old Marine he had once been, toward the witness stand. His eyes, thank God, were directed straight ahead, not at me. But that would change, and I readied myself.

He was sworn, and I began my questioning, still seated, not trusting my legs.

"You handled the SEC informal investigation in behalf of Synoptics, Jason Moncrief, and Deborah Hinton, is that correct?"

"Yes, teamed with an associate named Dana Mathews, the young woman seated in the back of the courtroom."

Seated in the back of the courtroom! Something exploded in my gut, then spread fire into my heart and my throat. Dana. Here? How had I missed her. *Jesus,* as if this wasn't hard enough already. Had Hale asked her during the lunch hour to come in to discourage me from putting him on the stand? He damn sure wanted me to know she was there.

Everybody turned to look at the "young woman," so I did, too, and was rewarded with a stare that would bend a spoon at a hundred feet. And who was sitting next to her but Rex Ashton. Fucking *Ashton.*

The judge cleared his throat, I turned back to face Hale, and remembered his warning. Had Ashton come to remind me how easy it was for him to drop a dime to a new Swarthy Man? Or to have his will carried out by the law, having set me up for Sheila's murder the way he'd done Darryl for Deborah's?

"We've had testimony that Ms. Hinton had improperly caused a run-up in the value of Synoptics stock. Is that true?"

"Yes."

"And that she, along with Jason Moncrief, his stepson, Jeffrey Casperson, and a woman named Sheila Anderson, all profited from this run-up, correct?"

"It would appear so."

"And both Hinton and Anderson have been murdered?"

"Yes."

"And both owned stock in Synoptics?"

"Yes." Although he looked grim, Hale's answers were consistently crisp and concise, betraying neither anxiety nor anger. Did he think I was merely laying a foundation? Still going after Moncrief?

"A company represented by you?"

"I'm the litigation lawyer in charge of Synoptics matters. My partner, Rex Ashton, handles their business matters, as you know."

I glanced at the jury. They were attentive, but watching me with narrow-eyed suspicion, as if not to be taken in. They wondered where I was headed. I knew where I was headed, and how much it would cost, but not how far I'd be able to get.

"The firm of Stanton and Snow has had some major financial reverses in recent years, haven't they?"

"Yes."

"And was saved by a bailout loan from you and Mr. Ashton?"

Hale hesitated, then quibbled with me about whether the firm was "saved," but finally admitted that their influx of capital had stopped the "hemorrhaging of good lawyers and clients."

The jury smiled at that, obviously enamored of the handsome senior partner. But neither Hale nor I were smiling. He was pretty sure where I was headed now. We were the matador and the bull, each respectful of the other, each in fear of the imminent pain that neither of us could avoid.

"The loans made by you and Mr. Ashton totaled approximately ten million dollars? Five million from each of you?"

Norma objected on her usual grounds, but the judge had become curious again and overruled her.

"Yes."

"Now, sir. Please tell the folks in the jury box the source of your five million dollars."

He flinched as if I'd struck him, for he knew it now, he knew it for sure. How can I describe the way he looked at me?

Hale cleared his throat, then said, "Various sources, savings, loans, an unexpected windfall, things of that sort."

He was going to fight, and I admired him for it.

"Can you document anything close to five million in loans and 'windfalls'?"

"They were from friends, relatives. Handshake sorts of things." A light sheen of moisture dampened his forehead, like the outside of a beer glass in hot weather.

I rose for the first time, stepped around my table, stood before the man I had once admired and respected as much as anyone in the world and said, "You're lying, sir."

"Objection!" shouted Norma. "Argumentative as well as irrelevant."

"*Sustained.*"

"Would you name one person, 'friend or relative,' Mr. Lassiter?"

"Objection. Your Honor!"

"Overruled. I'll allow him to answer, subject to a motion to strike and for sanctions if counsel does not tie it up."

Hale shrugged. "I'd have to think about it."

"Okay, but as you sit here now, you can't tell the jury one single, specific 'source' of this five million dollars?"

"I said I'd have to think about it."

Jesus, I was finally getting somewhere. How could the jury not recognize his evasiveness? The waffling?

"What was your net worth thirty days before you made the five-million-dollar loan to the firm, sir?"

He was reddening. "I don't recall."

"Something else you'd have to think about?"

"Objection, argumentative."

"Sustained," snapped the judge. "No sarcasm, Counsel."

Reel it in, kid. "I apologize, Your Honor, and to you Mr. Lassiter. You lost millions of dollars on a 1993 investment in a hotel computer company, correct?"

"Yes. HotelTech International."

"So would six hundred seventy-five thousand be a close estimate of your net worth approximately one month before you made the five-million-dollar loan to S & S?"

That surprised him. He looked to be waiting for an objection that didn't come, then shrugged and said, "Probably."

"Then let me see if I can refresh your memory as to where that five million came from."

Another glance at the jury told me that while they remained confused, their suspicious looks were no longer trained on me, but on the witness. I withdrew a sheaf of Barney's papers from my briefcase and showed several of them to Norma McCutcheon, then passed them to the clerk.

"May I have these documents marked *B* through *F* for identification, Your Honor?"

"My usual objection, Your Honor," said Norma.

"The usual ruling," said Judge Hernandez. "Defendant's Exhibits B through F for identification only."

I handed the documents to Hale.

"Have you seen that top document before, sir? Defendant's Exhibit B appears to be a detailed summary of trade confirmations as to various stock transactions involving Synoptics Corporation by a woman identified as 'Sheila Anderson, an unmarried woman.' "

Hale gave Norma McCutcheon an imploring look. Did the jury see it? Did she? There was no objection.

"I don't recall seeing this document."

"The rest of the documents appear to be trade confirmations from an offshore brokerage house, J. W. Westerhaus, Grand Cayman Islands, correct?"

"Objection, hearsay," said Norma.

"You may identify the document if you can," said the judge.

Hale shrugged, and I could tell he was fixing to lie again. "I've never seen this, Your Honor."

I then had another exhibit marked as Defendant's Exhibit G, and showed it to Hale. "This appears to be a record reflecting fund transfers from Sheila Anderson's account with J. W. Westerhaus to a numbered account also in the Cayman Islands 'for the benefit of "Project Salvation.' " The total sum was ten-point-three million dollars, nearly the same amount loaned by you and Mr. Ashton to Stanton and Snow."

Another glance toward the prosecutor, another objection.

"He may answer yes or no," said John Hernandez.

"I've never seen this document," said Hale. He was lying, he had to be. But could anybody else see it?

"You made your loan to the firm in November of 1998, correct?"

"That sounds about right."

"How were you to be paid back?"

"Monthly payments of thirty-five thousand dollars each."

"How much interest did you charge the firm?"

"The loans were interest-free."

"Because the purpose of the loan was 'salvation' of the firm, was it not?"

"Again, I can't say the firm would have failed without the loan, but the loan certainly reduced pressure."

"The bank had called the firm's line of credit, true?"

"Yes. I believe we owed six or seven million dollars."

"The firm was deeply in debt to suppliers, as well. In fact, the firm was heavily overextended?"

"We had experienced some . . . reverses, yes."

"Good lawyers were threatening to leave the firm?"

"Yes."

"Some had left?"

"Yes."

"And your loan and Mr. Ashton's loan to the firm were made within a month after Deborah Hinton was killed?"

He thought for a few seconds. "Yes."

"And, according to the documents I've shown you, *exactly eleven days after funds were distributed from Sheila Anderson's account to an entity called 'Project Salvation.'*"

"Objection, hearsay!" said McCutcheon.

"Sustained."

"Let me ask it another way, Mr. Lassiter. Would it refresh your memory, independent of the Project Salvation document, if I suggested to you that the loan you and Mr. Ashton made to the firm took place only weeks after Deborah Hinton's murder and in the very same month and in nearly the same amounts as were distributed to Project Salvation?"

"Objection," said McCutcheon, "compound, complex, argumentative, and irrelevant."

"Sustained."

Shit, Hale, let's get it over with. Look me in the eye. That's it. Here it comes.

"Okay, Mr. Lassiter. Let me be direct. Isn't it true that the funds you lent to the firm came substantially from funds transferred to you and Mr. Ashton from an offshore entity called Project Salvation?"

"Objection."

"Overruled," said Judge Hernandez, who then faced Hale. "You may answer that if you can, sir." The judge then turned his eyes on me and added, "After that, I think we've spent about enough time on this, Mr. Strobe."

"Yes, Your Honor," I said, "this should do it."

As Hale considered the question, the hushed tension in the courtroom was almost unbearable. At the counsel table, Darryl leaned forward, hands covering his head. I was afraid to look past him to the rear of the courtroom where Dana was seated. I turned back instead to Hale, who had never looked so grim. He held my gaze for a full ten seconds with feverish eyes that were sad but unyielding. He must know I had him.

"Mr. Lassiter?" Judge Hernandez said, and Hale blinked, as if awakened from a dream.

He then turned his head forty-five degrees, looked straight at the jury, and said, "No, sir, they most definitely did not."

His answer hit like a twister, with me standing at the vortex, naked—stark-ass naked, all eyes on me, waiting.

Why was I so shocked by his answer? Had I really thought he was going to confess the truth merely to avoid throwing an innocent man back into prison and me into the hands of his homicidal partner? Had I forgotten one of Soledad's cardinal maxims, that any of us would lie to save our own skin? Didn't I know by now that fear was the mother of falsehood, and hadn't I seen that Hale was drowning in fear?

Still, I had somehow expected more of Hale Lassiter, and was almost as devastated by this calm betrayal of his integrity as I was about having failed Darryl.

For I *had* failed. I had run out of cards.

"I offer the exhibits in evidence, Your Honor," I said, though even I knew the fate of unauthenticated car-trunk documents.

"Hearsay, Your Honor."

"Sustained. Have you any more questions, Mr. Strobe?"

"Just a few more, Your Honor," I said, "Did you know Deborah Hinton?"

"Hardly at all. I met her once or twice in connection with the SEC investigation. That's it."

"You were not friends?"

"No. Barely acquaintances."

"Never exchanged gifts?"

"Objection!" said Norma McCutcheon, recovering from a momentary languor. "Argumentative, irrelevant, and immaterial."

"You may give the obvious answer, sir," said the judge, "and we'll be finished here."

"No, we did not."

Was he gambling I didn't have the lighter? Had Dana returned it to him? Another betrayal?

"You deny that Deborah Hinton gave you a sterling silver cigarette lighter with two emeralds and diamonds surrounding the base?"

"I do deny it," he said, with a confidence that confirmed he was sure at least that *I* didn't have it.

I was out of gas, and he knew it.

I turned and stole a glance at Dana. She looked away.

"Do you also deny offering me a light with a lighter of that description in your office just last month?"

He gave me the kind of sympathetic look you give to a foreigner you'd like to help out but can't understand what he needs.

"If I've never owned such a lighter, sir, how could I have offered you a light with it?"

"Your Honor," said Norma McCutcheon, "I hate to interrupt Mr. Strobe's self-immolation, but might we move on?"

"Yes, Mr. Strobe," said the judge. "Please do move on."

"I have no further questions, Judge," I said, and retreated to my chair, mindful of the hostile glare of the jurors and unable to look Darryl in the eyes.

"Your Honor," continued the deputy DA, "I move to strike the entire testimony of this witness on grounds of irrelevance. We're here to determine whether Mr. Orton killed Ms. Hinton, not whether somebody else may have killed Ms. Anderson."

"I must agree with you, Counsel," said John Hernandez. "The Anderson documents are indeed hearsay and without foundation as to authenticity, and it's not her murder we're concerned with here. . . ."

I saw that the judge's gaze had moved out over our heads and into the gallery and the juror's eyes followed his as one. I was too dejected to notice at first, but realized that Hale's face had turned pale as parchment. I then heard a soft chink on the rail behind me and turned to see Dana standing there, her eyes wet and downcast.

On the rail was the lighter.

I started to thank her, but she turned and walked straight away from me.

42

I picked up the lighter from the rail with trembling fingers, got up, and handed it over to the clerk.

"Defendant's H for identification only, Your Honor?"

"It may be so marked."

Holding the lighter in plain view of the jury, I approached Hale, whose features had suddenly sagged into old age, despair. And why not? First his surrogate son, now his surrogate daughter, the mother of his only child—both turned against him.

"Your Honor, I'd like to interrupt Mr. Lassiter's testimony in order to get Deborah Hinton's parents in here, Mr. and Mrs. Breckenridge, to testify concerning this lighter, and then to call to the stand Dana Mathews, the woman who handed me the lighter, to testify as to where she got it."

I was speaking more to Hale than to the judge, but I could see that both got the message. Norma rose to make her objection, but I walked straight up to Hale and blurted out my next question: "You know who killed Deborah Hinton, don't you?"

"Yes." The double betrayal had drained the fight out of him.

"It wasn't Mr. Orton, was it?"

"No."

A rustle swept through the gallery as if windows had been blown out by the winter gale outside. Hale's tortured eyes avoided mine and stared down at the white knuckles of his clenched fists.

"How do you know that, sir?"

He didn't answer, just stared hopelessly at his hands, and I realized the courtroom had gone stone silent. Even Norma McCutcheon froze in midobjection and stared at the witness. Waiting.

I looked up at the judge and cleared my throat. He caught my drift.

"I'm afraid, sir," said Judge Hernandez, "that you'll have to answer the question, sir. Or, of course the protection of the Constitution is available to you sir—"

"No, Your Honor, I won't be taking the Fifth Amendment," Hale murmured, "I know . . . because . . . I was present when Ms. Hinton was . . . "

"You were there, sir, when she was murdered?"

I heard movement behind me and glanced over my shoulder as Rex Ashton began making his way across a row of people, on his way toward the aisle.

"Who killed her, sir! Will you point him out?"

Hale nodded grimly. "Yes. It was my partner, Rex Ashton," he said, and the words froze Ashton in his tracks; in fact, the whole damn courtroom made itself into a still photograph. "That gentleman there."

It was Jaxon who moved first, gliding up the center aisle, blocking Ashton's intended path and signaling him to resume his seat. Ashton sat, his face red and menacing. Then all eyes were back on me and Hale.

"You witnessed Deborah Hinton's murder at the hands of Mr. Ashton?" I said.

"I did," Hale said simply, his voice becoming firm again, his head and his shoulders erect.

"Did he plant hair from the head of the defendant onto Deborah Hinton's body?"

"He did."

"Did he tell you how he obtained Mr. Orton's hair follicles?"

"He said he recovered the samples from the barber shop at the TechnoCenter after Mr. Orton had been there."

"Did he also order the deaths of my investigator, Mr. Klinehart, and Sheila Anderson?"

"He did."

In a vast silence of the courtroom, I swear I could hear Dana's tears falling, feel them fall, each one burning into my heart like acid. I looked up at Hale, and his expression was calm. It was like he and I were alone in the courtroom. I loved him again in that moment, forgave him his weakness, forgave him everything.

"I'm finished, Hale," I said.

"I'm finished, too, Billy, as you know. But for what it's worth, I'm glad it's over."

Though barely audible, these words nearly cleared the courtroom of reporters as they raced against deadlines and each other. Hale and I continued to regard each other through moist eyes, and I swear I saw him nod his head slightly, a token of respect that was like a punch in the stomach. As I returned to my chair, I heard the judge ask Hale if he would please remain seated until the police had secured Mr. Ashton. He then cleared the gallery of all but police and bailiffs. Dana was permitted to stay.

I felt Darryl's firm touch on my arm. Norma was staring at me as if I'd emerged dockside after being tossed in deep water wrapped in canvas and chains.

"The defense," I said quietly, "rests."

Within minutes, two new police officers escorted Hale off the witness stand and into the gallery. After both sides waived argument, the judge instructed the stunned jurors and ordered them to retire to the jury room, select a foreperson, and return when they had reached a verdict. But we were in for one last surprise. They refused to leave the courtroom, which I later learned was a first in San Francisco history. They simply huddled together in the jury box and came up with swiftest verdict since Sir Thomas More's in *A Man for All Seasons*. Mrs. Meagher, juror number eight, stuck her head out of the pack of twelve and announced their unanimous verdict of not guilty. Darryl and I hadn't even had a chance to get to our feet.

The judge tried to excuse the jubilant jury with thanks, but they were so worked up the bailiff had to practically force them to leave. Darryl still hadn't said anything, probably because it was happening so fast, or maybe he could see I was hurting, struggling for control.

I turned to see Jaxon and another officer standing close to Hale Lassiter as he was given a moment to console Dana.

"Mr. Orton," said the judge, recapturing my attention, "you are free to go, with the apologies of the State of California. Please follow the marshal back to the seventh floor to recover your possessions."

I looked at Darryl, and for the first time since that day a hundred years ago when he had boldly walked into the rec yard at Soledad, he appeared stunned and confused. I doubt he had expected to be freed, and now he had no idea what to do next.

"I'll be damned," he said, and then said it again. "You did it, kid."

"*She* did it," I said, "That was Dana who walked up and gave me the lighter."

"I figured. Well, she made a hell of a first impression on me. Give her my thanks."

"I'll try."

"This is the only time you're gonna hear it, kid, so pay attention. Thank you."

"I owed you," I said. "Always will."

Darryl shook his head. "Nope. Anything good I might have done for you in prison has been more than offset by the bad turn I did to you today."

"Bad turn?"

"Looks like this case has made you into a trial lawyer. May God forgive me."

I returned his smile. "I'll wait for you right here, Darryl. Then we'll go to my apartment and figure out what we're going to do with the rest of our lives."

He followed the deputy into the holding area, still shaking his head in wonder.

I turned as Ashton was being led toward the holding cell, hands already cuffed behind him. He gave me his most chilling look, but it had lost its power, and I gave him one back. Challenged, he paused, and by the sheer force of his will, stopped his guards in their tracks and maneuvered both of them to within several feet of me.

"What could be more demeaning," he said through clenched teeth, his face florid with rage, "more *degrading,* than being imprisoned by a hayseed jailbird like you?"

"Well, Mr. Ashton," I said smiling into his nuclear gaze, "you're soon going to find out."

He snarled something back I couldn't understand, and they led him off.

Then the judge addressed me. "Needless to say, Mr. Strobe, I've quashed the warrant for your arrest. It is clear, however, that you have walked very close to the edge today at times, notwithstanding to good effect. I realize you are inexperienced, but do not let this become a pattern."

"I know it's no excuse, Your Honor. I was not only inexperienced, but desperate. I'll be more careful in the future."

Hernandez nodded and said, "I expect that both states—your inexperience and your desperation—have been altered for the better as a result of your efforts today. Welcome to the trial bar, Mr. Strobe."

I thanked him, and he entered his chambers, shaking his head with mixed curiosity and amusement, much like Darryl had. Norma McCutcheon came over to congratulate me.

"You," she said, "should be a prosecutor."

I looked past her to where Hale, his lips alarmingly purple in hue, remained in conversation with Jaxon and some other gray suits. "Thanks, Norma," I said, "but I think I'll stay on the side of the angels."

I looked back to Hale's group and saw that Dana had left. Hale looked over Jaxon's shoulder in my direction, and our eyes met and held for just a second. He was saying something to one of the cops, but gave me a rueful smile, another gesture that pierced my heart. Then, they turned him toward the jail holding area and led him away.

43

Darryl decided he wanted to spend some time alone, so I picked him up some toiletries and the guitar I'd saved for him, lent him some cash, and put him up in a hotel for the night, the Juliana, not the Premier. I told him I'd take him wherever he wanted to go the next day.

Dana wasn't picking up her phone.

I suddenly remembered Vic James in New York had probably sent someone to pick me up at JFK. I called him, told him what had happened. He was shocked about Hale and Ashton, of course, and also seemed disappointed about me not coming. He said a job would be waiting for me if I ever changed my mind.

Next, I called Lisa, who sounded upbeat and well. She was down to monthly mixantrone IVs and getting stronger. She told me that Ma was finished with the DTs and doing great. She would be there for another four to six months. I told Lisa I'd come out soon to help her rent out the house and get stuff stored while we figured out what was going to happen next. She agreed.

I couldn't get Dana out of my mind, but knew she wouldn't want to see me. She would be hurting ten times more than I was over what we had done to Hale and would need time.

I'd forgotten that my apartment had been turned upside down. I began putting it back together, glad to have something to do that didn't require thought.

Around four o'clock I got a call from Mace Rothschild, telling me that the shit had hit the fan at S & S. The cops had a team going through Hale's and Ashton's files.

"Dana's called in sick," Mace said, "but I guess you know all about that."

"I'll call you tomorrow, okay, Scarecrow? I'm crapped out."

"Sure. Sorry. Will you still be leaving the firm?"

"I never really joined it, Mace. I'll let you know what I'm up to as soon as I know myself."

"What about Hale?"

"I'll stop by and try to speak with him in the morning."

"Maybe he'd let you represent him."

Despite my despondent mood, I flashed on to Charles Laughton in *Witness for the Prosecution,* taking on the defense of Marlene Dietrich after she'd killed his client right in front of him.

"I doubt he wants to even see me."

I hung up, feeling tired and restless at the same time. I put on my running shoes and took off for Aquatic Park, where I ran and walked my way into total fatigue, then entered my apartment around 7:30 P.M. I had hoped for a message from Dana, and there it was, along with several others from the press, TV, and people from S & S. I grabbed the phone and punched in her number.

"It's me."

"Hello, Billy."

"You okay?"

"Not really," she said, and I could hear her trying to control her sobbing. A kid's program blared in the background.

"Dana, you did the right thing. We both did. I truly believe that Hale knows it, too."

"That's what he told me. Why am I having so much trouble believing it?"

"I'm coming over."

"*No!*" she said, then, more gently, "No, not now."

"I need to see you, Dana. We should be together tonight. He was my friend, too."

"I know, Billy, but I need some time."

"All right," I said, feeling my eyes tearing up. "I'll come by in the morning."

"I'm sorry, Billy. Give me a few days. I'll call you."

Don't call me, I'll call you.

"Sure," I said.

She murmured a good-bye, and I heard the phone go dead. I lowered the receiver into the cradle, staring at it as if it was to blame for everything. I was beginning to give out and wished I could fall into bed and sleep for about a year or two.

I looked up and saw myself in the small mirror on the kitchen wall. Was I only twenty-six years old? I leaned my head into the sink and splashed water on my face.

I wondered if Darryl had called Bess Padgett. Had it sunk into his head yet that he was a free man?

Three days later, the phone rang. *Dana?* I grabbed it.

"Hello?"

"Yes, hello, Mr. Strobe, it is Mr. Bharani speaking from the downstairs?"

"Oh. Hello, Mr. Bharani."

"Yes, and to you a most Happy New Year's."

"Thank you, sir, same to you."

"Another favor I must ask of you, Mr. Strobe. The central heating it is again very poorly working. Would you please to come to the first floor and with me take a look at the thermostat?"

My landlord had invested his father's wealth acquired during the Shah's regime in an old wood-frame and stucco apartment building that had been knocked out of whack by the '87 quake. The place needed a full-time super just to keep the doors opening and closing and the inferior plumbing, electrical, and heating systems working. It seems I had become it.

"I'll be down in a minute, sir."

I put on a clean shirt and walked down the stairs on heavy legs and saw, in order, the balding head of Mr. Bharani, staring at the inner workings of the first-floor thermostat, and outside, on the street, the back of a woman with legs I'd recognize anywhere, helping her young child out of the backseat of her car. The child carried a large, stuffed rabbit.

"I am most grateful to you, Mr. Strobe," Mr. Bharani was saying, "and so very sorry to always be bothering you. I have a friend who is a designer of buildings who says that it is sometimes best to let the old structure go and build a new one on the old foundation."

Dana was straightening Sarah's dress on the sidewalk.

"Yes, sir," I said. "I had a friend tell me that once, too. I reckon that's sometimes best."

I glanced in the hallway mirror, saw that my hair had finally grown out and that the cut on my head had healed.

And that the face looking back at me was smiling.

Epilogue
Six Months Later

SYNOPTICS MURDER VERDICTS
Ashton, Lassiter convicted

DEAN J. COHN

San Francisco, Ca. (Jul.10)—Following only two days of deliberation, less time than it took for the various lawyers' closing arguments, a jury of eight women and four men rendered their verdicts late last night in a trial that has attracted national attention, convicting the defendants of 14 counts of fraud, murder, and accessory to murder.

"We're very pleased that justice has been carried out," declared Norma McCutcheon, lead prosecutor on a case that had sent a shudder through the blue-stockinged Montgomery Street financial district. Convicted are Rex Ashton, 49, and Hale Lassiter, 58, highly respected local attorneys who co-chaired Stanton and Snow, one of San Francisco's oldest and most prestigious law firms. "This verdict should send a message to the rest of the country that no amount of wealth and status can buy immunity from the reach of the law," added McCutcheon.

Some might argue that this was not the case with Lassiter, who escaped the more serious murder charge and was only found guilty of securities fraud and as an accessory after the fact to murder.

Citing Lassiter's early cooperation with police and the jury's leniency, legal observers expect Lassiter to receive a relatively light sentence that could set him free in as few as three to five years with good behavior. Ashton, however, will face a second trial to see if he will be sentenced to death or life imprisonment without possibility of parole for the murder of Deborah Hinton and contracting for the murder of two others.

The case was fraught with ironies. Ashton could end up in Soledad prison in a space previously occupied by the very night janitor whom Ashton himself had originally framed for Ms. Hinton's murder. Even more ironic, it was during the retrial of the janitor that Lassiter's current lawyer, William Strobe of the Urban Poverty League, then representing Orton, exposed Lassiter's criminal involvement.

Ashton's lawyer was unavailable for comment, but the jubilant Strobe echoed the prosecutor's praise of the judicial system by paraphrasing Winston Churchill's comment on democracy: "Our justice system is the worst, in the world," said Strobe, "except for all the others that have been tried."

Among the character witnesses for Lassiter was the president of the American College of Trial Lawyers, a State Supreme Court justice, and Dana Mathews, a friend and former law associate of Lassiter's, and now the fiancée of defense counsel Strobe.

John Martel is an ex–U.S. Air Force pilot, a lawyer in the San Francisco firm of Farella, Braun & Martel, and a veteran of more than one hundred trials (with only four losses). He has been hailed by the *National Law Journal* as one of the top ten trial lawyers in America. He is the author of *The Alternate, Partners,* and *Conflicts of Interest.*